Sugar and Spice

Books by Fern Michaels

ABOUT FACE * ANNNIE'S RAINBOW * CELEBRATION
CHARMING LILY * DEAR EMILY * FINDERS KEEPERS
THE FUTURE SCROLLS * THE GUEST LIST * KENTUCKY
HEAT * KENTUCKY RICH * KENTUCKY SUNRISE
LISTEN TO YOUR HEART * PLAIN JANE * SARA'S
SONG * VEGAS HEAT * VEGAS RICH * VEGAS SUNRISE
WHAT YOU WISH FOR * WEEKEND WARRIORS
WHITEFIRE * WISH LIST * YESTERDAY * VENDETTA
PAYBACK * PICTURE PERFECT * THE JURY
SWEET REVENGE

Books by Beverly Barton

AFTER DARK * EVERY MOVE SHE MAKES * WHAT
SHE DOESN'T KNOW * THE FIFTH VICTIM * THE LAST TO
DIE * AS GOOD AS DEAD * KILLING HER SOFTLY
CLOSE ENOUGH TO KILL

Books by Joanne Fluke

CHOCOLATE CHIP COOKIE MURDER * STRAWBERRY
SHORTCAKE MURDER * BLUEBERRY MUFFIN MURDER
LEMON MERINGUE PIE MURDER * FUDGE CUPCAKE
MURDER * SUGAR COOKIE MURDER * PEACH COBBLER
MURDER * CHERRY CHEESECAKE MURDER

Books by Shirley Jump

THE BACHELOR PREFERRED PASTRY * THE DEVIL
SERVED TORTELLINI * THE ANGEL CRAVED LOBSTER
THE BRIDE WORE CHOCOLATE

Published by Kensington Publishing Corporation

Sugar and Spice

FERN MICHAELS
BEVERLY BARTON
JOANNE FLUKE
SHIRLEY JUMP

ZEBRA BOOKS
KENSINGTON PUBLISHING CORP.
www.kensingtonbooks.com

ZEBRA BOOKS are published by

Kensington Publishing Corp.
850 Third Avenue
New York, NY 10022

All Kensington titles, imprints, and distributed lines are available at special quantity discounts for bulk purchases for sales
promotion, premiums, fund-raising, educational, or institutional
use.

Special book excerpts or customized printings can also be
created to fit specific needs. For details, write or phone the
office of the Kensington Special Sales Manager: Attn. Special
Sales Department. Kensington Publishing Corp., 850 Third
Avenue, New York, NY 10022. Phone: 1-800-221-2647.

Zebra and the Z logo Reg. U.S. Pat. & TM Off.

First Printing: November 2006
10 9 8 7 6 5 4 3 2 1

Printed in the United States of America

Contents

The Christmas
Stocking

FERN MICHAELS

Chapter One

Los Angeles, California
October, Two Months Before Christmas

It was a beautiful five-story building with clean lines, shimmering plate glass and a bright yellow door. A tribute to the architect who designed the building. An elongated piece of driftwood attached to the right of the door was painted the same shade of yellow. The plaque said it was the Sara Moss Building. The overall opinion of visitors and clients was that the building was impressive, which was the architect and owner's intent.

The young sun was just creeping over the horizon when Gus Moss tucked his briefcase between his knees as he fished in his jeans pocket for the key that would unlock his pride and joy, the Sara Moss Building named after his mother.

Inside, Gus turned off the alarm, flicked light switches. He took a moment to look around the lobby of the building he'd designed when he was still in school studying architecture. He thanked God every day that he'd been able to show his mother the blueprints before she'd passed on. It was his mother's idea to have live bamboo plants to match the green marble floors. It was also her idea to paint clouds and a blue sky on the ceiling. The fieldstone wall behind the shimmering mahogany desk was a must, she'd said. Fieldstones he'd brought to California from Fairfax, Virginia, in a U-Haul truck. There was nothing he could deny his mother because he was who he was because of her.

There was only one picture hanging in the lobby: Sara Moss standing next to a sixty-foot blue spruce Christmas tree that she had his father plant the day he was born. That tree was gone now from the Moss Christmas Tree Farm, donated to the White House by his father the same year his mother died. Over his objections.

He'd gone to Washington, DC, that year and took the Christmas tour so he could see the tree. He'd been so choked up he could hardly get the words out to one of the security detail. "Can you break off a branch from the back of the tree and give it to me?" For one wild moment he thought he was going to be arrested until he explained to the agent why he wanted the branch. He'd had to wait over two hours for one of the gardeners to arrive with a pair of clippers. He'd had a hard time not bawling his eyes out that day but he'd returned to California with the branch. Pressed between two panes of glass, it now hung on the wall over his drafting table. He looked at it a hundred times a day and it meant more to him than anything else in the world.

Gus stared at the picture of his mother the way he did every morning. As always, his eyes grew moist and his heart took on an extra beat. He offered up a snappy salute the way he'd always done when she was right about something and he was wrong. At this point in his daily routine, he never dawdled. He sprinted across the lobby to the elevator and rode to the fifth floor where he had his office so he could settle in for the day.

As always, Gus made his own coffee. While he waited for it to drip into the pot, he checked his appointment book. A light day. He really liked Fridays because they led to the weekend. Still, it was the middle of October and business tended to slow down as a rule. He wished it was otherwise, because the approaching holiday season always left him depressed. He told himself not to complain; he had more business than he could handle the other ten months of the year. When you were named "Architect of the Year" five years running and "Architect to the Stars" six years running, there was no reason to complain. His burgeoning bank balance said his net worth was right up there with some of Hollywood's finest stars. He wasn't about money, though. He was about creating something from nothing, letting his imagination run the gamut. *Architectural Digest* had featured eleven of his projects to date and called him a "Wonder Boy."

Everyone in the business who knew or knew of Gus Moss were aware that when the new owners moved into one of his custom-designed houses, Gus himself showed up wearing a tool belt and carrying a Marty Bell painting, his gift to the new owners, that he hung himself.

Gus loved this time of the day, when he was all alone with his coffee. It was when he let his mind go into overdrive before the hustle and bustle of the day began. He ran a loose ship, allowing his staff to dress in jeans and casual clothing, allowing them to play music in their offices, taking long breaks. He had only three hard and fast rules. Think outside the box, never screw over a client, and produce to your capability. His staff of fourteen full-time architects, four part-timers, and an office pool of seven had been with him from day one. It worked for all concerned.

As Gus sipped his coffee he let his mind wander. Should he go to Tahoe for some skiing over Christmas? Or should he head for the islands for some sun and sand and a little snorkeling? And who would he ask to accompany him? Sue with the tantalizing lips, Carol with the bedroom eyes or Pam the gymnast with the incredible legs? None of the above. He was sick of false eyelashes, theatrical makeup, spiky hair, painted on dresses and shoes with heels like weapons. He needed to find a nice young woman he could communicate with, someone who understood what he was all about. Not someone who was interested in his money and had her own agenda. At thirty-seven, it was time to start thinking about settling down. Time to give up takeout for homecooked. Time to get a dog. Time to think about having kids. Time to think about putting down roots somewhere, not necessarily here in California, land of milk and honey, orange blossoms and beautiful women.

Gus settled the baseball cap on his head, the cap he was never without. Sometimes he even slept with it on. It was battered and worn, tattered and torn but he'd give up all he held dear before he'd part with his cap that said Moss Farms on the crown. He settled it more firmly on his head as he heard his staff coming in and getting ready for the day.

Gus finished his coffee, grabbed his briefcase and headed for the door. He had a 7:15 appointment with the Fire Marshall on a project he was winding up. He high-fived several members of his staff as he took the steps to the lobby where he stopped long enough to give Sophie, the Moss Firm's official receptionist/greeter, a smooch. "How's it going this morning, Sophie?"

"Just fine, Gus. When will you be back?"

"By nine-thirty. If anything earth shattering happens, call me on the cell. See ya."

As good as his word, Gus strode back into the lobby at 9:27. Out of the corner of his eye he noticed an elderly couple sitting on a padded bench between two of the bamboo trees. Sophia caught his eye and motioned him to her desk. "That couple is here to see you. They said they're from your hometown. Their names are Peggy and Ham Bledsoe. They don't have an appointment. Can you see them? They're here visiting a daughter who just graced them with their first grandchild."

Gus grinned. "I see you got all the details. Peggy and Ham here in California! I can't believe it."

"We're of an age, darling boy. Go over there and make nice to your hometown guests."

Gus's guts started to churn. Visiting with Peggy and Ham meant taking a trip down Memory Lane and that was one place he didn't want to travel. He pasted a smile on his face as he walked over to the patiently waiting couple. He hugged Peggy and shook Ham's hand. "Good to see you, sir. Miss Peggy, you haven't changed a bit. Sophie tells me you're grandparents now. Congratulations! Come on up to the office and have some coffee. I think we even have sticky buns. We always have sticky buns on Friday."

"This is a mighty fine looking building, Augustus. The lady at the desk said it's all yours. She said you designed it."

"I did," Gus mumbled.

"Mercy me. I wish your momma could have seen this. She was always so proud of you, Augustus."

They were in the elevator before Gus responded. "Mom saw the blueprints. She suggested the fieldstone and the bamboo trees. Did you see the picture?"

"We did, and it is a fine picture of Sara. We tell everyone that tree ended up in the White House," Ham said.

Gus was saved from a reply when the elevator came to a stop and the doors slid open. Peggy gasped, her hand flying to her mouth. "This is so . . . so grand, Augustus."

Gus decided he didn't feel like making coffee. He was too nervous around this couple from home. He knew in his gut they were going to tell him something he didn't want to hear. He pressed a button on the console. "Hillary, will you bring some coffee into my office. I have two guests. Some sticky buns, too, okay?"

Gus whirled around, hoping to delay the moment they were going to tell him why they were *really* here. "So, what do you think of California?"

"Well, we don't fit in here, that's for sure," Peggy said. "We're simple people, Augustus. All those fancy cars that cost more than our farm brings in over ten years. The stores with all those expensive clothes where they hide the price tags made my eyes water. Our son-in-law took us to Ro-day-o Drive. That was the name of it, wasn't it, Ham? Hollywood people," she sniffed. "I didn't see a mall or a Wal-Mart anywhere."

Will you just please get to it already. Gus licked at his dry lips, trying to think of something to say. "I just finished up a house for Tammy Bevins. She's a movie star. Would you like to see a picture of the house?"

"No," the Bledsoes said in unison. Gus blinked and then blinked again just as Hillary carried in a tray with an elegant coffeepot with fragile cups and saucers. Linen napkins and a crystal plate of sticky buns were set in the middle of a long conference table.

"Will there be anything else, Gus?"

"Nope, this is fine. Thanks, Hillary. Hey, how's the new boyfriend?"

"He's a hottie." Hillary giggled. "I think I'll keep this one." Gus laughed.

Peggy Bledsoe pursed her lips in disapproval. "Shouldn't that youngster be calling you Mr. Moss?"

"Nah. We're pretty informal around here, Miss Peggy. Sit down. Cream, sugar?"

"Black," the Bledsoes said in unison.

Gus poured. He filled his own cup and then loaded it with cream and four sugars. *I hate coffee with cream and sugar. What's wrong with me?* He leaned back in his chair and waited.

"We stopped by the farm before we left, Augustus. Your father isn't doing well. I don't mean healthwise. The farm has gone downhill. Business is way off. Last year he sold only two hundred Christmas trees. This year if he sells half that he'll be lucky."

Gus was stunned. Moss Farms was known far and wide for their Christmas trees. People came from miles around to tag a tree in September. Normally his father sold thirty to fifty thousand trees from November first to Christmas Eve. He said so.

"That was before your momma died and you lit out, Augustus. Sara was the heart and soul of that farm. She did the cider, she did the gingerbread, she managed the gift store. She did the decorations, she made the bows for the wreathes and the grave blankets. She even worked the chain saw when she had to. All that changed when she passed on. You should have gone back, Augustus. That farm is falling down around your father's feet. The fields need to be thinned out," Peggy snapped.

Gus snapped back before he could bite his tongue. "I did go back. Pop didn't want me there. Told me to get out. I call three times a week—the answering machine comes on. He never calls me back. I send money home and he sends it back."

Ham drained the coffee in his cup. "I don't think he's going to sell *any* trees this year. The Senior Citizens group rented the old Coleman property and are setting up shop. Tillie Baran is spearheading the effort. They ordered their trees from North Carolina. They're going all out to raise money to re- furbish the Seniors' Building. Just last week at our monthly meeting, Tillie said her daughter is coming home from Phila- delphia to take over the project. Little Amy has her own pub- licity company. That means she's the boss. When you're the boss, you can take off and help your momma," he said point- edly.

"You wouldn't believe how good that little girl is to her momma," Peggy said with just a trace of frost in her voice.

Gus reached for a sticky bun he didn't want. "And you think I should go home to help my father and save the day, is that it? Like little Amy Baran is doing."

"The thought occurred to us," Peggy said. "I think your momma would want you to do that."

Before Gus could think of something to say, Ham jumped into the conversation. "Tillie went out to the farm and asked your father if he would sell her the trees at cost if he wasn't going to promote his own farm. It would have been a good way to thin out the fields but he turned her down flat. So now the Seniors have to pay a trucking company to bring the trees from North Carolina."

Gus searched for something to say. "Maybe the farm is getting too much for him. It's possible he wants to retire. It sounds to me like he's had enough of the Christmas tree business."

"Moss Farms is his life, Augustus. Your father can at times be a cantankerous curmudgeon," Peggy said. "He's all alone. With no business, he laid everyone off."

Gus felt sick to his stomach. He thought about his teenage years on the farm when his father worked him like a dog. That was when his father thought he was going to stick around and run the farm, but his mother was determined he go to college to make something of himself. How he'd hated the fights, the harsh words he heard late at night. All he wanted was to get away from the farm, to do what he was meant to do—create, design and see his creative designs brought to life. All he'd done was follow his mother's dream for him. He wanted to explain to the Bledsoes that he wasn't an uncaring son. He'd done his best where his father was concerned but his best wasn't good enough. He reached for another sticky bun he didn't want. He hated the sugary sweet coffee. He wished he could brush his teeth. Even as he decided that silence was a virtue at this point in time, he asked, "More coffee?"

"No, thank you, Augustus. We have to be going. It was nice to see you again."

"Yes, it was. Nice to see you too. I'm glad you stopped by. I'll take you down to the lobby."

"What are all those movie stars *really* like?" Ham asked.

"Just like you and me. Underneath all the glitz and glamour, they're real people. The glitz and glamour is what they do to earn a living. When they go home at night, they're just like you and Miss Peggy."

Peggy snorted to show what she thought of that statement.

The ride down to the lobby was made in silence. Gus stepped aside to allow the couple to walk out first. "Have a safe trip home. It was nice seeing you. Have a nice holiday." He extended his hand to Ham who ignored it. Gus shoved his hands into the pockets of his jeans. His gut was still churning.

"Just how rich are you, Augustus?" Peggy asked.

Stunned, Gus thought about the question and how his mother would respond. She'd say if a person had the guts to ask such a personal question, they deserved whatever answer you wanted to give. "Filthy rich!" he said cheerfully.

Peggy snorted again. Ham held the door open for his wife before he scurried through. Neither one looked back. Gus wondered how all this was going to play out back home when the Bledsoes returned.

Gus took the stairs to the fifth floor, his head buzzing. When he reached the fifth-floor landing, he sat down on the top step and dropped his head into his hands. For one wild moment he thought he could smell pine resin on his hands. He fought with his breathing to calm down. When his heartbeat returned to normal he let his thoughts drift. He thought about his dog Buster, his faithful companion during his childhood. He thought about Bixby, his buddy all through high school and college. He wondered where Bix was these days. He made a mental note to go on the Net to look him up.

Gus felt his eyes fill with moisture. The Bledsoes were right—his father was a hard man. A cranky curmudgeon pretty well nailed it. Because he'd been big for his age, six foot three at the age of twelve, his father thought him capable of a man's work—to his mother's chagrin. No amount of interference on her behalf could change his father's mind. He'd worked him from sunup until sundown. He'd get sick late at night and his mother would always be there promising his life would get better. And it did when he went off to college.

Gus's head jerked upright as he wondered if he hated his father or if he just didn't like him. More likely the latter, since he didn't hate anyone. He simply wasn't capable of hating anyone.

An hour later, Gus untangled himself and opened the door that led to his office. He felt like he was stepping onto foreign territory since his thoughts were back at Moss Farms. Nothing had changed in his absence. The tray with the coffee service and the leftover sticky buns was still in the middle of the conference table. The pine branch was still hanging over his drafting table. How strange that the Bledsoes hadn't asked what it was or why a dried pine branch was hanging on his wall. Everyone who entered the office asked sooner or later.

He decided right then and there that he didn't like the Bledsoes any more than he liked his father.

The phone on his desk rang. He picked it up and made small talk with a client who wanted to take him to dinner. "How about a rain check, Karl? I have to go out of town for a while. Let's pencil in the first week of the New Year. Okay, glad it works for you. I'll be in touch."

Gus whipped his day planner out of his backpack. He flipped through the pages to see what pressing matters had to be taken care of. Nothing that couldn't wait, he decided.

Five minutes later he made an announcement over the intercom. "Look alive, people, this is your boss. I'd like to see all of you in my office, STAT."

They came on the run the way they always did. When the boss called a special meeting it was of paramount importance. Gus Moss never sweated the small stuff.

Gus wasted no time. "Look, guys, I need to go out of town for a couple of months. Actually, I have to go home. My father needs me." He wondered if it was a lie or wishful thinking on his part. "Can you guys handle things?"

"Surely you jest," Derek Williams quipped. "It will be a vacation for all of us with you gone. We'll party up a storm and drink a toast to you every night."

Gus grinned. They wouldn't do any such thing and they all knew it.

"Hey, man, you said you were going to watch Cyrus for me while I go to Costa Rica next month." It was Max Whitfield who was Gus's right hand.

"Damn! Okay, okay, I'll take him with me if that's okay. He can run the farm all day. You okay with that, Max?"

"Oh no, my dog does *not* fly in the cargo hold. Dogs die on airplanes."

"Then I'll drive. Works for me if you're okay with it. I promise to coddle him just the way you do. I'll give him an apple and a carrot every day. I'll make sure to give him his vitamins and will give him only bottled water, just the way you do. What I won't do is dress him up in those designer duds you deck him out in."

Max, a string bean of a man, eyeballed his boss and then nodded. "When are you leaving?"

"In the morning. Bring the dog to the office and I'll take off from here. You guys sure you can handle things?"

"Yes, Dad," the little group said in unison.

"Swear you won't call us a hundred times a day," Derek said.

"I don't think you have to worry about that. Okay, it's all set then. Hillary, cancel the rest of my appointments. Reschedule."

Gus looked around at his loyal staff. A lump formed in his throat. They were the best of the best. He made a mental note to double their Christmas bonuses. He could do that tonight at home and hand them out in the morning. Loyalty was one thing he never skimped on. A long time ago his mother had told him a person was only as good as the people who worked for them. At the time he hadn't understood what that meant. He knew now, though.

Time to go cross-country.

Back to his childhood memories.

Back to his father's house.

He hoped he was up to the challenge.

Chapter Two

A week later and three thousand miles away in Philadelphia, Pennsylvania, thirty-four-year-old career woman Amy Baran was on an emotional high as she packed her already over-stuffed briefcase. She looked around her cluttered office and sighed. One of these days she really had to give some thought to organizing things. She knew it wasn't going to happen because she loved living in clutter, loved that she could instantly lay her hands on anything she needed.

Amy Baran owned a small public relations firm in the heart of the Main Line District. It employed two full-time staff members; two part-time moms whose schedules she worked around; a receptionist-slash-secretary; and a battle-scarred, bushy-haired orange tabby cat named Cornelia she had found half-starved in the basement of the building she rented. If anyone reigned supreme at the Baran Agency, it was Cornelia who greeted clients by purring and strutting her stuff.

Cornelia knew how to turn on the computer, flush the john, and even open the box of Tender Vittles when someone left it sitting on the kitchen counter.

"You going to miss me, Linda?"

"Does Cornelia need whipped cream on her catnip? Of course I'm going to miss you. That was a silly question, Amy. But things slow down at this time of year and you're only a cell phone call away. You said your mom has a fax machine so I think we're good to go in case something crops up. In a way, I envy you. Going home for the holidays is always kind of special and going all out on your mom's project to help the Seniors is the icing on top as far as good feelings go. If anyone can make it work, you can."

Amy flopped down on her swivel chair, her long legs stretched out in front of her. "Easy to say, Linda. Mapping out a PR campaign to sell cosmetics or corn flakes is a lot different from selling Christmas trees. I know zip about Christmas trees other than you put them in a stand, string lights and ornaments and flick the switch. Instant gratification."

"You got a plan, boss?"

Amy laughed, the sound ricocheting off the walls. "Sort of, kind of. I'm thinking three tents. One for the stuff Mom wants to sell. You know, ornaments, lights, gift wrap, the big red velvet bows. I ordered tons of stuff a week ago when Mom hit me with this. I jumped right on it. Mom's got the Seniors lined up to work the store, as she calls it. They're going to be serving gingerbread and hot mulled cider the way they used to do at Moss Farms. I told you about that wonderful place from my childhood. I hate it that Mr. Moss let the farm go to ruin. I have such nice memories of going out there with my father. He always made it a special event. One year it actually snowed the day we went to pick up the tree. I was so excited I could hardly sleep the night before. Memories are wonderful, aren't they?"

Linda flicked the long braid that hung down to the middle of her back. "Memories are super as long as you don't dwell on them. Maybe you'll meet Prince Charming when you go home. I see it now: he appears out of nowhere, asks you to help him pick out the perfect tree. You do, and then he asks

you to deliver it and help him set it up. You agree. You fall
into his arms in front of the tree and voila, you now have a
boyfriend!"

"In your dreams! I don't have time for boyfriends. I'm
trying to build this business and working sixteen hours a day
is more than any guy can understand. All in good time."

Linda eyed her boss. She would never understand how
someone as personable, as pretty, as intelligent as Amy didn't
have men falling all over her. "Your clock is ticking, Amy.
There's more to life than building a business."

Amy sniffed as she fiddled with the comb that controlled
her long, dark, curly hair. She fixed her green eyes on Linda
and said, "You're a year older and I don't see you in any
hurry to settle down."

"Yeah, well, at least I have a prospect. George loves me
and would marry me in a heartbeat if I said the word. I'm
thinking about it. I want us to have enough money saved up
to put a down payment on a house. There's no way I'm going
to live in an apartment with kids. I want lots of kids and so
does George. By next year we'll have saved enough for a
starter house. It's my plan. You don't even have a prospect,
much less a plan, Amy."

Linda was right even though she didn't want to admit it.
She longed for Mr. Right but so far he had eluded her.
Maybe Linda was right and she needed to cut back on the
hours she worked and get some kind of personal life. Or she
could go to the Internet and sign up on one of those matchmaking sites. *Like that was really going to happen.*

Amy shrugged as she continued to stuff her briefcase.
She had to sit on it so she could lock it. "I don't know why
I'm taking all this. Better to be prepared for anything and
everything. Okay, okay, I'll work on my social skills and try
to snag a guy when I get home. You realize single guys do
not buy Christmas trees. They buy artificial ones. Families,
moms and dads and kids, buy trees. Having said that, I will
do my best to find a man who will meet with your approval.

If I come back empty handed, I will explore one of those dating sites, okay?"

"Yeah. Look, if you need me, give me a call. I can take the train and be there in three hours. I'm going to miss Corny," Linda said as she scooped up the tabby to settle her in the carryall. She pulled the zipper.

Amy took a last look around. "It feels right, Linda. Going home, I mean. I hate leaving you for two whole months but like you said, I'm just a phone call away. You don't think I'm making a mistake, do you?"

"Am I hearing right? The famous Amy Baran is asking me if she's making a mistake? The short answer is, no. Look, my mom passed away. I'd drop everything, even George, to have her back calling me to help out. You always have to give back, Amy. If you don't, you're just a shell of a person. I expect you to be an authority on Christmas trees when you get back. I can go on the Net and research Christmas tree farms and send out some query letters asking if they want to use our services next year. That's assuming you pull this off and raise the money you need."

You don't know my mother, Linda. "Good idea. You know what bothers me the most is the trucking fees. We're starting out in debt. I don't like that. If bad weather sets in, the trees might not be cut in time. I'm at growers' and truckers' mercies. Mom did all the initial contacting. I wish she had left it up to me instead of going with the first person she contacted. You need to shop around to get the best price. Well, I gotta be going. I packed everything up last night. Yes, yes, I will call you along the way and will call you when I get to Mom's house. I'll miss you, Linda. Two months is a long time," Amy said wistfully.

Linda threw her arm over her boss's shoulder. "I think you're going to be too busy to miss this place. Go on now before we both start blubbering."

Amy picked up Cornelia's carrying case and threw it over her shoulder. The briefcase weighed a ton and she probably

24 *Fern Michaels*

wouldn't even open it once she got to Virginia. Her mother always said she overcompensated for everything. Her mother also said she was anal retentive, was an overachiever and needed to think inside the box instead of outside. So much for her loving mother.

Amy settled Cornelia on the passenger seat before she unzipped the carryall. Cornelia poked her head up just long enough to see her surroundings before she curled up to sleep. Amy slipped a disc into the player and settled down to make the trip to Fairfax, Virginia.

Four hours later with four stops along the way, Amy pulled into her mother's driveway on Little Pumpkin Lane. She leaned back and closed her eyes for a moment. She was home. The house where she'd grown up. A house of secrets. The house where she'd been lonely, sad, angry. So many memories.

Now why had she expected her mother to be standing in the doorway waiting to greet her? Because that's what mothers usually did when an offspring returned home for a visit. A stupid expectation, Amy decided as she climbed out of the car. She left Cornelia in the car while she unloaded her bags and the boxes of things she'd brought with her. Four trips later, Amy carried Cornelia into the house and settled her and her litter box in the laundry room. She called her mother's name, knowing there would be no answer. Her mother was a busy lady who did good deeds twenty-four/seven. All she did was sleep at the house. It was like that while she was growing up, too. Tillie Baran for the most part had always been an absentee mother with various housekeepers picking up her slack. When the housekeepers went home, her father took over, making sure she ate a good dinner, brushed her teeth, helped her with her homework and tucked her into bed at night. For some reason, though, she'd never felt cheated.

All of that changed when her father died of a heart attack in the lobby of the Pentagon on the day after she graduated from college. If her mother had grieved, she hadn't seen it.

Armed with her substantial inheritance, Amy had relocated to Philadelphia where she worked for a PR firm to get her feet wet before she opened her own small agency.

She called home once a week, usually early Sunday morning, to carry on an inane conversation with her mother that never lasted more than five minutes. She returned home for Easter, Thanksgiving and Christmas—just day trips, because her mother was too busy to visit. For the past two years, though, she hadn't returned home at all. Her mother didn't seem to notice. No matter what, though, Amy kept up with her early Sunday morning phone calls because she wanted to be a good daughter.

And now here she was. Home to do her mother's bidding. For the first time in her entire life her mother had asked for her help. She couldn't help but wonder if there was an ulterior motive to this particular command performance.

Amy carried her bags, one at a time, to her old bedroom on the second floor. It all looked the same, neat as always, unlived in, smelling like lemon furniture polish. A cold, unfeeling house. Her mother's fault? Her father's?

Amy hated the house. She thought about her cozy five room townhouse, chockful of doodads, knick-knacks and tons of green plants that she watered faithfully. In the winter she used her fireplace every single evening, not caring if the soot scattered from time to time or if the house smelled like woodsmoke. She had bright-colored, comfortable furniture and she didn't mind if Cornelia slept on the couch or not. Her garage was full of junk and she loved every square inch of it. There simply was no comparison between her mother's house and her own. None at all.

Amy stopped in the hallway and opened the door to her father's old room. It still smelled like him after all these years. How she'd loved her father. She looked around. It was stark, nothing out of place. A man's room with rustic earthy colors. She opened the closet the way she always did when she returned home. All her father's suits hung neatly on the double racks, exactly two inches apart. His shoes were still lined up against the wall. This was a room that didn't include her mother. Amy had always wondered why. She backed out of the room, closing the door behind her.

She had no interest in checking her mother's room. Instead, she opened the door to her room. A bed, a dresser, a bookshelf and two night tables on each side of the twin bed. The drapes were the same; so was the bedspread. She hated the patchwork design.

Long ago she'd taken everything from this room, even the things she no longer wanted. There was nothing here that said Amy Margaret Baran ever resided in this room. It was a guest room, nothing more. Well, she didn't do guest rooms. In a fit of something she couldn't explain, Amy carried her bags back down the hall and opened the door to her father's room a second time. She would sleep here for the next two months. The bed was king-size, and there was a deep reading chair and a grand bathroom, complete with a Jacuzzi.

As Amy unpacked her bags she wondered if her father's spirit would visit her. She didn't know if she believed in such things or not but she had an open mind. If it happened, it happened. If not, her life would go on.

She set her laptop on her father's desk, her clothes hanging next to her father's. The picture of her and her father on her sixteenth birthday—taken by the housekeeper whose name she couldn't remember—went on the night table next to the house phone. She looked around as she tried to decide what she should do next. She walked over to the entertainment center that took up a whole wall. Underneath was a minifridge. She opened it to see beer and Coca-Colas. She wondered when the drinks had been added. She popped a Coke and looked for the expiration date. Whoever the housekeeper was, she was up-to-date.

Amy settled herself in the lounge chair and sipped her drink. All she had to do now was wait for her mother.

Cornelia leaped into her lap and started to purr. Amy

stroked her, crooning words a mother would croon to a small child. Eventually her eyes closed and she slept, her sleep invaded by a familiar dream.

. . . She knew it was late because her room was totally dark and only thin slivers of moonlight showed between the slats of the blinds. She had to go to the bathroom but knew she wouldn't get up and go out to the hall because she could hear the angry voices. She scrunched herself into a tight ball with her hands over her ears but she could still hear the voices. . . .

Chapter Three

Exhausted from his long trip, Cyrus antsy to get out and run, Gus pulled up to the entrance of Moss Farms and looked at the dilapidated sign swinging on one hinge from the carved post. A lump rose in his throat. A few nails, new hinges, some paint, and it would be good as new. The lump stayed in his throat as he put his Porsche Cayenne into gear and drove through the opening.

Gus ascended a steep hill lined with ancient fragrant evergreens, their massive trunks covered in dark green moss. His mother always said it was so fitting because their name was Moss.

At the top of the hill, Gus shifted into park and got out of the car to look down at the valley full of every kind of evergreen imaginable. He saw the Douglas firs; the blue spruce field; and to the left of that, the long-needle Scotch pine. He shaded his eyes from the sun to better see the fields of balsam fir, Fraser firs, and Norway Spruce. To the left as far as the eye could see were the fields of white pines and the white firs. The Austrian pines looked glorious, and the three fields of Virginia pines seemed to go on to infinity. Thousands and thousands of trees. The lump was still in his throat when he tried to whistle for Cyrus, who came on the run.

Gus coasted down the hill to the valley where his old homestead rested. It looked as shabby and dilapidated as the entrance sign. *What does my father do all day?*

Gus wasn't disappointed at the lack of a welcoming committee. He really hadn't expected his father to run out and greet him. Still, it would have been nice. He parked the car at the side of the house and climbed out. He whistled for Cyrus, who was busy smelling everything in sight. "Hey, Pop!" he bellowed. Cyrus stopped his sniffing long enough to lift his head to see what was going on.

A tall man with a shaggy gray-white beard appeared out of nowhere. He was wearing a red plaid jacket with a matching hunting cap. "No need to shout, son. There's nothing wrong with my hearing. You on your way to somewhere or are you visiting?"

Gus licked at his lips. *What happened to, "Nice to see you, son" or "Good to see you, son"? Maybe a handshake or a hug.*

"I came for a visit. I thought I'd help with the trees this year. Looks kind of dead around here. What's going on, Pop?"

"Like you said, it's dead around here. I let everyone go. I'm retired now."

"Just like that, you retired? Why didn't you tell me?"

"Didn't much think you'd care. Nice looking dog. Not as nice as old Buster, though. Buster was one of a kind."

Gus jammed his hands into his pockets. "Why would you think I wouldn't care? If you needed my help all you had to do was ask. Are you just going to let those trees grow wild? That's just like throwing money down the drain."

"You're a little late in coming around, son. When I needed you, you were in California making fancy houses for fancy people. When you left here you said you didn't want to be a farmer. I took you at your word."

Gus flinched. The old man had him there. He didn't want to be a farmer; he wanted to do exactly what he was doing. *Well, I'm here now, so I'll just have to make the best of it.*

"I'm here to help. The first thing I'm going to do is fix the steps on the front porch before you kill yourself. Then I'm going to hire some people to thin the fields and then I'm going to set up shop and sell Christmas trees. I'll find someone to operate the Christmas store and then when you're back on your feet, you can take over."

"Don't need your help, Augustus. If that's why you came here, you can just climb into that fancy rig of yours and drive back to California and all those fancy people you like so much."

Gus dug the heels of his sneakers into the soft ground and rocked back. "I kind of figured you'd say that, Pop. So, let me put it another way. I came home to protect my investment, *my half* of Moss Farms. The half Mom left to me. If you don't want me staying in the house I can get a room at a hotel in town. It doesn't matter to me. The farm does matter. So, Pop, like it or not, I'm going to go to work."

"Won't do you any good. Some group of women in town will be selling trees this year. A lady all prissy and dressed up came out here to ask me to sell her my trees. She wanted them at cut-rate prices. I said no. You want to go up against her, go ahead. I always said you were a smart aleck," Sam Moss said as he turned to lumber away. "Stay in the house if you want; I don't care, just pick up after yourself."

"Yeah, Pop, you always did say that. And a bunch of other things that were even worse," Gus called to his father's retreating back. If the old man heard his son's words, he didn't show it. Gus wished he was a kid again so he could cry. Instead, he straightened his shoulders and climbed back into the Porsche, with Cyrus right behind him.

Gus backtracked and headed for town and a used car lot,

where he bought a secondhand pickup truck the owner said he could drive off the lot with the promise that one of his workers would drive the Porsche back to Moss Farms by mid-afternoon.

With Cyrus riding shotgun, Gus drove to Home Depot, where he loaded up the back of the truck with a new chain saw, hammers, nails, lumber, paint and anything else he thought he would possibly need. When he checked his loading sheet and was satisfied, he drove to the unemployment office and posted a notice for day workers paying five dollars over minium wage. All calls would go to his cell phone so as not to bother his father. The *Fairfax Connection* took his ad and promised to run it for a week. Again, he asked for day workers to run the Christmas store his mother had made an institution.

Gus made two more stops, one at a florist he remembered his mother liking. There he explained what he needed and was promised wholesale prices. The order, the nice lady said, would be delivered by the end of the week. His last stop was a gourmet shop, where he again explained his needs and was promised delivery in seven days.

On his way home, Gus pulled into a roadside stand where his mother used to buy fresh cider. Within thirty minutes, he signed a contract for a daily delivery of fresh cider, and for an extra hundred dollars the owner agreed to rent him a top-of-the-line cooler. His arms loaded down with vegetables, fresh apples, eggs and some frozen food, along with some dog food, he completed his shopping, and headed back to Moss Farms, feeling like he'd put in a hard morning's work. He was on a roll and he knew it. It was the same kind of feeling he always got when he presented a finished set of blue-prints to a client. He loved the feeling.

As he drove along in his new pickup truck, Gus wondered about the dressed-up prissy woman who wanted to buy trees from his father. Competition was a good thing, a healthy thing. Maybe he needed to come up with a jingle or something to be played on the radio. For sure he was going to need to do some advertising. Well, hell, he had a workforce back in California. He'd give them a call and let them run with it. Creative minds needed to be put to use. He made a mental note to order a fax machine.

"I'm paying my dues again, Mom," he whispered.

"I know, son, I know," came back the reply.

Gus almost ran off the road as he looked around, his eyes wild. Cyrus let his ears go flat against his head. He whined as he tried to get closer to Gus. *I must be either overtired or overstimulated.* He tried again. "Did you just talk to me, Mom? Or was I hearing things?"

The tinkling laugh he'd loved so much as a kid filled the car. "In a manner of speaking, Gussie. I told you I'd always be there for you when you needed me."

"Where . . . where are you, Mom?"

"Right beside you where I've always been. You just haven't needed me before. I'm so proud of you, coming back like this. Your father is a hard man, Gus. Be patient and things will work out."

"He gave our tree to the White House. I went there and got a branch. I hated him for that, Mom."

"I know. I saw you there. I don't want you to hate your father. He has difficulty showing affection. He loves you."

"Well, Mom, he has a hell of a way of showing it." Gus wondered if he was losing his mind. Was he so desperate for family affection he was imagining all this? He asked.

He heard the tinkling laugh again. "No, you aren't losing your mind. You're opening your mind. It goes with the upcoming season, Gus. You really need to fix that sign," Sara Moss said, as Gus pulled into the entrance of Moss Farms.

Gus stopped the truck. "I'm going to do it right now. I have everything in back of the truck. Mom, did you . . . what I mean is . . . ?"

"I saw the plaque on your office building. That was so

wonderful of you, Gus. I felt so proud of you. Go along now. Do what you have to do."

Gus climbed out of the truck, looked around. Then he shook his head to clear his thoughts. Cyrus was still whining. "Will you come back, Mom?"

"Only if you need me. Remember now, be patient with your father."

Gus didn't know if he should laugh or cry. He looked at his watch. High noon. His shoulders straightened and his step was firm as he rummaged in the back of the new pickup for the tools he would need.

By one o'clock, Gus had the sign fixed with a new coat of paint. By two-thirty, he had the front steps fixed, sanded, and painted. He jacked up the front porch with a two-by-four and had it back in place by three-thirty. By five o'clock he had the kitchen cleaned to his satisfaction. At six o'clock he was washing bed linens for his bed and was in bed between the clean sheets and blankets by eight-thirty. And he hadn't seen his father once since coming back from town. He was asleep the moment his head hit the pillow because he knew he had to get up at four, eat and head out to the fields, because that's what a farmer did.

Chapter Four

Amy jerked awake when Cornelia stirred in her lap. At the same moment, the front door slammed shut.

Her mother was home.

Groggy from the short nap, Amy combed her hair with her fingers, tightened the velvet bow at the back of her head, then knuckled her eyes as she steeled herself for what she knew would probably be an unpleasant encounter with her mother. She waited at the top of the steps to see if her mother would call her name, acknowledge her presence in some way. Such a silly thought. Evidently Cornelia was of the same opinion as she hissed and snarled, circling Amy's ankles. She bent down to pick up the unhappy cat and descended the steps. She called her mother's name twice before she entered the kitchen.

Tillie Baran waved airily as she babbled into the cell phone clutched between her ear and her cheek. She was opening a container of yogurt and sprinkling something that looked like gravel over the top. A bottle of mineral water was clutched under one arm as she juggled everything and still managed to sound animated to whomever was on the other end of the phone. Amy thought it was an awesome performance.

She eyed her stick-thin mother. She was, as usual, dressed impeccably. There wasn't a hair out of place. There never was.

Finally, the call ended. Amy reached for the cell phone and, in the blink of an eye, danced away and turned it off. "I need to talk to you, Mom. Without this stupid thing ringing off the hook."

"Oh, honey, don't do that. It's my lifeline to the world. I have to charge the battery for at least thirty minutes."

Amy wagged her finger. "No, no. Either we talk or I'm outta here. What's it going to be, Mom? I sure hope you aren't going to tell me this is one of your projects that you gave up on."

"Good Lord, why would you say such a thing, Amy? Everything is ready to go for the Seniors. All you have to do is set things up and make it work. I'm depending on you to pull this off. I'm working on the New Year's Gala the Rotary is sponsoring. I have so much to do and not enough hours in the day." All this was said as Tillie shoveled the yogurt and gravel into her mouth. After every bite she swigged from her water bottle.

"What exactly is ready to go, Mom? By the way, did you see that study someone did about people who talk on cell phones all day the way you do?"

"I don't believe I saw that, Amy?"

"You can get a brain tumor. Go to the library and look it up."

For the first time in her life Tillie Baran was at a loss for words. "You can't be serious."

"I'm serious. Now, what's there to set up?"

"The Christmas trees, of course. I ordered them. They will arrive on the Tuesday before Thanksgiving. I told you I rented the Coleman property."

"Mom, you rented a piece of land. A corner property on a

major highway. Did you give any thought to a structure of some sort? It gets bitter cold around here in November. Who did you hire to work, to make the wreathes, the grave blankets and all the stuff you have to do to get something like this under way? You're going to need a guard at night so people don't steal the trees. Where are you going to sell all the extras you told me about?"

Tillie looked puzzled for a moment. "That's your job, dear."

"No, Mom, that's not my job. It was your job. You said you had it ready to go and all I had to do was the PR stuff to get it off the ground. Are the Seniors going to help? Do you know how heavy a Christmas tree is? Who is going to work the chain saw to trim off the bottoms? Who's going to drill the holes in the trunks? Mom, did you think this through?"

"Good heavens, Amy, of course I did. We had seven different meetings about the trees. You're overreacting, aren't you?"

Amy watched as her mother tugged at the jacket of her Chanel suit. She noticed a worried look in her mother's eyes. "No, Mom, I'm not. Who is going to unload the trees from the trucks when they're delivered, and don't tell me the Seniors, because they won't be able to lift them. I hope you don't expect me to do it. How about you? Are you going to be helping?"

The worried look was becoming more intense. "I have this gala . . . there are so many details . . . hire people," she said vaguely. "The university . . ."

"Mom, the kids are studying for finals. They go home for the holidays. No one is going to want to stand out in the cold to sell trees and make six bucks an hour. It doesn't work that way these days. Kids spend all their time with their iPods."

"I'm sure you'll think of something, dear. I really have to go now. Can I please have my phone back?"

"NO!" Amy bellowed at the top of her lungs. "This is where the rubber meets the road, *Mother.* Either you sit down and hash this out with me or I'm leaving. I'll leave it up to you to explain how you failed. I won't be here to scrape the egg off your face either."

"You're just like a bulldog. Your father was that way," Tillie complained, but she did sit down and fold her hands.

"Don't go there, Mom. Right now I'm pretty damn angry, so tread lightly. Did you pay a deposit to the Colemans?"

"Of course not. We have to pay them $2,000 the day after Christmas."

"What? Why didn't you get them to donate the land? This is for the Seniors. Couldn't you have gotten a better rate?"

"They said they wouldn't take a penny less. I had no other choice."

"Did you look for a better place? You didn't, did you? You took the easy way out. Okay, we're now $2,000 in debt. What kind of deal did you make for the trees?"

Tillie started to wring her hands. "Well . . . it's $40 a tree. We have to sell them for $100 each. Some of the bigger trees will cost more. I ordered twenty thousand and put down a deposit of $5,000."

"Oh my God! If you don't sell all of them, you, Mrs. Baran, are on the hook for the balance. You do know that, don't you? I assume you signed an order for them. Did you sign it as Tillie Baran?"

"I did do that. And the lease with the Colemans."

"That's just great Mom. Why didn't you talk to me first? Right now you, *personally,* are $797,000 in debt, and we haven't even started. If there's something else, you better tell me now."

"Well . . . I did hear something today when I was having lunch with the secretary of the Chamber of Commerce. It seems . . . appears . . . it just might be gossip . . . but the rumor is Sam Moss is gearing up to reopen his farm to sell his trees this year. They're saying his fields need to be thinned out and he's going to sell each tree for . . . $40. Of course I never listen to rumors. I even made a trip out to his farm and the old geezer ran me off. I offered to buy his trees for $40 each. Which just goes to show you can't trust a man. Never ever!"

Amy jerked upright. She'd think about that last comment later. "Old geezer. Mr. Moss is as old as you are, Mom. That means he's sixty-four. He probably called you an old biddy. This is a disaster. Are you listening to me, Mom?"

"Of course I'm listening. Are you listening to me? I told you, it's just a rumor. Sam Moss is an angry, bitter old man. If he is indeed going forward, it's out of spite. He always hated how Sara got so involved with the Seniors."

"What about you, Mom? If Mr. Moss is bitter, what are you? You're a robot, a machine that goes twenty-four/seven. I never see you laugh or cry. You're always on automatic, you never stop. Well, you better stop now and think about this little project you just dumped on me. Either we partner on it or I'm bailing out on you. That means you failed. *You,* not me, Mom. Now, how important is all that to you?"

Tillie cleared her throat, then licked at her dry lips. "The Seniors are counting on me. I promised we would raise enough to refurbish the Seniors' Building before the town condemns it. I gave my word. It . . . it is important. I've never failed at any of my events. What . . . what should I do, Amy?"

Amy threw her arms in the air. "I don't know. I'm not a magician. I have a few ideas but I don't know if they'll work. We need to sit here and map out a plan of action, so don't get any ideas about leaving me holding the bag with the mess you created. See this," Amy said, holding up her mother's cell phone. She walked over to the sink, turned on the water, and let it cascade over the phone. "Don't even think about getting another one. Mine will be enough for both of us. Now, let's sit here and talk. First I'm going to make some coffee and order some food. I'm up for Chinese. From here on in, Mom, you are going to keep this refrigerator filled with food. I do not exist on yogurt and water. I want you to think of this little project as me saving you from a life of humiliation. Starting right now, it is my way or the highway, with me driving down it."

Tillie sniffed. She knew she was beaten. She kicked off her shoes and settled down with the paper and pencil Amy placed in front of her. She needed to have the last word. "You are just as mean and hard as your father."

After ordering dinner from Ginger Beef Chinese Food over on Telegraph Road, Amy spooned coffee into the paper cone on the coffeemaker. "We aren't going to go there, Mom, but rest assured before I leave here we will revisit the issue of your husband and my father, because it is long overdue."

Tillie bit down on her lip as she played with the cup and spoon that her daughter set in front of her. If she had anything to say about it, that particular little talk was never going to happen.

Amy risked a glance at her mother, wishing she could feel something other than aggravation. Her mother was copping an attitude. Well, she would just have to deal with it. How strange that this was turning into a role reversal. She felt like the mother admonishing a wayward child. She hoped she could remain tough and stern and not let her mother stomp all over her.

"Let's get our home base settled before we tackle anything else." Amy didn't wait for her mother to agree or disagree. She forged ahead. "We are going to have three meals a day. That means either your housekeeper makes it or you and I take turns. We will sit here at this very table and eat together and discuss what's going on with what I am now calling Tillie's Folly. There will be no more yogurt or that rabbit poop stuff you sprinkle on top of it. This refrigerator will be filled with meat, fish, and chicken. We will have cheese, fruit, and vegetables, along with bread and English muffins. And eggs. Good food. You, Mother, will be working alongside me, so I suggest you get yourself some warm boots, flannel-lined slacks, some heavy sweaters and a good warm hat. The first time I see a cell phone hanging off your ear, our deal is off and you can sink or swim. Do we have a deal, Mom?"

Tillie squirmed in her chair. "Yes, we have a deal. When did you get like this?"

"Do you really care, *Mother*?"

"No, I suppose I don't."

It was Amy's turn to squirm. There was a lot to be said for honesty.

"All right, let's get to it. We have an hour before our dinner arrives. Now, this is what I've been thinking. Give me your input and don't be shy about it. I don't care how bizarre something sounds. We might be able to make it work."

Tillie licked her lips. "Were you trying to scare me before when you said I was liable for all . . . for all those bills?"

Amy leaned across the table. "Read my lips, Mom. You signed the work orders. That means you are liable."

"That . . . that would wipe out my nest egg. I would have to get a job."

"That's what it means, Mom. Look at it this way, 'tis the season of miracles—or almost, anyway."

Chapter Five

Sam Moss sat on the top of the newly repaired steps that to the front porch. There was a time when the porch held pumpkins with lit candles, cornstalks, and a few scarecrows. So long ago. Now the porch was empty, just the way he was empty.

It was full dark now, an hour past supper. The only thing he'd eaten today was a frozen TV dinner at lunchtime that tasted like cardboard because the pot of stew he'd made wasn't done cooking. Sometimes he wondered why he even bothered.

Out of the corner of his eye he could see a line of headlights heading out of the fields. The drivers of the vehicles wouldn't see him sitting on the steps because the big blue spruce at the corner of the house blocked the view of the porch. Gus's workers, that's how he thought of them, wouldn't be gazing about anyway. They'd be in a hurry to get home to their families and a warm supper. Gus would be the last one to come down the road.

His son had been home six full days, and what the boy—which was how he thought of his son, the boy—had accomplished stunned him. In all of his sixty-four years he had never seen such single-minded determination to get the farm up and running. A river of guilt rushed through him at what he was allowing to go on. What *really* bothered him was the boy hadn't asked him for a penny. He knew from the talk in town that Gus was paying his workers more than a decent wage plus overtime. He'd never in his life paid overtime to an employee. Sara always said he was behind the times, a fuddy-duddy with tunnel vision. If she were here right now, sitting on the steps right next to him, she'd give him a poke on the arm and say, "See, Sam, I told you our son is the best of the best." Like he didn't know that.

How he wished he was more like Sara, who was so outgoing and loved by everyone. *Was* outgoing. *Was* loved by everyone. Especially by Gus. That hurt, but he'd accepted that the boy liked his mother more than him. Because of that, without really meaning to, he'd been extra hard on him. In his own defense, he'd said things like, hard work never hurt anyone, hard work builds character. He'd truly believed that because of him, Gus was the man he was today. Until yesterday afternoon, when it started to rain and Gus had come in for a slicker. They'd eyeballed each other until Gus finally said, "Yeah, I know, Pop, working in freezing rain won't kill me, and it will build my character. Well guess what, if your next line is 'I'm the man I am today because of you,' think again. I'm the man I am because of Mom. Not you. Never you." Then he'd stomped out in the cold rain to continue working the fields, to correct what his father had let go to wrack and ruin.

"So, I'm a horse's patoot," Sam Moss muttered as he got up to go into the house.

He'd cooked a pot of stew earlier in the day. It was the one thing he did well. It was simmering on the stove now, ready to be eaten. If he got into the kitchen in time, he could casually mention the stew and even set the table. Maybe they could talk. Maybe he could offer . . .

Sam removed the red plaid mackinaw and hung it on the hook by the back door. He was setting the table when Gus walked in. "Made some stew today. You're welcome to sit down and eat. Got some frozen bread warming in the oven," he said gruffly.

"No, thanks. I'm too tired to eat. Maybe later. Since you seem to be talking to me today, one of my guys told me he heard in town that you're going to be selling trees for $45 each to clear the fields. I sure as hell hope you're talking about *your half* of the farm and not my half. I'll be selling mine at market value. You better get it in gear, Pop, or you're going to look like . . ."

"A horse's patoot?"

Gus reared back. "I was going to be a little more blunt and say a horse's ass. That's if the rumor is true. If it isn't true, I'll take back my opinion." Without another word, Gus left the room.

Sam turned away to hide his grin. The boy had grit, he had to give him that. He ladled the fragrant stew in to his bowl and sat down to eat.

Sam's mind roamed as he ate. He now knew his son's habits at the end of the workday. He showered, slept for three hours, came downstairs to eat, did some paperwork and went back to bed. It was during Gus's three-hour nap that Sam went out to the fields to check the day's work. After his inspection, on the walk back to the house, he always felt like puffing out his chest. The boy had grit *and* promise. He frowned as he broke a piece of bread off the loaf on the table. He really hadn't expected the rumor he started to get back to Gus so quickly. He still couldn't believe he'd purposely started it. How stupid of him to think people would flock to buy the trees Gus cut down at a giveaway price. Gus's trees. He had to remember that.

Upstairs, Gus stood in the bathroom, staring at himself in the mirror. Who the hell was that wild-looking guy with the six-day growth of beard staring back at him? His face was

windburned and his eyes were bloodshot. The beard itched.
He was so cold he thought he'd snap in two before he could
get into the hot shower. Nothing, not even rousing sex, felt
as good as the hot water running over his body. He let his
shoulders droop as he turned this way and that in an effort to
get warm. Stew. Hot stew. He couldn't remember when he
smelled something half as good. Made by his father, who had
issued an invitation. Maybe he was finally coming around.
Or maybe his father thought he was going to fall on his face.
Maybe he thought he didn't have the stamina to carry through
on his plan. *Who the hell knew what the old man thinks.* Still,
an invitation was an invitation. His mouth started to water at
the thought of the savory stew and crusty bread.

Bone tired, Gus stepped out of the shower, dressed and
headed downstairs. He was stunned to see a place set for him
at the table. There was even a napkin. Salt, pepper and butter
were in the middle of the table. He helped himself. He'd
dined in five-star restaurants, eaten gourmet food, but nothing had ever tasted as good as what he was eating. He had
two bowls of the delicious stew, drank a bottle of beer and
ate half the loaf of bread. Beyond stuffed, Gus cleaned up,
transferred the contents of the pot into a huge bowl and set it
in the refrigerator. He wrapped the leftover bread in foil.

With no idea where his father was, Gus turned off the
light and switched on the night-light over the stove before he
headed upstairs where he turned on his laptop and proceeded to go shopping at L.L. Bean. He ordered thermal underwear, flannel shirts, foot warmers, hand warmers, several
wool watch caps, and four pairs of boots. He ordered his
own slicker, two shearling jackets, heavy corduroy trousers,
and a dozen pairs of wool socks. He completed his order and
hit the button for overnight delivery.

With the temperatures in the low forties, he wanted to be
prepared.

His eyes drooping, his stomach full, Gus fell into bed. He

slept soundly until the shrill of the alarm woke him at four o'clock. He groaned, rolled over, tussled with Cyrus for a few minutes, then climbed out of bed to get dressed. He sniffed. Was that coffee and bacon he smelled? He wondered if his father was making breakfast for himself. Or for him. *Nah, lightning doesn't strike twice. Yesterday had to be a fluke.* How could he possibly be hungry after all he'd eaten last night? Yet he was starved, his stomach rumbling.

Cyrus loped ahead of him and sprinted down the stairs. By the time Gus reached the kitchen, Cyrus was gobbling eggs and bacon from a bowl that used to belong to old Buster.

Gus blinked. The table was set. On his mother's place mats. A plate full of eggs, bacon, sausage and toast waited for him along with a huge mug of coffee. Next to his plate was a large thermos. "Looks good," Gus said, sitting down. He bowed his head and said a prayer the way his mother taught him to do before he dived in. It did not go unnoticed by his father.

Sam Moss raised his head and looked directly at his son. "Can you use another set of hands out there?"

Gus stopped chewing long enough to stare at his father. "I can use all the help I can get to clear the white pine field. How are you at taking orders?"

"'Bout as good as you are, Augustus. I can learn."

"We're clearing *my* half of the fields. If you want me to work on *your* half, you're going to have to ask me, Pop. That's how this has to work."

"Let's work on your half first. Don't expect big things out of me, Augustus. I haven't done any manual labor for a long time. I'm out of shape. I'll work your half of the farm. I don't have a problem with that."

"I hope not, because I'm going to work you the way you worked me."

The old man stroked his beard with a gnarled hand.

"Payback time, eh? I worked you as a kid until you dropped to try to make a man out of you. Now you're going to work this old man to prove . . . what?"

Gus stood up. "To prove to me you're good enough to be my father. We're running late. Time is money. Remember those words?"

"Yep." Sam pulled his mackinaw from the hook. He followed Gus and Cyrus out the door.

"Who's cleaning up that mess in the kitchen?" Gus called over his shoulder.

"The new housekeeper who starts today. I even gave her a menu for tonight."

Gus hunched into his jacket as he headed for the pickup truck. He was grinning from ear to ear in the darkness.

Chapter Six

It was ten o'clock when Amy pushed her chair away from the table. Earlier, she'd kicked off her shoes, and now she contemplated her pedicure as she tried to make sense out of her resentful mother. She hated being hard-nosed, but she really didn't have many options under the circumstances. She eyed her mother now as she tried to think of something nice to say. The words eluded her.

"Are we done here, Amy?"

"For now, Mom. Do you at least understand what a problem you created? I don't know if I can pull this off. I just wish you had consulted me when you first came up with the idea. It's a wonderful idea and if it works it will benefit the Seniors." *There, that was something nice. Now they wouldn't go to bed angry with each other.*

"But you don't think it will, is that it? Say it, Amy. Say what you're thinking. Let's get it all out in the open before we go any further."

"I don't think we should go there, Mom. Let's go to bed, sleep on it and tackle it again in the morning. I have some savings I can use. I still have most of Dad's insurance left.

My business is doing well, so I can cut some corners. I'm going to call the people you ordered the trees from and see if I can cancel the order in the morning. I just want you to know this is a seat-of-the-pants operation as of this moment."

"I have things to do tomorrow. My day planner is full," Tillie snapped.

"Not anymore it isn't," Amy snapped. "You're mine now, Mother. From now till December 26, you will be working right alongside me. I want your word. Your word, Mom."

"But . . . I can't possibly . . . I have plans . . . commitments. I don't know you anymore, Amy Margaret Baran."

Amy bit down on her lower lip to try to stem the words she was thinking about, but they spewed out of her mouth because they were long overdue. "Like I know you, Mom! You stopped being my mother when I was four years old. Housekeepers cooked for me, washed my clothes, fed me, put me to bed. I lost count of how many we had. God knows what would have happened to me if it wasn't for Dad. You were never here. You didn't even show up at my high school graduation. You never talked to my teachers. You showed up five hours late for my college graduation. I still can't believe you showed up for your husband's funeral. You were never here for Christmas. Dad and I always got the tree and decorated it. Oh, you posed in front of it, then off you went. Dad bought the presents. Dad wrapped the presents. Dad taught me to roller skate. Dad taught me to ride a bike, and he taught me how to drive. I've always wanted to know, Mom. *Where were you all that time?*"

"Not now, Amy. I'm very tired right now. Let's just both agree that I was a horrible mother and let it go at that."

Amy did her best to blink away her tears. "At least we can finally agree on something."

Amy gathered her books and ledgers and all the notes she'd made earlier together in a nice, neat pile. She set them on the counter out of the way. Her shoes in her hands, she made her way to the second floor, where she threw herself on the bed and had what she intended to be her last cry where her mother was concerned.

Down the hall and across the room, Tillie Baran sat down on the edge of the bed, her shoulders shaking, tears rolling down her cheeks. She should have told her. Why didn't she? Why didn't she defend herself against her daughter's onslaught of hateful words? Because she was guilty, that's why. Too little, too late. The best she could hope for now was a civil relationship with her daughter until this Christmas tree fiasco she'd created was over and done with.

Tillie could see her reflection in the mirror across the room. She looked haggard, and she looked every one of her sixty-four years. She was old, and she had no purpose in life except to do what she called good deeds. If the truth were known, she didn't even really do good deeds. She had ideas for good deeds that other people carried out with a lot of hard work, then she got the credit for those good deeds. She heard her name on the local radio and TV news, and it was always her picture in the paper, never the drones who brought her ideas to fruition. In a million years she never thought her daughter would bring her to task the way she had down in the kitchen just moments ago

Tillie knew she had to make things right with her daughter, somehow, some way, without damaging her thoughts and memories of her father. How could she possibly tell her daughter that three years into her marriage she'd found out her husband was a philanderer, that he needed a string of women to make his life happy. A wife at home tending the fires was just for photo ops in his political life as a roving ambassador to different countries. With offices in the Pentagon and access to the White House, there had been no shortage of young women to entertain and Aaron Nathaniel Baran entertained them all.

How well she remembered a well-meaning friend telling her she thought she should *know* about her husband's outside social activities. She'd gone into shock, became depressed and had a full-blown nervous breakdown. Amy had been five when she finally crawled out of her misery and started a life of her own. A life that didn't include her husband and the little girl who adored him. So long ago, and yet it was just like it was yesterday. The pain was the same today as it was then, only magnified now with Amy's attitude.

Tillie Baran knew she had some serious soul-searching to do. She wondered if it was too late to redeem herself in her daughter's eyes. Respect was all she could hope for. Love was simply out of the question and with no other options available to her, she would have to accept whatever Amy was willing to give her.

As Tillie prepared for bed, a plan started to form in her mind. Tomorrow, if Amy cut her some slack, she'd go out to Moss Farms and try to sweet-talk Sam. If she had to, she would trade on her old friendship with Sara and Sam. Then again, maybe she wouldn't do that. That was the way the old Tillie would have done it. This new Tillie was going to have to be up front and businesslike.

Tillie stared at herself in the mirror as she removed her makeup. *Why do I need all this glop?* If Amy's dire predictions came to pass, she wouldn't be able to afford it anyway. She didn't think twice about sweeping her arm across the vanity. She watched as bottles, jars, and tubes slid into the wastebasket. She didn't feel anything one way or the other. Tomorrow morning she would wash her face and put on some moisturizer and that would be that.

Bedtime reading. No novels tonight. Tonight it would be her latest brokerage statement and how she could make things right for Amy, for the Seniors and possibly herself. She shivered with guilt and humiliation when she recalled her daughter's tone and the expression on her face. That had to be right up there with the moment when she'd confronted her husband about his infidelities and his *so what* attitude.

It was almost midnight when Tillie slid the brokerage

statement into the current folder. Obviously, she was going to have to sell the house, which was nothing more than a status symbol anyway. She'd get a townhouse somewhere and maybe she could get a job as a tour guide. She'd be good at that, she thought. She'd start clean, with no debts. A ripple of fear skittered around in her stomach at the mere thought. She said a small prayer then, asking God to give her the strength to follow through on her plans.

Tillie tossed and turned all night long. In the end she finally gave up, showered, smeared on some moisturizer and dressed in clothes she dug out of a trunk and smelled like mothballs. Old clothes, the kind she used to wear before she became a social gadabout. Corduroy trousers, wool socks, a heavy sweater, and a pair of ankle-high boots she had to clean before she could put them on. She couldn't remember why she'd saved all these clothes. Maybe she knew one day she would need them. "I guess this is the day," she muttered to herself as she made her way downstairs to the kitchen where she would have made coffee if she had any. But since she didn't, she reached for her daughter's heavy jacket and left the house.

Tillie couldn't remember the last time she'd been out and about at four-thirty in the morning.

What would Sam Moss say when he opened the door to see her standing there? Well, she'd find out soon enough.

She stopped at the first fast-food establishment she came to, a Wendy's, and ordered two coffees to go. As Tillie sipped at the hot brew, she thought about the last time she'd gone to see Sam Moss and how it had turned out. Maybe Sam would be in a better mood.

Ten minutes away, Sam Moss was explaining to his son, Gus, that he would join him as soon as he picked up the new blades for the chain saw. "Henry doesn't open his shop till five o'clock. He told me he has two used saws. I want to take a look at them, and if he gives me a guarantee, I'll take them. I'll meet you in the Fraser fir field."

Gus waved, and a minute later was gone.

Sam sat down at the kitchen table, a second cup of coffee in front of him. He could see the clock on the wall across from the table. He was finishing the last of his coffee when he heard a knock on the kitchen door. He opened the door and then took a step backward. "Kind of early to be visiting, isn't it, Tillie?"

"Yes, it is early to be visiting. I was thinking about that on the drive out here. I wasn't sure . . . what I mean is, you all but ran me off the last time I was out here. I need to talk to you, Sam. Actually, the truth is, I need your help. I thought I could trade on our old friendship. It's cold out here, can I come in?"

Sam wiggled his nose. "You smell like mothballs, Tillie. Of course you can come in. Would you like some coffee?"

Tillie was glad she had left the coffee from Wendy's in the car.

"Yes, that would be nice. The smell . . . well, that's part of my problem. Do you think you can ignore it?"

Sam turned away, his mind racing. This visit couldn't be a good thing. He poured coffee into a mug and set it down in front of his old friend. That wasn't quite true, Tillie had been his wife's friend more than his. She'd always been nice to him, though. Sara had loved going to the Senior Citizen meetings and helped plan the social calendar with Tillie. He sat down across from her. He should apologize to her for running her off his property the last time she'd been out here to the farm. There was something different about her today, and it wasn't just the mothball smell.

"I've managed to get myself into some trouble, Sam. I know if I tell you, you won't go spreading my business all over town. That was one of the things I always liked about you—you didn't gossip like the rest of us. I'm here for advice and if you can see your way clear to helping me, that will be fine, but if not, I'll settle for the advice. Will you hear me out?"

Sam poured himself some more coffee before he settled down to listen. When Tillie finally wound down it was five-thirty. "All these years, and you never told your daughter about her father? Why, Tillie?"

Tillie shrugged. "She loved him, Sam. When I had my nervous breakdown, I abandoned her. He was all she had. He might have been a lousy husband but he was a good father to Amy. I screwed up. Everything she said about me is true. I don't know how to undo all those years. For now, I can do everything she wants me to do, but what about afterward? I'm going to cancel the tree order, pay for my mistake, sell my house and get something smaller. I don't need that big house. I should be okay if I get a job. I need some of your trees, Sam. I need you to sell them to me at cost. It's the only way I can make this work. It's not for me, Sam, it's for the Seniors." Tillie's eyes filled with tears. She swiped them away with the back of her hand. "The young can be so cruel, Sam. What Amy said was all true, it was how she said it that burned to the quick. By the way, how is that son of yours who lives in California? Sara was so proud of him. Did you two make peace?"

It was Sam's turn to open up. When he finished, Tillie stared at him wide-eyed. "Oh, Sam, how wonderful for you. He came back to help you. That means he's forgiven you. That's what it means, isn't it?"

"Your girl came to help you. Do you think she's forgiven you?"

Tillie shook her head. "No. She's doing what she thinks a daughter should do. I guess your son is doing the same thing. How did we get to this place in time, Sam? We should be taking cruises, buying little treasures in gift stores, going to afternoon matinees, going to friends for dinner." A lone tear rolled down her cheek. "We let it happen, Sam. We can't blame anyone else but ourselves. It's almost light out. I have to get back to the house. Will you think about what I asked and get back to me? I don't have a cell phone any longer. Amy took it away and ran it under the water because she said it was growing out of my ear. Call me at home even if the answer is no."

Sam nodded, stood up, then stunned himself by saying, "Would you like to go out to dinner this evening?"

Tillie jammed a fur-lined hat on her head. "Sure, Sam. I'd like that. Is it a date?"

Sam had to think about the question. A date was where you got dressed up, rang the lady's doorbell. "Yep," he said. "Just don't wear those clothes."

"Okay," Tillie said as she opened the kitchen door. "It might be better if I met you wherever it is you want to go for dinner. Amy doesn't need to know all my business."

Sam nodded, understanding perfectly. "Do you like the Rafters?"

"I do. I'll meet you there at seven. Or is that too late?"

"No, that will work for me, Tillie. I'll have some answers for you tonight."

Tillie didn't know why she did what she did at that moment. She stood on her toes and kissed Sam's cheek. Later she thought it was because she was just so relieved to have finally told someone her problems, someone who had actually listened. "I'll see you this evening. Have a nice day, Sam."

Have a nice day, Sam. She'd kissed his cheek. He could still smell her mothballs. Sam Moss laughed then, a belly laugh that was so deep the floor under his feet rumbled.

When he hit the Fraser fir field at seven-thirty, Gus looked at his father suspiciously. "Did something happen, Pop?"

"No, why do you ask?"

"You smell like mothballs."

Sam burst out laughing as he picked up one of the chain saws and moved off. When had he last heard his father laugh? Never, that was when.

Chapter Seven

The scents emanating from the kitchen were tantalizing as Amy set the table. She was so tired she could hardly see straight. All that aside, she'd put in a productive day's work along with her mother who was chirping about this and that, finally winding down with, "I'm sorry, Amy, but I'm going out to dinner. I guess I should have told you sooner but my head is just swimming with all we've done today."

Amy looked at her mother, at the flowered dishes on the table, the lit candle, the wineglasses just waiting for her to pop the cork. She sniffed at the aromas coming from the stove, the mixed salad, and the baby carrots in the warming bowl. That was when she really noticed her mother. She smelled good. Her hair was pulled back from her face into a bun. She wore no makeup other than a little lipstick. She wore flannel slacks with a bright yellow sweater and low-heeled shoes. She looked like a matron, so unlike Amy's always-fashionable mother that her daughter could hardly wrap her mind around the new Tillie Baran she was seeing.

What could she say other than, "Okay. I guess we'll be

eating this stuff for the rest of the week. By the way, thanks for going shopping. You certainly were up and out pretty early this morning."

"Umm, yes. The early bird gets the worm, that kind of thing. You said you wanted me here in the kitchen at eight o'clock, so I had to take care of some business early to be back here on time. We *old* people don't sleep much."

Amy reared back. This was the first time in her memory that she could remember her mother using the word *old* in reference to herself. Other people were old, not Tillie. Maybe this was where she was supposed to say, "*You're not old, Mom.*" She turned away to fiddle with the lid on the pot roast. "Don't stay out too late."

Tillie laughed, a delightful sound. Amy realized she'd never actually heard her mother laugh out loud. How in the world was that possible? She'd seen her smile but that was it. There must be a man lurking somewhere in the picture. "You smell good," she blurted.

"Do you think so? I have to be going. I'm sorry I didn't tell you sooner about my plans, Amy. Everything looks and smells delicious. I'll look forward to the leftovers tomorrow."

Amy poured herself a cup of coffee and sat down to think about her mother and all that had transpired during the day. Her mother had behaved like a trooper to her surprise. She did everything Amy suggested, even more. She followed through on every single detail by making copious notes. The things they'd accomplished in a mere ten hours boggled her mind. They'd opened a business bank account, with both of them depositing sizeable checks to activate it. They'd ordered two large tents that would be set up on the Coleman property over the weekend. The power company promised electric hookup first thing Monday morning. Portable heaters were ordered along with all the Christmas decorations from the Curiosity Barn. The wholesaler she'd contacted had promised delivery of the wreath wires, the lath, the florist wires, the speciality bows, and everything else she needed for assembling the wreaths and grave blankets. Trial and error was the order of the day as she tried to figure out where to get a barrel and the netting for the trees. Several Seniors had come to the rescue, and there was now a huge metal rain drum sitting on her mother's back porch. The bails of netting would be delivered on Tuesday along with tree trimmers and chain saws.

She was going to have at least fifty volunteers but no real workers. Tomorrow she would go on the hunt for actual employees. Tonight she had to get started on her PR campaign.

Damn, she was tired. Detail tired, not physically tired. Maybe she needed to get dressed and go for a run to clear her thoughts.

Amy looked at the dinner she'd prepared. Just the thought of mashing the potatoes and making gravy left her weak in the knees. She'd do that when she served leftovers. Instead she made herself a sandwich with the meat and ate it, along with a second cup of coffee. The minute she finished eating, she tidied up the kitchen, wrapped everything up, turned on the dishwasher and then stared at the huge chart she'd pasted to the kitchen wall. The bit red X in the middle of the chart glared at her. *I can pull this off. I really can. All I need are Christmas trees.* The grower her mother had signed on with was not an easy man to deal with even after she threatened him. Finally, in desperation, she'd told him to keep the five-thousand-dollar deposit and cancel the order. He in turn threatened to sue Tillie. That's when she told him to get in line with all the other people waiting to sue Tillie Baran. He's squawked and threatened some more, but at the end of the conversation he'd agreed to cancel the order. She'd been light-headed with her victory, but the elation was short-lived. Now she had to find Christmas trees, and the only place that had what she needed was Moss Farms. Maybe Mr. Moss would remember her and agree to sell her some trees. If not, this whole thing was going to go down the drain.

Well, that wasn't going to happen, not on her watch.

Amy looked at the kitchen clock. It was only 6:45. She could drive out to the farm in fifteen minutes. Mr. Moss would be done with his dinner and settled in for the evening. Maybe he would be more agreeable to her than he was with her pushy mother. Then again, maybe the cranky old man would run her off his property the way he'd run her mother off. *Oh well, nothing ventured, nothing gained. If he won't help, maybe out of the kindness of his heart he'll steer me in the right direction.*

Without stopping to think about it anymore, she reached for her jacket and was out of the house before she could change her mind.

Gus Moss stepped out of the shower, towel dried, and pulled on a pair of beat-up sweatpants and his first Tulane sweatshirt, which was full of holes. He stared at himself in the mirror and burst out laughing. He'd shaved his beard yesterday and he now looked like himself. He slicked his curly hair back but knew the moment it dried it would be all over the place. *Maybe I'll get a buzz cut over the weekend. If I can find the time.*

Cyrus, who dogged him everywhere he went, barked sharply. "Yeah, yeah, I know, Cyrus, we're running behind schedule, but Pop threw me for a loop when he said he wouldn't be here for dinner. Did you see him, Cyrus? He looked like a dandy, all duded up and wearing aftershave! I think he's stepping out on me is what I think. Okay, okay, let's see what Mrs. Collins left us for dinner."

Everything, including Cyrus's dinner, would be in the warming oven. It was the best move his father could have made. With all the different smells, Gus liked coming into the house. He liked the sweet-smelling sheets and clean blankets Mrs. Collins put on his bed. He liked that there was a fire blazing in the kitchen fireplace when he came in from work. He liked the whole gig. Cyrus liked it too. The dog had made friends with Gus's father. Out of the corner of his eye he'd see Gus's father scratch Cyrus behind his ears and call him Buster from time to time. He knew at night that the retriever spent part of the night with him and part of the night with his father. He grinned at the thought.

"Here we go, big guy. You get chicken, mashed potatoes, a little gravy, lots of broccoli and even a buttered roll. I get the same thing, but just a little broccoli because I hate it. That berry pie looks pretty good, too." Cyrus woofed, gobbled down his food and then went to the door. He knew when he got back he'd get his dessert.

Gus filled his plate twice, saving just enough room for a slice of pie. When he finished, he leaned back in the captain's chair at the head of the table and let his mind go back over the day's work. Another week of hard work with his crew and he'd be ready to cut the trees to go on sale the day after Thanksgiving. He felt so proud of himself he decided he would have an extra large slice of pie—as soon as Cyrus pawed at the door to get in. While he waited he added two more logs to the fire. A shower of sparks raced up the chimney.

Outside, Cyrus was barking his head off. Gus listened to the tone. It wasn't a playful bark, or an I-treed-a-racoon bark, or an Okay, I'm-done-and-ready-for-dessert bark. This was a bark that meant there was an intruder on the premises. He reached up and turned on the outside floodlights. The entire backyard was suddenly bathed in a blinding white light and Cyrus was escorting a young woman to his back door. *Cyrus must like her,* Gus thought, because his tail was swishing back and forth at the speed of light.

Gus opened the door and stared at the young woman in the purple hat and scarf. She smiled. He smiled—and fell in love on the spot.

His love opened her mouth and spoke. Suddenly he wanted to shower her with diamonds and rubies. Maybe pearls. "I know it's late, but is it possible to speak with Mr. Moss?"

"Uh, sure. I'm Mr. Moss. Gus Moss. Come in, come in."

His love spoke again. "I'm sorry. I meant the other . . . Mr. Moss senior."

"Oh, *that* Mr. Moss. He isn't here. Will I do?"

Cyrus, never known for his patience, barked and pawed at the kitchen counter where the pie was. "Excuse me. Cyrus is relentless. He won't give up until he gets his pie. I was just about to have some. Will you join me?"

Amy stared at the good-looking young man. She thought her blood was boiling in her veins. "You know what, I think I will join you. I have a sweet tooth."

His love had a sweet tooth. "Me too. All my teeth are sweet." Gus grimaced, showing his teeth. His love laughed.

"Is that good for a dog?" Amy asked pointing to the pie Gus just put in Cyrus's bowl.

"His owner refuses to give him dog food. I'm just dog sitting old Cyrus. People food seems to agree with him. Do you want ice cream on your pie?"

"Well, sure. What good is pie without ice cream? Do you have any coffee to go with that pie?" He watched, mesmerized when the purple hat and scarf came off, then the jacket. Lean and trim. Just the right kinds of curves. His love was perfect, and she was standing right there in his father's kitchen.

"Absolutely. Big slice or little slice?"

His love laughed again, a tinkling sound that sent shivers up Gus's spine. "Oh, a big slice. If you're going to eat pie and ice cream, you need a big piece to really enjoy it. I haven't had pie in a long time. What kind is it?"

"Berry. What should I call you?" Gus said, turning his back on her to cut the pie.

"I'm sorry; my manners are atrocious. Amy Baran. Nice to meet you, Gus Moss. I didn't know Mr. Moss had a son. I used to come out here every September with my dad to tag a tree. Then we'd come back around Thanksgiving to take the tree home. It was the highlight of my life back then. Dad would always give me ten dollars to spend in the Christmas shop. I felt so grown-up when I'd sit down to eat the ginger-bread and cider. Then I really grew up, and we didn't do it anymore. Your mother always took time with the kids. Where were you?"

"Out in the fields I guess." *Amy Baran*. This was the young woman Peggy and Ham Bledsoe talked about. The same Amy Baran who returned home to help her mother. His competitor. He turned around, his expression blank. "Nice to meet you, Amy Baran." Gus extended his hand and she grasped it. It was no wishy-washy handshake either. She gave as good as she got.

Gus ate his pie as he tried to figure out what this . . . *spy* was doing sitting in his kitchen. He decided his eyes were bigger than his stomach. Suddenly, the pie and ice cream lost their appeal. He set the dish down on the floor for Cyrus. Amy continued to eat. She appeared to be enjoying every mouthful.

"So what did you want to see my father about?"

"To buy some trees. A lot of trees. My mother told me she heard in town that your father is selling all his trees this year for $45 to thin out his fields. We'd be happy to buy about ten thousand. For buying that many we'd like a dis-count of maybe 5 percent. It's for the Seniors. No one will be making money off this deal, and that includes me and my mother. My mother asked me to come home to help out and to map out a PR campaign to sell the trees. I have to admit it was all a good idea, but my mother didn't think it through and made some major goofs. It was left to me to pick up the pieces. When do you think I can talk to your father? Or do you make the decisions? That was certainly good pie. I en-joyed it."

"The housekeeper made it. I'll pass on the compliment. That would be a loss of $55 a tree to Moss Farms. I don't know who started that rumor. Moss Farms is in business to *make* money, not give it away. What are you planning on selling them for? A hundred bucks a pop? That's a lot of money, Miss Baran. So you would still make a 25 percent return on the investment if I sold to you at $80 a tree."

"Yes, it is a lot of money, but it's for the Seniors' Building. There's no other place to get funding. As it is, the building was left to the Senior Citizens in a member's will. Are you following me here?"

"I'm on the same page. Only half the fields will be ready to harvest. The half you're talking about is overgrown. They haven't been fertilized or irrigated. There are a lot of dead trees in those fields. I don't have enough help to get them in shape for this season. Ah, I see by your expression that you aren't following me. Let me explain. My father let the farm go to wrack and ruin. I came home last week from California to help out. A lot of people his age don't want to hear from their whippersnapper sons, who think they know more than they do. My father . . . my father felt the same way. Push came to shove and, Miss Baran, I exercised my option to take over the half of the farm left to me by my mother, that wonderful lady who was always so nice to you. *My* trees will be ready to cut Thanksgiving week. If my father sells to you, you are going to have a lot of disgruntled customers. As they stand now, I wouldn't pay twenty bucks for one of them. Business is business, and time is money. I learned that at my father's knee," Gus snapped.

Amy's jaw dropped as she tried to absorb what Gus Moss was telling her. Her back stiffened. "Let me be sure I understand what you've just said. As far as you know the $45 per tree is a rumor. Moss Farms is divided into two parts. You own half, your father owns half. You are working your tree fields, and your father's are nothing but garbage. You're willing to sell your trees to me for $80 a tree which is a 20 percent discount to the Seniors. Did I get that all right?"

"That's about it. We'll trim the base, clip the straggly

branches, drill the hole in the trunk and net the trees. We'll divide the lot into three categories—small, medium and large trees. You can sell them for whatever you want. We'll even deliver them to your site. That's all gratis. Labor is expensive. It's the best I can do."

"Well, that isn't good enough, Mr. Moss. This is for charity, for the Senior Citizens of our town. Your father is a senior citizen, and so is my mother. One day you and I will be seniors. Shame on you, Gus Moss. I wouldn't do business with you if you paid me my weight in gold. Who do you think you are?"

His love was angry. Well, he was angry too. "I'm an architect. I'm not a tree farmer. I came here to help my father and to protect my interest in this farm. I put my personal life on hold to come here to do this and to make it work. And it is working. My fields are ready to go."

"Helloooo, Mr. Moss. I did the same thing. I'm going to make it work, but for all the *right* reasons. Not to make money for myself and to protect my investment."

The purple hat was suddenly on her head, the muffler whipping past his nose as she wrapped it around her neck. "You . . . you . . . *Scrooge*. Shame on you, Gus Moss. I hope you enjoy your ill-gotten gains. Thanks for the pie." The door slammed behind Amy. Cyrus let out a shrill bark and slammed against the back door as he tried to understand the young woman's angry tone.

Gus flopped down on the chair he'd been sitting on during Amy Baran's tirade. *Scrooge! Scrooge!* She'd called him, Gus Moss, a scrooge.

Chapter Eight

The Rafters was a secluded restaurant perched high on a hill. In the fall and winter when the trees were bare, the nation's capitol could be seen in the distance. It wasn't necessarily the kind of eatery where one went to be seen—just the opposite, as it afforded privacy and small rooms where one could dine without worrying about people stopping by to say hello. It was rumored that more than one senator and congressmen had dalliances in the private rooms. The owners of the establishment, the ladies Harriet and Olivia Neeson, were quick to deny all such rumors.

Sam Moss had called ahead for a reservation and was assured by Harriet, who had been a dear friend of his wife, Sara, that she would reserve the best table in the house.

Sam and Tillie were halfway through the meal when Sam realized he was enjoying himself. He liked the witty, sharp-tongued Tillie Baran. He knew he was going to be sorely disappointed if this outing turned out to be solely about Christmas trees.

It had been ages, years actually, since he'd dined out. He always felt like a fish out of water sitting down in a restaurant by himself. When Sara was alive, they ate out every Saturday and Sunday to give her a break from cooking. He'd liked the fact that they both got slicked up. Sara preferred to say they got dressed up. Before his date with Tillie he'd dithered about what to wear and had trouble deciding if he should get dressed up. Finally, he settled on one of his vintage sport jackets. He was glad now that he hadn't gone the suit-and-tie route, because Tillie was dressed casually. She smelled so good he kept sniffing her over the delectable aromas emanating from the kitchen. Yes sireee, he was enjoying himself.

Tillie looked up from her pecan-crusted salmon she was eating and said, "I can't help but notice how you keep sniffing, Sam. Do I still smell like mothballs?"

"No, no. I'm trying to decide which smells better, the aromas from the kitchen or your perfume. It's been a long time since I smelled perfume. The truth is, I haven't been out with a lady since Sara died."

Tillie pushed her plate away. "I can top that, Sam. I haven't been with a man in twenty-eight years. What I mean is, I haven't . . . never mind. It must have been very hard on you when Sara passed away. My husband . . . it was different. I know you and Sara were very happy."

Sam saw that his dinner companion was becoming agitated. "That was all a long time ago. Life goes on whether we like it or not. Let's talk about more pleasant things."

"How about we get down to business and talk about trees?" Tillie said bluntly.

"I can do it, Tillie, but it's going to pose a big problem for me. Unless we can come up with some way . . . Look, I'm on shaky ground where my son is concerned. We're being civil to one another but our relationship is very strained. He hasn't forgiven me for a lot of things I really don't want to go into right now. What that means to you is, he is working his half of the farm. He hired people to thin out the trees. He did some irrigating and fertilizing. His half. My half of the fields is in poor shape. If we can find a way to get the trees thinned and cut, I'll donate as many as you want to the Seniors' fund-raiser."

"Sam! Really! You'll donate as many as we can sell? That's wonderful. We'll just have to find people to help us. We have over seventy members to our chapter. The members have sons, nephews, grandchildren. Surely we can convince them to help us."

Sam toyed with his wineglass. "We have to do it at night, Tillie."

Tillie reared back in her chair. "At night! Right off, I see that as a problem. Why?"

Sam looked embarrassed. "I don't want Gus to know. Right now the boy doesn't have a very high opinion of me. Like I said, we're on shaky ground. He left his business to come here to help me. I reacted like the old fool I am, said and did a lot of things Sara would deplore, but I did them anyway. He wants to prove to me he can get the farm back on its feet. He just might succeed at the rate he's going. It's too late to get my fields in shape, so while I'm donating them to you, you won't be able to charge much for them. That means they aren't going to be perfect trees. If I donate them to you, whatever you do sell them for will be all profit. Perhaps less than you planned, but you'll make something. If you can get the volunteers, I think we can make it work. Maybe you can bill them as Charlie Brown trees." Sam guffawed at what he thought was his witticism.

"Why are you doing this, Sam?" Tillie asked suspiciously. "When I came out to see you weeks ago you all but ran me off your property."

"I'm sorry about that. I wasn't in a good place mentally at the time. Then Gus came home with a major attitude. I had to fall back and regroup. At my age it's damn hard to admit when you're wrong, especially to your son. There are things . . . I don't know if I can ever make right."

Tillie reached across the table to take Sam's hand in her

own. "I know all about that, Sam. I really do. Amy and I are in the same position. I think we're two old fools that stepped off the road and are trying to find it again. My daughter is so . . . efficient, so smart. She's detail oriented. She follows through. That's important, as she pointed out to me. She doesn't like me, Sam. She as much as said I wasn't mother material. Do you know how hard that was to hear? Worse, she's right. She ran my cell phone under water. She said it was growing out of my ear." This last sentence was said with such outrage, Sam burst out laughing. He squeezed her hand.

"My son doesn't like me either. He needs to show me up, prove that he can run the farm and make money. He's trying to show me that even though he hates it, he's good at it. Does that make sense?" Tillie nodded. "I understand he's a damn fine architect and makes tons of money out there in California. Gets all kinds of awards. Sara would have been so proud of him. He never forgave me for donating 'his' tree to the White House. Sara always said when it got to a proper growth, she was going to donate it to the White House in Gus's name. She was so proud of that tree. Gus thinks I did it for spite."

Tillie was aghast. "And you never told him?"

"No, I never told him, just the way you never told your daughter about your husband."

"Not only are we old fools, Sam, we're stupid old fools. Why do we always think we know best just because we're older? Do you think we can pull this off, Sam? Won't your son hear or notice the activity out in your . . . your half of the fields?"

"No. What he considers my half is down more in the valley. We can drive in from the back end. He's busy working *his half*. He goes to bed at eight o'clock and sleeps so soundly the house could fall down around him and he wouldn't hear it. How are you going to explain it to your daughter?"

"I'll think of something. It's the season of miracles, isn't it? Every morning when Amy gets to the site she'll see whatever we put there during the night. She did tell me this was a seat-of-the-pants operation. I think she's right. A mysterious Good Samaritan delivers trees in the middle of the night. She'll find a way to run with that. She's a PR person and will play that up to the public. *I think she's right.* Can we really do this, Sam? I'm starting to get excited."

Sam stared across the table at his dinner partner, saw the sparkle in her eyes, felt her hand squeeze his again. He was starting to get excited himself. "Yes, we can do it. When you go home, start making phone calls. I'll do the same. We'll start work tomorrow night. We'll all meet at the back entrance at eight-thirty and take it from there. Do you care for dessert?"

"No, Sam, I don't think so. I think we should go home and get to work. I have one small question. If we work all night, when are we going to sleep?"

Sam threw his head back and laughed again. "We might have to pretend we're sick. Old people get sick all the time. We can say we got our flu shots and like a lot of people, got sick."

"Oooh, Sam, you're so devious. I think that might work. I don't see your son or my daughter fussing over either one of us, do you?"

Sam grinned from ear to ear. "Nope." He squeezed Tillie's hand. When she squeezed back, he laughed again. "Okay, partner, let's hit the road and get to work. I think we should do this again sometime, Tillie."

"I'd like that, Sam. I really would. It was a lovely dinner. Thank you."

Amy was sitting at the kitchen table nursing a glass of wine she really didn't want. Every time she thought about Gus Moss, her cheeks burned. The man was a scrooge. An out-and-out California guy who thought only about money. The arrogance of the man!

Amy was startled out of her reverie when she noticed her mother standing in the doorway. "Did you have a nice time wherever you went, Mother?"

"I suppose so. Dinner is dinner. You eat, you chat, you pay the check. Dinner. Is something wrong? You look angry."

"I am angry. After you left, I drove out to Moss Farms to talk to Mr. Moss, only he wasn't there. His know-it-all son was there. Mr. Moneybags Moss. I offered to buy his trees and asked for a discount. The best he could do was 20 percent. We can't operate and make money at that rate. We had words. I called him a scrooge. I think I might have screamed that. He gave me some pie that was very good. He's in charge of the farm these days. He was so arrogant, Mom. But boy was he good-looking. I'm really pissed off right now."

Tillie felt so weak in the knees she had to sit down. Her daughter poured a glass of wine for her, which she drained in one long gulp. "I see."

Amy bolted off her chair and started pacing the kitchen from one end to the other. "What do you see, Mother?"

"That . . . that you're upset. I'm . . . ah . . . feeling a little slow today. I got a flu shot the other day and for some reason I always get sick afterward. That happens to a lot of people my age for some reason. I could . . . ah . . . be laid up for as long as a week. I'm sorry, Amy. I'll do what I can, even if I have to do it in bed. It's not easy getting old. Not that you would understand that."

"Oh, I understand, Mother. It's called a cop-out. Good night. I'll see you in the morning. I'll make breakfast if you can see your way to getting out of bed."

Tillie felt her shoulders stiffen. "I'll do my best, Amy," she said cooly.

Tillie poured herself another glass of wine as she contemplated what the coming days would bring. "This is all my fault," she mumbled to the silent room. "All my fault."

Chapter Nine

The silvery flakes of frost on the windows of Amy's car alarmed her. She hoped she was dressed warm enough. To her way of thinking it was too cold for this time of year. They shouldn't have a frost until Thanksgiving, but then what did she know about weather conditions? Not a whole lot, she decided as she climbed into her car to head to the Coleman site, where the tent people would be erecting the tents three days ahead of schedule. Nothing was working right. Everything had a glitch. Even her mother was under the weather. Sometimes, life wasn't fair.

She had to find some Christmas trees or she was going to fizzle like a dead firecracker. She'd been talking a good game to her mother but it wasn't working for her. Someone, somewhere had to have some Christmas trees they were willing to sell for a discount for a worthy cause. She'd beaten the bushes, banged the drum, and the tree growers had laughed at her. None to spare, she'd been told. Orders were placed months in advance, not weeks like she was doing. If push came to shove, she might have to resort to dealing with the crook her mother had signed on with. If she didn't pull this off, she'd be a failure in her eyes, and her mother's as well. Amy thought about her bank balance as she drove to the Coleman site. It wasn't exactly robust, but it was healthy. She'd dipped into it for deposits, and now it looked like she might have to do more than dip the second time around.

She thought about Gus Moss and how nice it had been sitting in the kitchen at Moss Farms. Everything had gone so well until she told him what she wanted. Such a scrooge. Why couldn't people be more generous? Money wasn't the answer to everything. Christmas was supposed to be a time for giving, for helping one's fellow man. What was it Gus Moss had said? *Time is money, business is business.* Maybe that was her problem, she was taking this personal. The tired old cliché of all PR people came to mind. Fight fire with fire. Preempt your opponent. Strike first. Amy shivered. Was she a match for Gus Moss? Probably not. What she knew about Christmas trees would fill a thimble, whereas Gus Moss could write the book on the subject. One of the sharpest PR people she'd ever come across told her she had to subscribe to his credo: dazzle them with rhetoric and baffle them with bullshit, and you win the game. Like she was really going to do that? Not in this lifetime.

Amy swerved into the vacant lot and was surprised to see three trucks and men hustling about, driving stakes into the ground. She was pleased to see that the tents were made from a shiny white plastic that would lend itself well to the red and green Christmas colors, colors that would stand out and draw attention. Another plus was the site, which was a corner property with an entrance from both roads and more than ample parking. She would have plenty of room to line up her trees if she ever got any to line up.

Amy watched the workers for a few minutes before she drove off down the road to a Burger King, where she bought a honey biscuit and two cups of coffee to go.

Back at the site she opened her laptop and logged on. Time to find some Christmas trees. An hour later, Amy was jolted from her search by a knock on the car window. She looked at the bill, winced, and wrote out the check. She went back to her search as the men drove off. She looked at the tents and was impressed. At least she'd done one thing right.

It was midmorning when a whoop of pleasure echoed in the car. A man named Ambrose McFlint had trees for sale in McLean, Virginia. The banner ad running across the flat screen said the trees were reasonably priced, and free delivery went with the deal. Within minutes, Amy had the car in gear and she was headed for McLean.

Ten miles away Gus Moss was tagging trees he judged ready to be cut in two weeks' time. Orange tags were tied onto the branches for the first cutting. Red tags meant the second cutting. Purple tags were balled trees to be dug out with the backhoe, but only when the trees were paid for.

As Gus tromped from the Douglas firs to the Balsam firs to the Virginia pines, he let his mind run wild to the young woman he'd shared dessert with last night. Even though he was bone tired, he hadn't slept well, tossing and turning all night long. He couldn't get Amy Baran's expression out of his mind. She'd been shocked, dismayed at his callousness. Then she'd added insult to injury and called him a scrooge. Would it kill him to sell her a few trees at a healthy discount for the Seniors' cause? All his life he'd been a generous person, so why was he suddenly turning into a skinflint? He didn't have to prove anything to anyone except maybe his father. The why of it simply eluded him.

"Jack, Bill, come over here," he called to two of his workers. See this grove of Virginia pine? I want you to trim the trees, cut away the brush and tag them with these red tags. We'll cut these trees the Tuesday before Thanksgiving and deliver them after dark. Don't look at me like that and don't ask any questions. Just do it."

"All of them? There must be over two hundred," Jack, his foreman, said.

"Yeah, all of them. We'll stagger the deliveries, fifty at a time. I'll pay you overtime."

Gus felt his shoulders lighten a bit as he prowled his fields. An anonymous donation of two hundred trees should take him out of the scrooge category.

Every so often Gus glanced over his shoulder to look for his father, but he was nowhere to be seen. He'd had to make his own breakfast that morning. He felt a grin stretch across his face. His father must have had a really busy night. He'd heard him come in, heard him going up and down the stairs all night long. Obviously he wasn't the only one who hadn't had a good night's sleep.

As he worked through the day, all he could think of was Amy Baran. He suddenly loved the color purple. *Where is she? What is she doing right now?* He wished he knew.

He wondered what she would do if he called her up and asked her out to dinner. He nixed that idea as soon as it popped into his head. He knew in his gut Amy Baran would never go out with someone she considered to be a scrooge. *So why did I even think about it?*

It was noon when Gus made his way back to the farmhouse. He needed some hot soup and a cup of strong, black coffee. He looked up when he felt something brush his cheek. Rain? He was stunned when he realized what he felt was a snowflake. Thick gray clouds scudded across the sky. Snow this early? He hoped not.

Gus almost swooned at the delicious scents that assailed him the moment he and Cyrus entered the kitchen. A fire was roaring in the fireplace. *The only thing missing is the girl with the purple hat and scarf,* Gus thought as he washed his hands. He ladled soup into a bowl, cut a chunk of crusty bread and fell to it. He was careful to only eat two bowls of soup; otherwise, he'd be sluggish all afternoon. The strong, black coffee made his eyeballs stand at attention. As he sipped the brew he walked around the house calling his father's name. He craned his neck to stare out the window. His father's truck was gone. He must have gone to town for something. He shrugged.

Gus set his dishes in the sink, gave Cyrus a rawhide chew, put on his jacket and hat and was out of the house, all within five minutes. Instead of walking out to the white pine field, he climbed into his pickup. If the weather held he could clear at least two rows of the beautiful white pines that would bring him top dollar. As he bumped along the rutted fields his thoughts returned to Amy Baran. He felt like a sixteen-year-old again with his first crush.

On the seat next to him, Cyrus growled as he fought with his chewie, which wasn't crumbling to his satisfaction. "You see, Cyrus, you have to work for everything in this life. There's no free lunch, even though Miss Amy Baran seems to think there is." Cyrus ignored him as he continued fighting with the rawhide bone.

Gus stood in awe as he gazed at the white pine grove. How beautiful, how pungent it smelled. Suddenly, he didn't want to cut the trees. They were just too majestic. Even though his father hadn't fertilized or irrigated the beautiful trees, they had survived. All the grove needed was to be thinned out. Maybe he would cut every third one instead of all of them. It broke his heart that once the magnificent specimens were cut, decorated by someone in a house that was probably too warm, the tree would slowly die and be discarded. *You live, then you die,* he thought bitterly.

Angrily, Gus walked among the stately trees, tying long, yellow strips onto the branches. Long strips of the bright yellow tape meant the trees were not to be touched.

Why, he asked himself, was he so angry? Was he angry that his mother died, that his father let everything go to hell, that he'd killed *Gus's birth tree* by cutting it down and donating it to the White House? Or was he angry at the young woman in the purple hat and scarf for calling him a scrooge and hurting his feelings? All of the above, he decided as the

chain saw in his hand came to life. He worked then like there
was a devil on his shoulder, cutting away the thick under-
growth and dead branches. He broke a sweat but continued
until it was too dark to see what he was doing. He was sweat-
ing profusely and every bone in his body ached as he drove
back over the same bumpy fields. He looked down at his
watch and was surprised to see that it was six-thirty. His father would be waiting dinner for him.

His father wasn't waiting for him when he opened the
kitchen door. The table wasn't set either. The huge pot of
soup was still simmering on the warming burner. The oven
showed a golden roast chicken dinner complete with stuffing
and mashed potatoes and gravy. Cyrus barked.

Gus shed his outer clothing, and that's when he noticed
the red blinking light on his father's answering machine. No
voice mail for Sam Moss. Gus pressed the button to listen to
the message. His eyebrows shot up to his hairline when he
heard the sweet, melodious voice of his love. "Mr. Moss . . .
ah, Gus, this is Amy Baran. I'm . . . ah, calling you to apologize for calling you a scrooge last night. I was upset when I
called you Scrooge. At the time I meant it because I was
angry. I don't mean it today because I'm no longer angry.
Even though we're competitors of sorts, I hope you sell all
of your trees and that you make a lot of money. Again, I'm
sorry for my rude behavior."

"Well, hot damn! Did you hear that, Cyrus?" Gus slapped
at the kitchen table as he danced a little jig while Cyrus
nipped at his ankles. His love apologized. She wasn't angry
with him. Maybe now he could call her for a date. He played
the message again and listened to the end of it. A frown built
between his brows. She hoped he sold all his trees and made
a lot of money. She thought this was all about money. She
thought he was a money-hungry Christmas tree salesman.
How could she think that about him? It was never about the
money.

A niggling voice whispered in his ear, a voice he didn't

want to hear. *Sure it's about the money. It's about proving to your father you can do in two months what he didn't do in the last ten years. This is your way of getting back at him. It all translates to money—$$$. Who are you kidding, Gus Moss?*

You didn't put it behind you. You're kidding yourself if you think you've moved on. You haven't. You are a scrooge.

The phone found its way to Gus's hand. He dialed Information and asked for the number to the Baran residence. His shoulders slumped when he heard the voice mail click on. "This is Gus Moss, a.k.a. Scrooge. I just want to say I accept your apology and would like you to know I'm really a stand-up guy. I'd like to invite you to dinner if you have some free time. If you're agreeable, we should probably schedule it before we both get busy selling Christmas trees. The apology wasn't necessary. I would have said the same thing if I had been standing in your shoes. I think you should give me an opportunity to defend myself. I hope you have a nice evening."

Chapter Ten

It was eight-thirty when Amy Baran dialed Gus Moss's phone number. She hated herself for what she was about to do but she had no other choice. Ripples of anxiety raced up and down her arms. "Gus, this is Amy Baran. I just got your message. I appreciate the return phone call. Listen, I was just about to go out to Tony's to grab a pizza. Would you like to join me?" *Liar, liar, pants on fire.*

Gus looked down at his worn sweatpants, then at the oven where his dinner sat. He'd been in no hurry to eat earlier. "Well, sure. Thirty minutes?"

"That works for me. I'll meet you there."

"Wear that purple hat and scarf, okay?"

Amy laughed, a jittery sound, but Gus didn't pick up on her nervousness. He was beyond excited as he raced upstairs to change his clothes, with Cyrus right behind him, nipping at his heels. It took him four minutes to change into acceptable clothes for a pizza date. He used up another five minutes filling a plate for Cyrus. Two minutes later he was out the door. It only took a minute for him to realize how cold it was. He cranked on the heater and sailed down the road.

Gus was ten minutes early when he parked his truck and headed for the pizzeria. It was warm and steamy, the rich scent of garlic and cheese wafting about. The place was full of chattering customers chomping down on Tony's pizza. He looked around at the red leather booths for a sign of Amy. He saw her in the back. She waved. He grew light-headed as he made his way to the booth.

She smiled.

He smiled.

She motioned for him to sit opposite her.

He obliged.

"I took the liberty of ordering. I got the works except for anchovies. If you want them, now's the time to ask. I hope you like Corona."

"I do. Like Corona and no, I don't like anchovies. I guess we have something in common. I love pizza. Three food groups you know." He needed to stop acting like a young teenager and act like the successful man he was. He struggled for something to say that sounded intelligent. "It's cold out." *Wow, that was brilliant.*

"I felt some snow flurries when I got out of the car. Usually it doesn't get this cold this early. How do you handle this cold coming from California?"

"I bought a lot of warm clothing. The truth is, today I was so cold I was numb. How was your day?"

Amy picked at the napkin in her hands. It was almost shredded. Here it was, the question she'd been dreading. "Listen, I want you to know something about me, Gus. By nature I am not a devious person. I have ethics. I'm pretty much up front and in your face if anything. I called you back . . . under false pretenses. I was sincere about the apology the first time I called you. I'm not going to beat around the bush. I need your Christmas trees. I went out to McLean to a guy who said he would sell me some. It didn't work out. I'm asking you to help me. Well, not me really, the Seniors."

She was so frustrated, so embarrassed, her eyes filled with tears. She blinked them away. She squared her shoulders. "I was wondering . . . hoping you would consider the two of us pooling our efforts to help the Seniors. I know you want to make money, so here is my proposition. I'll take on your loss as my own personal debt. It might take me a few years to pay it off, but I will pay it off."

Gus stared at the agitated woman sitting across from him. Whatever he'd been expecting, this wasn't it. Her eyes looked luminous with unshed tears. He wanted to bolt over to her side of the booth and wrap his arms around her. He grappled for something to say. "Why is this so important to you?"

Amy brushed at the corners of her eyes. "I'm not sure. If you absolutely need an answer, the only thing I can say is I'm trying to . . . to . . . prove to my mother that I turned out okay even though she was never around when I did things she should have patted me on the head for. I suppose that sounds silly to you. I don't know, maybe it's a girl thing. I never got . . . what I mean is . . . I always wanted her approval. I never got it. So, while it is about the Seniors, it's all about me, too. Does any of this make sense to you?"

Well hell yes, it made perfect sense to him. Wasn't he living through the exact same thing? Maybe they were soul mates. He nodded, his eyes sober as he handed her a paper napkin. "It makes sense," he said quietly. "I'm doing exactly what you're trying to do. So, do you have an idea, a plan?"

Amy leaned across the table. Her eyes sparkled with hope. "Does that mean you'll help me?"

Gus didn't trust himself to speak. He nodded.

"Well, I thought I could . . . I have a campaign all worked out. That's my speciality. It's what I do for a living. I'll have to get rid of the tents, suck up the deposit, and relocate to your farm. People, according to Mom, don't know you're back in business, so I can make that happen. I'll work alongside you. I'll do whatever you want. You don't have to worry about me carrying my weight. I'll work around the clock if that's what you want. We can draw on the Seniors to set up your store. I can make the wreaths and grave blankets. This will free up your people to handle the trees. Does . . . do you think . . . ?"

Gus leaned back in the booth to allow the waiter to set a steaming pizza in the middle of the table. "Okay."

Amy's face lit up like a neon sign. "Do you mean it, Gus? What . . . what about time is money and business is business? Are you sure?"

Was he? Suddenly he realized he'd never been more sure of anything in his life. He nodded. "Let me ask you a question. What happens if when this is all over and done with, your mother and my father don't understand what we're all about?"

Amy sat up straighter in the booth. "Then, Gus Moss, it's their loss, not ours."

Ah, his love thought just the way he did. He nodded again. He stretched his arm across the table. "Okay, partner, let's put our heads together, but first we eat this pizza."

His love laughed, her eyes sparkling like diamonds. She squeezed his hand. Gus felt like he was on fire. He watched as she loaded her pizza with hot peppers, just the way he liked his. He said so. They both laughed in delight.

Gus Moss was in love. It never once occurred to him that Miss Amy Baran might be using him for his Christmas trees. He told himself his heart would know if that was the case.

Amy Baran tried to still her pounding heart. It never once occurred to her that Gus Moss might be using her and her PR campaign to sell his Christmas trees. If that were the case, she told herself, her heart wouldn't be pounding the way it was.

At one point, Gus moved to the other side of the booth, where they talked in low whispers about everything and anything. Without realizing it, he reached for Amy's hand. She exerted a little pressure to show she didn't mind this close-ness.

It was eleven-thirty when Gus paid the check and walked Amy to her car. He wanted to kiss her so bad his teeth ached with the feeling. Something told him this wasn't the time.

Suddenly he was jolted forward when Amy grabbed the lapels of his shearling jacket and pulled him to her, where she put a lip-lock on him that made his world rock right out from under him. When she finally released him, she smiled. "I'll see you at six o'clock tomorrow morning, Gus Moss." She leaned forward and whispered in his ear. "Dream about me, okay?"

Gus stood statue-still as he watched his love drive away. His fist shot upward. "Yessss!"

Sam Moss looked down at the oversize watch on his wrist, a gift from Gus a few years ago. It was almost mid-night, and his well-meaning Seniors were pooped to the nth degree. Tillie, at his side, looked like she was going to col-lapse any minute, but she was still wearing her game face. "This isn't working, Tillie. They mean well, their minds want to do this but their bodies aren't willing. I think we need to fall back and regroup."

"I know, Sam. Can we go someplace where it's warm and talk about it? I'm worried about some of them. Let's all go over to the all-night diner and decide what we're going to do. I didn't think getting old was going to be this devastating. My daughter was right, making arrangements via cell phone and doing the actual work are two different things. I owe her an apology. Actually I owe her more—"

"Shhh," Sam said as he put his finger near her lips. "We'll figure something out. I'll talk to the men, you talk to the ladies. If nothing else, we have enough branches and limbs to make a good many wreathes and grave blankets. Three and a half hours, and all we managed was to cut down six trees, and even with all our manpower we can't get the trees into the trucks. You're right, Tillie, we're old. Where in the hell did all the wisdom we're supposed to have go?"

How sad he sounds, Tillie thought. She tried then to do what all women had done since the beginning of time—bolster up the big man standing next to her. "I think, Sam, we transferred our wisdom to our children because they turned out to be know-it-alls."

Her words had the desired effect. Sam guffawed as he drew her to him with his arm. Tillie felt light-headed. "Let's get our work crew and head for the diner. Breakfast, dinner, whatever, is on me. Snap to it, little lady. I'll meet all of you at the diner."

Tillie found herself giggling. *Dear God, have I ever giggled like this? Never, as far as I can remember.* Suddenly, she felt warm all over as she herded the female Seniors to cars for transport to the diner. She felt guilty as she realized not one of them would have given up, even knowing they weren't carrying their weight.

"Look, we didn't really fail. We're going to rethink this. When we're warm with some good food, we'll come up with a better idea." Tillie wondered if what she was saying was true.

They were a weary, bedraggled group as they trooped into Stan's Diner, which was open twenty-four hours a day. Two police officers were paying for take-out coffee and Danish. Otherwise, the diner was empty.

The women all headed for the restrooms to wash the pine resin off their hands. Tillie sat down, her shoulders slumping. How had it come to this? She hoped she was strong enough not to cry.

Within minutes, Sam and the weary male Seniors blew into the diner. Stan, the owner, greeted them, his eyes full of questions. Sam took him aside to speak with him. Within minutes, the waiters had the tables pushed together and Stan had his marching orders. Hot chocolate, tea and coffee were brought. Taking into consideration the Seniors' health, Sam ordered Egg Beaters omelets, turkey bacon, oven-baked potatoes, and toast.

When they were all seated with hot drinks in front of them, Tillie looked around. Her friends, and they were her friends, looked shell-shocked. She wondered if she looked the same way. Probably. She decided she really didn't care how she looked. She had to give her friends some hope, some encouragement. She couldn't let them return to their homes thinking that just because they were old, they were failures. With a nod from Sam, she used her spoon to tap her water glass for attention.

"I want you all to listen to me. Like Sam said, our minds are willing but our bodies aren't in tune. This was an over-whelming project. Most of us don't see well at night. That's strike one. Strike two is we aren't twenty, thirty, forty or fifty. We simply cannot do the things we used to do even though we want to do them. Strike three is the cold weather. We aren't used to manual labor. Been there, done that. We all had good intentions but they aren't working for us. I'm going to turn it over to Sam now in case he has some ideas, I, for one, am not giving up."

The Seniors clapped their approval of Tillie's little speech.

Sam stood up and looked around the long table. "I have an idea but I don't know if it will work. When I go home tonight, I'm going to wake up my son and *talk* to him. I think most of you know about . . . about how things are with me. I'm going to ask him to help us. The boy has a lot of ill feel-ing toward me. I'm going to try and make that right. Will it work? I don't know. I've never . . . I've never had to actually ask him for anything. It's going to be a new experience for both of us. If Augustus turns his back on me, I am prepared to donate whatever you would have netted from selling trees to the Senior project."

"But if you donate the money that means we still failed," Ian Conover said. "We wanted to earn the money, Sam. If your son turns his back on you, can you handle it? No man wants to see his son turn against him."

"I'm prepared for that, Ian. Nothing can be worse than all the years since Sara died. I'm going to do my best, and if my best isn't good enough, then so be it."

The Seniors clapped and raised their mugs to toast their leader.

Sam Moss walked into the kitchen at one-thirty in the morning. Cyrus greeted him with a soft woof of pleasure. His son was asleep at the kitchen table. Sam took a minute to stare at his Gus, remembering the day he was born. He'd been so crazy with happiness, he'd left the hospital, raced home to plant a tree, and named it Gus's tree. Then he headed for Wheeler's Hardware store and bought a child's John Deere tractor for his newborn son. That was probably his first mistake. He should have bought him an easel or a drafting board.

Sam sighed as he hung up his jacket and hat. If there was a committee that handed out a prize for the most mistakes made by a father, he'd win it hands down. He poured himself a cup of the strong, bitter coffee that was still in the pot. He sat down at the table to wait for his son to wake up. One taste told him the coffee was bad, so he threw it out and made a fresh pot. He was into his second cup when Gus woke up.

"Dad!"

"It's me, son. I've been sitting here wondering if by some chance you were waiting up for me. I seem to recall that was my job. It's funny how things turn around when you least expect it. Were you waiting up for me? I want to talk to you about something, Gus."

"I was waiting for you. I guess I'm not used to you going out at night. Yeah, I remember the nights I came home and you and Mom were sitting here pretending you weren't waiting for me. I need to talk to you about something too. How would you feel about me donating all my trees to the Seniors?" he blurted. "I had a pizza with Amy Baran this evening, and they really are in a bind. Nothing worked out for them. She brought me up short. She told me she would partner up with me, do the public relations campaign, and she would make the grave blankets and wreaths herself. She said the Seniors would man the shop, bake the gingerbread and hand out the cider. She has some really grand ideas. It will put Moss Farms back on the map, Dad.

"I want to apologize to you about that . . . my-half-of-the-farm crap I spouted when I first got here. This is your farm. It was always yours and Mom's. I came here to help you, Dad. Then you dug in your heels, and I, in turn, dug in my heels. I let old . . . hurts and memories take over. So, if you're okay with Moss Farms working with the Seniors, I'll stay on through the holidays and give it all I've got."

Sam Moss could feel his insides start to shake. He knew how hard it was for his son to say what he'd just said. He nodded. He finally managed to get the words out. "I regret the things I've done, Gus—for so many things that went wrong. I was selfish. I wanted a chip off the old block. I wanted you to love this farm the way your mother and I loved it."

Gus reached down to scratch Cyrus behind the ears. "I do love the farm, Dad. I just don't want to farm it. There are other people who can do it better than I ever could. All I ever wanted was for you to be proud of me. You never ever, by thought, word, or deed, indicated that you were. Mom said you were, but I thought she was just saying what she knew I wanted to hear. I'm a damn good architect, Dad."

"Come here, son," Sam said, going into the living room. He opened a chest that served as a coffee table. Gus looked down and saw copies of all his awards, stacks of *Architectural Digest* where his designs were featured, piles and piles of newspapers that carried his picture and write-ups about him. "Does this answer your question, son?"

Gus was so stunned he didn't know what to do or say. He knew in his gut this was as close as he was going to get to a real, gut-wrenching apology. The words "I'm sorry" simply were not in Sam Moss's vocabulary. He decided he could accept that. "Yeah, Pop, except for one thing. If you were so damn proud of me, if you loved me, why did you chop down my tree and give it to the White House? Mom said an hour after I was born you planted my tree. Then you chopped it down and sent it away."

Sam Moss dropped down on his knees to rummage in the bottom of the chest until he found an envelope. He held it out to Gus. Gus read his mother's letter addressed to the White House and the reply that was sent to her accepting her offer of Gus's tree for display during the Christmas season. "Why did you let me think . . . why didn't you tell me . . . ?"

"That's where I am guilty, son. I wasn't in a good mental place that year. Your mother and I were invited to the White House. Your mother wanted it to be a surprise for you. It was what she wanted. If it means anything to you at this point, I tried arguing her out of it. I dearly loved that old tree. Another year or so and it would have gotten straggly looking. Just so you know."

And then his father said the magic words Gus had waited a lifetime to hear. "No father could be prouder of his son than I am of you. I'm sorry, son."

Chapter Eleven

Operation Christmas Tree, as Gus referred to it, kicked into high gear the following Monday morning. His work crew, numbering twelve, arrived at the crack of dawn. Sam's crew of Seniors arrived minutes later. Both Moss Senior and Moss Junior issued orders like the generals they pretended to be. OCT was under way.

Tillie stepped forward and led the Senior Ladies to the gift shop where they proceeded to set up shop opening box after box of ornaments, ribbons, Christmas toys, bells and everything else she had ordered at the last minute for opening day.

Amy arrived breathless, wearing sturdy work boots, tight-fitting jeans, a bomber jacket and a bright orange hat and scarf. Gus Moss fell in love all over again. When she waved her clipboard at him and winked, he thought he would go out of his mind. Suddenly, all he wanted to do was cuddle, to snuggle, to hold her hand, to whisper in her ear. What he didn't want to do was go out in the tree fields and wield a chain saw. When she winked and waved again, he groaned and climbed into his truck.

Sam and Tillie poked each other and grinned at these go-ings-on.

"Seven days to Thanksgiving, then the fun starts," Sam said happily. "It gets pretty wild around here, Tillie. Are you sure you're up to it?"

"We'll soon find out. Did you have anything in mind for Thanksgiving, Sam? If you don't, I have an idea."

"Let me hear it, little lady."

"We always have a turkey dinner at Seniors' headquarters, as you know. Adeline McPherson makes the best turkeys in the county. I'm sure you know that too. Let's do the dinner out here at the farm. I know Addy would be more than happy to work in your kitchen and you have those two, big double ovens. We'll invite everyone—Gus's crew, their families, all the Seniors, and us. I think it would be a good incentive and a great way to kick things off. Everyone will be in the mood to give 100 percent on Friday morning when the trees go on sale. You'll have to pay for it, Sam. Can you see your way clear to doing that?"

Sam beamed. It had been a long time since anyone asked for his opinion or for a donation to anything. Giving his trees away simply didn't fit into this particular equation. "It would be my pleasure. You sounded like my Sara just then, Tillie."

Tillie looked up at Sam, a stricken look on her face.

"What? What's wrong? What did I say?" Sam asked anxiously.

"I'm not Sara, Sam. I'm me, Tillie. Please don't compare or confuse us. I have to go now, the ladies need me. Lunch will be promptly at noon. We need to keep to a schedule."

Sam ambled off scratching his head. "That was kind of blunt, Mom, don't you think?" Amy asked.

"Well . . . I just don't . . . I wouldn't want . . . Never mind. What's on your agenda for today?"

Amy settled her knit cap more firmly on her head as the wind kicked up. "I'm going into town. I have appointments lined up through the whole day. My first stop is the local radio station. I already contacted the stations in the District, and one of them agreed to play my jingle and advertise for Moss Farms every hour on the hour. It's all free, Mom. The station manager's parents live in an assisted living facility, and she's all for anything that benefits senior citizens. On Wednesday two billboards are going up where you can see them from I-95. I had to pay for those but got a 40 percent discount. Local TV is in the bag, all four channels. A new Christmas sign is going up at the entrance to the farm tomorrow. It's an eye popper—bright red.

"Tomorrow I pick up the Christmas Stocking. For a hundred bucks the Canvas Shop made this twenty-foot stocking out of bright red canvas. It's going to be weatherproof. We'll hang it from the tree next to the gift shop. I'm going begging today, asking for donations to fill the stocking. Everyone who comes out here to buy a tree gets to fill out an entry form, and Sam or Gus will pick the winner at noon on Christmas Eve. We're not actually going to put the donations in the stocking, but we will have a scroll next to the stocking so people can see which store donated what item. I think this is a biggie, Mom. It's going to draw people like crazy. The radio and television stations will be announcing who gave what. Free advertising for the donors. Win–win!"

Tillie looked at her daughter in amazement. "Oh, Amy, that's wonderful. In a million years I never could have come up with an idea like that. I am so proud of you. You're right, it's a biggie." Impulsively, she reached out and hugged her daughter.

Amy grew light-headed. This was the closest her mother had ever come to showing any kind of affection toward her. She hugged her back, and suddenly her world was right side up. Feeling shy at this show of affection, she waved her arms about. "I think we make a good team. We're going to make so much money for your Seniors they might be able to add that new wing to the building you were talking about."

"Well, my dear, Sam and I can't take credit for anything.

It was you and Gus who brought all this together. Sam, me, the Seniors are just the elves. You two are Mr. and Mrs. Santa. I think he *really* likes you, Amy," Tillie whispered.

"How . . . how can you tell?"

"Silly girl. Open your eyes. Good luck, honey. I'll see you when I see you. Lunch is at noon if you make it back in time."

Honey. Her mother had called her honey. Another first. She said Gus *really* liked her. Mothers never lied to their children. She wondered if that was a myth made up by some disgruntled mother who had lied to her child and then tried to salvage the lie. She discounted the thought immediately.

As Amy made her way to her car she knew, just knew, it was going to be a dynamite day.

Sam Moss was thinking the same thing as he chugged his way over the frozen fields in his battered pickup truck. He couldn't remember the last time he'd felt this alive, this good. He looked down at the cell phone on the seat next to him. A gift from Gus, who had said, "You need to get with it, Dad. I'll program it for you, and you just hit the button. It's a new world out there, and you need to join it." Sam snorted when he remembered Tillie telling him her daughter ran her cell phone under the faucet because it was growing out of her ear. Well, if his son said he needed a cell phone, then he needed a cell phone. He stopped the truck as he diddled and fiddled with the gadget in his hands. Finally, he simply called Information for the number to the butcher shop in town.

"Elroy, Sam Moss. I want you to come out here and fill my three freezers. A whole side should see us through the holidays. On second thought, maybe a side and a hindquarter. And I want to order six fresh turkeys for Thanksgiving. Big turkeys, twenty-five pounds each. Go on that fancy computer of yours and send everything else times ten that Sara used to order."

Sam listened to the voice on the other end of the phone. "Well, hells bells, Elroy, I want it now, like today. Why else do you think I called you? Be sure you come out here for your tree now. They go on sale the day after Thanksgiving. I just might throw it in for free if I don't get voted down. I'm not really in charge anymore. My son, Gus, is issuing the orders these days."

Sam listened again. "You're right, Elroy, it's the best feeling in the world."

Sam pressed the Off button. He wished there was someone else to call, but he didn't have many friends these days. Then again, he didn't want the darn thing to grow out of his ear. He guffawed at the thought.

Sam blew the horn on the old truck, and waited. It took the golden streak two and a half minutes to arrive and hop into the truck. Cyrus barked happily as he tried to nuzzle Sam's neck. Sam laughed all the way out to the Norway spruce field.

Life was suddenly so good he was scared.

Gus was waiting for him, the chain saw that he never seemed to be without in his hands. "Dad, I've been waiting for you." He pointed to the narrow row of trees. "I think these particular trees can use another year of growth. What do you think? I don't want to tag and cut them if they won't sell. I say we tag them, let the buyers choose the ones they want, then cut them. Two hundred bucks for one of these beauties. By the way, I just got a call on my cell from someone at Super Giant. The supermarket chain wants to order a thousand Christmas wreathes and five hundred grave blankets for their different stores. Ten minutes ago a call came in from a Boy Scout troop asking to buy two hundred trees to sell for a fund-rasier. I said we'd donate them. You okay with that, Dad?"

His son wanted his opinion. Sam wondered if it was a test of some kind. "That's pretty pricey for a tree, don't you think? I don't have a problem with the Scouts or the supermarkets. I just hope we can handle it."

Sam rubbed the whiskers on his chin as he pondered the situation. "The only people willing to pay that kind of money are the Beltway's politicos. I say we sock it to them good. Mark them at $250, and they'll kill themselves trying to get one so they can brag about how much they paid for their Christmas trees. Good thinking, son."

Gus looked at his father and burst out laughing. "Okay, Dad, you're the boss."

Sam thought he was going to black out at the kind words. He had to get past the moment and think about all this later. He could hardly wait to talk to Tillie and tell her. He had to think about *that* later, too. "You sweet on that little gal, Amy?"

A smart-ass retort rose to Gus's lips, but he stifled it. "She's okay, Dad. She's got a good work ethic."

"Well, that sure as hell doesn't sound very romantic, son. Do I need to take you into the woodshed and explain the facts of life? I asked you if you were sweet on her. I'm kind of sweet on her Momma. You wanna run with that one, son?"

Son of a gun! "Yeah, Dad, I am kind of sweet on that little gal. You want to run with that one?"

Sam threw his arm around his son. Father and son started to laugh like two lunatics as they slapped each other on the back.

"I'm going over to the balsam fir field. Is it okay if Cyrus goes with me?" Sam gasped as he wiped at his wet cheeks.

Gus nodded. Banner days like this were something he'd only dreamed of.

Chapter Twelve

Gus Moss hung up the dish towel just the way his mother had taught him. He looked around at the tidy kitchen. It was hard to believe they'd fed over seventy people today. Seventy happy people, who left the cleanup to Gus and Amy.

It was eight o'clock now, time to sit down with a nice glass of wine and stare into the fire. At least for a little while. Then the mad rush would begin in less than twelve hours. "Thanks for helping with the dishes. I don't mind the dishes as much as the pots and pans." *Such a titillating conversation,* Gus thought.

Amy flopped down on the couch. "You want to hear something, Gus? I've never been this tired in my whole life. I'd never admit it to my mother, though. Right now she thinks I walk on water. It's such a good feeling, but, God, I am beat. Eating all that food sure didn't help. Aren't you tired?"

Gus grinned. "If I leaned up against the wall, I'd go right to sleep. The only thing that keeps me going is the same thing that drives you. I don't want to disappoint my father. I can design houses in my sleep. I can't swing a chain saw in my sleep." He yawned to make his point.

"That's a great fire. I use my fireplace every day during winter." She yawned, then Gus yawned. A second later, they were both asleep, Amy's head on Gus's shoulder.

Sam Moss returned an hour later and covered up the couple with an afghan his wife had made one winter when the snow was so deep they were snowbound for over a week. If memory served him right, she'd made two afghans that week. He smiled at the sleeping couple, wondering what the future held in store for both of them. Gus lived and worked in California. Amy lived and worked in Philadelphia. No matter what he thought or wanted for them, he wasn't about to stick his nose into his son's affairs. He'd learned a bitter, hard lesson, and he wasn't going there ever again.

In the kitchen, Sam poured the last of the coffee into a cup and cut a slice of pumpkin pie. He had no idea how he could still be hungry after all he'd eaten today. He needed to think, and he always thought best when he was eating, which just proved Sara had been right when she said that meant he could do two things at one time.

Sara. He'd promised himself that he was going to do some hard thinking. He wondered what Sara would think if she knew what he was feeling where Tillie Baran was concerned. He wondered if she was proud of him for the way things were turning out with Gus. He wished he knew.

"You had a nice turnout today, Sam."

Sam whirled around, but no one was in the kitchen. He was so tired now he was hearing voices. A voice from beyond. *Maybe I've overdone it. Time to go to bed.*

"It's time to move on, Sam. I want you to be as happy as our son is right now. Are you listening to me, Sam?"

Sam didn't trust himself to speak. He nodded.

"Then clean up your mess and go to bed."

"Are you sure it's okay, Sara?" Sam whispered.

"It is very okay. I'm proud of you, Sam. Now, get on with your life."

Sam jolted forward when he felt Cyrus stick his wet nose

against his hand. "Thanks for waking me up, boy. I was dreaming there for a minute. Want some pie?" Cyrus woofed softly.

Sam moved by rote then as he washed his plate and cup. He couldn't shake the feeling that he had spoken to his dead wife. He never dozed off while he was eating. *Is it possible Sara just visited me? Or is it wishful thinking?*

Sam stopped in the living room to check on his sleeping son. Out for the count. His chest puffed out with pride. A little late, but Sara had always said it was never too late to make things right.

As he climbed the stairs to the second floor he decided Sara had indeed visited him and told him to get on with his life. A tired smile lit up his face. She was proud of him. He knew in his old heart that it didn't get any better than that.

The weather cooperated the following morning. The storm clouds of the day before had moved on. It was cold and brisk, with a hint of snow flurries to come, perhaps later in the day.

Gus woke first and wondered why he felt so cozy and warm. Then he saw Amy burrowed under his arm. A loud sigh escaped his lips, loud enough to wake Amy. She didn't wake in stages either. She bolted wide awake, looked at him with wide eyes, and burst out laughing. "I hope you respect me this morning."

"We didn't . . ." Flushing a bright red, Gus jumped off the couch and held out his hand for her to grasp. He pulled her to him and kissed her the way she'd kissed him once before. When he finally broke free, he said, "If that didn't make your teeth rattle, I have to tell you that was my best shot."

Amy tweaked his cheek. "Oh, my teeth are rattling all right. But . . . I know you can do better. You know how I know this, Gus Moss?"

Somehow, Gus managed to get his tongue to work. He sounded like a bullfrog in acute distress. "How?"

"Because the next time, I'll cooperate and give it 110 percent. I only gave you 50 percent this time. Now you have something to look forward to." Gus watched her, his mouth hanging open as she sashayed out of the room.

"Promises, promises," Gus muttered as he made his way upstairs to his bathroom. She was right, though, it was definitely something to look forward to.

The only lull in business that day happened shortly after lunch when Gus's crew returned to the fields with the flatbed U-Haul to replenish the eight foot trees. The gift shop absorbed the lull with the antique cash register ringing constantly. Children came back for seconds for the gingerbread men and the hot cider. To the children's delight, Sam's old-fashioned Victrola, sitting outside on the back porch, played "Jingle Bells."

Cyrus, decked out in Buster's old reindeer ears, the bells on his collar tinkling when he walked, allowed himself to be petted and chased by the little ones. When the cars left the compound, trees tied to their roofs, one of the Seniors handed out little cellophane bags to the children. The bags said REINDEER TREATS in bright red letters. The children squealed and giggled as their trip to Moss Farms ended on a happy note.

It was clear to everyone that the Moss Christmas Tree Farm was back in business.

Tillie worked the kitchen, making coffee and sandwiches that she handed out during free moments, which were few and far between.

The cash register continued to ring. Sam said it was the sweetest sound in the world.

Amy looked up from the work table, where she was busy making wreathes and grave blankets. "Gus! How's it going out there?"

"I don't have much to judge by, but to my mind it's the

biggest day after Thanksgiving I can remember. I gave up counting a couple of hours ago. I just stopped to get some coffee. Your mother is like a chicken on a hot griddle."

Amy giggled. "She's having the time of her life. Trust me."

"So is my dad. Two people are waiting for their blankets. They asked me how much longer it will be."

"I know. I can't make them fast enough. I'm not too proud to tell you I need some help. I ran out of wreaths two hours ago. We need more of an assembly line here. I can't do the wiring and the bows. My hands are raw from the wire."

"You need to wear gloves," Gus said as he took her hands in his. They were black from the resin and bark, and he could see specks of blood on the palms of her hands. How well he remembered the days when he'd done the same thing. His mother had always put something called Bag Balm on his hands and wrapped them in warm flannel at night when he went to bed. Then he would wake and do it all over again. To this day he still had scars on his hands from the baling wire.

"There's no easy way to do it, Amy. Can you work with gloves?"

"I'm not complaining, Gus. It's too awkward working with gloves. I have to be able to feel the wire. I just said I could use some help. Someone to make the bows and tie them on will make things go a little faster. I hate the idea that people will go somewhere else for their wreaths and blankets. You know, time is money. Don't worry about me."

"I'll see if I can find you some help. I don't think any of us were prepared for such a busy day. Your ad campaign is really working. Your mother told me she ran out of patches for the Christmas Stocking. Everyone wants the plasma TV Zagby's donated. Whoever wins that stocking is going to need a truck to haul it off. That was one of the best ideas I ever heard of."

Amy glowed with Gus's praise. "Okay, I have to get back

to work. I'm going to need some more greenery in about ten minutes."

"Okay, see you later." Amy's mind raced as she worked the wire through the wreath hoop and then threaded it back through the pine boughs. The Seniors all had arthritis and while they might try to help her, they would do more harm to themselves. Where could she find someone willing to cut their hands to shreds to help the Seniors?

Volunteers.

At four-thirty, just as it was starting to get dark, Amy had a brainstorm. She stopped what she was doing, not caring if two dozen people were waiting for her creations. She stepped out of the barn and made an announcement: "Leave your name in the store, and we'll deliver your blanket or wreath." There was a little grumbling, but for the most part, people were understanding. "I'll try to get them to you by Sunday afternoon. Mr. Moss and the Seniors appreciate your business and your patience."

Back in the barn, Amy whipped out her cell phone. An hour later she'd called every church in town asking the priests and ministers if they could send their youth groups to help after school next week. She promised to make donations to each church. All promised to get back to her later in the evening.

Amy looked at her work table. She was fresh out of greenery. Time to take a break. She wanted to wash her hands, which would probably be a mistake since the thick resin was coating the cuts. She didn't care. All she wanted right now was to soak her hands in soothing warm water and sip a hot drink through a straw. She was just closing the door when Gus pulled up in his pickup, the trailer full of greens.

"I'm going to pretend I didn't see you. I'm going into the house to get some coffee and wash my hands. I think I might have a lead on some volunteers."

"I'll join you. I'll pretend I didn't get here." In the time it took his heart to beat twice, Gus scooped her up in his arms and carried her across the compound to the kitchen, where he sat her down on one of the kitchen chairs.

Tillie stopped what she was doing long enough to pour her daughter a cup of coffee.

"Put a slug of something in it, Mom."

That's when Tillie noticed her daughter's ravaged hands. She wanted to cry. She looked up at Gus, who could only shrug.

"I had no idea what a hard business this is," Tillie said softly. She quickly ran a dishcloth under warm water. She gently wrapped it around her daughter's hands.

Gus eyed both women. "This is only day one, ladies. We have thirty-three more days to go. It won't get any easier."

"I'm no quitter," Amy said vehemently.

"And neither am I," Tillie said with spirit.

"So what's the lead you have?" Gus asked.

"I called all the churches in the area and asked the priests and ministers if they would ask their youth groups to come out and help after school. They all promised to get back to me this evening. I just hope I can stay awake long enough to take the calls. If it works out, we can build up an inventory. If that doesn't work, I'm all for using that liquid cement to glue the boughs together. I'll make it work . . . so will both of you stop looking at me like that?"

"What's for dinner?" Gus asked as he slipped back into his jacket.

"Stew and fresh bread. Addy made it all this morning. Store-bought pie."

"Works for me." Gus grinned as he headed out the door.

"What's the deal here, Mom?"

"Everyone eats here, we're taking turns cooking. Breakfast, lunch, and dinner. We close the gates at five-thirty. Everyone goes home to sleep in their own beds. Sam and I pick everyone up in the morning and we do it all over again. Are you coming home with me, Amy?"

"Of course. Why would you think otherwise?"

"Well . . . you didn't . . ."

"Mom, I was so tired yesterday I fell asleep on the couch. No one woke me up. Don't read into something that isn't there, okay?"

"Okay. Just thirty-three more days to go. We can do this, can't we, Amy?"

Amy closed her eyes. "We have to do it. Thanks for the coffee, Mom."

"Oh, Amy, I almost forgot. A reporter from the newspaper was here earlier to take pictures of the Christmas Stocking. They're going to run it in tomorrow's paper on the front page. Above the fold! Isn't that great?"

"Super, Mom! Just super!" Amy said wearily as she headed back to the barn.

Hours later, the workday finally ended, and Amy, a can of Bag Balm in hand, followed her mother to the car. She waved to Gus and Sam. "Burn rubber, Mom!"

"Gotcha, kiddo. Heigh-ho, Heigh-ho, it's off to home we go, with only thirty-three more days to go! Heigh-ho, Heigh-ho. I can't wait to go home."

Amy laughed hysterically. Tillie wondered if she should slap her daughter. She decided she was too tired to do anything but drive. Then she, too, started to laugh. "This is where the rubber meets the road, Amy. A month ago if someone had told me this would be happening, I would have laughed in their face."

"Yeah, me too. You can't sing worth a damn, Mom."

"I know. Sad, isn't it?"

"Boo hoo." Amy giggled. "I meant it back there when I said I was no quitter."

"I know, Amy. I'm no quitter either. We'll do it." She looked over at her daughter, who was suddenly sound asleep. *How pretty she is,* Tillie thought. *How dedicated. How warm and caring my daughter is.* Then she cried for all the lost years.

Chapter Thirteen

Amy's alarm buzzed at six o'clock. A second later, the local radio station came to life with a rousing rendition of "Jingle Bells." Then the announcement for Moss Farms invaded her bedroom. She pulled the covers over her head, but she could still hear the cheerful voice announcing the latest gift to go in the Christmas Stocking, a gift certificate to the China Buffet for a free dinner for two every week for a full year.

Amy swung her legs over the side of the bed. She smiled in spite of herself. Her PR campaign had taken off like a rocket. Instead of the television and radio announcers doing a countdown of days left till Christmas, they started the top of each hour by announcing the latest contribution to the Christmas Stocking. Estimates were running high as to the value of the contents. Fifty thousand dollars' worth of merchandise and gift certificates seemed to be the magic number. Amy thought it was much higher, because shops and business professionals dropped by with gift certificates on a daily basis. Just yesterday a local plastic surgeon stopped on his way to the office to drop off a gift certificate for a free

face-lift. She'd giggled over that all morning, as did all of the
Senior ladies.

Then there was the mystery gift that the announcers played
up every day. A gift valued at ten thousand dollars. The different stations had call-in periods during which people called
in trying to guess what the mystery gift was and who had donated it. So far no one had come close to guessing the mystery gift was a seven-day Carnival Cruise for a family of four.

Just three more days, Amy thought as she lathered up
under the shower. Three more days and she could sleep until
the New Year. Then it was back to her own world in Philadelphia. Gus Moss would be returning to his life in California,
and her mother and Sam would probably start "keeping company" once they wound down from this little adventure. And
it *was* an adventure. Tillie was dressed and waiting by the
front door with a cup of coffee and a Pop-tart. Amy wolfed it
down and could have eaten another one. "Three more days,
Mom!"

"Don't talk with your mouth full, Amy," Tillie said in a
motherly tone.

Amy looked up at her mother. No one had ever said that
to her before. Then again, maybe she never talked to anyone
with her mouth full. "Let's go. Time is money, Mom. Pastor
Mulvaney is sending out three college kids from his choir to
help me this morning. I've got kids coming this afternoon
too. We have a great inventory now for all the people who
stop by at the last minute."

They quickly walked to the car and climbed in. Tillie settled herself behind the wheel and backed out of the driveway. "I'm going to miss you when you leave, Amy."

"I'll come home more often, Mom. You know what, I
think Sam is going to be taking up a lot of your time once
Christmas is over."

"I hope so. I really like him. We're comfortable together.
You know, that old sock-and-shoe routine. He told me yesterday that he's making plans to take every single person

who worked at the farm, their families, and even the school-kids who volunteered on a cruise at the end of January. Just four days. He said the cruise line gave him a great deal. You and Gus are invited, of course."

"Hmm," was all Amy could think to say.

"I know this is none of my business, Amy, but I'm going to ask you anyway. Are you and Gus . . . are you going to stay in touch?"

That was the question Amy had been asking herself for days. She tried for a blasé attitude. "Don't know, Mom. California is across the country. I'm thinking, 'out of sight, out of mind.'"

"Does that bother you?"

Amy was tempted to fib to her mother but couldn't. "Yes," she mumbled over the rim of her coffee cup. "Oh, look, it's starting to snow."

"Then do something about it," her mother snapped. Amy looked over at her mother, who looked grim and determined.

"Just like that! Do something! Takes two to tango, Mom."

Tillie took her eyes off the road for a moment. "Yes, just like that. Haven't you learned anything in the last two months? It's all about communication, giving off mixed signals, ignoring the obvious, being afraid to say what's on your mind and in your heart. Like Sam says, you snooze, you lose. I say, go for the gusto!"

"Is that what Sam says?" Amy drawled. "Gusto, eh?"

"Yes, that's what Sam says, and that's what I say. I can't believe I'm giving you relationship advice."

"Yeah, me too. You're pretty hip these days, Mom."

"I know. I want my cell phone back. I think I earned it."

"I got you one for Christmas. It's purple. It takes pictures and everything. You can even text message. Play your cards right and I might throw in an iPod."

Tillie turned on the right-turn signal and swerved into Moss Farms. She drove slowly over the old road and came to a stop at the top of the rise. "That's one kick-ass Christmas stocking, daughter! I like sitting here looking at it every morning. Did you ever call those people from *Money* magazine who called you?"

"Nope. I'm playing hard to get. C'mon, Mom, time to get to work. What's on the menu today?"

"Addy said she was making waffles for breakfast, corn chowder for lunch, and pepper steak for dinner. With buttered noodles. Does that work for you?"

"It does," Amy said, hopping out of the car. She loved this time of the day, when she could sit next to Gus eating breakfast. They weren't too tired to talk about anything and everything, unlike at the close of the workday, when they were red-eye tired with only one thought—sleep.

"Morning, everyone," Amy said cheerfully.

Gus looked around to see who "everyone" was. She must be referring to Cyrus and him. "Good morning to you, too, Miss Baran."

"Three more days!" Amy said as she filled her plate with waffles from the warming oven. Gus poured coffee for her, and Cyrus dogged her steps, no doubt hoping for a sliver of bacon. She obliged.

"It will be over before you know it," Gus said, trying to be as cheerful as Amy sounded. He knew he wasn't pulling it off. He was simply too damn tired to be cheerful at this hour of the morning.

"Are you and your dad going to put up a Christmas tree here in the house?"

"I don't think so. He didn't say anything about it. Are you and your mom putting up a tree?"

Amy eyed the man she secretly thought of as her destiny and laughed, a forced sound. "Not if I can help it. I don't want to see a pine tree of any kind until next year and maybe not even then. I think I turned into a grinch. It's snowing out. Looks like it might lead to some of the serious white stuff. You know, an accumulation." Such a scintillating conversation.

Gus groaned. "Do you know what snow means, Amy?"

"Yeah, I have to shovel Mom's driveway."

"No, it means all the procrastinators will be trooping out here to buy a tree in the snow. Snow means Christmas. People get the spirit the minute the snow starts to fall."

"I can help with that, Gus. We have a good amount of inventory in the barn. For the most part, I think my end is done. I can't imagine selling 200-some wreaths and 125 grave blankets over the next few days. Tell me what you want me to do and I'm all yours."

Gus jerked to attention. "Do you mean that?"

"Uh . . . well, yes. Just tell me what you want me to do. I can bale the trees. I can saw off the bottom branches and I can drill the holes. I don't have the upper-body strength to lift the trees."

"Oh, I thought . . . what I mean is . . ."

Tillie's words rang in Amy's ears. *Then do something about it. Go for the gusto!* "You thought I meant I was all yours as in us, as in a team, as in a couple. . . . I did mean that. I meant the other part too. What are you going to do about it, Gus Moss?" she asked boldly. Surely that counted as going for the gusto.

Gus decided to take the high road. "What do you *want* me to do about it?"

Amy stood up and stomped her foot. "I want you to tell me whatever the hell you want to tell me. I'm too tired to play games. I like you. I am very attracted to you. You're a great kisser, and you said yourself you were a stand-up kind of guy. I see us as a couple. I can see myself married to you with a bunch of kids. Well?"

Cyrus barked so loud Amy thought her eardrums had ruptured.

Amy felt her eyes start to burn. So much for saying what was on her mind. She was going to strangle her mother as soon as she found her. She shrugged into her jacket. "Your silence tells me all I need to know. You can just kiss my . . . my . . ."

"Mouth? I'd be happy to oblige, but do you see that SUV out there with all those squealing kids? Jeez, they even brought the dog with them. I told you, it's a family thing the minute it starts to snow. I will kiss you later, and you said it all better than I ever could. Start thinking about moving out to the Golden State. Five kids, two dogs, a cat, a bird, and some hamsters. You okay with that?" Gus called over his shoulder as he rushed out the door. "I'll design us a house around you, Amy Baran."

Amy stood rooted to the floor. "I think that was a proposal of sorts. Don't you, Cyrus? If so, I'll take it." She wrapped her muffler around her neck and marched outside to greet the family with the squealing kids and barking dog.

"We want four trees," Amy heard the father say. She watched as the mother rolled her eyes as she did her best to herd the six kids to the gift shop. "Don't forget the four wreaths and the four grave blankets." Amy laughed. She knew immediately who was the boss of this rambunctious family. She continued to laugh as the dog chased Cyrus, trying to get his reindeer ears.

The rest of the day was no better. By four o'clock three inches of snow covered the ground. The trees were coated with it, which only made them heavier. At five o'clock, when Gus closed the gate at the entrance, Amy thought she would collapse. She knew if she closed her eyes even for a second she'd be out for the rest of the night.

While she waited for the Seniors to come in for supper, Amy drank three cups of black coffee, one after the other. She was so wired from all the caffeine she'd consumed that she thought she was going to explode. The minute Gus walked in the door, she eyeballed him and said, "So when are we getting married?"

"How about tomorrow?"

"I'm too tired."

Gus laughed. "Did you just propose to me? I thought I was supposed to do the asking."

"You did. This morning. I'm just . . . I'm just confirming it. I'm a detail kind of gal. You should know that about me." Suddenly, Amy looked around and was stunned to see the room was full of Seniors, her mother, and Gus's father.

"We're getting married," Gus said.

Everyone clapped. Even Amy.

"When?" the Seniors asked.

"New Year's Day," Gus said.

Amy yawned. "Works for me," she said before she slid to the floor and was out like a light.

"Looks like your daughter might be spending the night, Tillie. Guess I'll be driving you home after supper."

Tillie smiled. What was the point in telling Sam she'd driven to the farm this morning? There were all kinds of being tired. She smiled up at Sam. "I'd really appreciate that, Sam. I was going to put my tree up tonight as a surprise for Amy. Maybe if you aren't too tired, you could help me."

Gus sidled up to his father. "Go for it, Dad; that's the best offer you're ever going to get." He bent over to pick up Amy. Cyrus barked as he slung the sleeping girl over his shoulder. She felt like a rag doll. The Seniors clapped again. Gus felt like a caveman as he made his way through the gauntlet of helpers to the living room.

Gus covered the sleeping girl and built up the fire. He was staring into the flames, his thoughts a million miles away, when one of the Seniors brought two plates of food, one for him and one for Cyrus.

Harvey Jenkins poked his head into the living room. "We're going to put a tree up for Sam if you don't mind, Gus. Is there anything special you want in the way of ornaments, or should we use some from the gift shop?"

"I have no idea where Mom kept the ornaments, Harvey.

Just put some lights on the tree and use the ornaments from the shop. I appreciate it. You've all done so much already. This is above and beyond what any of us expected."

"Can't have Christmas without a tree in your living room. We want to do it. We'll have it up in no time and be out of your way. You can sit here and enjoy it. It's snowing pretty heavy out there right now. Most of us are staying the night, because if it snows all night we won't be able to get back here. Sam said it was okay. We'll be upstairs if you need us. Later on, that is," the old man said gruffly.

"Okay," Gus said as he leaned back in his father's favorite chair. He was asleep the moment his eyes closed. He didn't open his eyes again until six o'clock the next morning. He could smell bacon and coffee, but it was the sight of the beautiful tree in the corner of the living room that made him suck in his breath. This was the tree he'd never had as a kid. All lit up with shiny ornaments and a ton of gaily wrapped packages nestled under it. He had to blink his eyes several times to ward off the tears. How beautiful, how awesome, how generous of the Seniors. He knew he would remember this moment for the rest of his life.

He turned around to see the Seniors watching him like a cluster of precocious squirrels, big smiles on their faces. "Does it look like the kind your Momma used to put up?" Addy asked.

Gus had no trouble with the lie he was about to tell. "Exactly," he said, going over to hug each one of them. He loved how they fussed over him, patting him on the arm, on the back, then hugging him.

"Wake up Amy. I hope she likes it," Harvey said.

"Hey, sleepy head, wake up," Gus said, poking Amy on the arm.

Amy bolted upright. She looked around in a daze. "Did I sleep for three whole days? Is it Christmas? It's gorgeous. It takes my breath away. Oh, Gus, it's just beautiful."

"The Seniors did it while we both slept. Thank them, not

me. I couldn't have done that even on my best day. But to answer your question, you did not sleep for three days, and it is
not Christmas."

"Oh, well, we'll manage somehow," Amy said as she ran
over to the Seniors, who hugged and kissed her. "It's like
having a bunch of mothers, fathers, and grandparents all
rolled into one." She winked at Gus. "I don't think it gets any
better than this."

Time lost all meaning as Gus, his crew, Amy and the
Seniors got their second wind as the countdown to the noon
hour on Christmas Eve began. Sam's Victrola continued to
play Christmas carols over the jury-rigged sound system as
all the Christmas tree procrastinators showed up to buy their
trees at the last minute while the kids romped in the snow
and chased Cyrus all over the compound.

Christmas Eve morning, Sam and Tillie arrived with what
Gus called sappy expressions on their faces. All Amy could
do was giggle. She'd never seen her mother so happy. Gus
said the same thing about his father. All morning, as they
worked side by side, they kept poking each other and pointing to their parents.

"I don't know why I say this, but I think the two of them
are up to something," Gus said as he picked up a twelve-foot
tree to shove into the barrel. Amy pulled it out from the other
side and tied the bailing plastic in a knot. Two of Gus's crew
plopped it on top of an SUV, its engine still running. They
both waved as the car drove out of the compound, the kids
inside bellowing "Jingle Bells" at the top of their lungs.

"One more hour and it's all over. Then all we have to do is
deal with the media and the drawing, and the rest of the day
is ours. Did I mention lunch? Addy said Dad's freezers are
about empty, so lunch and dinner will be a surprise."

"I wonder who's going to win the contents of the stocking," Amy said. "I hope it's someone who can use a face-lift."

"The snowblower is what everyone is talking about. Whoever wins is going to need an eighteen-wheeler to cart it all away." He grew serious when he turned to Amy. "This was . . . an experience I wouldn't trade for anything in the world. If you hadn't showed up that night in your purple hat and scarf, I don't know which direction I would have gone in. I feel so damn good right now. All thanks to you, Amy Baran." Amy blushed as she squeezed Gus's arm.

"I wouldn't trade it either, but you did all the hard work. All my wreaths and blankets sold. We have two trees left. I think that says it all. Look, here comes the media, and it's starting to snow again. I guess we better get ready."

"What does that mean, get ready?"

"That means we comb our hair and get ready to smile. I'll do that while you close the gates. Business is officially over."

Gus loped off. As he struggled through the snow with the huge, slatted, iron gate, he looked up at the sign he'd repainted when he first arrived. He blinked, then rubbed the snow from his eyelashes. It was a different sign. This one said, MOSS & SON CHRISTMAS TREE FARM. A lump the size of a lemon settled in his throat.

The snow was too deep; the damn gate wasn't going to close. Suddenly, it started to move. "Need some help, son?"

Maybe he should have answered, but he couldn't get his tongue to work. Suddenly, he was eight years old, running to his dad because he couldn't close the gate by himself. His father's words were crystal clear in his memory. "You need some help, son?"

Gus threw himself at his father, and together they toppled into a snowdrift. "Yeah, Dad, I need some help."

"Then let's put our shoulders to the wheel and close this gate. The media people will have to open and close it on the way out. We're done here."

How easy it all was when you worked together. Gus wished he could think of something profound to say but he couldn't come up with the words. Then again, maybe actions and not words were all that was necessary.

His father's arm around his shoulder, Gus walked with his father back to the compound.

The Victrola was still playing, the Seniors were bundled up in their winter gear, and Amy and her mother were standing between the giant Christmas Stocking and the mile-long scroll that Amy was starting to unroll. Cameramen snapped and snapped their pictures, close-ups of the awesome scroll and the giant stocking. Amy pointed to the glittering letter on the stocking. An obliging cameraman focused his camera and took his shot.

MERRY CHRISTMAS TO ONE AND ALL!

In smaller letters, each Senior's, each worker's, each volunteer's name was listed. At the bottom, it said, THANKS FOR YOUR SUPPORT. The names Sam, Tillie, Amy, and Gus ran across the toe of the stocking.

"I think this is the most exciting moment of my life," Tillie whispered to Sam.

"I *know* it's the second most exciting moment of my life," Sam whispered back. "The first was the day Gus was born."

Gus smiled. If he had been a bird, he would have ruffled his feathers and taken wing. Since he was a mere mortal, he punched his father lightly on the arm as he moved forward to stand by Amy, who was getting ready to pick the winner from the bulging stocking.

A microphone was shoved in Amy's face as she stood on top of a ladder and dug deep into the stocking for one of the entries. "And the winners are . . . Janet and Ed Olivetti!"

The Seniors buzzed. Gus caught phrases as they chirped and chittered among themselves. *They sure can use it . . . Ed was laid off the whole summer . . . Two kids in college . . . two more getting ready to go . . . and the littlest one with major health problems . . .*

After the media pack up and left, Gus turned to Amy and said, "Now."

"Okay." Amy turned to the assembled Seniors and proclaimed, "Listen up, people. There was an unannounced gift not listed on the Christmas Stocking scroll. Let me tell you about it."

She took a piece of paper out of her pocket and read, "In honor of all the effort put in by the Senior Citizens, a prizewinning architectural firm has donated its services to supervise the building of an additional wing."

Before anyone could react, Gus turned to his father and said, "Please, Dad, can we turn off your Victrola?"

"I can do better than that." Within minutes, Sam had the old contraption and the scratchy records in his hands. With a wild flourish, he dumped the machine and the records in the trash. "As a very wise person said to me just recently, it's time to move on. I could use a little Bing Crosby or Nat King Cole. Now, let's have some lunch."

Gus reached up to help Amy down from the ladder.

"Merry Christmas, Amy."

"Merry Christmas, Gus."

"Do you realize in seven days I'll be calling you Mrs. Moss?"

"Yep," Amy said linking her arm with her soon-to-be-husband's. "Until then, you won't mind if I sleep the days away."

"Not as long as I'm sleeping alongside you."

Gus opened the door to the kitchen. Everyone shouted, "Merry Christmas!"

"To one and all!" Amy and Gus called out in return.

Epilogue

Amy Baran slipped into her mother's wedding gown, which fit her to perfection. "I didn't know you saved your gown. You never said . . ."

"I never said a lot of things, Amy. I was happy the day I wore that gown. What came after . . . well, it no longer matters. A wedding gown is something you save for your daughter. You look beautiful. Do you have something old, something new, something borrowed, and something blue?"

"I do. The Seniors were more than helpful. Mom, I am so happy. I wish there was a way for me to thank you for asking me to come home. I did what you said, I went for the gusto. I hope Gus doesn't think I'm pushy."

"He doesn't think any such thing. He loves you. Sam told me he talks about you in his sleep. He's a fine young man, Amy. Sam . . . Sam can be stubborn, but he finally came around. We've had such long talks. He's become a good friend. A really good friend."

"Is that your way of asking me if I approve?"

"I guess. This room we're standing in was Sara and Sam's

room. I feel like she's still here. Sometimes I have these . . . doubts. My situation was different from Sam's. He dearly loved his wife. I'm not . . ."

"Mom, Sam knows his own heart. He's moved on. He found you. You don't have to live here in this house if you don't want to. You have your own house but you need to ask yourself if Sam feels the same way about our house. Dad's room is the same. You didn't change a thing. Sam cleared all of Sara's things out of here. Hey, you could move down the hall to another room."

"I guess. It's time to go downstairs. Where's your veil? Amy, do you think I'll make a good grandmother?"

"The best. Mom, I know about Dad. I want to thank you for never telling me. I think if you had, I would have run amuck. Now, we're never going to talk about that again."

Tillie nodded. "Did something happen to the veil?"

"I'm not wearing it. I'm wearing this"—Amy said, plopping her purple hat on top of her curly head—"and this scarf," she said twirling the purple scarf around her neck. "Whatcha think, Mom?"

Tillie laughed so hard she cried. "I think you're going to give those California gals a run for their money. I hear the music. Sam's waiting outside the door to walk you down the steps and give you away to his son."

"Then let's do it."

She saw him standing next to the minister. She paused, waiting for him to see her. He turned, his eyes popping wide as both his fists shot in the air. Amy started to laugh as all the Seniors clapped their hands. She sashayed forward, twirling the end of the purple scarf this way and that. Gus howled with happiness as wedding protocol flew out the window.

This, he decided, just like the last two months, was a memory he'd keep with him for the rest of his days.

Ten minutes later, the minister said, "I now pronounce you man and wife. You may kiss the bride."

The Seniors clapped and hollered, whistled and stomped their feet.

"I promise to love you forever," Gus whispered in Amy's ear.

"And I promise to love you even more."

Ghost of Christmas Past

BEVERLY BARTON

Dear Reader,

December is one of my favorite months and Christmas is my favorite holiday, so I found it a real treat to write a romantic novella set during this special time of year. Here in the southern part of the United States, we don't get a great deal of snow during the winter and seldom in December—except in the mountains. I chose the Great Smoky Mountains, specifically the Gatlinburg, Tennessee, area, as the setting for my story about two lonely people in need of their own Christmas miracle. When Kate Hadley wrecks her late husband's Mustang in the mountains during a snowstorm, she never dreams how drastically her life will change when former Army Ranger Mack MacKinnon rescues her. Haunted by memories of her former husband, Kate is greatly disturbed by her instant attraction to the tall, dark and handsome stranger, a man she thinks of as her white knight. Trapped together in Mack's cabin, the sexual tension between them heightens as they become better acquainted. But is what they feel only lust or is it true love? Can it become the forever-after kind of relationship that Kate needs?

I hope you enjoy reading Kate and Mack's love story as much as I enjoyed writing it. I'm a believer in second chances and in love being triumphant over all obstacles, even the ghost of Christmas past, as in Kate's situation.

Those of you who have read my novels for Zebra know that I write romantic suspense, so I want to tell you just a little about two upcoming books. In February 2007, look for a very special Valentine's Day present from Lisa Jackson, Wendy Corsi Staub and me. We have joined forces to write an exciting romantic thriller about love, revenge and deadly secrets that three women hold to a brutal murder. You will not want to miss MOST LIKELY TO DIE.

In April 2007, look for my next romantic suspense novel, THE DYING GAME, with a twisted, psychotic villain to whom murder is simply an amusing game. But for his victims—all former beauty queens—the game is a terrifying end to their lives. When Judd Walker (a secondary character from my July '05 novel, KILLING HER SOFTLY) loses his wife to the killer, he turns vigilante, using his wealth and power to conduct an independent search for his wife's murderer. Former Chattanooga police officer Lindsay McAllister, who fell hard and fast for Judd when she worked as a detective on his wife's murder case nearly four years ago, is now employed by the private P.I. firm Judd hired. With the dying game accelerating and the body count rising, Lindsay must put her own life on the line to catch a maniac and save the soul of the man she loves.

I enjoy hearing from readers. You may write to me in care of Kensington Publishing Corp. or through my website at *www.beverlybarton.com.*

Warmest regards,
Beverly Barton

lined up through the whole day. My first stop is the local

Chapter One

Katie Hadley gripped the steering wheel with white-knuckled pressure, doing her level best to keep the car from skidding on the layer of ice that coated the winding mountain road. Why hadn't she checked the weather forecast before heading out on this last-minute trip?

Because you weren't thinking straight. You're running away, remember? All you thought about was escaping while you could.

Suddenly, the white Mustang veered right, spun halfway around, then slid off the side of the road. Trying everything she could think of to stop the car's sideways descent down the steep slope, Katie uttered a succinct prayer for help. Instead of stopping, the car picked up speed in its downward plunge.

Bam! Crash! Shatter!

The Mustang's passenger side slammed into a towering pine tree, crushing in the door and breaking the window. The driver's air bag exploded, temporarily trapping Katie. Stunned and slightly winded, she sat there immobile, her mind rioting with a jumble of thoughts. Was she injured? Could she get out of the car? Could she get help if she needed it? How bad was the damage to her car?

Darrell's car.

He'd been so proud of their new Mustang, like a kid who had received the Christmas present of his dreams. Please God, let the car be repairable. She couldn't bear the thought of losing Darrell's car. It was something tangible of his, like his clothes and wristwatch and collection of CDs, that kept him alive for her.

Her husband had been gone four years, two months, and seven days. And not one day passed that she didn't miss him. If only . . .

Katie realized that she couldn't just stay here, inside the wrecked car, alone in a rocky ravine in the Smoky Mountains. But if she got out of the car, what could she do and where would she go?

Cell phone, Katie thought.

Slipping her hand between her seat and the door, she found the mechanism that released her seat, allowing her to shove it backward as far as it would go. There, that was better. Then she unsnapped her safety belt and reached over in the other seat to search for her purse. Her leather shoulder bag wasn't there. Squeezing her body away from the air bag, she managed to move halfway into the passenger seat; then she reached down to the floorboard and felt around for her purse. When she found it, she unzipped the top flap with trembling fingers and grappled about inside until she found her cell phone.

Holding the phone up near the window, in the twilight of early evening, she turned it on. She had deliberately turned it off when she left home a few hours ago. She hadn't wanted to talk to anyone, hadn't wanted her mother or her sister trying to persuade her to return home. As soon as her cell phone came on, she started to hit the emergency number, then stopped. What if she didn't phone for help? What if she stayed right here? How long did it take a person to freeze to death?

Damn it, Katie, you can't think that way. Darrell would be so disappointed in you for even considering suicide. That knowledge was the single reason she hadn't done anything foolish in the weeks and months following Darrell's death.

Katie hit the preprogrammed emergency number and waited for a response. Nothing! She checked to see if she had coverage this high up in the mountains. She did. Why hadn't the call gone through?

A repetitive beep alerted her that her battery was low. Great. Just great. She couldn't call for help, so that left her with only one alternative. She had to get out of the car, climb up the embankment, and try to find help.

Think. Had she seen any cabins in the past few miles? She wasn't sure. By the time she had left downtown Gatlinburg, it was already snowing to beat the band. The cabin she'd rented, for a two-week stay that would save her from her well-meaning family during the holidays, was a mountaintop retreat. She was about three-fourths of the way there, or she had been before the wreck. If she had driven by any cabins in the past few miles, it was unlikely she could have seen them because of the heavy snowfall. If she hadn't been so damned and determined to escape at all costs, she might have realized the narrow, hazardous mountain road was becoming icy and therefore dangerous.

She had one escape route from inside the Mustang—her driver's side door. The other door was totally smashed in against the tree. After unlocking the door, she grasped the handle. To her amazement, the door opened, but only partially. When she pushed on the door, a scraping sound alerted her that the door was hung on something. Glancing outside, she saw nothing but white, as if the world was covered in an enormous frosted blanket. Realizing the door was caught on a slanted section of the ground, she used her shoulder, shoving as hard as she could. The door gave way only a few inches, but maybe it was enough for her to squeeze through, if she held her breath.

After she yanked her purse off the floorboard and stuck her cell phone back inside, she tossed the purse out the door, then slipped through the tight opening. Her breasts raked against the door's edge, not painfully but uncomfortably. Once free from the car, Katie lost her balance immediately, fell into the snow, and started tumbling down the embankment. Grasping at thin air, she kept rolling but finally caught hold of what she assumed was either a very low tree limb or a bush of some sort. Breaking her free fall, she held on tightly and gasped for air. She lay there shivering, drenched through and through by the fresh, wet snow.

How could she have been stupid enough to get out of the car and leave behind her coat, cap, and gloves? Thank goodness she'd worn a heavy sweater over her blouse. But her hands were already like ice.

Turning onto her back, Katie stared straight up at the grayish white sky. Snowflakes fell in glistening abundance. Knowing she had no other choice, Katie tried to stand, but she kept slipping because of the ice beneath the snow. Finally she gave up and began climbing up the hill, grasping anything in her path she could use as leverage.

Crack. Snap. Chink.

Katie stopped and listened. What was that odd sound? Without warning, a small, bare tree limb, laden with ice, broke off a nearby tree and, like a sharp spear, pierced through the snow and into the ice-covered ground. Dear Lord, she was surrounded by trees, each bearing deadly branches that might break and stab their icy tips into her.

Crawling faster in an effort to escape the killer trees, Katie passed by her car, stopping only long enough to grab the strap of her shoulder bag and drag it along behind her on her climb up the ravine. Before she reached the road above, two more small limbs broke off a nearby tree and pierced the frozen ground, one missing her by a few feet, another by mere inches.

Finally, she made her way to the road, but not before she fell backward at least three times, slipping and sliding because of the ice. Once she reached the roadside, she struggled to stand, wishing she could brace herself against a tree, but thought better of that idea. Damp, shivering cold, and more than a little frightened, Katie staggered out into the middle of the road.

Mack MacKinnon's SUV crawled slowly up the mountain road. If he hadn't been almost out of supplies, he wouldn't have risked the trip into Gatlinburg, but he'd had no choice. It had been stupid of him to let his supplies run so low, but he hated like the devil to go into town, to have to interact with other people, so he put off trips to the grocery store as long as possible. He had thought he could make it there and back before the worst of the storm hit, but the predicted storm had moved in a lot quicker than the weathermen thought, the freezing ice a forerunner of the heavy snow. The ice had hit while he'd been in the supermarket, so he'd come outside to discover that the weather had turned deadly. After packing away a two-week supply of groceries in the back of his nondescript black Jeep, he'd headed home. What usually took him less than twenty minutes was going to take a good hour at the rate he was going. But better to be safe than sorry. Within minutes of pulling out of the supermarket parking lot, he'd turned on his headlights. The farther he went up the mountain, the more obscured the visibility through the windshield became.

It was a good thing he'd made Destry come inside before he left; otherwise the old Lab/collie mix-breed dog would be frozen solid by now. When he'd first bought a cabin up in the mountains eighteen months ago, he'd wanted to be alone, thought he needed complete solitude. Then after six months, this mongrel mutt, looking like he hadn't eaten in weeks, had shown up on his doorstep. Mack had fed him, and that had been that for both of them. Within a few days, the dog was his. He'd named the flea-bitten pooch Destry, after the old western movie *Destry Rides Again,* one of his favorites.

Except for his dog, Mack still preferred being alone, liking the solitude and serenity of the mountains. That's why he had paid a small fortune to buy several acres that surrounded his cabin. Luckily, he'd been saving his money for the past fifteen years, which now allowed him the luxury of not working. At least not at a regular nine-to-five job. He hadn't planned on retiring from the army quite so soon, but when his last Ranger assignment had ended in the deaths of half his men and his being critically wounded, he'd opted for early retirement after he recovered.

If he ever really recovered.

Physically, he'd never be 100 percent, but he could deal with a slight limp and ugly battle scars. What he didn't want, didn't need, and couldn't endure was pity from well-meaning people. He was no damn hero. He'd been doing his job. Beginning and end of story.

Suddenly, a hazy figure appeared directly in front of Mack's Jeep. In that first startling moment, he thought he was seeing things, but he eased down on the brakes all the same and brought the Jeep to a standstill in the middle of the road. Then he glared through the windshield, thinking surely that what he'd seen had been an illusion. But no, she was still standing there in the road, waving her hands frantically. Good God, what was she doing out here in the middle of nowhere?

Mack grabbed his fur-lined gloves off the passenger seat, put them on, and opened the door. Once outside, he slid his parka hood up over his head and marched toward the woman, who, though slipping and sliding, was apparently trying to make her way to him. He stopped and waited for her to come to him. No point in both of them skating around on the slick, snow-covered ice.

"Please, help me," the woman called to him.

As she came nearer, he noticed she wasn't wearing a coat, hat, or gloves. Her cheeks were pink from the cold, and fresh snow glistened in her long, blond hair.

He glared at her, thinking she must be out of her mind. "What the hell are you doing—"

"I wrecked my car," she told him as she approached. "It skidded off the side of the road. Over there." She indicated with a toss of her hand.

"Are you hurt?" He stared into a pair of panicked brown eyes.

"No, I don't think so, but my car . . . I need to call a wrecker. My cell phone battery is dead and—"

"Lady, forget about your car for now. It'll still be down there when this storm passes and the roads clear."

"But you don't understand about my car." She stumbled when she reached him, either unsteady on her feet or slipping again on the ice.

When he grabbed her shoulders, intending only to steady her, she crumpled like a limp rag, falling against him. Damn! He eased her off his chest and shoved her backward. Noting her eyes were closed and she was unnaturally still, he gave her a gentle shake.

"Lady?"

No response.

He shook her a little harder. She moaned.

Shit! She'd passed out, either from injuries she suffered during the wreck or from exhaustion and exposure. Either way, he couldn't leave her here, as much as he might have wished he could.

Sizing her up, he figured she was a lightweight, about five-four and maybe 125 tops, including her jeans, sweater, boots, and oversized shoulder bag. Doing what had to be done, he lifted her into his arms and carried her to his Jeep. The extra weight, light as it was, bared down on his bad leg, making his usual limp more severe. After managing to open the passenger door, he tumbled her inside and strapped her in, then shut the door and went around to get in on the other side.

Was she nuts, driving up the mountain in the middle of a snowstorm? Mack chuckled silently to himself. He'd gotten caught in that same storm, hadn't he? Maybe she'd thought she could beat the storm, just as he'd thought he could. But at least he knew how to man these treacherous mountain lanes, even with an inch of ice coating the asphalt. Apparently this woman had been driving too fast or simply hadn't been able to control the slippery effects of driving on ice.

When Mack tossed the hood off his head, melting snow from the hood and parka scattered over him and into the backseat. He removed his gloves, restarted the engine, and eased the Jeep forward. Slowly. Carefully.

What the hell was he going to do with this woman? He hadn't had an overnight visitor, male or female, since he'd moved here, and if he had his way, he never would. He couldn't leave her, and there was no way anybody could make it up the mountain now to retrieve her. So it looked like he was stuck with her, at least until the storm passed and the cleanup crew made it up to his cabin. That could be to-morrow or several days from now, depending on just how much snow fell overnight.

Every now and then, while he maneuvered his Jeep up the winding mountain path, which would soon turn from asphalt to gravel as he neared his place, Mack stole a quick glimpse of Sleeping Beauty. And she was a beauty. Her features were small, delicate, and feminine. Something basically male within him stirred to life just looking at her. No big deal, he told himself. Nothing to worry about. After all, he *was* a man and it wouldn't be normal if he didn't react to a pretty woman. Besides, it had been a long time since he'd had sex.

Cursing under his breath, Mack forced himself to concentrate solely on the task of getting home.

Just as he turned off on the gravel drive that led to his cabin, the woman stirred. She moaned. Her eyelids flickered.

"Are you awake?" he asked, his voice gruffer than he'd intended.

Her eyes popped wide open; she lurched forward, her body stopped from hitting the dashboard only by the tug of her seatbelt. "Where am I? What—" She gasped. "Oh God, I wrecked Darrell's car. Did you call a wrecker to come get it?"

"Sit back and relax," Mack told her.

"Did you call a wrecker? I have to make sure Darrell's car is all right."

"Lady, did you hit your head? You're talking crazy worrying about a car when—"

"But it's Darrell's car," she told him, a catch in her voice, almost a whimper.

"Who the hell is this Darrell and why is his car so damn important?" Mack didn't have much patience when it came to pacifying other people's nutty whims. He wasn't the type of guy who found silliness cute in a woman.

Silence.

Had she passed out again?

He caught a glimpse of her in his peripheral vision, enough to make him take his eyes off the road for a split second. Oh great, she was crying. Not out-loud boo-hooing, but quiet, restrained tears that glistened on her eyelashes.

"Our first concern is making it to my cabin," he said, ignoring her emotional state. "If you're hurt, I'll do my best to patch you up. You'll need some rest, then later food."

When he paused and she said nothing, he felt a sense of relief. He wasn't good at small talk either.

The Jeep crawled along the icy, gravel lane leading to the overlook where his cabin nestled on the edge, giving him a spectacular view. The snow was coming down heavier; bigger flakes and occasionally an ice crystal battered the windshield.

"Here we are," he told her when he pulled the Jeep to a stop in front of his cabin. "Let's get you inside by the fire, then I'll come back out and unload my supplies."

When he turned to open his door, she reached across the console and grabbed his arm. "Thank you for rescuing me."

"Yeah, sure."

She squeezed his arm. "Darrell is my husband . . . was my husband."

Mack stared at her. "Divorced?"

She shook her head. "He died."

"Sorry."

"He'd just bought the Mustang new a few months before . . ."

"Look, when the weather clears, I'll get a wrecker up here to haul your husband's car out of the ravine."

"Thank you." She squeezed his arm again.

"Come on, let's get you inside." Once again his voice was gruffer than he'd intended, but damn it all, her gentle touch had stirred something inside him, something he didn't like. Sympathy for another human being? Attraction to a lovely woman?

Don't go soft, MacKinnon.

He wouldn't let his normal male attraction to a pretty woman affect his common sense. Besides, there was nothing soft and sentimental about his reaction. He was horny as hell, and that's all there was to it.

When he went around the SUV and opened the passenger's side door, he asked, "Do you think you can walk?"

She nodded. "Yes, I think so. I'm pretty sure I don't have any broken bones. I'm just scraped up a little from crawling up the ravine. And I'm exhausted and cold."

He helped her out of the Jeep and onto her feet. She swayed slightly toward him, her breath warm, her hands still cold. With his arm around her waist, he led her to the cabin's side entrance, up two wooden steps covered in snow and ice, and onto the porch. They both slid a little on the icy surface.

"Stand still a minute," Mack told her. "Let me get the door unlocked."

Nodding, she offered him a weak smile.

The minute he opened the door, Destry came barreling toward him, but he stopped when Mack called him to a halt. "Go back inside, old boy." The dog obeyed instantly. Mack held his hand out to the woman; she took it, and he led her inside.

"Make yourself at home. And don't mind Destry. He's a pussycat."

Again she simply nodded, then entered the cabin.

"If you think you'll be okay for a few minutes, I'll go back for my supplies."

"I'm all right," she said.

Mack had to make three trips to bring all the supplies from the Jeep to the house. His bad leg hurt like hell. All this extra walking, plus the winter cold, was doing a number on his old injuries. Balancing a few plastic sacks at a time while he tried not to slip on the ice was a major task. After he brought in the last of the sacks, he called out to Destry.

"Go out now, before dark." Destry bounded outside, slid across the porch, then stopped, a puzzled look on his face. Mack laughed, then closed the door.

He found the woman standing in the middle of his living room/dining room combination, her head tilted to one side as she gazed up toward the open loft space that housed his bedroom.

"You should probably get out of your wet clothes," Mack said.

She gasped, then whirled around to face him. Her big brown eyes were quite expressive.

He grunted. "I have no intention of attacking you. It's not my style. It's just that you might be more comfortable in something dry." He glanced upward. "My bedroom is up there. My clothes will be way too big for you, but you can use one of my flannel shirts for a nightgown, if you'd like, and a pair of my socks might stay on you if you fold them several times."

"Thank you, Mr.—? I don't know your name."

"MacKinnon. Mack MacKinnon."

She held out her slender, delicate hand. "It's nice to meet you, Mr. MacKinnon."

"Under the circumstances, why don't you just call me Mack."

"All right. And I'm Katie. Katie Hadley."

"Hello, Katie."

"Is there any chance I might take a warm bath before I borrow one of your flannel shirts?" Her gaze focused over his shoulder, as if she were too shy to make direct eye contact.

Oh great, he had rescued the bane of a horny guy's existence—a good girl.

"Sure thing. All my appliances are gas, including the water heater. You can shower or take a bath in the claw-foot tub. Towels are stacked in an open case in the bathroom."

"And your shirts?"

"The flannel shirts are in the closet, and the socks in the top dresser drawer."

She nodded, then headed toward the stairs.

"While you're doing that, I'll fix us some supper," he called. "What's your choice—tomato soup with grilled cheese sandwiches or vegetable soup with bologna sandwiches?"

She paused on the third step, glanced over her shoulder, and replied, "Either will be just fine. I'm not picky."

"Okay." He swallowed hard. He couldn't remember the last time a woman had gotten to him the way this one did. Usually he wasn't a sucker for the damsel in distress type, but there was something about Katie . . . something different.

"And Mr. MacKin—Mack, about Darrell's car . . ."

He growled.

"I was just going to apologize for making such a big deal about rescuing the car. I realize that there's nothing we can do about it right now."

He grimaced. "Yeah, sure."

"And thank you again for rescuing me. You probably saved my life."

He shook his head. "Okay, okay. Enough thank-yous. And I didn't save your life, so don't go making me out to be some big hero." The role of hero had always set uncomfortably on his shoulders, and he sure as hell didn't want this doe-eyed, little blonde to get any romantic notions about him. He was no white knight, not by a long shot.

Chapter Two

Katie stayed longer in the huge claw-foot tub than she'd intended, but every muscle in her body ached and the hot water, now tepid, had felt incredibly soothing. As she climbed out of the tub and reached for a huge white towel, she sighed contentedly. How odd that she did not feel ill at ease all alone in this house, with a man she didn't know. After all, he could be an ax murderer or a crazed psychopath. Or he could be just what he appeared to be—her rescuer.

She knew two things about him. One: his name was Mack MacKinnon. Two: he had been kind to her, despite being a bit gruff.

You know something else about him, a pesky inner voice reminded her. *You know he is devastatingly attractive.*

Mack was handsome in that rough and rugged way that appealed to most women. Tall. Probably six-three. A big guy, with huge shoulders. And she'd noticed he had gorgeous blue eyes, which were a striking contrast to his jet black hair.

It wasn't that she was blind to good-looking men. She wasn't. But since Darrell's death, she had not met one single man who interested her. When her older sister, Kim, had suggested she was still in love with Darrell, she'd had no choice but to agree. She did still love her husband and probably always would.

"You can't spend the rest of your life alone," Kim had told her. "You're only thirty. Don't you want to get married again and have children?"

The first year after Darrell's death, she had barricaded herself from the outside world, barely allowing her parents and siblings entrance. During those first few months, she had longed to die. Living had been sheer torture.

The second year she had reemerged from her protective cocoon and went back to work at the interior design firm that she and Kim had founded together right after she graduated from college. How Kim had kept the firm solvent during the year Katie had deserted her, plus took care of then-year-old twin daughters, Katie didn't know.

The third year, her siblings—Kim and younger brother, Kit—had set her up on a series of blind dates. And her mother had introduced her to every single man in the county. Her family had wanted her to find love again, to be happy again, and she loved them for it. But they tried too hard, pushed too hard.

They simply didn't understand.

Katie dried off, hung the towel on the wide iron-bar rack on the wall, and lifted from the door hook the green and tan plaid flannel shirt she'd found in Mack's closet. After slipping into the huge 2X shirt, which hit her just above the knees, she buttoned every button and rolled up the long sleeves; then she sat down on the commode to put on the pair of thick gray socks she'd dug out of a cluttered sock drawer in his dresser. The calf-high socks hit her at the knees. She rolled them down, forming a fat band around her ankles. Once dressed, and feeling rather awkward because she wasn't wearing a bra or panties, Katie glanced into the small mirror over the pedestal sink. She ran her fingers through her damp hair and sighed.

After picking up her wet clothes, including her under-wear, which she'd washed out in the sink, she hung all the items over the shower door. How would Mack react when he came into his bathroom and saw her pink silk panties and matching bra? Mentally chastising herself for being silly—after all, Mack wasn't a teenager who'd drool over women's unmentionables—Katie opened the door and walked into the bedroom. One bedroom. One bed. If he were a real gentle-man, he'd probably offer her the bed. Naturally, she'd decline the offer, assuring him that she'd be perfectly fine on the sofa. He'd insist, she'd refuse. He'd tell her that he wouldn't take no for an answer and she'd demurely accept his kind offer.

While the scenario concerning tonight's sleeping arrange-ment played through in her mind, her nose caught a whiff of something utterly delicious. As if on cue, her stomach growled. She hadn't eaten a bite since breakfast, and suddenly she was ravenous.

Mack lifted Destry's bowl, dipped a ladle filled with hot tomato soup from the pot on the stove, and poured the con-tents over the dog's dry food. By the time Mack set the bowl on the kitchen floor, Destry had his nozzle stuck in the bowl and instantly started eating. Mack reached down and patted the dog's shaggy head. He had no idea how old Destry was, but the vet guessed around seven or eight, which was far from young for a large-breed dog.

Lifting the metal spatula, Mack flipped the grilled cheese sandwiches so they would brown on the other side. After checking on the brewing coffee, he glanced at the table set for two. He felt an odd tightening sensation inside his gut. Wouldn't you know the first person to interrupt his solitary existence would be a gorgeous blonde in need of a white knight.

"Hmph." Mack was no white knight. He had rescued her because he'd had little choice. It was either bring her along with him or leave her to freeze to death.

If he was lucky, Katie Hadley wouldn't be the good girl he thought she was. What he needed was a woman who'd be interested in a temporary fling for the day or two they'd be trapped here, then leave and never look back. But the way his luck ran, Katie would be just what she appeared to be—a sweet, young widow who was still in love with her husband. After all, why else would she be so attached to the man's car, attached to the point of obsession?

Don't know. Don't care. Don't ask. That was Mack's motto. Do not become involved.

Lost in his own thoughts, he hadn't heard her come down the stairs, so when she cleared her throat, the sound startled him. He glanced into the living room, then sucked in a deep breath; the sight of her wearing his old shirt and knowing she was naked beneath ignited a fire in his belly. God, how he'd like to strip her out of that shirt, toss her down on the sofa, and—

"Hi," she said, her voice soft and much too sweet.

"Hi." His voice had been gruff. This time, he'd meant it to be.

"Something sure does smell good."

"Yeah, it's just soup and sandwiches." He turned his back on her and busied himself pouring the soup into huge, brown cups. "Just come on in and sit down. Everything's ready."

"What can I do to help?" she asked.

"Not a thing."

"I don't expect you to wait on me while I'm here." She came into the kitchen area and glanced into the iron skillet where the sandwiches were browning. "I can put these on plates and—"

"Just go sit down, will you?" He practically growled at her.

Startled, she gasped. "Sorry."

"Look, we're going to be stuck here together for a couple of days, so let's set up some ground rules."

"Of course." She walked over to the table, pulled out one of the chairs, and sat, then folded her hands in her lap. "Whatever you say is fine with me. After all, this is your house, and I'm a guest."

"An unwanted guest." He carried the two big cups of soup to the table, then placed one in front of her and the other on the opposite side of the table.

When she didn't respond to his grumbled comment, he glanced over his shoulder and noticed she was staring pointedly at his legs. A dark rage welled up inside him. Why were people so damn fascinated by other people's handicaps? He hated the way people reacted to his limp. Some simply stared at him, while others actually asked him about it.

"Polio?"

"Car wreck?"

"You were in the military, huh?"

"Birth deformity?"

"Are you an amputee?"

"Does it hurt?"

"Is one leg shorter than the other?"

Women found his limp either fascinating or repulsive in fairly equal measure. Some cringed when they saw the horrible scars; others wanted to touch them, to soothe away his pain.

"What are you staring at?" He glared at Katie.

"I'm sorry. I know staring is impolite, but I just now noticed that you have a limp."

He didn't respond; he simply removed the sandwiches from the skillet, dumped them on a plate, and took them over to the table.

"I've got fresh coffee or there's water, cola, and milk," he said.

"Water will be fine." She scooted back her chair. "I can get it."

"Sit!" he bellowed.

She sat. Her cheeks flushed bright pink. Tears glistened in her eyes.

Damn! She was one of those women. Sensitive. Emotional. Weepy.

"Ground rules," he said. "If I want your help, I'll ask for it."

She nodded.

He got her a glass of tap water, then placed it on the table before he poured himself a cup of black coffee.

He dug into the meal, spooning the soup into his mouth and following with huge bites of the grilled cheese. They ate in silence, the only sounds the creaking of the cabin, the ice-coated limbs occasionally breaking off trees, and Destry's contented snore. The old dog lay spread out in his favorite winter spot—right in front of the fireplace.

Mack deliberately didn't look at Katie. He didn't want her asking questions, being friendly, putting ideas in his head. All he wanted was to get through the next couple of days without acting on his basic instincts. He might not be a gentleman, but he wasn't the kind of man who took advantage of a woman.

When he finished his meal, Mack glanced at her plate. She'd eaten half the sandwich. Setting his two empty cups on his plate, he scooted back his chair, picked up the plate, and asked, "Are you finished?"

"Yes, thank you. It was quite good."

"I've got some chocolate chip cookies and some fruit, if you want dessert," he said.

"No, thank you. I'm fine."

"Coffee?"

She shook her head. "Do you have a telephone here?"

"Just my cell phone."

"May I use it?" she asked.

"Sure. It's over here on the counter. I'll get it for you."

He handed her the phone, then cleared away her plate and cups. She hadn't eaten more than a few bites of the soup. And it was damn good soup.

"There's not much privacy here," he said. "It's a small cabin. If you want to talk in private, go upstairs in the bathroom."

"That won't be necessary. I just want to call my sister and let her know I'm okay. I left town without telling anyone where I was going. I planned to phone Kim after I got here, but I wanted to leave without my family trying to stop me."

"Why would they try to stop you? You're a grown woman."

"I'm planning on staying away during the holidays. I won't be there for Christmas with my family."

He narrowed his gaze and stared at her. "So, you ran away from home, huh?"

"Something like that."

"Look, if you need to, give your sister my cell phone number and tell her my name and assure her you're safe with me. Tell her that I make a habit of steering clear of nice girls."

Katie cocked her head to one side and smiled. "What makes you think I'm a nice girl?"

"Oh, I don't know. Instinct I guess."

"You know what, Mack MacKinnon?"

He shrugged.

"I think maybe underneath that gruff exterior, you're a nice man."

Mack chuckled sarcastically, the sound a mixture of laughter and grunt. "I'm not. Consider yourself forewarned."

Her smile vanished. She studied him for a couple of minutes, apparently trying to figure out which to trust—her instincts or his warning.

* * *

Katie understood that Mack was trying to warn her off, but she wasn't quite sure of his reason. Maybe he thought she had romanticized their meeting and had some foolish notions about the two of them getting together. Had Mack lost someone he loved, just as she had, and wasn't prepared to love again? Or had some woman broken his heart and left him afraid to care about someone new?

"I won't be a minute." Katie clutched the cell phone in her hand. "I don't want my family to worry."

"Go ahead," he told her. "I'll clean up in here."

She went into the living room and sat down in one of two large, overstuffed leather chairs flanking the fireplace. She chose the one at the opposite end of the cabin. After sitting, she dialed Kim's number. The answering machine picked up.

"Hi Kim. It's Katie. Look, I've left town for a while. I've gone to the mountains until the first of the year. I'm fine, so don't worry about me. And don't let Mom and Dad call out the National Guard. It's just . . . I couldn't face Christmas this year. Silly of me, I know. But . . . I love you. All of you."

Katie flipped the phone closed. A lump lodged in her throat. She wouldn't cry. Not now. Not with Mack probably watching her. How could she explain to him—a stranger—that she'd run away from home so she wouldn't have to spend Christmas with her happy, loving family? That first Christmas after Darrell died, her family had been sympathetic and understanding and hadn't insisted she join them for the usual Brown family rituals. Christmas Eve began with all the girls in the family— mothers, daughters and grand-daughters—going to Grandma Brown's to make cookies. Then there was church together on Christmas Eve, followed by a trip to Great-Aunt Rebecca's, where dozens of Katie's mother's family members congregated every year. Then there was Christmas Day, which Katie had once looked forward to the most but now dreaded the most.

Darrell had proposed to her on Christmas Day, eight years ago.

Katie had been so lost in her thoughts, surrounded by memories of the ghost of Christmas past, that she hadn't heard Mack walk into the living room, sit down opposite her, and lean over to pet his dog.

"Finish talking to your sister?" Mack asked.

"Oh." Katie gasped. "I left a message. If you don't mind, I'll try to call her again tomorrow."

"Sure."

"So, his name is Destry?" She glanced at the big furry dog.

"Yep."

"Like in *Destry Rides Again*?"

Mack looked right at her. "Yeah. How'd you know about that old movie?"

"My dad's an old western movies buff. I've seen both Destry movies, the old black-and-white version with James Stewart and the fifties one with Audie Murphy."

"Your dad and I would get along just fine. If he's a UT fan and likes to fish, we could be buddies for life."

Katie laughed. What were the odds that two people could have so much in common? "My Dad lives and breathes UT football, and since he retired last year, he bought a fishing boat and he and Kit, my brother, go fishing a lot."

"You have a brother and a sister. Or is that brothers and sisters?"

"One sister, Kim—Kimberly Diane—who's three years older than I am. She's married to a dentist, and they have five-year-old twins, Betsy and Becky. Kim's a great mother, just like our mom is. And Kit, short for Kittwell, our mother's maiden name, is two years younger than I am. He's married, and he and his wife are expecting their first baby in February."

When Mack didn't respond, she glanced at him. He had this odd expression on his face, which she interpreted as aggravation.

"TMI?" she asked.

"Yeah, a bit too much info. Just because we're stuck here

together doesn't mean we have to become buddies and share cute little stories about our families."

"You're certainly working awfully hard to convince me that you're a mean-spirited sourpuss."

"What you see is what you get."

"Is it?"

He ignored her question.

She glanced around the room. This wasn't a new cabin, not one built recently for tourists to rent. The wooden walls possessed a mellow, aged patina, as did the floors. The rock fireplace was huge, the mantel made of rough-hewn wood. The furniture was new, the two massive chairs leather, the long sofa a dark brown chenille. The entire room, indeed the entire cabin, didn't have a single feminine touch. It all but screamed "a man lives here alone."

"You haven't decorated for Christmas yet," she said, thinking aloud, and when she noted the scowl on his face, she wished she'd kept her thoughts to herself.

"I don't decorate for Christmas." His big hand continued stroking the sleeping dog's back.

"Not even a Christmas tree?"

"Not even."

Why should it bother her that he wouldn't have a tree or a wreath on the door or a stocking hung on the mantel? Hadn't she left home, left her family, so she wouldn't have to face another Christmas with all the fanfare, hoopla, and decorations? Yes, but she had a good reason to boycott Christmas. The season brought back too many memories of a time when she'd been happy. So very, very happy.

"Why don't you like Christmas?" she asked.

"Why don't you?"

Tossing the question right back at her startled her momentarily. But it achieved the desired effect.

"You made your point. Your personal life is none of my business."

"And yours is none of mine," he told her.

"If we're trapped here together for a couple of days, it's going to be difficult not to talk to each other about something. We'll have to find things to do to pass the time."

The corners of Mack's wide mouth lifted in a hint of a smile. "If you weren't a nice girl, I could think of plenty we could do to while away the hours. Any chance I misjudged you?"

Katie knew she should be offended, maybe even slightly shocked by the innuendo, but she was neither shocked nor offended. "Unfortunately, you were right about me being a nice girl, so making out on that fur rug"—she tapped the edge of the large, brown fur spread out before the fireplace—"is out of the question."

The minute the words were out of her mouth, she wished them back, because they conjured up an image in her mind that did shock her. It had been only a flash, only a ten-second glimpse of Mack and her, both of them naked, lying on the rug, wrapped in each other's arms.

"Ah, shoot. I had such high hopes of your helping me christen that rug. I thought we'd open a bottle of wine and put on some soft music. You could do a striptease for me and then we'd get all hot and sweaty—"

Jumping in to stop him from going any further, but doing it in the same teasing tone he had used, she said, "I don't put out on a first date. Sorry. You know how we nice girls are."

"Yeah, I do. That's why I prefer not-so-nice girls."

"Too bad one of those girls didn't wreck her car and need rescuing this evening."

Mack chuckled under his breath. "Just my luck that it had to be you."

"Yes, it had to be me, didn't it?"

He cleared his throat. "I have a TV, a radio, and a CD player, if you'd like to—"

"Not tonight. Maybe tomorrow."

"Sure."

"Actually, after that warm bath and hot supper, I'm getting kind of sleepy. I wouldn't mind going to bed early, if that's all right with you."

"Sure, if that's what you want." He rose from his chair and limped over to the staircase.

She wanted to ask him when and how he had acquired such a pronounced limp, but she didn't dare. He'd made it perfectly clear that he didn't want to share personal information.

He disappeared up the stairs rather rapidly. She heard him thumping around up there in the loft; a few minutes later, he reappeared carrying a blanket, a thick quilt, a sheet, and a pillow.

She jumped up and rushed over to him. "Here, let me help."

He tossed the pillow onto the sofa, then handed her the other items. "Just make yourself a bed there on the couch. I'll add some more logs to the fireplace, so it should stay toasty warm in here all night."

She stood there holding the folded sheet, blanket, and quilt, her mouth wide open, her brain processing the fact that Mack had not offered her his bed.

"I'll take Destry and go upstairs. You can turn out all the lights down here before you settle in. We'll try not to wake you when I let him out again later tonight."

She said, "Thank you," but what she really wanted to say was "You're right, Mack MacKinnon. You most definitely are no gentleman."

Chapter Three

Katie woke to the smell of fresh coffee and frying bacon. For a few sweet moments she thought she was at home, a little girl again, and the aroma was coming from her mother's kitchen. But when she opened her eyes, she discovered she was not lying beneath her canopied twin bed situated across from Kim's. Instead, the first thing she saw was a large, dark man standing over her, his shirt unbuttoned to reveal a spectacular chest. He cradled a brown mug in his big hand.

"Morning," he said as he held out the mug to her.

As she sat up, she remembered she wore nothing except this man's flannel shirt, so she kept the blanket and quilt covering her from the waist down. "Thanks." She accepted the mug, which she quickly discovered contained some of that delicious smelling coffee. After taking a sip, she sighed.

"Did you sleep okay?" he asked.

After taking another sip of coffee, she looked up at him and smiled. "Yes, thanks. Actually, I slept quite well."

Stop staring at him, she told herself, but for some reason she couldn't take her eyes off him. His short, black hair was slightly tousled, and it was obvious from his dark beard stubble that he hadn't shaved this morning. Where his shirt hung open, she saw his well-muscled chest, covered with just a sprinkling of curly black hair.

"Like what you see?" He grinned mockingly.

"Oh, sorry. I—I wasn't really staring at you," she lied. "I'm just a bit dazed and not quite awake."

He chuckled, as if he knew she was lying. "Breakfast will be ready in a few minutes. The scrambled eggs and toast are ready, and the bacon is just about done. I like crisp bacon."

"Crisp is fine."

"From the looks of you"—he gave her a quick once-over—"I'd say you're the type who eats yogurt for breakfast, or maybe a protein bar."

She drank more coffee before she replied. "You make a great cup of coffee, Mack. And I'm sure breakfast will be just as good. I'm not picky about my meals. And you're right, I often eat yogurt for breakfast and sometimes skip breakfast completely."

"You shouldn't do that. Don't you know breakfast is the most important meal of the day?"

She laughed, relieved by his teasing manner this morning. "What time is it?"

"A little after seven."

"Really? I seldom sleep this late. Actually I seldom sleep well, certainly not the way I did last night."

Mack walked into the kitchen, separated from the living room and dining area by a short bar topped with the same rusty-brown granite as the counters. She watched him as he removed the hot bacon and placed two pieces on one plate and four on the other; then he turned off the gas burner and carried the two plates over to the table.

"Come get it while it's hot," he called to her as he returned to the kitchen to refill his coffee mug.

Katie carefully removed the covers from her lower body,

taking her time as she stood, making sure the flannel shirt didn't hike up in the back and that it covered her as much as possible.

"You're decent," Mack said.

"What?"

"Look, Ms. Nice Girl, I got the message loud and clear last night. You're not going to hop into the sack with me, so stop worrying that I'll try to jump your bones."

"Is that why you didn't offer me your bed?" The question just popped out. "I mean—"

"I didn't offer you my bed last night because I'm six-three and weigh in at two-twenty-eight. I don't fit on that couch. You do. You're what? Five-four and weigh about one-twenty-five soaking wet."

"Oh." Of course, that made sense. He was a big man and wouldn't have fit comfortably on the sofa, where she had, in fact, fit perfectly and slept like a baby.

Katie carried her coffee mug into the dining room and placed it on the table. She and Mack exchanged glances. Moving quickly, he came over and pulled out her chair.

"Thank you." She sat.

He grunted. "I figured you expected it."

Instinctively reaching for a napkin, she found there wasn't one. Hmm, no napkins, not even paper ones. Oh well, she'd make do.

After he sat down across from her and lifted his fork, she said, "I weigh one-twenty-two."

"I stand corrected." He speared a cluster of scrambled eggs and shoved them into his mouth.

Katie glanced down at her plate and surprisingly enough realized she was hungry. She took her butter knife and sliced her single piece of toast in half, then picked up a section and took a bite.

They ate in relative silence, Mack finishing off his meal before she did. When he got up, he asked, "I'm getting more coffee. Do you want a refill?"

"Yes, please."

He retrieved the glass pot from the coffeemaker, brought it to the table, and refilled their mugs, then set the empty pot on the bar behind him. "You sure do have good manners, Ms. Nice Girl. I'll bet you say *ma'am* and *sir* to your elders, don't you?"

"You're making fun of me."

"Nah, just having a little fun *with* you."

"My mother drilled good manners into all three of her children. It took with Kim and me, but the verdict's still out on Kit. Although, since he married Molly, his manners have improved."

"That happens to a guy when he hooks up with just one woman and is fool enough to marry her. He gets whipped pretty fast."

Katie glared at Mack. "You don't have a very high opinion of marriage, do you? What happened to you? A really nasty divorce?"

Mack sat, cupped his coffee between his big hands, and looked at her over the rim of the mug. "I've never been married. But I've seen what it's done to other guys."

"Good marriages are based on love and mutual respect. And on compromise. When you're with the right person, there's nothing more wonderful than . . . I'm sorry. I didn't mean to lecture you."

"It's okay." He took a hefty swig of his coffee. "I take it that you had one of those marriages?"

"Yes, I did."

"Good for you."

"Someday, when you meet the right woman—"

"That's not going to happen. I'm thirty-six, and Ms. Right hasn't come into my life, so I doubt she's out there somewhere waiting for me."

"You never know."

"Lady, you're a dyed-in-the-wool romantic, the most dangerous type of female."

"I've never thought of myself as dangerous. I kind of like the idea."

"Just like a woman. Give her a little compliment and it goes to her head." Concentrating on his mug instead of on Katie, Mack drank more coffee.

"Have you heard a weather report this morning?" she asked

"It's quit snowing for now," he said. "We've got an inch or so of ice, topped off by six inches of snow, and we're due for more ice and snow before nightfall."

Katie moaned. "I guess that means there's no way to get out of here today, is there?"

"Nope. And if we get the ice–snow mix they're predicting, we're bound to lose power lines. We're lucky that hasn't already happened. And more ice and snow means we could be stuck here for several days."

"Several days? You're kidding."

"What's the matter, you don't like sleeping on my sofa, wearing my shirt, and eating my cooking?"

"Oh, no, Mack, don't get me wrong. I appreciate your coming to my rescue yesterday, and I appreciate your hospitality. It's just I didn't expect to spend the holidays with anyone. I wanted to be alone." Katie gasped. "Oh shoot, that didn't come out right."

"I hadn't planned on sharing my cabin with anyone, certainly not a woman, now or ever. But, honey, it looks like we're stuck with each other for the time being."

"What did you mean by 'certainly not a woman'?" Katie asked, curiosity overcoming common sense. "You can't expect me to believe that a man like you hasn't had women up here—"

"What do you mean, a man like me?"

"Young, virile, handsome—" Oh drat, she'd done it now. She gone and said the first thing that popped into her head. Again!

Mack grinned. "You think I'm handsome? And virile?"

Katie felt her cheeks warming and prayed they weren't bright pink. "You've got a mirror. You know you're attractive. And the virile goes along with your being young. It's just an assumption, of course."

"Of course. But if you'd like to find out, firsthand, I'd be glad to—"

"Mack, will you stop doing that!" Katie scooted back her chair, stood, planted her hands on her hips, and glared at him.

With a half-smile on his lips, he looked up at her, his expression one of total innocence. "Aren't you the girl who, just a couple of minutes ago, told me she liked the idea of being a dangerous woman?"

"Well, yes, but there's dangerous and then there's dangerous."

Mack rose from his chair. Swallowing hard, Katie dropped her hands from her hips. He came around the table, directly toward her. Despite the fact her mind issued her feet orders to back away from him, she froze to the spot.

Oh God, he was coming closer and closer. Mr. Tall and Dark and Sexy. Katie's heart did a nervous little rat-a-tat-tat, and rapid flutters danced in her stomach.

When he was so close that they were almost touching, he stopped and looked down at her. She swallowed again, took a deep breath, and looked up at him. He had the most fabulous blue eyes, a rich, midnight blue.

"How long's it been?" he asked, his voice low and deep.

"How long's what been?" Her heartbeat rumbled in her ears.

"How long's it been since you've . . ." Dramatic pause. ". . . been kissed?"

She breathed a sigh of relief, because no sooner had the question come out of her mouth than she had assumed he would ask how long it had been since she'd had sex, only he would have used a cruder expression. She'd had no intention of telling him something that was none of his business.

But a kiss was something different. A kiss wasn't dangerous. People kissed other people all the time. Friends kissed. Parents kissed their children; brothers kissed sisters; nieces and nephews kissed aunts and uncles. The list was endless.

"I was kissed a few days ago," she told him.

"You were? By whom?"

"By my twin nieces."

She really hated his cocky grin.

"I meant when was the last time you were kissed by a man? And I don't mean your father or your brother."

"Oh."

He leaned his head down and looked her right in the eyes. She held her breath, certain that he was going to kiss her. Her lips parted. Her breathing accelerated. She really should say or do something to stop him. But for the life of her she couldn't. Feeling like a fly caught in a spiderweb, she stood there, gazing into his eyes, and waited for his kiss.

His breath was warm and smelled of coffee. As his mouth hovered over hers, Katie closed her eyes.

He caressed her cheek with the back of his hand and said, "It's been a long time, hasn't it?"

"Yes," she gulped the one-word reply.

He caressed her cheek again, then said, "I'd be happy to kiss you anytime you'd like. All you have to do is ask."

Her eyelids flew open. He had already lifted his head and taken a step back away from her. Their gazes met and locked.

"I'll keep your offer in mind," she replied, "if I ever get that desperate."

Chuckling, he turned around and headed back to the table. Katie wanted to scream. Arrogant bastard! What made him think she'd ever ask him for a kiss? *Well, maybe because you were standing there, with your eyes closed and your lips practically puckered.*

God, she felt like a fool!

* * *

This is what happens when you allow a woman to stay with you in your home, Mack thought. Katie had been in his house less than twenty-four hours and already she had taken over as if she had every right to invade his private domain. She'd washed and dried her dirty clothes and his, made his bed, cleaned the bathroom, swept the kitchen, dusted the furniture upstairs and down, and now she was in his kitchen making cookies. Christmas cookies! And it was only a little after three in the afternoon.

The worst of it was that Destry had taken a liking to her, from the moment she fed him her leftover slice of bacon and talked baby talk to him this morning. Bundled up from head to toe, Mack stood on his porch and watched Destry stomping around in the snow, heading back toward the house, after he finished doing his business.

Destry galloped up on the porch, went to the door, and scratched, completely ignoring Mack.

"You're a traitor, you know that, don't you," Mack told him. "A piece of bacon and a little sweet talk and she won you over, didn't she?"

Destry gazed up at him with dark, soulful eyes.

"Yeah, I know, she's hard to resist."

But he had resisted the temptation to kiss her. She'd been willing. He knew enough about women to know when a woman wanted to be kissed. Hell, Katie Hadley needed to be kissed. He didn't know how long it had been for her—since she'd been kissed or since she'd had sex—but he had an odd notion that she hadn't been with anyone since her husband died. And just how long could that have been? Months? A year at most? After all, it seemed obvious she hadn't gotten over her precious Darrell.

A stupid twinge nipped Mack in the gut, some odd sensation that he hadn't felt in years. Jealousy?

Man, he was an idiot. Why should he be jealous of Katie's dead husband?

I'm not jealous. I'd have to care about Katie to be jealous. I don't care about her. She's nothing more than an unwanted houseguest.

"Come on, boy, let's go in. It's freezing out here."

Mack and Destry entered through the back door, both man and beast making damp tracks across the floor. He halfway expected Katie to scold them, as if she had every right to. But she seemed totally absorbed in her baking, so much so that she ignored them completely.

Mack's kitchen smelled faintly of vanilla and cinnamon. "Cookies ready yet?" he asked as he hung his parka up on a rustic hall tree in the living room, near the front door.

As if on cue, she bent over the oven and, using two pot holders, opened the oven door and pulled out a pan filled with big, round cookies. "The first batch is just now coming out of the oven."

"They sure do smell good."

"You didn't have any confectioners sugar, so I can't make icing for them," Katie told him. "Instead, I added cinnamon and nuts to half the cookies and left half plain. I like them both ways."

She looked perfectly at home in his kitchen, from the smudge of flour on her cheek down to the large dish towel she had tucked inside the front waistband of her slacks in lieu of an apron. While she removed the hot cookies from the pan, one by one, and placed them on a plate, he watched her. Katie was a pretty little thing. Her wrists showing from beneath where she'd rolled up the sleeves of her red knit sweater were small and delicate, as were her hands and fingers. His gaze traveled downward, over her nicely rounded butt and trim legs to her small feet. Size six, he surmised.

"Like what you see?" she asked without glancing up from her chore.

"Huh?" Then he realized she'd caught him gawking at her and was simply tossing his own question right back at him. "Yeah, honey, I do. I like it very much."

"Thank you. I've been told I make very good cookies."

"Did you think I meant the cookies?"

"Didn't you?" She set the pan in the sink, tossed the pot holders on the counter, and turned to face him.

"May I have a bite?" he asked.

She smiled. "A bite of cookie or a bite of me?" she inquired jokingly.

"Is it an either/or question? I'd really like a bite of both."

"You'll settle for the cookie," she told him.

"Okay." For now. But sooner or later, he intended to have a taste of her.

Katie tore a paper towel from the rack, placed two warm cookies on it, and brought them to him where he stood in front of the fireplace. When she held out the paper towel to him, he reached out and grabbed both cookies. She stood there looking at him, apparently waiting for him to sample the goodies. He took a bite out of one cookie and tasted butter and vanilla.

"Mmm . . ."

He took a bite out of the other. Cinnamon and nuts.

After munching and swallowing, he said, "I like this one best. I'm a sucker for cinnamon."

"Would you like a glass of milk?" she asked.

"I'd rather have coffee."

"You drink too much coffee."

"You women are all alike," Mack said. "Spend one night with a guy and you think you can tell him what to do, how to live—"

Katie went dead still. Her smile vanished. "I'm sorry, Mack. I didn't mean to be bossy. Of course, it's none of my business how much coffee you drink."

Crushing the paper towel in her hand, she whirled around

and rushed back into the kitchen. He stood there feeling like a heel. He'd been joking with her, or at least halfway joking. One thing for sure, he hadn't meant to hurt her feelings.

Should he apologize?

Mack remembered he still held the remainder of the two cookies in his hand. He wolfed down the cinnamon cookie, then tossed the plain one to Destry, who gobbled it up in one bite. Wiping his hands off on his jeans, he looked into the kitchen at Katie, who was patting out the remainder of the dough and placing the cookie circles on a baking pan.

He meandered across the living room and into the kitchen, came up beside Katie, and glanced over her shoulder. She stiffened, but didn't acknowledge his presence.

"I was just kidding, you know," Mack said.

No response. God, was she pouting?

"Besides, you were right," he told her. "I do drink too much coffee."

She placed the final cookie on the pan, picked up the pan, and shoved him out of the way as she headed for the stove. He stood there, waiting for her to turn around and face him. But instead, she came up from where she'd bent over the oven and went straight to the sink, once again ignoring him completely.

When she delved her hands into the soapy water, Mack tried again to apologize. Coming up behind her, he laid his hand on her shoulder. She tensed. He lowered his head and whispered in her ear.

"I'm sorry, honey."

He heard her deep sigh and thought surely everything would be all right now. When she turned around, he was halfway certain she would smile and maybe even kiss him on the cheek. From past experience, he'd learned that women love it when a man apologizes.

But when she turned to him, she wasn't smiling. Instead, her face was pale, and tears glistened in her eyes. "I'm the one who should apologize. I knew you were joking. It's just that . . . that the morning before Darrell died, before the company car he was driving was T-boned by an eighteen-wheeler, we had a disagreement about—" Katie gulped down several tiny sobs. "You see, I worried about the way he ate, and I made too much of the fact that he preferred cheeseburgers and fries to grilled chicken and steamed vegetables. It was such a stupid disagreement. One we'd had before, and it didn't amount to anything. But—but he told me that I had to stop trying to run his life."

"Katie . . . honey . . ." Mack wanted to pull her into his arms and hold her. She looked so miserable.

"Oh, we'd have made up that evening when he came home. We always made up. But he didn't come home. He never came home again. He was killed instantly."

"Katie, I'm sorry that you lost your husband, and I'm sorry that I said something that brought back unpleasant memories." He curled his hands around her shoulders and gently pulled her toward him, intending to wrap his arms around her.

She stared at him, her eyes wide and round, watery with tears, and leaned into him. But the minute her breasts pressed against his chest and he eased his hands down her arms, she gasped and jerked away from him.

"Katie?"

She ran from him, straight to the back door. Realizing she was running scared, he simply stood there and watched while she flung open the door and hurried out onto the porch. After giving her a couple of minutes, he retrieved his parka from the hall tree, walked outside, and came up behind her.

With her blond hair blowing in the frigid afternoon wind and her slender shoulders trembling, Katie stood gazing out at the falling snow.

The next wave of snow and ice was coming in earlier than predicted. They could easily have downed power lines and up to a foot of snow by morning.

Mack walked up behind her, draped his parka over her shoulders, and stood there, not touching her again, waiting for her to respond.

She didn't move, didn't speak.

He waited for a good five minutes before reaching out, taking her hand in his, and saying, "Come on, honey, it's time to go inside now."

Chapter Four

While the weather grew worse outside, the wind howling as a fresh blanket of ice and then snow covered the already frigid, white ground, Mack and Katie stayed warm and safe inside his cabin, thanks to the gas heat. Periodically, Mack checked the weather radio for updates, and the news wasn't good. As he had predicted, power lines were beginning to go down through not only Sevier County but neighboring counties too. Roads throughout the region were becoming impassable, and residents were being warned to stay indoors. It seemed the worst winter storm to hit the Smoky Mountains in a couple of decades had descended on northeast Tennessee. A storm of this magnitude was almost unheard of in December.

After Mack had escorted her off the porch and back into the house several hours ago, Katie had busied herself finishing the cookies, making dinner for them, and then cleaning up the kitchen. Their conversation had been limited to little more than yes and no whenever the other made a comment. By eight o'clock, she'd been able to use needing a bath to escape from Mack. And she so desperately needed to get away from him, from those midnight blue eyes that seemed to see directly into her; away from the sympathetic looks he gave her; and away from his gruff, cold attitude. It was as if as long as she stayed in a jovial mood, joking around with him, he was fine, but when she became emotional and weepy, he put up a wall between them because he didn't want to deal with anything unpleasant.

She'd stayed in the bathtub until her water turned cold and her fingertips wrinkled. Now, she was dressed in Mack's big flannel shirt and standing in the middle of his bedroom, wishing she didn't have to go downstairs and face him.

You won't have to talk to him, won't have to carry on a pleasant conversation, she reminded herself. She should just go downstairs, grab a novel from his collection of hardbacks and paperbacks stacked in a bookshelf by the fireplace, and act as if she was totally absorbed in reading. He'll probably be grateful for the solitude. After all, that's what he is used to, isn't it?

Doing exactly as she had planned, Katie tiptoed down the open staircase and quietly entered the living room. Mack sat in the overstuffed chair to the right of the fireplace, Destry curled at his side. Both man and dog glanced up when she walked over to the bookshelf. She looked at Mack and nodded. He returned her silent greeting, then focused on the forty-two-inch flat screen hanging across the side wall in the wide living room. He kept his gaze glued to the John Wayne western, which was playing on the satellite channel he was watching.

Katie found a copy of an older David Baldacci novel, one she'd read several years ago but wouldn't mind rereading. She took the book with her, sat down on the sofa, lifted her feet off the floor, and settled in comfortably. She was well into chapter three when Mack rose from his chair. She deliberately kept her gaze riveted to the book.

"Want some popcorn?" he asked.

"Oh, no . . . well, sure. Popcorn would be fine. Thank you."

"Beer or cola?" he asked as he headed for the kitchen.

"Cola, please. I don't really care for beer."

He removed a bag from the popcorn box and placed the bag, right side up, in the microwave. "Are you a teetotaler?" Mack asked.

"No. I enjoy an occasional glass of wine or a mixed drink, but I really don't care for the taste of beer."

"Hmm . . ."

Within minutes, the microwave timer beeped. Katie hazarded a glance into the kitchen, and when her gaze connected with Mack's, she gasped. Caught! Her heart fluttered erratically. Why was he staring at her that way? His hard glare made her nervous. But she shouldn't be nervous. She knew she was safe with Mack.

Physically safe—yes. Emotionally safe—no.

Katie simply could not deny the fact that she found Mack attractive. Very attractive. There was something so innately masculine, so fundamentally male about him that she found it difficult to resist the primeval feminine urge to respond to his masculinity. And that was the last thing she wanted—to respond to him the way a woman responds to a man who attracts her. She had not been with a man in the four years since Darrell's death. She hadn't wanted anyone. How could she give her heart to another man when it still belonged to her husband? She couldn't possibly love two men at the same time, could she? Besides, what she felt for Mack was hardly love. After all, she didn't really know him. No, what she was feeling for him was pure, old-fashioned lust. The hot, sweaty, passionate, nasty kind of desire.

Suddenly, a loud chinking sound followed by a whooshing thump came from outside the cabin. A second later, the room went dark. Katie cried out, startled by the unexpected darkness, despite the fact that Mack had told her it was only a matter of time before the heavy accumulation of ice on the trees and power lines would send many crashing to the ground. And that's just what had happened, aptly finishing the job of cutting them off from the rest of the world.

"It's okay," Mack told her. "A tree limb probably hit the power line."

"I'm fine," she said. "The sudden darkness just startled me."

"If you want to continue reading, I've got some battery-operated lanterns upstairs."

"Oh, no, that's okay. I've already read the book, but it was a good one and I knew I'd enjoy rereading it."

Mack came back into the living room, but instead of sitting in the chair by the brightly glowing fire, he sat beside Katie. She tensed. He held out the bag of hot popcorn to her.

"Here, take this, will you? I need to light a few candles so we can have a little more light than the fire puts out."

She grabbed the warm paper bag and held it when he got up and went in search of candles. Within a few minutes, he had placed fat jar candles around the room, and the candlelight cast a shadowy, golden glow over the semidark room.

Mack came back to her and deposited himself on the opposite end of the sofa, in a slouchy, relaxed sprawl, his knee brushing her thigh as he maneuvered into a comfortable position. Tension spiraled from her thigh to her entire body rather quickly. Her reaction to the accidental touch of his jean-covered leg warned her that she couldn't let him get close, really close. This man was dangerous, even in small doses, and probably lethal if taken in as a whole.

"If you'd like to go to bed early, I can go upstairs and give you some privacy," Mack said. "I'll have to bring Destry back down in a couple hours, but we'll try not to disturb you."

Say yes, thank you, so you can be alone, the sensible part of Katie's brain told her. But for some reason, she didn't listen to logic and instead went with her emotions, which were all over the place.

"I don't think there's any way I can go to sleep this early," she said. "Not after sleeping so well last night."

"Okay. Destry and I will just stay put for a while longer."

When he heard his name, the big dog raised his head and glanced in their direction, then came up on all fours and ambled across the room. After Mack rubbed his head and behind his ears, Destry lay at Mack's feet.

"He's very devoted to you. Did you raise him from a puppy?" Katie asked.

"Nope. He just showed up here one day about a year ago. He was scrawny and hungry, and I made the mistake of feeding him. He never left."

"Why would he? If he was lost and lonely and hungry and you were kind to him, there would be no reason he'd ever want to leave you. And it's obvious that you're fond of him too. Y'all seem to share a real bond."

Mack grunted. "He's company for me. All the company I want."

Mack didn't mean that remark as an insult, she told herself, but the comment still hurt her feelings. Then again, it didn't take much to hurt her feelings these days. For weeks now, as Christmas approached, she had gotten increasingly sensitive about every little thing. And nobody understood, after Darrell being gone for four years now, why she had been unable to move on, why Christmas couldn't just be Christmas and not the anniversary of their engagement.

"I have a battery-powered radio in the kitchen," Mack told her. "I can get it so we can have some music, if you'd like."

"All right. A little music might be nice." And it would prevent him from having to talk to her. She understood that this was his subtle way of reminding her that he didn't want to get into a personal discussion, didn't want to become buddies and swap childhood memories and share each other's favorite colors, songs, and food.

Mack stepped over Destry when he rose to his feet. The dog snorted, as if aggravated that Mack wouldn't stay in one place. Feeling edgy, Katie got up and roamed around the living room, stopping by the front window. She couldn't really see much of anything except darkness beyond the frosty windowpane.

Soft music filled the cabin. She didn't instantly recognize the tune, but the soothing melody sounded familiar.

"I figured you for the type who'd like something mellow," Mack said as he approached her. "I've got it on one of those stations that plays semiclassical stuff, along with some fifties and sixties cool jazz. If you'd like something else, just say the word."

"No, it's lovely, whatever it is."

He stood beside her, not touching her, and yet she could almost feel him, his presence so powerful. They remained silent, neither moving nor speaking for what seemed like forever.

Why did this have to happen? If she had to be caught in a winter storm, wreck Darrell's Mustang, and need to be rescued, why couldn't some elderly couple have come along and rescued her? Why did he have to be some gorgeous hunk who oozed sex appeal from his pores? And why did he have to be the first man since Darrell died who stirred to life such strong, long-dormant sexual longings? She had almost forgotten what it felt like to want a man.

Damn! She couldn't want Mack. She just couldn't. And for lots of reasons, the least of which was that she was one of those throwbacks from another generation, a woman who wanted to be in love before she had sex.

"We might as well face it," Mack said. "It's not going away. If anything, it's getting stronger."

She could say that she didn't know what he was talking

about, but that would be a lie. She knew. God in heaven, every cell, every nerve, every muscle in her body knew.

"It's just our being confined alone together this way," she told him.

"You think so?"

"Yes, probably. After all, we're both young, healthy people with all the normal needs and wants and—"

"So, you think if we'd met under different circumstances and weren't trapped alone together, we wouldn't find each other the least bit attractive?" he asked, but he didn't move, didn't glance her way.

She took a deep breath and let it out slowly. "No, I didn't say that. I imagine we might find each other attractive under normal circumstances, but the . . . the . . . er . . . feelings wouldn't be so intense."

She knew the minute she'd spoken, she had said the wrong thing, had admitted too much. Tensing, Mack became deadly silent. She thought she could actually hear his heartbeat, then realized it was her own heartbeat drumming like mad inside her head.

"Mack?"

"Whatever you do, honey, don't touch me."

She clenched her teeth. *Don't say another word. Don't move. Don't do anything except breathe.*

They stood side by side as the soft music swirled around them and the sound of crashing tree limbs exploded outside on a fairly regular basis. One moment turned to ten and ten to a hundred. Katie wasn't sure how long they simply listened to each other breathe, each practically in rhythm with the music. A log in the fireplace burned down, and the charred pieces dropped away, making a thumping sound that startled her. When she jumped, Mack turned around, grabbed his heavy parka off the hall tree, and flung open the front door. Destry raised up, but when Mack slammed the door, the dog lay back down, apparently knowing it wasn't time for him to go outside.

Wrapping her arms across her chest and gripping her elbows, Katie hugged herself. She wouldn't cry. There was no point. It would accomplish nothing except give her a headache.

There was no need to worry about Mack. He'd come back inside when he got good and ready. He just needed to cool off, figuratively and literally. And so did she. After all, that hot, sizzling passion wasn't a one-sided affair—it went both ways.

Katie made her bed on the sofa, fluffing her pillow repeatedly until she was beating her fists into it. Crying out in frustration, she grabbed the pillow and hugged it to her. *Damn you, Mack MacKinnon. Damn you for making me feel alive again, for making me want you.*

Mack walked the length of the porch several times, allowing the frigid night air to assault him, and with every step, he called himself a fool. Why hadn't he just grabbed her and kissed her? She'd wanted it. She wanted him By now, they could have been in his bed, naked and fucking their brains out. Instead of taking her the way he'd wanted to do and to hell with tomorrow and any consequences, he'd gone all noble and warned her off. What man in his right mind tells a beautiful woman who wants him that she shouldn't touch him? A crazy man, that's what kind. An idiot. A fool. Sometime between rescuing his damsel in distress yesterday and admitting to himself that she was as hot for him as he was for her, he'd gone soft in the head.

His head was the only thing soft. The rest of him was wound tight as a coiled spring ready to snap and he had the hard-on from hell. What he should be doing was closing himself off in the bathroom and eliminating his problem instead of standing out here, freezing his butt off.

It wasn't that Katie was the first woman he'd ever wanted this much, but she was the first he'd ever had to force himself not to take. If they had sex, she might regret it come morning. But what difference did that make? It wasn't as if Katie meant something to him, as if he cared about her . . . loved her. She was just a pretty woman he was trapped with in his own cabin. What would be so wrong with the two of them working off a little sexual energy?

He should go back in the house, confront her, and then tumble her onto the sofa and take here right there. She might whimper a lame protest, but it wouldn't take more than a few kisses, a few caresses, and she'd be his. He knew the signs. Katie was as horny as he was.

You'll be doing her a favor. She has all that bottled-up passion inside her. She's on the brink of exploding. You could be the guy to set off that explosion and enjoy the fireworks and the aftershocks.

Katie was vulnerable. She had wrecked her dead husband's car, one she had a strong sentimental attachment to. She'd suffered a shock, been picked up by a stranger, and was now stranded with a guy she barely knew in his cabin during a winter storm. This woman was still grieving for her husband. And right about now, she was probably hating herself for wanting Mack, for being consumed by sexual need. If he took advantage of her tonight, he'd be a real heel.

Mack stayed outside for as long as he could, until he was nearly frozen. If not for his military training, he wouldn't have been able to withstand the cold for that long. But enough was enough. He had talked himself down off that sexual high. He'd go inside, say good night to Katie, and call Destry to follow him upstairs. He could shower and shave by candlelight and find something to occupy his time until he went back downstairs to let Destry out for the final time tonight.

When Mack opened the door, he glanced over at the sofa and noticed that Katie had already bedded down for the night. He whistled for Destry, who came galloping toward him.

"Good night, Katie," Mack said.

"Good night." Her voice was a mere whisper.

Destry followed Mack up the stairs and settled down at the foot of his bed. Feeling around in the dark, Mack opened the bottom drawer of his dresser and removed a couple of fat candles he kept there for emergency use. He pulled a book of matches from his pocket, struck one and lit both candles, then picked up one candle and carried it with him into the bathroom. After placing the candle on the back of the commode, Mack stripped off, tossed his clothing into the corner, and turned on the water in the shower. Rubbing his hand over his beard stubble, he grunted. Often, he didn't shave for days, occasionally for weeks. So, don't shave. Who cares? It's not as if he'd be shaving for Katie.

Mack pulled open the shower door and stepped under the warm spray. Man, it felt good. But not as good as Katie's body would feel next to his. Not as good as being buried deep inside her would feel.

Chapter Five

Katie didn't sleep well the second night in Mack's cabin. She tossed and turned all night. Waking and sleeping. Waking and sleeping. And when she slept, she dreamed all sorts of crazy things. In one dream, Darrell was alive, and he and Mack were fighting over who Katie belonged to; she'd ended the fight by informing both men that she didn't "belong" to either of them. In another dream, she and Mack were making love—in the snow! Both of them naked, writhing and panting on the frozen ground. How ridiculous. She had awakened from that dream on the verge of an orgasm. But it was the last dream, the one that had awakened her at a little after five that had kept her awake. In that dream, she was sitting beneath a huge Christmas tree, a toddler in her lap. She was helping the child—her child—open his presents. And standing over them, a camera in his hand, was Mack. The proud papa.

Katie tiptoed into the kitchen, trying her best to be quiet and not disturb Mack and Destry, who were both still asleep upstairs in the loft bedroom. She had to erase those ridiculous dreams from her mind. And she had to find a way to get through today and tomorrow, or however long it took for the roads to clear, without giving in to her sexual needs. As she prepared the coffeemaker in the semidarkness, she went through several different possibilities that might create a peaceful coexistence for Mack and her.

As soon as there was a cupful of coffee in the pot, she removed the pot and poured the coffee into a mug. She needed caffeine, needed to wake up fully and send some energy to her brain. After sitting down at the table, mug in hand, Katie continued thinking. By the time she had drunk her first cup of coffee, she knew what she had to do. When Mack came downstairs later this morning, she would confront him, be honest with him, and hope he would be reasonable.

Katie took her refilled coffee mug into the living room, sat on the sofa, and pulled the covers over her lap. Sitting there waiting for daybreak, she went over what she planned to say to Mack. Went over it again and again.

"Despite the fact that I'm very attracted to you, it's not something I will act on. We're strangers. We have no emotional ties to each other. And I am the type of woman you think I am. I'm that throwback—a good girl who needs to be in love to have sex. And although no one, not even my family, understands . . . well, the truth of the matter is that I still love my husband.

"We're stuck here together until the roads clear. I'd like for that time to be pleasant for both of us. I'm sorry that I've invaded your privacy, but I'll be gone as soon as possible. In the meantime, why can't we act like civilized adults?"

Deep in thought, worrying about how her well-plotted scenario would actually play out, she didn't hear Mack and Destry coming down the stairs—not until Destry bounded across the room and almost knocked the empty mug from her hands.

Mack whistled for his dog. Katie placed her mug on the end table, then reached out and petted Destry. Glancing over her shoulder, she smiled and said warmly, "Good morning."

Mack grunted.

Destry ran to Mack, who opened the back door for him so he could go outside and do his business.

"There's coffee, if you'd like a cup." Katie tossed aside the covers, stood, and faced the kitchen. "It's stopped snowing."

Mack grunted again before reaching for the coffeepot.

Katie sauntered leisurely into the kitchen, determined to be friendly to Mack while resisting the urge to have her way with him. She was a smart, successful woman of thirty and despite having endured a tragedy no young woman should have to go through, she finally had her life on track. Eventually she'd find someone. A nice, easy-going guy like Darrell, a man she felt comfortable with, not one who sent her hormones into overdrive. Darrell had been the love of her life. There was no place in her heart for a greater love, a more passionate love. Instinctively, she knew Mack was the type of man who would expect everything from a woman. Everything and then some.

"I've been thinking about making pancakes for breakfast," she said. "I notice you have all the fixings, including two kinds of syrup."

"Knock yourself out." Cradling his mug in one hand, Mack walked over and stood near the back door, his gaze fixed on the nearby window.

"You're grumpy this morning," she told him in a teasing tone. "Did you get up on the wrong side of the bed?"

He huffed loudly. "I didn't get much sleep."

"Oh, I'm sorry."

"You should be."

"Pardon?"

"It's your fault I didn't get much sleep."

"Oh."

He kept his back to her as he continued gazing out the window. "You mean you aren't going to pretend you don't know what I mean?"

"What's the point of pretending when we both know there's a strong sexual attraction between us." She took several hesitant steps in his direction. "In all honesty, I didn't sleep well last night either. And that was your fault."

Mack glanced over his shoulder, an inquisitive glint in his eyes. "There's a simple solution to our problem."

"I know."

"But?" he asked.

"But I can't take the easy way out. I don't have casual sex. It's just not something I do. It's not me."

"And you can't make an exception in this case?"

Katie shook her head. "Good girls don't have one-night stands, especially not with a stranger."

Destry scratched at the back door and barked once. Mack let him in, stopping him just inside the kitchen to wipe off his wet feet. The dog rushed over to his bowl, and when he found it empty, he cocked his head to one side and stared at Mack.

"Yeah, I know. You're hungry," he told Destry, and promptly dragged a sack of dog food out of the pantry and filled the bowl to overflowing.

Despite his gruff exterior, Mack had a good heart. At least he loved his dog. That fact was quite apparent. Katie's feminine instincts told her that when Mack loved, he loved without restraint, completely, with everything in him.

Stop that! Don't go giving the man attributes that you don't know he has. You can't romanticize him. There's no point. You are not getting involved with him. The two of you have no future.

"I'll start those pancakes," Katie said, but before she reached the refrigerator, intending to remove the milk and eggs, Mack grabbed her arm. She stopped and looked directly at him.

"We're going to be stuck here with each other until the roads clear," Mack said. "The sexual tension between us is so thick you could cut it with a knife. I figure if we just screwed our brains out for a couple of days, we'd work it out of our systems. But since you don't like that idea, we're going to have to find another solution."

I do like the idea. I like it way too much. She couldn't figure out what was happening to her. She had loved Darrell with all her heart. She still loved him. But she couldn't remember ever being so hungry for Darrell or any other man. Maybe it was true that women didn't reach their sexual prime until they were in their thirties and that's why she was "in heat" for Mack. *Yeah, sure, whatever you have to tell yourself.*

"Maybe if we concentrated on getting to know each other . . ." When she saw the skeptical look on his face, she paused. "Yes, I know you don't want to do that, but it's the way people become acquainted, the way to make friends."

Mack's lips twitched, a hint of a smile. "Okay."

She stared at him, not quite sure she'd heard correctly. "Okay? Did you really say okay?"

"Yeah, honey, I said okay."

An odd sensation tingled through Katie, a peculiar combination of relief and disappointment. That sex-starved part of her had wanted Mack to say "no way in hell" and drag her off to his bed. But the sensible, rational part of her, the real Katie Hadley, was glad he'd agreed to her suggestion.

"Thank you, Mack. Thank you so much." She almost ran to him, her first instinct being to hug him. Wrong move! She stopped herself cold but kept her smile in place, then got busy preparing pancakes.

During breakfast, Katie talked nonstop about her parents, her siblings and their mates, and her twin nieces. Thankfully, Darrell's name didn't enter the conversation. Mack tried his best to act interested, to pay attention to what she was happily chattering about, just in case there was a quiz later. And knowing Katie—or as he was getting to know her—she would expect him to at least remember these people's names.

After breakfast, they both got dressed for the day, then bundled up, Katie in one of his old coats, and took a short hike around his house. The air was clean and crisp, the wind cold, the sun bright. Icicles hung from the tree branches, and numerous limbs were stuck in the ground where they'd fallen during the night, piercing through the layers of snow and ice.

Mack's bad leg suddenly gave way and buckled on him. Without thinking he grasped the closest thing, which just happened to be Katie's arm. She grabbed hold of him with one hand and slipped her other arm around his waist. He hated letting anyone see a weakness in him, especially women. Especially this woman.

"May I ask how you got that limp?" Katie stood at his side, providing a momentary prop for him.

"I was an Army Ranger," he told her.

Her eyes widened. "You mean you were wounded in battle?"

"Yeah." He hated talking about his wartime experiences.

"How long ago?" she asked.

"I came out of the hospital and left the army eighteen months ago."

"Then you're a career soldier."

"Not any longer."

They walked back toward the house in silence, taking it slow and easy. Mack's leg ached like hell. What had possessed him to go walking in the snow? Oh yes—their jaunt into the woods around his cabin had been Katie's idea. Something to keep them busy so they wouldn't think about sex. Yeah, right.

When they reached the cabin, Destry came leaping past them up the steps to the porch. Panting, he sat on his hind legs and waited for them.

"I believe he's ready to go back inside," Katie said.

"Me too." Mack grabbed hold of the railing and boosted himself up the steps. "It's about lunchtime, isn't it?"

She checked her wristwatch. "Yipes. It's after one. I thought I'd take a couple of cans of tuna and make tuna salad. How does that sound?"

Mack opened the back door and stood aside to let Katie enter first. "Sounds fine to me."

Once inside, divested of their coats, caps, and gloves, their damp shoes placed by the fireplace, Katie went to work preparing lunch.

"I'll set the table," Mack told her.

"Thank you." She offered him a big smile. "See how pleasant things can be between us, if we both try?"

"And pleasant is preferable to passionate, right?"

When her sweet smile vanished and her smooth brow wrinkled, Mack knew he should have kept his big mouth shut. But playing house with a woman as if they were a couple of ten-year-olds wasn't Mack's idea of a good time.

"You promised." Her pink lips puckered slightly into a little pout as she spoke with just a hint of a whine in her voice.

Mack grimaced. "All right, all right."

She sighed heavily, then offered him a fragile smile. "Why don't you see if you can get an update on the weather radio?"

"I doubt anything's changed since earlier," he told her. "And the news I got off the regular radio said that road crews have already begun clearing the streets in Sevierville, Pigeon Forge, and downtown Gatlinburg."

"How long do you think it will take them to get up here?"

"I'm not sure. This is just my second winter here, and we didn't get anything half this bad last winter."

"Then I might be here for Christmas."

"You might be."

She sighed again. "If that happens, may I use your cell phone to call my family on Christmas Day?"

"Sure."

After giving him another smile, she used the manual can opener to remove the lids from the tuna cans, then dumped the contents into a large bowl and took several items from the refrigerator.

An hour later, lunch eaten and dishes hand-washed, dried, and put away, Katie suggested they play checkers.

"I noticed a checkerboard in that bookcase, along with a deck of cards and several games," Katie said.

"They were here when I moved in," he replied. "I'd meant to throw them out but never got around to doing it."

"Come on, let's play checkers. It'll be fun."

Fun? He doubted it. Then a devious thought hit him. "Okay, we'll play checkers, but we need to decide on the stakes."

She eyed him quizzically. "You mean play for pennies or matchsticks or—"

"Or each of us names what we want if we win."

After being hesitant at first, her mind obviously mulling over the idea, Katie nodded. "Okay, just as long as sex is not involved."

Mack chuckled, then using his forefinger marked an X across his chest. "I swear."

They set up the board on the kitchen table. He took black; she took red. She won the first game. Hell, she was a lot better at this than he was. He hadn't actually played checkers since he was a kid.

"Okay, what do you want for winning the first game?" he asked.

"I want to know if you've ever been married, engaged, or in love."

She studied his face as he glared at her. "Yeah, I see how it's going to be. You'll use this game to worm all sorts of information out of me."

"It works both ways," she told him. "If you win, you can ask me anything you'd like."

"Hmm . . . What if that's not what I want when I win?"

"Aren't you the least bit interested in finding out more about me?"

He knew a trick question when he heard one. "Okay, I know when to give in and play the game by your rules."

Mack got up and walked over to the small pantry. After he opened the door, he reached inside and pulled out a bag of Katie's homemade cookies. "No, I've never been married or engaged. As for being in love . . . maybe once or twice, when I was younger."

"Remind me again, just how old are you?" she asked teasingly.

"That's another question."

"That one should be free," she said. "I'm thirty."

"Thirty-six." He held out the bag to her as he sat back down. "Cookies?"

She shook her head and set the board up for their second game. When she won for the second time, she seemed quite proud of herself.

"Where were you born and raised?" she asked.

"I was born in Valdosta, Georgia, but after my mother died when I was nine, my dad moved us around a lot, going from job to job. I pretty much grew up all over the South and Southwest."

"I was born and raised in Cleveland, Tennessee, not two hours from here. I've never lived anywhere else, except when I went off to college. Darrell was from Cleveland, too, so naturally we stayed there after we got married."

"So, when you ask me a question and I answer it, you're then going to give me the same information about you?"

She nodded. "That's called conversation, getting to know each other."

Mack grunted.

"You grunt a lot, you know that, don't you?"

He chuckled.

"Ready for another game?"

"Set 'em up."

When he won the third game, but just barely, he made a big show of being excited about winning. Katie laughed at his antics.

God, he loved her laughter.

"For my prize, I want to know something personal about you," Mack said.

She sat up straight and placed her hands in her lap. "Ask away."

"What color are your panties?"

"Mack!" Widening her eyes, she forced a shocked expression, but she couldn't keep from giggling. Hadn't he seen her panties drying in his bathroom that first morning? Surely he had.

"White? Red? Black?"

"You're not supposed to ask about anything that has to do with sex," she reminded him. "Sex is taboo."

"Hey, I didn't ask to see your panties," he said. "I just asked what color they are."

"Pink."

"Hmm. And your bra too?"

"Stop that."

"Ah, come on. Tell me."

"It's pink, too, as you darn well know. You saw them."

"Good girls don't wear black or red underwear, huh? And as for seeing your underwear—I didn't see them on you."

"You asked your questions and they've been answered." She reset the board, then reached over and stuck her hand in the open cookie bag. "I'm going to make some hot chocolate to go with these cookies. Do you want some?"

He wanted some all right, but not hot chocolate. "Yeah, thanks. I'll help you. You get the cocoa mix and I'll get the milk."

She offered him another of her sweet smiles, and for some stupid reason he felt as if he'd been poleaxed. What the hell was it about Katie Hadley that made him want her so damn much?

After eight games of checkers, with Katie winning five of the eight, they put the board away and Mack went outside with Destry. She had won the answers to a great many questions that gave her some insight into who Mack MacKinnon was. Giggling to herself, she thought about one question in particular.

"Is Mack your real name or just a nickname, short for MacKinnon?"

He'd stammered a few times, then admitted that his name was Cletis Hobart MacKinnon and he'd been named for both of his grandfathers.

"No wonder you want to be called Mack."

She'd also found out that he'd joined the army straight out of high school, that he had no siblings, and his father had died ten years ago. He had no close family ties. Mack was a loner. He claimed he preferred the solitary life here in his mountain cabin. She wondered, given the choice, whether he might not choose having a family over the isolated bachelor life he'd been living.

They had prepared supper together, cleaned up afterward together, and talked the whole time. At least Katie had talked. He had listened, replying whenever necessary. The lady was an open book—about everything except her husband. Saint Darrell, who'd been dead for four years. How many women mourned a man for four years?

Katie should be remarried and having babies. She was the type who wanted and needed domestic bliss. So why hadn't she found her second Mr. Right by now?

What worried Mack was the fact that he didn't like the

idea of Katie with another man. In forty-eight hours, she'd gotten under his skin. He knew it wasn't anything to worry about, that his jealous thoughts were all tied up with the fact that he wanted to screw Katie. If he could just work her out of his system, he'd be fine.

"You need to bring in more firewood," Katie said. "I'll go with you and see if I can find some twigs."

"What?" *Had she said twigs?*

"You weren't listening to me, were you? My dad does that to my mother all the time. She's always saying, 'David, you're not listening to me.' Why are all men—"

"Tell me again, honey, and I promise I'll listen."

"We'll need twigs to stick the marshmallows on."

What was she talking about?

Katie explained. "I told you that we should roast marshmallows while we listen to the radio and swap stories about our childhoods."

Mack groaned.

Katie frowned at him.

"You stay here," he said. "I'll find you some twigs."

Grumbling to himself the entire time he was scouring near the porch for twigs, Mack asked himself why, if he knew for certain that he wasn't getting in Katie Hadley's pink panties, he was jumping through hoops to try to please her.

An hour later, sitting in front of the roaring fire, their bellies filled with marshmallows, the sticky twigs burning in the fire, Mack leaned his back against the nearby chair. When Katie scooted closer, he maneuvered her around so that she sat between his spread thighs and eased closer and closer until her back pressed against his chest.

Once she was cozily situated, he released his hold on her upper arms and allowed her to simply lay against him on her own. What he wanted was to put his arms around her and hold her.

"This probably isn't a good idea," she told him.

"I'm not touching you," he said. "We're just a couple of people getting acquainted, sitting back and enjoying the fire and the music on the radio."

"Mack?"

"Huh?"

"Thank you for today. You've been wonderful."

"You're pretty wonderful yourself."

She glanced over her shoulder and up into his face. "I like you a lot, you know."

"I like you a lot too."

"Maybe when I go home, back to Cleveland, you could drive down and visit me sometime."

"Maybe."

"We could have a real date. Go out to dinner, go to the movies. That sort of thing."

"We could."

"And after we've dated for a while, we could discuss our relationship becoming more"—she swallowed—"intimate."

"Katie?"

"Hmm . . . ?"

"I'm going to kiss you. Just kiss you. Nothing else. All right?"

"All right."

He lifted her onto his lap, turned her toward him, and then cupped her face between his open palms. Her eyelids fluttered, then closed. He took her mouth in a tender kiss.

God, she tasted good.

He kissed her and kissed her and kissed her. She sighed, parting her lips, inviting him in. With her full cooperation, he devoured her mouth, his body tightening, demanding more.

Katie responded, returning the kiss with equal passion.

When they were both breathless and came up for air, they stared at each other for one endless moment. Then Mack released his hold on her face and slipped her off his lap and onto the floor.

"I think I'd better take Destry out and then go on up to bed," Mack said.

Gazing at him with a dazed expression, she didn't reply, simply nodded.

He had to get away from her. Now. If he didn't, he wouldn't be able to walk away from the temptation to claim her completely. His body ached with wanting her.

Damn, it was going to be another long, restless night.

Chapter Six

Katie had dreamed about Mack again, the two of them making love with wild abandon in various positions and odd places. She'd never in her entire life climaxed in a dream, not until she'd dreamed about Mack MacKinnon. What was it about him that appealed to her so much? Why him and not the dozens of other nice, attractive men she'd met in the four years since Darrell died?

Because he's the one, an intuitive inner voice said.

Had Fate sent her to the mountains, up that specific road, on that specific day, for a reason? Had the worst winter storm to hit the area in decades been sent from above just for Mack and her?

As Katie cleared away their breakfast dishes while Mack was outside with Destry, she considered her options. She could keep things safe between Mack and her or she could give in to temptation and they would become lovers. Either way, the end results would be the same. As soon as the roads cleared, possibly by tomorrow, the next day at the very latest, she would leave and go home to Cleveland in time for Christmas with her family. And Mack would stay here, alone and isolated from the world. He didn't want a long-term relationship with her or any other woman, and she couldn't give him or any man all of herself, all of her love, not when a part of her still belonged to Darrell and always would.

The back door flew open and Destry bounded into the kitchen, with Mack right behind him. As he bent to clean the dog's paws, Mack glanced up at Katie and smiled.

"It's already getting warmer," he said. "The icicles hanging from the roof are melting. If the weather forecasters are right, it'll get up to thirty-six degrees today."

"Do you think the roads will be clear by tomorrow?"

"Maybe." He rose to his full six-three height. "Tomorrow's Christmas Eve. You want to go home, don't you?"

"Yes, I do." Her gaze locked with his. "I thought I wanted to get away from my family, that I couldn't bear to spend one more merry, merry Christmas with them. Not when all Christmas means to me is memories of Darrell and how happy we once were. But I was wrong. I need my family."

"You're lucky to have a family, people who really care about you."

"You're right. I am. It's just that Darrell proposed to me on Christmas Day."

Mack came over to her but stopped short of touching her. "You have to let him go, honey. Put him where he belongs— in the past."

Fighting to keep her smile in place, she swallowed hard. "You don't understand. You've never loved someone the way I loved Darrell."

Mack frowned. "Probably not." He lifted his hand and gently caressed her cheek. "But my old man loved my mother that way. When she died, he went to pieces. He started drinking and moving from job to job. Women came and went in his life. I had four stepmothers in the span of eight years."

"Oh, Mack, how sad."

"Just as I was getting used to a stepmom, she'd be gone

and another one would show up a few months later. But I survived. I learned not to get attached to any of them."

She wrapped her hand around his where he held it to her face. "It must have been terrible for you."

Mack sucked in a deep breath. "Yeah, but not half as bad for me as it was for the old man."

"I don't understand how it could have been worse for him."

"He kept trying to find my mother. Every one of his wives resembled my mom, but none of them were his Leah. He couldn't let her go, couldn't free himself from her ghost." Mack turned his hand over and grasped Katie's. "He eventually drank himself to death, grieving over her. My mother wouldn't have wanted that for him."

"No, I'm sure she wouldn't have."

"Do you think Darrell would want you to stop living and loving?"

"No, of course he wouldn't, but—"

"You don't have to stop loving Darrell. But you can't feel guilty if another man comes into your life, a man you love just as much or maybe even more than you did him. The right man won't feel threatened by your memories of Darrell. He'll be grateful that you're the kind of woman who can love that deeply and completely."

Katie couldn't bear to hear another word. Tears filled her eyes and lodged in her throat. She shook her head and turned away from Mack, but he held fast to her hand, stopping her from running.

"Just in case you're still here for Christmas, do you want to do something to make the cabin a bit more Christmasy?" he asked.

Swallowing her tears, she stared at him, totally taken off guard by his question.

"Do you mean decorate the cabin? Put up a tree? Exchange presents?"

"Yeah, I guess. Whatever you'd like."

"Do you mean that?"

He tugged on her hand, slowly pulling her toward him. "Sure. We could bundle up right now and go find a small tree. I don't have any decorations, but maybe we—"

"We could string popcorn to use for garland and we could make stars out of aluminum foil. Oh, I know what else—we could tear colorful pages out of magazines, cut them into pieces, glue them into rings and make a chain and—"

Mack whirled her around, patted her on the butt, and said, "Get your coat, woman. If we have to do all that, we need to start now."

Not until she was bundled in Mack's old coat and cap and they were trudging through the nearby woods did she realize how adeptly he'd maneuvered her from tears and sadness to laugher and joy.

"I've never done this before," she told him.

"What—stomp around in a foot of snow?"

"No, silly, I've never cut down my own Christmas tree. We had live trees when I was little, but Mom's used an artificial tree for years."

"It'll be a first for me too," he said. "The last time I had a Christmas tree was before I left home to join the army. Dad's wife at the time put up a tree my senior year in high school. It was one of those silver trees, and she hung purple satin balls all over it. It was the ugliest thing I've ever seen."

They both laughed. It felt so wonderful to laugh, to truly enjoy the moment, to find pleasure in being with someone.

"How about this tree?" Mack reached out and shook the snow from a five-foot cedar. "The shape is good and it's not so big it'll take up a lot of room."

Katie stepped back and surveyed his choice. "It's perfect."

Mack hoisted the ax that he'd taken from where it had been covered with a tarp, inside the wood box on the porch. "Stand back."

Katie watched while Mack chopped down the tree, one hard, powerful lunge after the other, until the cedar toppled into the snow. Mack grinned triumphantly. Katie clapped her glove-covered hands together, gleefully praising him for his hard work. He handed the ax to Katie, then grabbed the tree by the trunk and dragged it to the cabin. After placing the ax back under the tarp, she rushed up the steps and opened the front door. Mack pulled the tree into an upright position and carried it into the living room.

"Where do you want it?" he asked.

"In the corner, away from the fireplace," she told him. "If we had lights to put on it, we'd put it in front of a window."

Mack hauled the tree over to the corner and laid it flat on the floor. "I'll have to get some wooden strips and build a stand, then attach it to the tree."

"Oh, I'd forgotten all about a stand."

"I'm in charge of practical, manly stuff. You're in charge of decorations." He winked at her.

Katie laughed, once again reveling in the marvelous sensation of pure happiness. She felt alive—totally, completely, gloriously alive. Thanks to Mack.

If anyone had told him a week ago that he'd be helping string popcorn for Christmas tree decoration, Mack would have told them they were crazy. But here he sat, on the floor in front of the fireplace, following Katie's instructions as he slipped one piece of popcorn after another over the needle and onto the long string. He glanced over at the tree, already filled with aluminum foil stars and ringed with colorful paper chains.

"I appreciate your going back outside to gather some greenery for the wreath we made and hung over the fireplace and to put in all the windows," Katie said. "Don't you think it's beginning to look a lot like Christmas in here?"

"Absolutely. Who'd have thought you could use the red ties from plastic garbage sacks to make bows for the wreath? Honey, you're incredible."

"Why, thank you, sir. But it's no big deal. I've got that magic interior designer's touch. I can take a few inexpensive items and decorate a room."

"You love it, don't you, being an interior decorator?"

She cleared her throat. "That's interior designer, if you please." She giggled. "And yes, I love it. Kim and I both do."

"You and your sister are really close, huh?"

"Very. She's my best friend as well as my sister. Of course, we adore Kit, too, and his wife is fast becoming like a real sister to us."

"You're lucky."

Damn, why had he said that again? Now she'd get all mushy and sympathetic. He didn't want her sympathy. He hated the very thought of anyone feeling sorry for him. That was one of the reasons, after he'd come out of the hospital with a bad leg, he'd bought this place up in the mountains. He didn't want to have to interact with people any more than necessary.

Katie laid down her popcorn garland, a work in progress, and reached over to squeeze his hand. "If I didn't know it before how lucky I am, I know it now. I just wish you had a family. You need someone to love you."

Mack cleared his throat. "As soon as we finish up here, how about I grill us some steaks for supper?"

"Sounds great. And you know what I want to make for dessert?"

"I don't have the foggiest."

"Snow cream."

"You're kidding."

"No, really. I don't know why I haven't thought of it before today. We have all that wonderful clean snow outside and we have sugar and milk and vanilla. All the ingredients we need."

A peculiar, surprising thought flickered through his mind. *We have all the ingredients we need to make this thing between us work. I make you happy. You make me happy. We're sexually attracted to each other. We're both single and available.*

What had gotten into him? You'd think he was in love or something. Here he was thinking about Katie and him as a couple. And not just in bed, not just a one-night stand.

How the mighty have fallen! And the one who'd brought him down hadn't even been trying. Katie had crashed into his life unexpectedly and totally unwanted. She hadn't chased him, hadn't pursued a relationship with him, hadn't tried to trap him. And on top of everything else, she was still hung up on her dead husband.

So don't get any more involved with her than you already are. If you can keep your hands off her for another day or two, she'll be gone and out of your life forever.

Why did the thought of never seeing Katie again bother him so damn much? The answer was simple—he *was* an idiot. He'd gone and gotten hung up on a woman who would settle for nothing less than forever after.

"Mack? Mack!"

"Huh?"

"Where did you go? You looked as if you were a million miles away," Katie said.

"Just thinking about what else we can do to make this a good Christmas for you. Just in case you're stuck here past tomorrow."

"I've decided that even if the roads are clear tomorrow, I might stay over until Christmas morning."

"Why would you do that?"

It was pitiful how badly he wanted her to stay.

"Well, we could have Christmas Eve together and then you could drive me home to Cleveland and spend Christmas Day with me and my family."

"I don't know, honey, your folks wouldn't be expecting an uninvited guest and—"

"You would be my *invited* guest."

What would it be like to spend Christmas with Katie and her family? It wouldn't change anything between them, wouldn't obligate either of them to more than that one day. And it might be great to sit down to a big home-cooked Christmas dinner.

"Mack, please say yes." Katie looked at him pleadingly. "Remember, you did rescue me and open up your home to me. It's only right that my family should return the hospitality."

"I don't know. Maybe."

"Ah, come on. Say yes."

"If I do drive you home and stay for the day—"

"No strings attached," she told him. "Come home with me for Christmas and you don't have to come back to Cleveland to see me ever again . . . unless you want to."

Yeah, that was the kicker. The problem was he'd want to see her again and again and again.

"What if I decide later on that I do want to come back to see you?" he asked.

She looked him square in the eyes. "Then you'd come back and we'd take things slow and easy and see what happens."

Slow and easy wasn't Mack's style. When he wanted something as badly as he wanted Katie Hadley, he usually didn't wait. He was accustomed to reaching out and taking what he wanted. If she was talking about a long courtship where they held hands and kissed good night after a date, then she had the wrong guy. He wanted Katie in his arms, in his bed, and the sooner the better.

She was his woman. She just didn't know it yet.

But she would. And soon.

Katie curled up on the sofa, pulled the covers to her neck, and burrowed in for the night. Everything was set. She had called Kim and explained that she was bringing Mack to Christmas dinner and that she wanted everyone to be very nice to him.

"Is there something going on between you two?" Kim had asked.

"We've become friends."

"Just friends?"

"I like him a lot and I think he feels the same."

"How much is a lot?"

"No more questions," Katie had said. "Just tell Mom and Dad. Okay?"

Katie gazed at the corner where they had put their tree. Although in the dark it was difficult to see just how beautifully they'd decorated it with homemade items, in her mind's eye Katie could see every aluminum foil star, every strand of popcorn and paper rings, and all the twigs of holly leaves and red berries.

Today had been such a lovely day. Moments out of time.

The snow cream she'd made had been almost as good as her mother's. Mack sure had liked it. He'd eaten three helpings. She loved doing things with him, loved doing things for him. Despite his size, his occasional gruffness, and his military background, Mack really was a kind, gentle man. He was the sort of man who should be married and a father instead of being holed up in the mountains all alone. What he needed was the right woman.

But she wasn't the right woman for him, was she? Mack deserved a woman who could love him with her whole heart.

If only I could be that woman.

How could she give Mack what he deserved when she still loved Darrell?

You don't have to stop loving Darrell, but you can't feel guilty if another man comes into your life, a man you love just as much or maybe even more. Mack's words echoed inside her head. Was it possible that she could actually love Darrell and love someone else too? Could she keep on loving Darrell and love Mack?

Did she love Mack?

The right man won't feel threatened by your memories of Darrell. He'll be grateful that you're the kind of woman who can love that deeply and completely.

It took a man with a great deal of self-confidence not to be threatened by the memory of a woman's dead husband. Could Mack really accept that a part of her heart would always belong to Darrell?

Wasn't that what he'd said, in a roundabout way? So did that mean Mack was the right man for her? And was she the right woman for him? Would loving Mack be a betrayal of the love she'd shared with Darrell?

Katie tossed back the covers, stood up, and took a deep, fortifying breath. Before her courage deserted her, she climbed the stairs, one slow agonizing step at a time, until she reached the loft bedroom. The wall of windows at the front of the house and across the back at the loft level allowed moonlight to flood the area. Katie tiptoed closer to the bed where Mack lay sleeping, the covers pulled up to his shoulders.

Oh God, can I do this? Will I regret it later?

She moved to the side of the bed and stood there, her pulse accelerating with each wild beat of her heart.

"Mack?"

Without saying a word, he reached out from beneath the covers and grabbed her wrist. She froze.

"I thought you were asleep," she said.

"I haven't slept much since you came into my life."

"I did that first night, but—"

He yanked her down, into the bed and on top of him. She yelped as she fell against him. They lay there eye to eye, nose to nose.

"Mack . . . I—I think we should talk."

"Honey, we've done enough talking."

Chapter Seven

Not even for a moment did Katie think about resisting. In her heart of hearts, she knew she hadn't come up to Mack's bedroom to talk. She had come to him because she wanted him, needed him, yearned for him. Right or wrong, good or bad, she had fallen in love with this man, and the feelings were unlike anything she'd ever known. She had loved Darrell, all her young hopes and dreams wrapped up in a neat, happily-ever-after package with him. Her relationship with Darrell had grown by slow degrees, through months of dating, a yearlong engagement and had deepened after they married. But this thing with Mack was more basic. It was raw and passionate, and she'd gone from meeting him to loving him in a matter of days.

Mack grasped the back of her head and brought her mouth down to his. As she lay on top of him, their bodies separated by the flannel shirt she wore and the heavy bedcovers, he ravaged her mouth. She moaned softly, his tongue inside her, mating with her tongue. The kiss deepened, intensifying with each passing second, until Katie couldn't breathe. She was connected to Mack as if they were one entity.

Every nerve in her body tingled, every muscle melted, and her feminine core ripened with moisture, tightening and releasing in preparation. She ached unbearably with the need to have him inside her.

When they stopped kissing, both of them breathing heavily, she rested her forehead against his and whispered his name. "Mack . . ."

"I'm going to make love to you," he told her, his voice husky with desire. "All night long."

She sighed, her body more than ready to accommodate him, longing for the feel of him on her, under her, around her, and inside her. She wanted to touch him, taste him, look at every big, hard inch of his body.

"I want that," she told him. "I want you . . . more than I've ever wanted anything in my life."

"God, Katie!" He shoved her to his side, tossed back the covers, and pulled her on top of him again, their bodies now touching. "I want you as much as you want me. Probably more."

"That's not possible." She rubbed herself against him and discovered that he was totally naked and already aroused. His sex, large and hard, pulsed against her bare thigh.

He ran his hands up beneath the flannel shirt she wore—his shirt—and caressed her naked buttocks. She whimpered when he slipped his fingers in the crevice.

"Your skin is like silk," he told her, his mouth against her neck. "Let's get you out of this shirt so there's nothing between us."

She straddled him, her mound against his sex. He reached up and undid her shirt, then spread it apart. When he looked at her breasts, he groaned deep in his throat. Hurriedly, he slid the shirt down her arms and off, then tossed it onto the floor. While she sat astride him, feeling as if she would go out of her mind if he didn't take her soon, he cupped her breasts, then covered them with his big hands.

She tossed back her head. Her hair swayed across her

shoulder blades. Mack rose up enough to flick her nipples with his tongue.

Katie keened as pure pleasure and pain radiated from her breasts—up, down, and out, until her whole body vibrated with the sensation.

"You like that, don't you? You like my mouth on your breasts." He covered one nipple with his mouth and sucked greedily. When she whimpered and squirmed and grasped his head, he suckled at one breast while he lifted his hand to the other breast, using his forefinger and thumb to pinch repeatedly.

Katie came apart, crying, begging, on the verge of an orgasm—and he wasn't even inside her yet. "Now . . . please . . ."

"Not yet," he told her. "You're going to have to wait."

"Mack, please."

He tumbled her onto her back, sideways across the bed, then spread her thighs and kissed a hot, damp path from her breasts, gliding over her belly and down to the thatch of blond hair at the apex of her legs. His fingers delved first, two going deep inside her, testing her readiness. Moisture gushed against his fingers.

When his tongue went to work, laving, licking, sucking, Katie cried out as unbearably intense sensations rocketed through her. Within minutes, she came. Wild and explosive. Her body trembled with release.

Mack rose from between her spread thighs and straddled her hips, all the while skimming his hands over her. She jerked and panted, her hot, perspiration-damp body incredibly sensitive to his touch. When he moved away from her, she reached out for him.

He took one hand, kissed each fingertip and said, "I need to protect you, honey."

Despite being in a climactic daze, she understood what he was telling her and waited patiently for him to retrieve a condom from wherever he kept them in the bathroom.

Within a minute, Mack returned. He dropped a handful of

condoms onto the top of his nightstand. She looked up at him, drinking him in, appreciating all that masculine beauty, all that macho power. It was then that she noticed the thick, ugly scars marring his otherwise perfect leg.

Realizing she was staring at his flawed leg, Mack hesitated.

She understood now. The injury was a brand of honor, one he preferred to go unmentioned. Katie held open her arms and smiled. Mack heaved a deep sigh and smiled.

Katie continued her appreciative appraisal of his manly attributes. He possessed broad shoulders, muscular arms, and a wide chest sprinkled with curly black hair that pointed downward in an arrow that led to the thicket of black curls surrounding his impressive penis. Reaching up, she circled his condom-clad erection.

"I want you inside me," she told him.

"I plan to give you what you want."

He came down over her, kissed her, then lifted her hips upward and thrust into her. They both moaned with the sheer satisfaction of being united in the basic way a man and woman can become one.

"I knew it would be like this," he said, his voice a rough whisper. "I knew this is what it would feel like to be inside you."

"I love it," she told him. "I love your being inside me." She clutched his shoulders and lifted her hips, inviting him to move.

"I can't make it last. I've wanted this so much that I'm ready to come right now."

She kissed him. He rammed in and out of her several times. She bucked up, meeting each lunge. And when he came, she came at the same moment. Mack grunted and groaned and shook from head to toe.

"Damn, Katie! Damn!"

She clung to him while the aftershocks of their orgasms vibrated through them. Breathing hard, he eased off her and rolled onto his back, then pulled her up against him so that she lay on his outstretched arm.

After removing his used condom and tossing it into the wastebasket next to his nightstand, Mack reached down and yanked the covers up and over them. Nuzzling her cheek with his nose, he said, "Get some rest, honey. I'm going to be all over you in a couple of hours."

Katie sighed contentedly and within minutes began drifting off to sleep, happier than she'd been in a long time.

Happier than I've ever been in my entire life.

Mack woke sometime during the night, and when he felt a warm body lying next to him, it took him a full minute to remember that Katie had come to him and they had made love. God, had they made love. It had been a while for him, and he realized it had been a lot longer for her. She was about as hungry for loving as a woman could be, and he'd tried his best to satisfy her in every way. He'd never wanted to please a woman more than he wanted to please Katie.

Now that she was his . . .

Mack grinned. He liked the sound of that. Katie was his.

He leaned over and kissed her cheek. She sighed deeply. He kissed her forehead. She moaned. He kissed her lips. Her eyelids fluttered.

"Wake up, Katie," he whispered against her ear.

She swatted at his head.

He laughed. "If you want some more good loving, you'd better wake up."

Her eyelids flew open. She gazed up at him and smiled.

He ran his hand beneath the cover and caressed her breasts. Her nipples peaked instantly. She stretched like a lazy cat in the sun.

Mack slid his hand over her belly and between the thighs, then inserted his fingers inside her and rubbed his thumb pad over her nub.

Katie gasped.

"Do you want on top this time?" he asked.

"Uh-huh." She threw back the covers and attacked him, hoisting herself on top of him and straddling his hips.

"You're awfully eager."

"You bet I am." She circled him with her hand and pumped up and down. "I want more. Lots more."

"Honey, I'm just the man to give you what you want. More. Lots more." Mack reached over and grabbed a condom. After removing the foil covering, he handed it to Katie. "Need any help?" he asked teasingly.

She took the condom and worked it over his penis; then she lifted up and positioned her body so that she could impale herself on his sex. Bringing him deep inside her, she took him to the hilt. He clutched her hips. She moved up and down several times, riding him with a slow, steady rhythm.

"It wasn't a dream the first time," she said breathlessly. "It really is this good, isn't it?"

Pressing the small of her back, he urged her to lean forward, just enough for his mouth to reach her breasts. "If it got any better, I couldn't stand it. But I'm willing to risk my life, if you are."

"I'm willing."

He played with her breasts, using his hands and his mouth to excite her. He felt the tension inside her growing, expanding, reaching the limit. As she increased the speed, he continued his attention to her breasts and within seconds, she came. Shivering. Moaning. Her release triggered his. He came with a vengeance. His ears rang. He felt as if his head had exploded. Goddamn, what a climax!

She collapsed on top of him. He kissed her temple as he caressed her buttocks. Mine! Every masculine instinct within him claimed her. All his possessive, protection impulses kicked into overdrive.

How could he ever let this woman go?

* * *

When they had made love for the third time, at dawn, Mack had asked her if she was sore and she'd lied and told him she wasn't. But now, at seven-thirty, after they'd made love for the fourth time—in the shower, no less—Katie had to admit her body felt well used and more than a little sore. Her nipples ached from all Mack's attention, and her femininity felt raw and slightly bruised.

"You are sore, aren't you?" he asked when she cringed as he ran a washcloth between her legs.

"Just a little."

"I'm sorry, honey. Was I too rough?"

"I loved your being rough," she told him. "I loved every second of our lovemaking. Everything you did to me . . . everything I did to you."

He dropped the washcloth to the floor of the shower, forked his fingers through her wet hair, and held her head as he kissed her.

She clung to him, her soaked body glued to his.

"No more," he said. "Until you're—"

She kissed him quickly, to hush him. "Next time"—she wrapped her hand around his penis—"I'll use my mouth."

Mack grinned. "And I'll go down on you again."

Her cheeks flushed. Mack laughed.

"Lady, how can you be such a sweet, good girl and at the same time be hot as a firecracker when we make love?"

She shrugged. "You bring out the firecracker in me."

"Oh, I like the sound of that."

Half an hour later, with Destry outside frolicking in the melting snow, Mack and Katie prepared breakfast together, sharing kisses and intimate touches while the bacon fried and biscuits baked.

"If you'd like, after breakfast, we can walk down the road a ways and see how things are looking," Mack said. "Even if the snowplows don't make it up here today, I figure with the warmer temperatures, the roads will be passable by morning."

"Let's not waste the day checking out the road," Katie said. "I'd rather cuddle by the fire and talk and . . ." She leaned back against him. He had positioned himself directly behind her as she cooked scrambled eggs. "Mack?"

"Huh?"

"You're still going to drive me home and spend Christmas Day with me and my family, aren't you?"

"Sure. My plans haven't changed."

All my plans have changed, Katie thought. *I want more than just Christmas Day with you. I want the rest of our lives. But what if it's not what you want?*

"What about after tomorrow?" she asked.

Mack wrapped his arms around her waist and kissed her neck. "You want to take things slow and easy, right?"

"Mmm . . ."

She had told him that she wanted to take things slowly, hadn't she? But she'd been wrong. She wanted to dive head-first into forever after with Mack. She was crazy in love with him. And strangely enough, loving Mack with every fiber of her being didn't change the fact that she still loved Darrell. She loved everything she'd shared with her husband, every day they'd been together. She loved her memories of a wonderful man who would be a part of her as long as she lived. But she finally knew in the depths of her soul that Darrell was her past. And Mack was everything to her. Here. Now. The only thing she didn't know was if Mack was her future.

"I suppose you're going to want me to drive down to Cleveland on a fairly regular basis and take you out on dates." Mack gave her an affectionate squeeze.

Katie removed the bacon from the pan, laid it out on a couple of paper towels to drain, and turned off the stove eye.

No, I don't want you to take me out on dates. I want you to marry me as soon as possible. I want to be with you every day for the rest of our lives.

"Is that what you want, for us to date?" she asked.

"I want whatever you want," he told her. "Just as long as you stay a part of my life, I'm not going to be demanding."

Damn it, Mack, be demanding! Sweep me off my feet, rush me to the nearest minister, and make me your wife.

She shoved him aside, then dumped the finished eggs, half on his plate, half on hers. "The biscuits should be done any minute, so go call Destry and fix his breakfast while I put everything on the table."

"Yes, ma'am." Mack saluted her. "Oh, shit!"

"What?"

"Destry. I can't leave him here all day tomorrow. It hasn't warmed up that much. I'll have to take him with us."

"That's no problem. Mom and Dad have a fenced back-yard and a nice warm basement."

"They won't mind—"

She tapped his lips. "My parents are going to be so thrilled that I came home for Christmas and that I brought a handsome young man with me that they wouldn't care if you brought a herd of buffalo with you."

Mack laughed. "I take it that they've been wanting you to find a suitable young man."

"At first, that's what they wanted. But now, I think they'll settle for any man who makes me happy, suitable or not." She wrapped her arms around his neck. "As far as I'm concerned, not only do you make me happy, but you're very suitable."

"In or out of bed?" He cupped her butt, shoved her against him, and rubbed her intimately.

Katie's body tingled. "Well, I have to admit that I'm quite fond of you in bed. You're a very talented lover. But you're pretty wonderful out of bed too."

"You, honey, are just plain wonderful."

"Are you saying you like being with a good girl?"

"Oh, baby, do I ever."

They both laughed, then suddenly as they stared at each other, they both grew quiet. Katie's heart beat like mad. How could she be so sexually aroused all the time, every minute she was near Mack? This was certainly a new experience for her.

"It's all new for me too," he told her, just as if he'd read her mind.

"Mack . . . I—I don't know—"'

"It's okay, Katie. You're confused because you've enjoyed having sex with me and yet you still love Darrell. You shouldn't feel guilty for enjoying being alive."

She'd been about to say that she didn't know how it had happened, how she'd fallen so hard so fast, that she was madly in love with him. But Mack hadn't mentioned the word *love,* had he?

"You're right—I shouldn't feel guilty."

"That's my girl." He hugged her. "Now let's eat. I'll call Destry in later."

The day went by quickly. Too quickly. They had cuddled by the fire and talked, the way Katie had wanted to do. They had shared childhood stories and memories of their teen years, and they'd both touched on their professions. She loved being an interior designer as much as he had once loved being an Army Ranger.

"Would you believe that while I've been playing hermit up here in the mountains for the past eighteen months, I've been writing a book?" Mack hadn't told another living soul about his writing. The first book was finished, the protagonist a hardened soldier turned P.I., and he was half-finished with the second book. Now all he needed to do was find a publisher.

Late in the afternoon, they had shared oral sex as they lay in front of the fireplace on the dark fur rug while Destry rambled around in the woods. Mack couldn't get enough of Katie. If he took her a thousand times, he'd still want her. Again and again.

After dinner, they'd listened to Christmas songs on the portable radio, then he'd opened a bottle of wine and they'd toasted the season. It had been the best Christmas Eve he'd spent since he was a kid, before his mother died.

And here it was Christmas Day. He stared at the lighted numerals on his battery-operated digital clock on the nightstand. One-twenty a.m.

Katie lay beside him, sleeping soundly. After they had made love, he'd slept for a couple of hours, then woke, his mind whirling, wondering what today would bring. A part of him wanted to keep Katie there, in his cabin, isolated from the world. But she wasn't an introvert like he was. She needed interaction with other people. Besides that, she had a family back in Cleveland. Parents, a sister, a brother, a couple of nieces.

One thing he knew for certain—he couldn't lose her. He'd do whatever it took to keep her in his life.

And if she can never let go of the past? What will you do then? Katie couldn't have a future with anyone until she accepted the fact that Darrell was the ghost of Christmas past.

Chapter Eight

The minute Mack pulled his Jeep into the driveway at her parents' home in Cleveland, Katie noticed that the drapes in the living room moved and she got a glimpse of her sister, Kim, peeking out the window.

"We've been spotted," Katie told Mack. "Brace yourself."

"For what?"

The front door of her parents' seventies brick ranch house flew open and out came Kim, followed by her twins. Kim was the spitting image of their father. Chestnut hair and chocolate eyes, tall and slender. She appreciated inheriting his lean frame but hated her prominent nose and square jaw.

While Kim and the girls rushed down the sidewalk, Kit came outside and stood on the porch. He lifted his hand and waved. Kit was his mother's son. Blond, blue-eyed, and stocky. Of the three children, Katie had inherited equally from both parents: her mother's blonde hair, her father's brown eyes, her mother's five-four height and petite facial features.

"Brace yourself for the onslaught," Katie said. "Here comes Kim and her twins, and Kit's on the porch."

Before Mack could reply, Katie opened the passenger

door and got out, hoping to head her sister off before she reached Mack and bombarded him with questions.

Kit hollered, "Need any help with your luggage?"

"I don't have any," Katie replied as she reached out and hugged Kim, stopping her instantly. "My suitcase is still in my car, and the wrecker service won't pull it out of the ravine until tomorrow."

Kim's eyebrows lifted in a just-what-have-you-been-wearing accusation. Katie's smile told her sister that she had a secret. Kim mouthed the word *you* as she grabbed Katie by the shoulders and surveyed her from head to toe, then hugged her again. "You look wonderful," Kim whispered, for Katie's ear's only. "Having a man in your life agrees with you."

Mack got out and rounded the Jeep's hood, Destry at his side. Betsy and Becky stared up at Mack, their brown eyes filled with curiosity, then studied Destry as if the old Lab–collie mix was a wild animal.

"Is that your dog?" Betsy pointed to Destry.

"Yes he is," Mack said.

"Are you Aunt Katie's boyfriend?" Betsy asked.

"Betsy Diane Reid!" Kim scolded.

Grinning, Mack knelt down to Betsy's eye level. "As a matter of fact, I am. My name's Mack." He held out his big hand. "Who are you?"

"I'm Betsy."

Mack shook her hand. "Well, Betsy, it's nice to meet you."

"My name is Becky." The shyer twin peeked out from behind Kim's leg.

"How do you do, Becky."

Both girls giggled.

"Goodness me, come on inside you two," Kim said. "It's cold out here."

Kim rounded up her girls and herded them toward the

porch. Katie smiled at Mack. He slipped his arm around her waist.

"What do I do with Destry?" Mack asked Katie.

"Open that gate"—she pointed to the wooden gate at the side of the house—"and let him have free rein in the back-yard. You can come out later and put him in the basement if you think it's too cold out here for him."

"He should be fine outside until the sun goes down. He'd rather be outside than inside."

Katie waited for Mack to get Destry situated before she headed for the porch. He put his arm around her again and they shared a private smile, each understanding that the other was remembering their time together in Mack's cabin.

"Mom's in the kitchen putting the finishing touches on dinner," Kit said as they approached the porch. "And she's got Dad carving the turkey and ham."

When Katie and Mack stepped up on the porch, Kit held out his hand to Mack. "I'm the baby brother, Kit Brown. I hear we owe you our thanks for rescuing Katie. Be prepared for a hero's welcome from Mom and Dad."

Katie felt Mack tense at the word *hero*. He'd told her how much he disliked being thought of as a hero, of having people fawn over him. She had asked Kim to forewarn everyone not to ask Mack about his limp, because it was a battle injury that he preferred not to discuss.

"I'm the one who owes your folks my thanks." Mack's arm tightened around Katie's waist, drawing her closer to him. "I should thank them for producing a wonderful daughter like Katie."

Kim cleared her throat as she opened the storm door and ushered her little ones inside the house. Mack and Kit shook hands, and Katie breathed a sigh of relief because her brother smiled at her and winked. That meant Mack met with his approval, that his first impression of the new man in her life was positive.

By the time Katie and Mack followed Kit into the foyer, her parents had come out from the kitchen, her mom busy wiping off her hands on her apron.

"Mack, these are my parents, Janice and David Brown," Katie said. "Mom, Dad, this is Mack MacKinnon."

"You two made good time," her father said, his dark gaze studying Mack, reserving judgment, as he offered his hand. "Are the roads pretty clear between here and Gatlinburg?"

"Seventy-five is completely clear," Mack replied, shaking hands with Katie's father. "The roads between Gatlinburg and Pigeon Forge were still a bit slippery, but it was clear sailing after that."

"My, my." Katie's mom stared at Mack, then went up to him and gave him a hug. "Thank you for taking care of our girl." She pulled back and smiled broadly, showing off the deep dimples in her cheeks. "We're tickled to death to have you here today to share Christmas with us."

"Thank you, Mrs. Brown."

"Mercy, hon, you call me Janice."

Okay, her brother liked Mack and so did her mother. Two down and two to go. Kim would come around pretty quickly, once she understood how happy Mack made Katie. Her dad was a different matter.

"We waited till y'all got here before opening presents, except for the girls," Kim said. "Mom insisted."

When they entered the living room, Kim's husband, Greg, came forward and shook hands with Mack. Kit's very pregnant wife, Molly, hugged Katie and offered Mack a welcoming smile.

"I'm afraid I don't have any presents for—" Mack tried to explain.

"Oh, goodness me, don't you worry about that," Janice told him.

Katie could tell that Mack felt uncomfortable as the family gathered in the living room. At her insistence, he sat on the sofa between Katie and her mother. Family tradition dictated that their father hand out the gifts, and one by one he distributed the gaily wrapped presents. When he handed Mack a box, Mack looked downright shocked, and by the time he had three gifts in his lap, his shock had turned to amazement.

If she knew her mother—and she did!—Janice Brown had sorted through the gifts she'd purchased for Greg's December 31st birthday and Kit's January 5th birthday for the items she'd given Mack: a beer stein—Kit collected steins, a pair of one-size-fits-all black leather gloves, and a book on antique firearms—Greg's hobby.

Once all the gifts were opened, Katie's mom popped up off the sofa. "Girls, come help me get dinner on the table."

Katie gave Mack a "it-will-be-okay" look. He nodded and grinned, letting her know that he thought he could hold his own with the men in her family. God, she hoped so. She wasn't worried about Kit and Greg. But she wasn't sure about her father.

Mack liked Katie's family, especially her plump, bubbly mother. He understood how Katie turned out to be such a nice girl. Her brother was a cutup, the kind of guy that put you instantly at ease. And her brother-in-law, though rather quiet, was friendly. He had expected the third degree from David Brown, but he'd simply asked Mack guy things, like his profession—retired army; his favorite sport and school team—definitely football and UT, which gained him a smile from the old man; and if he liked fishing—which he did.

By the time dinner ended and everyone was stuffed to the gills, Mack had begun to relax. Odd how quickly these people had made him feel like a part of the family. He'd forgotten how good that felt. He hadn't been part of a real family since his mother died.

David Brown shoved back his chair and stood. "Okay, boys, let's head down to my rec room before the womenfolk put us to work."

Without hesitation, Kit and Greg rose to their feet. Mack glanced at Katie, who gave him a nod, indicating he should go with the others.

"Thank you for a wonderful meal, Mrs. Brown... Janice," Mack said.

"You're quiet welcome," she replied.

David Brown's rec room was in the basement—actually it covered almost half the basement and contained a large leather sofa, two armchairs, a big-screen television, a pool table, a computer, and two old arcade games. A stocked bar with a counter and three stools lined the back wall.

During the next hour, Mack played pool with Greg and then Kit, while David opened bottled beer and passed them around. It was apparent that Kit and his dad had a good relationship, despite the difference in their personalities. Kit had his mother's fun-loving, outgoing personality, while David was more introspective, more guarded. A bit like Mack was himself. Greg had a quiet, easygoing way about him, and it was plain to see that there was mutual respect and genuine caring between him and his in-laws.

When Mack excused himself to go the bathroom, Greg told him to use the powder room upstairs. "My girls were playing down here earlier today and decided it would be fun to flush a deck of their Go Fish cards down the commode. We haven't had time to make repairs yet."

Chuckling, Mack nodded and headed upstairs. When he reached the door opening into the hallway leading to the bedrooms, he heard Kim's voice coming from nearby.

"While Mom's reading to the girls, I want you to tell me everything," Kim said. "And I mean everything."

"No way," Katie said. "What happened between Mack and me is a private matter."

Like a moth led to a flame, Mack eased the door closed

behind him and walked quietly down the hall to where the voices were coming from. The bedroom door stood partially ajar.

"Then something did happen," Kim said. "I knew it. I could tell just by looking at you that you and Mack made love. And it must have been great. The chemistry between you two is sizzling."

Mack eased closer to the bedroom door, then leaned against the wall, out of sight, and listened. He knew he had no right to eavesdrop this way, but there was a good chance Katie would admit to her sister the truth about how she felt about him.

"He's incredible," Katie told Kim. "And he makes me feel incredible."

"You're in love with him!"

Mack held his breath.

"Yes, I am. God, Kim, I'm crazy in love with him. It wasn't exactly love at first sight, but pretty darn close."

She was in love with him! Mack's gut tightened.

"I'm so happy for you. I knew that sooner or later, the right man would come along and help you get over losing Darrell."

Silence.

"I'll never get over losing Darrell," Katie said.

Mack clenched his jaw.

"But Mack understands. At least, I think he does. He said the right man would be able to accept the fact that I'd always love Darrell, that he wouldn't feel threatened by my memories but would be grateful that I was the kind of woman who can love that deeply and completely."

"My God, can your Mack actually be that wonderful?"

"He is pretty wonderful," Katie said.

"Oh, sweetie, you've got it bad, don't you?"

"Yes, I do. I'm so in love with Mack that if he asked me to marry him today, I'd say yes and run off to the far ends of the earth with him."

"Don't you think you two should date for a while and get to know each other just a little bit better before you—"

"I'm not sure Mack loves me. Not the way I love him. I don't know if . . . well, he might not want marriage and children."

"Then take your take time with him and see where it leads."

"I guess."

Mack heard the uncertainty and the underlying sadness in Katie's voice. Without making his presence known, he slipped back down the hall and found the powder room.

A few minutes later, as he made his way back to the basement, Mack wondered what he should do. When he left to go home tonight, should he ask Katie for a date? Should he give her the time and space her sister thought she needed? Would it be fair to sweep Katie off her feet before she changed her mind, before she realized that maybe he wasn't Mr. Right, that he wasn't as wonderful as she thought he was?

Greg and Kit were in the middle of another pool game when Mack returned. David Brown sat on a barstool at the far end of the room, his gaze switching back and forth from a sports channel on the TV to the game between his son and son-in-law. He glanced up, saw Mack, and waved him over his way.

Here it comes, Mack thought. *The old man is going to warn me off, tell me I'm not good enough for his little girl, that I'm not half the man Darrell Hadley had been.*

After crossing the room, Mack sat on the stool next to David.

"Want another beer?" David asked.

"No, thanks."

David grunted.

Silence.

"It's taken Katie a long time to come to terms with losing her husband," David said. "He was a good man, and they had a good marriage."

"Yeah, she told me."

"It'd take a real man to accept the fact that his woman had loved someone else and that a part of her always would."

"Are you trying to tell me something or ask me something?" Mack understood that this man loved his daughter, that it was not only his duty but his right to look out for her.

"Just how do you feel about my daughter?"

Mack took a deep, closed-mouth breath and released it through his nose. Truth time. "I'm in love with Katie."

"Does she know how you feel?"

"I haven't told her, if that's what you're asking."

"Hmph. You should have told her before you told me."

"She didn't ask. You did."

"So, you love my daughter," David said. "What do you plan to do about it?"

"We discussed dating for a while."

"Hmm . . . Is that what you want to do?"

"No, I don't want to spend the next year dating Katie," Mack said. "To hell with the fact that Darrell proposed to her on Christmas Day. What I want is to go upstairs right now, tell her that I love her, and ask her to marry me just as soon as we can get a license."

David chuckled. "So what's stopping you?"

"Katie and I just met a few days ago."

"If you ask her to marry you and she says yes, then nothing else matters. Janice told me that she knew I was the man for her the first day we met. If Katie's chosen you, and I think she has, then the results will be the same if you get married next week or next year."

"Are you giving us your blessings?" Mack asked.

"If Katie says yes, then you've got my blessings." David reached over and grasped Mack's shoulder. "There's just one thing I need to ask you to do for me."

"What's that?"

"Don't wait too long to give me a grandson," David told him. "I've got two granddaughters and another one on the way. If we don't do something soon, the females are going to take over completely."

Mack grinned. David laughed out loud and slapped Mack on the back.

Katie had to get away from her mother, if only for a few minutes. She'd thought Kim had been relentless in her questions and advice, but no one knew how to put a person through an inquisition the way Janice Brown did.

"If you love Mack, you should tell him," her mother had said. "And let him know that he has no reason to be jealous of Darrell."

"But Mom—"

"I know you loved Darrell. We all did. He was a fine young man. But you're not an in-love-with-love young woman now. And I do think you were as much in love with love as you were with Darrell." Her mother had held up a restraining hand. "Don't argue with me. I see the way you and Mack are together. My goodness, hon, your whole family is aware of the electricity between you two."

"Oh, Mom, I do love Mack and it's different from the way I loved Darrell. Is that wrong? Should I be—"

"You should be happy," Janice had told her.

Needing a break from her well-meaning mother and sister, Katie went outside and found solace in her mother's backyard greenhouse. The moist warmth inside was a drastic contrast to the crisp, cold outside, as was the lush green of numerous plants surrounding her to the barren ground covered in spots of melting snow.

Just as Katie leaned over to sniff one of her mother's hothouse rose bushes, the greenhouse door opened, letting in a whoosh of cold air. Katie turned to face the intruder and found Mack walking toward her.

"How did you know where I was?" she asked.

"Your mother told me."

"Oh."

"She said you came out here to do some thinking. What are you thinking about—me?"

"Why, Mr. MacKinnon, what a big ego you have."

Mack moved in on her, backing her up against a table lined with pots of herbs. She looked up at him and saw something wild and unnerving in his eyes.

"Mack?"

He grabbed her shoulders.

She gasped.

"I love you. I love you so much it hurts."

"You do?"

"Yes, ma'am, I do. And what's more, I don't want to date you for months and months. I don't want to spend one more day without you."

"You don't?"

He gave her shoulders a possessive squeeze. "Marry me, Katie. Marry me just as soon as we can get a license."

She stared at him in disbelief. "You just asked me to marry you." On Christmas Day.

"Yes, ma'am, I did, and I want an answer."

Katie felt as if she'd burst with happiness. Was it possible to die from sheer joy?

"Oh, Mack!" She threw her arms around him and kissed him. "Yes, yes, yes, I'll marry you."

"Does this mean you love me?"

Spreading kisses all over his face, she said between smacks, "I love you more than anything in this world, more than I ever thought it was possible to love someone."

Mack devoured her and she him. Finally, both of them breathless, he said, "We'd better stop now or we'll wind up making love, and I'm not quite ready for your father to find me ravaging his daughter in her mother's greenhouse."

*   *   *

Katie became Mrs. Mack MacKinnon on New Year's Day. They married in a small private ceremony at the Browns' home and honeymooned at Mack's cabin in the mountains. Two weeks later, Mack and Destry moved to Cleveland, but Mack kept the cabin for weekend getaways.

The following Christmas, one-month-old David Hobart MacKinnon—Davie—stayed in his grandparents' rec room with his father, grandfather, and two uncles, while his mother, grandmother, aunts, and cousins went to Grandma Brown's to make cookies Christmas Eve morning. Then that night, he attended church with his family, and afterward, his parents showed him off proudly to all the relatives at Great-Aunt Rebecca's Christmas Eve get-together.

Christmas morning, his father recorded the event while he sat propped in his mother's lap as she opened the twenty-five presents Santa had left for him. By noon, the threesome drove up to Grandma and Granddaddy's to celebrate the day with Katie's family, who was now Mack's family too.

The memory of a long-ago marriage proposal on Christmas Day lay deep in Katie's heart, something to be treasured, and her love for Darrell would always be a part of her. But just as Mack was the love of her life, the man she was destined to grow old with, his Christmas Day proposal was the one that brought joy to her heart and had fulfilled all her dreams.

Twelve Desserts of Christmas

JOANNE FLUKE

If you enjoyed reading about Hannah Swensen and the gang at The Cookie Jar, I've got some wonderful news. Hannah has her own cozy mysteries series that revolves around cookies, crime, and local color in Lake Eden, Minnesota. Filled with two scoops of love, a heaping cup of humor, a sprinkling of suspense, and a delightful assortment of nuts, I think you'll agree when *Romantic Times Magazine* calls Hannah's books, "A calorie-laden delight . . . comfort food for the reader's soul."

There are eight Hannah mysteries on your bookstore shelves. From the first to the most recent, the titles are: *Chocolate Chip Cookie Murder, Strawberry Shortcake Murder, Blueberry Muffin Murder, Lemon Meringue Pie Murder, Fudge Cupcake Murder, Sugar Cookie Murder, Peach Cobbler Murder,* and *Cherry Cheesecake Murder*. I'm currently working on Hannah's ninth adventure, *Key Lime Pie Murder,* to be released in hardcover by Kensington Books in March 2007.

If you'd like to find out more about Hannah, her life, her loves, and her recipes, drop by www.MurderSheBaked.com—you can e-mail me through the website, or directly at Gr8Clues@aol.com.

Sorry, but I've got to run. My stove timer's about to ring and I have two dozen Black Forest Cookies to take out of the oven. If they're perfect, the recipe will be in a future Hannah book.

One more thing . . . you never know what's waiting for you around the corner, so . . .

Eat Dessert First!

Joanne Fluke

Chapter One

It was a mild day by Minnesota standards. The temperature was in the low teens, and there was no wind to kick up the foot and a half of snow on the ground. The skies were leaden gray and more snow was predicted before the day was over, but Julie Jansen didn't have time to think about the weather.

She fairly flew across the quad, sprinting for the oldest and most impressive brick building on the campus. Only the corrugated rubber soles on her snow boots kept her from wiping out as she hit the patch of ice that always formed near the flagpole. Julie was breathing hard as she pulled open the heavy door to the main building and stopped at the cloakroom to make a lightning-fast switch from boots to shoes. Then the race was on again and she dashed down the hallway, breaking the school rule about running in the halls, her dark blond ponytail whipping from side to side the way it had when she'd been a cheerleader at Jordan High. There'd been no time to braid her hair and put it up in the elaborate style she wore in the classroom to make her look older. She'd slept through her alarm, and there had been barely enough time to dress. It was departure day at Lakes Academy and Julie was late for the final faculty meeting before Christmas vacation.

Julie skidded around the corner, the ends of her silk scarf flapping, and headed into the home stretch. Perhaps they hadn't started yet. Maybe Dr. Caulder had gotten a last-minute call and she could slide into her chair before he came in. But her hopes died a quick death as she neared her destination. The door to the conference room was standing open and she could hear the headmaster's stentorian voice. His head was turned away from the door and Julie did her best to slink in unnoticed, but just as she thought she was going to succeed, he turned to look her way. Julie sank into her chair, her cheeks hot and her breath coming in little puffs from the exertion. Could her students possibly be correct when they claimed that Dr. Caulder had eyes in the back of his head?

"We're so glad you decided to join us, Miss Jansen," Dr. Caulder intoned, and thirteen pairs of eyes turned to stare at her disapprovingly. The fourteenth pair, a warm brown color that reminded Julie of melted chocolate, held only compassion for her embarrassment and what Julie hoped was the beginnings of romance. Matt Sherwood, the second-newest teacher at Lakes Academy, knew exactly why she was late. They'd attended the Christmas program in the auditorium and after their students had left, they'd taken a stroll under the tall pines that stood like sentinels outside the main gate of the academy and he'd held her close to his side. Shivering a bit after the cold excursion, Julie had suggested sharing the thermos of hot chocolate the cook always left out for teachers who worked late, and they'd stayed up until almost three in the morning.

Julie tore her eyes away from Matt's and turned to the headmaster to apologize. But instead of scowling, Dr. Caulder was smiling at her! That was ominous, and Julie clamped her lips shut and let her gaze skitter away. When she'd first arrived at the academy in September, one of the older teachers had told her that the only time Dr. Caulder ever smiled at a teacher was when he was getting ready to put one over on her.

"Ah, the enthusiasm of youth!" Dr. Caulder's smile grew a bit wider. "I happen to know that Miss Jansen was up very late last night, but here she is, only five minute late, ready to share her love of learning and her zest for life with us."

Uh-oh, Julie groaned under her breath. Dr. Caulder must have had his spies out last night. It was recommended that teachers retire before midnight and most of the older staff did just that. But someone had spotted her with Matt and squealed on them. If Julie ever found out who the rat with the big mouth was, she'd . . .

"This is one of the reasons I'm sure Miss Jansen won't mind filling in for us this year. If my wife and I weren't expected at her sister's, we'd be glad to shoulder the responsibility. Unfortunately, it's a bit late to change our plans. We'll be back here the day after Christmas to assume charge."

What's he talking about? Julie shot a silent question to her co-conspirator in late-night conversation, but Matt gave a little shrug of the broad shoulders she found so attractive. It seemed her partner in after-curfew crime didn't know either.

"As always, we're the last to know," Dr. Caulder said with a sigh. "The reasons are varied, some legitimate and others . . . shall we say, impossibly lame?"

There were several titters from the older members of the staff. Julie shot another glace at Matt and was pleased to see that he looked almost as puzzled as she felt.

"Six unfortunate children will be staying here over the semester break," Dr. Caulder went on to explain, "three girls and three boys. That means two teachers, one male and one female, must be in residence to supervise them. This is where you enter the picture, Miss Jansen. Because you're unmarried and have no pressing family obligation, I would appreciate it if you'd stay with the girls. Of course you cer-

tainly have the option to decline. And if ~~you~~ do, we'll simply
have to make other arrangements."

Julie thought about it for a moment. She didn't have anywhere she *had* to go for Christmas. Her parents were taking
the Christmas cruise they'd always dreamed of, and she'd
planned to spend the holidays with her older brother. They'd
never been close, and David and his wife would probably be
relieved if she canceled. Then her nieces wouldn't have to
double up to give her a bedroom.

"Miss Jansen?"

Julie drew a deep breath and jumped in with both feet.
"I'll be glad to stay, Dr. Caulder."

"Excellent! All of us appreciate your sacrifice."

Julie noticed with surprise that there were smiles and
nods around the table. It seemed all she had to do to be accepted by the rest of the staff was to take a job nobody else
wanted. She smiled back and waited for the other shoe to
drop. Dr. Caulder needed a male teacher for the boys and
there were only two unmarried male teachers on the staff.
One was Mr. Leavenger, the math teacher. He was only a
year or two away from retirement and a bit of a curmudgeon.
Spending Christmas vacation with Mr. Leavenger as her sole
adult companion would seem endless, but she could handle
it if she had to. The only other unmarried teacher was . . .
dared she hope?

"Mr. Sherwood," Dr. Caulder voiced the name that was
dancing across the screen of Julie's mind. "I notice that you
have no family commitments. Would you mind staying here
with Miss Jansen and supervising the boys?"

"Not at all."

"I thought not," Dr. Caulder said dryly.

Matt had answered so quickly, Julie's cheeks felt hot and
she hoped she wasn't blushing. The kiss they'd shared at her
door had been a lot more romantic than casual. And as far as
Julie was concerned, it certainly beat their former colleague-
to-colleague friendship. A little tingle of anticipation swept

from the top of her head right down to her toes. If the speed of Matt's answer was any indication, perhaps he was starting to feel about her the way she already felt about him.

There was the usual bustle as the parents arrived. Suitcases were dropped and spilled open, apologies filled the crisp air as parents collided in a headlong rush to hug their children, and students hollered out their good-byes to their friends. The first car left, followed by the second, and less than an hour later the last car drove away through the freshly fallen snow, leaving six dejected children and two concerned teachers in their wake.

Julie glanced down at the three girls she was shepherding. Six-year-old Hope looked more dejected than hopeful, her older sister Joy wasn't at all joyful, and Serena, the oldest of the girls at almost thirteen, was about as far from serene as a girl could get. One look at Matt's boys and Julie knew they were in big trouble. Spenser, who'd just turned fourteen, and Gary and Larry, ten-year-old twins whose parents were getting a divorce, didn't look any more cheerful than the girls. She had to do something to take their minds off the fact that they wouldn't be with their families this Christmas.

"Let's plan something special for this afternoon," Matt said, beating Julie to the punch. "We've got the whole place to ourselves and we can do anything we want."

"Anything?" Julie asked him, winking at the girls.

"Well . . . almost anything. What did you have in mind, Miss Jansen?"

Julie gave him a mischievous smile. "I want to borrow a pair of roller skates and skate down the main hallway."

"But that's against the rules, Miss Jansen," Serena pointed out. "It's double demerits."

"Then it should be double the fun. What do you have to do to get a single demerit?"

"Well . . . you get one if you eat in your room, and one if you run in the hall."

"Okay. Let's do those too! We'll eat ice cream in our rooms straight out of the carton." Julie noticed that this drew smiles from all the kids, so she went on. "I ran in the halls this morning when I was late to the teacher's meeting, and it was great. We can line up and have a race from the front door all the way to Dr. Caulder's office and back again. And when we're done with that, we'll let Hope decide what's next. How about it, Hope? What would you like to do?"

"I want to talk real loud in the library." Hope's eyes began to sparkle. "That's against the rules."

"And I want to dance on top of my teacher's desk," Joy chimed in. "What do you want to do, Serena?"

"I want to draw a mustache on Dr. Caulder's picture."

Larry gasped loudly. "You can't do that! He'll find out . . ."

". . . you did it," Gary took over his twin's thought, "and he'll give you a million demerits!"

"No, he won't, not if I wash it off before he gets back. What do you want to do, Spense?"

"I want to climb up to the bell tower and throw snowballs."

"Us too!" Gary seconded it. "Larry and I . . ."

". . . always wanted to do that," Larry finished the sentence for him.

"No way," Matt said, and everyone turned to look at him. Was he going to be a stickler and enforce the rules? But then Matt started to grin, and everyone knew he'd been teasing. "I won't let you climb up to the bell tower unless I get to throw the first snowball."

"Deal!" the boys shouted, and Julie noticed that everyone was wearing a smile . . . everyone except Hope, who looked worried again.

"What is it, Hope?" Julie asked her.

"I saw Mrs. Dryer leave. Are we going to starve to death before she comes back?"

"Of course we won't!" Julie reached out to give her a hug. "Mrs. Dryer made lots of dinners before she left, and she put them in the freezer for us. Dr. Caulder told me she even baked a ham for our Christmas dinner."

"How about Christmas cookies?" Larry wanted to know. "The ones with colored . . ."

". . . frosting that look like Santas, and Christmas trees, and stars and stuff," Gary finished the description.

"Yes," Hope chimed in. "It won't be Christmas without cookies."

"I'm sure she made those too," Matt said, stepping up to take Julie's arm. "Come on men. Let's escort the ladies to the kitchen so we can find out what goodies Mrs. Dryer left for us."

"Uh-oh." Julie gave a little groan as she read the note the school cook had taped to the refrigerator.

"What's the matter?" Matt left the children exclaiming over the menus Mrs. Dryer had written out for them and walked over to join Julie. "Mrs. Dryer didn't bake your favorite?"

"Mrs. Dryer didn't bake *anyone's* favorite."

"What do you mean?"

"She left a note apologizing, but she barely had time to make the entrees. She ordered Christmas ice cream rolls, with little green Christmas trees in the middle, but they didn't come."

"You mean . . . no desserts?"

Julie nodded, holding up the note. "She says there's a whole case of Jell-O in assorted flavors and some canned fruit cocktail in the pantry, but that's it."

"No Christmas cookies?" Hope asked, tears threatening again.

"Of course there'll be Christmas cookies," Matt assured her. "Since Mrs. Dryer didn't have time to do it, we'll bake them ourselves. You bake, don't you, Miss Jansen?"

"Actually . . . no," Julie admitted, feeling a bit like crying herself. "I'm the world's worst baker. I took home economics in high school. All the girls did. But the only one who could burn things faster than I could was Andrea Swensen. We were cheerleaders together at Jordan High, and they called us the Twinkie Twins."

"Why?"

"Because every time they held a bake sale to raise money for the pep squad, every girl was supposed to bring something to school to sell. Andrea and I used to bring Twinkies, until her sister found out about it and then Hannah . . ." Julie stopped speaking and started to smile.

"Why are you smiling like that?" Matt wanted to know.

"Hannah baked like a dream, and all we had to do was tell her when the bake sales were and she'd bake for us. I can still taste her lemon meringue pie. It was just fantastic. But here's the good part. The last time I talked to Andrea, she said Hannah was back home and she'd opened a bakery and coffee shop in Lake Eden."

"Lake Eden?" Matt began to smile too. "That's only twenty miles away."

"Exactly. Why don't I call and see if Hannah would bake us some desserts?"

"Great idea!" Matt said, and the kids all nodded.

"Okay. Then the only question is, how many desserts do we need?" Julie flipped over Mrs. Dryer's sad little note about the absence of desserts and pulled out a pen.

"One for every night," Matt said.

"Got it," Julie said, her pen moving quickly across the paper. "Do you think we should order extra desserts, like cookies and muffins and cupcakes, for snacks? Or is that too much?"

Matt glanced at the kids and saw the six hopeful expressions. "It's not too much. Let's order an even dozen."

If extra-wide smiles and grateful expressions could have been translated into dollars, Matt would have been a rich man. As it was, he and Julie were heroes of the day, and that pleased him much more than anything else he could think of.

"Counting Mr. Sherwood and me, there are eight of us," Julie went on, "and that means everyone can choose a favorite dessert. Then we'll decide on four others together, and that'll make twelve. We'll have the Twelve Desserts of Christmas, almost like the song."

"That's right." Matt flashed Julie a smile that included their whole group. "We could even change the lyrics and sing it for our friends when they get back."

"Willie's gonna wish he stayed here," Spenser said, grinning widely.

Serena nodded. "Liz too. She kept telling me about all the presents she was getting, but I bet she won't have twelve desserts."

"That means we're special," Joy added.

"We certainly are," Julie confirmed it, smiling at each child in turn. "Let's get busy so I can call Hannah. Now who wants to choose tonight's dessert?"

It seemed to be the morning for running late. Twenty miles away in the little Minnesota town of Lake Eden, Hannah Swensen was almost an hour behind schedule. "I'm really sorry, Lisa," she apologized to her partner for the fourth time since she'd dashed into the kitchen at The Cookie Jar, their bakery and coffee shop. "I really didn't mean to saddle you with all the baking this morning."

"That's okay," Lisa said, passing a tray of Chocolate Chip Crunch Cookies to Hannah. "Herb gave me a ride to town this morning in his squad car, so I got here early. Mayor Bascomb asked him to figure out how many tickets he gave for speeding in the school zone in front of Jordan High."

"Why does Mayor Bascomb need to know that?" Hannah asked, placing the pan of baked cookies on the baker's rack.

"The city council's voting on speed bumps this morning and the mayor wants to prove that we need them."

"Do you know what they call speed bumps in the Bahamas?" Hannah asked, turning to face her partner.

"No, what?"

"Sleeping policemen." Hannah delivered the information and then stared hard at her partner. Either Lisa had developed a facial tick or she was doing her utmost to stifle a laugh. "You think sleeping policemen is funny?"

Lisa shook her head. "It's more cute than funny."

"Then why are you trying so hard not to laugh?"

"It's your hair. It's poking up out of your cap again."

"Just call me Medusa." Hannah gave an exasperated sigh and tucked her unruly red curls back under her health board mandated cap. "The phone started ringing while I was washing it and I didn't get a chance to put on the conditioner. What do we have left to bake?"

"Just the Cherry Winks and we're through."

"Right. I'll get the cherries." Hannah headed off to the pantry to fetch the essential ingredient for the cookies her customers loved at the holidays. "Do you think it's too early to do half red and half green?"

"I don't think so. Almost everyone is already decorated for Christmas. Gil Surma put his lights up over three weeks ago."

"Gil and Bonnie are always early. They want everything to look nice for their Christmas parties."

Lisa glanced at the calendar that hung on the wall by the phone and saw the three new entries that Hannah had made. "Bonnie called you to set dates for the parties?"

"That's right. We're catering everything, just like last year."

"She gave you the order for her Brownies?"

"Yes. And yes."

Lisa looked a bit confused. "Why did you say two yeses?"

"She wants brownies for her Brownies."

"Oh. I guess that makes sense. Let's make them in bon-bon papers the way my mother used to do. Then I can frost them and put half a pecan on each one."

"The girls would love that, but are you sure you want to go to so much work?"

"I'm sure." Lisa glanced at the calendar again. "What does she want for the Cub Scout party?"

"Old-Fashioned Sugar Cookies. But the party's not just for the Cub Scouts. It's one huge party for the Boy Scouts and the Cub Scouts together, and it's going to last all afternoon."

"That's nice. I'll do the scout logo in frosting on the sugar cookies. The boys really like that. How about the Girl Scouts?"

"Bonnie's driving them to the mall so they can shop for their parents. Then they're going back to her house for hot chocolate and Cinnamon Crisps."

Lisa glanced at the calendar again. "I can help you cater the Girl Scout party. Herb's got bowling league that night."

"Great." Hannah smiled at her young partner. Lisa had more energy than anyone she'd ever met. Of course age might have something to do with it. She had just turned twenty, and Hannah was a decade and a bit past that. Not that she wanted to think about age, especially when her biological clock was ticking and her mother delighted in reminding her that she didn't have many childbearing years left. And now it was almost Christmas, and everyone was talking about families and kids.

Hannah's smile took a wistful turn. Soon her newest niece, Bethany, would be old enough to give her that wonderful wide baby grin and reach up to pat her face. Babies were delightful with their chubby little hands, their squeals of utter delight when you tickled them, and their warm, sweet scent.

"What?" Lisa asked, noticing that Hannah had stopped at the pantry door and was staring at the wall.

"Oh! Uh . . . nothing. I was just thinking, that's all."

"Don't forget to save the red cherry juice for the dough," Lisa reminded her as Hannah got out the cherries. "Green juice makes them look really yucky."

"Yucky's not good in a bakery," Hannah said, heading back to the workstation. "People want things to taste good, but they also like . . ." She stopped abruptly and turned to eye the phone on the wall as it began to ring. "Mother!" she said with the same inflection she would have voiced if she'd slid off the road into a ditch. It wasn't that she disliked her mother. It was just that Delores had already called her three times this morning.

"You're sure it's your mother?"

"I'm sure. Nobody places orders this early and we don't open for another forty-five minutes. Who else could it be?"

"But I thought your mother called you at home and that's why you were late."

"She did."

"I see. But she has to call again because she's got something she forgot to tell you?"

"You got it." Hannah turned to eye her partner suspiciously. "Has my mother been calling you too?"

"No, Marge has."

Hannah was amazed. She'd always thought calling back several times was a trait unique to her mother. "Marge does that too?"

"Yes, but I don't mind. Marge is the best mother-in-law in the world."

Warning lights flashed in Hannah's logical mind. "Hold on. You can't make that kind of a value judgment without a standard of comparison."

"Sure I can." Lisa waved away her breech of logic. "I'm perfectly happy married to Herb, and there's no way I'm ever going to get another standard of comparison. That means this is it and Marge is the best mother-in-law in the world." Lisa stopped speaking and turned toward the ringing phone. "Are you going to get that, or do you want me to?"

"Will you?" Hannah asked, heading for the workstation. She'd have to talk to her mother eventually, but at least she could get in another sip of coffee before she had to do it.

"The Cookie Jar. Lisa speaking." Hannah watched as her partner grabbed a piece of paper and a pen. "Of course we can. We just baked a big batch of Chocolate Chip Crunch Cookies and we'll put them away for you. But . . . if you don't mind me asking . . . why do you need twelve dozen chocolate chip cookies?" There was a silence and then Lisa shrugged "Okay. We'll package them up for you right now."

"Who was that?" Hannah asked when her partner had hung up the phone.

"Your sister."

"Andrea?" Hannah guessed, and she wasn't surprised when Lisa nodded. Hannah's youngest sister, Michelle, was knee deep in final exams at Macalister College in Minneapolis. "What did Andrea say when you asked her why she needed twelve dozen cookies?"

"She told me it was a crisis and the whole thing was just awful."

"*What* whole thing?"

"I don't know. She said she was driving right over and she'd tell us all about it when she got here."

CHOCOLATE CHIP CRUNCH COOKIES

Preheat oven to 350 degrees F.,
rack in the middle position.

1 cup butter *(2 sticks, ½ pound)*
1 cup white *(granulated)* sugar
1 cup brown sugar *(pack it down in the cup)*
2 teaspoons baking soda
1 teaspoon salt
2 teaspoons vanilla
2 beaten eggs *(you can just beat them up in a cup
    with a fork)*
2½ cups flour *(not sifted—pack it down in the mea-
    suring cup)*
2 cups cornflakes
1 to 2 cups chocolate chips

Melt the butter, add the sugars, and stir them all together in a large mixing bowl. Add the soda, salt,
vanilla, and beaten eggs. Mix well. Then add the flour
and stir it in. Measure out the cornflakes and crush
them with your hands. Then add them to your bowl
and mix everything thoroughly.

Let the dough set on the counter for a minute or
two to rest. *(It doesn't really need to rest, but you
probably do.)*

Form the dough into walnut-sized balls with your fingers and place them on a greased cookie sheet, 12 to a standard sheet. *(I used Pam to grease my cookie sheets.)* Press the dough balls down just a bit with your impeccably clean hand so they won't roll off on the way to the oven.

Bake at 350 degrees F. for 10 to 12 minutes. Cool on the cookie sheet for 2 minutes, then remove the cookies to a wire rack until they're completely cool. *(The rack is important—it makes them crisp.)*

Yield: approximately 6 to 8 dozen, depending on cookie size.

Hannah's Note: If your cookies spread out too much in the oven, either chill it in the refrigerator before baking, or turn out the dough on a floured board and knead in approximately ⅓ cup more flour.

BON-BON BROWNIES

Preheat oven to 350 degrees F.,
rack in the middle position.

1 cup butter *(2 sticks, ½ pound)*
4 squares unsweetened baking chocolate *(for a total of 4 ounces)*
4 beaten eggs *(you can just beat them up in a glass with a fork)*
2 cups white *(granulated)* sugar
½ teaspoon salt
¼ teaspoon baking soda
2 teaspoons vanilla
1 cup flour *(don't sift—pack it down in the cup)*
1 cup chopped pecans *(walnuts will work also)*
Paper mini-muffin cupliners *(mine were marked 1⅝ inches on the package)*

Put the butter and the baking chocolate in a medium-sized microwave-safe bowl and heat it on HIGH for 2 minutes. Stir to see if it's melted. If it isn't, microwave it in 20-second intervals until it is. Set the bowl on the counter to cool to room temperature.

Beat the eggs. Add them to the cooled chocolate mixture and stir until they're thoroughly incorporated. Then add the sugar, salt, baking soda, and vanilla and mix well. Add the flour in two half-cup increments, mixing after each addition. Stir in the chopped pecans.

Set out paper cups *(I use double papers)* on a cookie sheet, 12 to a standard-size sheet, and spoon in the brownie dough until they're ⅔ full. *(Don't use mini-muffin pans—you need the papers to spread out a little as they bake.)* Bake them at 350 degrees F. for 15 minutes, or until a toothpick inserted in the center comes out clean. Cool them by placing the cookie sheet on a wire rack.

When the brownies are completely cool, count out one pecan half to top every brownie and make the Milk Chocolate Fudge Frosting.

Milk Chocolate Fudge Frosting:
2 cups milk chocolate chips *(a 12-ounce package)*
One 14-ounce can sweetened condensed milk

If you use a double boiler for this frosting, it's foolproof. You can also make it in a heavy saucepan over low to medium heat on the stovetop, but you'll have to stir it constantly with a spatula to keep it from scorching.

Fill the bottom part of the double boiler with water. Make sure the water doesn't touch the underside of the top.

Put the chocolate chips in the top of the double boiler and set it over the bottom. Place the double boiler on the stovetop at medium heat. Stir occasionally until the chocolate chips are melted.

Stir in the can of sweetened condensed milk and cook approximately 2 minutes, stirring constantly, until the frosting is shiny and of spreading consistency.

Spread the frosting on the Bon-Bon Brownies, mounding it up nicely in the middle.

Place a half-pecan on top of each brownie before the frosting is set.

Give the frosting pan to your favorite person to scrape.

Leave the Bon-Bon Brownies on a cookie sheet, uncovered, until the frosting is dry to the touch. This should take about 25 minutes or so. *(If you're in a real hurry, put the brownies in the refrigerator to speed up the hardening process.)*

Yield: Makes approximately 6 dozen attractive little brownies.

Hannah's Note: If you have any frosting left over, place it in a small container, cover it tightly, and refrigerate it. The next time you have ice cream, just heat the frosting in the microwave and spoon it over the top for a terrific milk chocolate fudge sauce.

Chapter Two

"Oh my!" Lisa gasped, staring at Andrea in shock. "That's just too sad for words."

"I know. I practically cried when Julie told me." Andrea settled herself on a stool at the workstation. She was wearing a soft rose-colored suit under a white fur jacket. Her shining blond hair was swept up in an elaborate twist, and the white fur hat that was perched on her head was far too small and dainty to protect her from the cold. Hannah glanced down at her own jeans and logo sweatshirt and quelled a small stab of jealousy. Her younger sister always dressed like a fashion model, and looked like one too.

Hannah pushed the plate of cookies closer to her sister. A few more calories wouldn't hurt Andrea's perfect figure, and it might make her feel better. "It does sound like a real tragedy."

"Absolutely," Andrea agreed, reaching for a cookie. "Christmas is for families. No child should have to spend the holidays at boarding school."

"Oh, that's not the tragedy. Spending Christmas vacation at school is bad, but kids can survive something like that.

Spending Christmas vacation without dessert is the *real* tragedy!"

"You're right." Andrea took a bite of her cookie and smiled her approval. "So you're going to bake desserts for Julie and the kids?"

"Of course. Was there ever any doubt?"

"Not really. Thank you, Hannah. I knew you'd come through for me. You remember Julie, don't you? We were on the cheerleading squad together."

"Of course I remember her. She was the only girl who could do five cartwheels in a row without getting dizzy."

"That's right. I really hate to ask, but could you run the cookies out to the academy this morning? Julie said the kids were really depressed when their friends left this morning and they need something to cheer them up. I'd do it myself, but I'm showing the old Goetz place at noon today."

Hannah was surprised. Andrea was a great real estate agent, but the Goetz place had been vacant for a year and it was practically falling down. "But the Goetz place is a real dump."

"Never say *dump*. Real estate professionals call a house like that *unloved*."

"*Unlovable* is more like it."

"Maybe to you, but these people are interested. So can you go out to the school with the cookies? Or should I take them later?"

"Hannah can take them," Lisa said. "The baking's done and the coffee's on in the shop. I don't have to open for another twenty minutes, and that gives me plenty of time to fill the serving jars and set up the tables."

Hannah wavered. She really wanted to see Julie again. "Well . . . if you're sure . . ."

"I'm sure. And while you're there, see if you can talk them into ordering apple crisp."

* * *

Julie must have been watching for her to arrive. When Hannah pulled up in the circular driveway of the school in her cookie truck, the front door opened and Julie stepped out. Hannah rushed to meet her and gave her a hug. "Hi, Julie. You haven't changed a bit."

"Yes, I have." Julie ginned widely. "See? No braces."

"That's true. So where are these poor little tykes who've been left without dessert?"

"Next door at Aames House. We thought separate dorms would be too lonely, so we're all staying there together. The kids are in the lounge, watching a movie with Matt."

Hannah went on alert as Julie said her fellow teacher's name. There was a slight breathless quality to her voice that turned the name into something approaching a vocal caress. Hannah was willing to bet the farm that whoever Matt was, he was more than just a fellow teacher.

"Who's Matt?" Hannah asked, preparing to listen for more vocal clues. Her cat, Moishe, could swivel both ears independently to pick up every nuance of sound, and for the first time in her life, Hannah wished she had that ability.

"Matt's the teacher who's staying with the boys. I'm taking care of the girls."

"And Matt is . . ." Hannah paused, trying to figure out how to phrase it. Everyone always accused her of having no tact. "Young? Handsome? Unmarried?"

Julie gave a little chuckle and her cheeks turned pink. "He's three out of three."

"And you didn't really mind giving up your Christmas vacation as long as Matt was staying here too?"

Julie gave the type of smile that Hannah associated with Moishe, right after she'd presented him with a bowl of vanilla ice cream. "I don't mind at all," she said.

"And Matt doesn't mind either?" Hannah guessed.

"I don't think so. He's marvelous, Hannah. Tall, handsome, bright, caring, and absolutely great with children."

Hannah just grinned. It was clear that Julie had fallen

harder than a novice ice-skater for Matt. She just hoped that Matt felt the same way about Julie.

"Andrea called and said you were bringing cookies. Do you want me to help you carry them?"

"Good idea." Hannah opened the back door of the cookie truck and loaded Julie up with three bakery boxes. She took the other two boxes, closed the truck door, and followed Julie to Aames House.

"Let's take them straight to the lounge," Julie said, leading the way down the long hallway with a spring in her step that reminded Hannah of a colt frolicking in a green pasture.

"We have to stop at the kitchen first. I brought dessert for tonight and it needs to go into the refrigerator."

"What is it?" Julie gave a little skip that made Hannah laugh.

"Lemon meringue pie. You used to always ask me to bake it when you were in high school."

"You remembered!" Julie looked delighted. "It's still my favorite, Hannah. And it's on the list, because I chose it for my dessert. Nobody makes it like you do."

When they reached the large kitchen, Hannah headed straight for the refrigerator to stash the pies on a shelf. Then she glanced around at the gleaming appliances and nodded. "Nice kitchen. It's arranged just right to be really efficient."

"Is it?" Julie frowned slightly. "I really wouldn't know. Kitchens are still unexplored territory to me."

"What do you do when you're home alone? Go out to dinner every night?"

"No, that's too expensive. Teachers aren't exactly rolling in money, you know. I fix meals for myself, but if it doesn't come in a package with microwave directions, I don't buy it."

"I figured as much," Hannah said, remembering that Andrea and Julie had tied for the bottom of the class in home economics.

"Come on, Hannah." Julie started for the door. "I really

want you to meet Matt. I'm hoping . . . well . . . I guess I might as well tell you."

Hannah was silent, even though she thought she knew what Julie was about to say. Her sister's cheerleading buddy was blushing again.

"I think Matt might be Mr. Right. I'm pretty sure he feels the same way, but teaching full-time is a demanding job and there's not much time for dating. This is the first time we've ever had the chance to be alone together."

"You're not alone here," Hannah couldn't help pointing out.

"I know that. We've got six chaperones, but the kids go to bed early. And then Matt and I have the whole rest of the night together."

"Really?"

Julie gulped and her already pink cheeks turned scarlet. "I didn't mean it *that* way!"

"Of course not," Hannah said, holding back a chuckle with real effort.

"Anyway, I really want to know what you think of Matt. I spent so much time with Andrea while I was growing up that you've always been like a big sister to me. Mom and Dad aren't here, so . . . you'll tell me what you think of him, won't you?"

"Absolutely," Hannah said, hoping that Matt would be everything Julie thought he was and she wouldn't have to deflate the only Jordan High cheerleader who'd ever been able to do a flip from the top of a five-person pyramid and land on her feet smiling.

LEMON MERINGUE PIE

Preheat oven to 350 degrees F.,
rack in the middle position.

One 9-inch baked pie shell

The filling:
3 whole eggs
4 egg yolks *(save the whites in a mixing bowl and let
    them come up to room temperature—you'll need
    them for the meringue)*
½ cup water
⅛ cup lime juice
⅓ cup lemon juice
1 cup white *(granulated)* sugar
¼ cup cornstarch
1 to 2 teaspoons grated lemon zest
1 tablespoon butter

*(Using a double boiler makes this recipe fool-
proof, but if you're very careful and stir constantly so
it doesn't scorch, you can make the lemon filling in a
heavy saucepan directly on the stove over medium
heat.)*

Put some tap water in the bottom of a double boiler
and heat it until it simmers. *(Make sure you don't use
too much water—it shouldn't touch the bottom of the*

pan on top.) Off the heat, beat the egg yolks with the whole eggs in the top of the double boiler. Add the ½ cup water, lemon juice, and lime juice. Combine sugar and cornstarch in a small bowl and stir until completely blended. Add this to the egg mixture in the top of the double boiler and blend thoroughly.

Place the top of the double boiler over the simmering water and cook, stirring frequently, until the lemon pie filling thickens *(5 minutes or so)*. Lift the top of the double boiler and place it on a cold burner. Add the lemon zest and the butter, and stir thoroughly. Let the filling cool while you make the meringue.

The meringue *(This is a whole lot easier with an electric mixer!)*
4 egg whites
½ teaspoon cream of tartar
⅛ teaspoon salt
¼ cup white *(granulated)* sugar

Add the cream of tartar and salt to the egg whites and mix them in. Beat the egg whites on high until they form soft peaks. Continue beating as you sprinkle in the sugar. When the egg whites form firm peaks, stop mixing and tip the bowl to test the meringue. If the egg whites don't slide down the side, they're ready.

Put the filling into the baked pie shell, smoothing it with a rubber spatula. Clean and dry your spatula. Spread the meringue over the filling with the clean spatula, sealing it to the edges of the crust. When the pie is completely covered with meringue, "dot" the pie with the flat side of the spatula to make points in the meringue. *(The meringue will shrink back when it bakes if you don't seal it to the edges of the crust.)*

Bake the pie at 350 degrees F. for no more than 10 minutes.

Remove the pie from the oven, let it cool to room temperature on a wire rack, and then refrigerate it if you wish. This pie can be served at room temperature, but it will slice more easily if it's chilled.

(To keep your knife from sticking to the meringue when you cut the pie, dip it in cold water.)

Chapter Three

"That went well," Julie said, giving a huge sigh of relief. "The kids didn't even seem to notice that I used sour cream instead of mayonnaise in their tuna salad sandwiches."

Matt squelched the urge to pull her into his arms and kiss her on the tip of her nose. There were times when Julie reminded him of a wayward elf. Of course she didn't *look* like an elf. Far from it!

He'd noticed Julie the moment she stepped out of her car on the first September morning of classes. She'd been wearing a brown tweed suit that was meant to be subdued, but it had done nothing to detract from her figure. She'd been perfectly sedate as she'd walked around her sensible black compact car and opened the trunk to take out her suitcase. But when she'd set it down on its wheels on the sidewalk and closed the truck, she'd done something that had struck a cord in his bachelor heart. She'd glanced around, decided that no one was watching, and put her hand on the handle of the rolling travel case. Then she'd danced the first few steps of the number Gene Kelly had done when he'd partnered the lamppost in *Singing in the Rain*.

That was the beginning of their relationship, Matt decided. He adored her spontaneous sense of fun. One day, after her class had left for the afternoon, he'd found her spinning merrily away in her desk chair, humming the theme from *Carousel*. And that was another thing that he found so pleasing. Julie liked the same classic movies that he liked. She could quote whole sections from *Desk Set,* and they'd found themselves reciting Tracy–Hepburn dialogue from three different movies last night under the pine trees.

Once Julie had captured his attention, he'd watched her whenever they were in a meeting together. And although she'd been perfectly circumspect around every male member of the staff, including him, Matt suspected that Julie Jansen had hidden passions. That suspicion was based on personal observation. One telling factor was the way she licked her lips right before she tasted chocolate ice cream. Another was the way she dug into a piece of pepperoni pizza on the rare occasions Mrs. Dryer served it at a late-night staff meeting. The third factor, the one that had proven his theory beyond a shadow of a doubt, was the way she'd responded to his kiss last night.

Matt smiled just thinking about it. And then he did his best to put the memory completely out of his mind and concentrate instead on straightening the pile of napkins that were stacked on the counter. He was supposed to be supervising the kids while Julie put the cookies in a basket. If he continued to think about kissing Julie, they could have a food fight right in front of his nose and he wouldn't even notice.

Something was going on. Matt saw Serena move a little closer and accept a package wrapped in napkins from the two younger girls. They contained sandwiches, no doubt. He'd warned the kids about Julie's mistake, and they'd promised to clean their plates anyway. Matt suspected that this was the way they intended to do it, because Serena passed her package to Spenser and he stacked it on top of the one he'd taken from the younger boys. Then he stood up and headed toward the restrooms in the hall. Matt hoped he'd tear the sandwiches into small enough pieces before he flushed them. It would be embarrassing for Julie if they had to call the plumber to fix a commode plugged with tuna sandwiches.

"Earth to Matt," Julie said, reaching out to touch his shoulder. "I asked you three times if you wanted to pass around the cookies."

"Sorry," Matt said, picking up the basket Julie had lined with paper napkins.

"Don't be sorry. Just tell me what you were thinking about. You looked like you just heard the best joke in the world."

"Close," Matt said and left it at that. There was no way he was going to tell Julie that her sandwiches might even now be surfing in the sewer. "What time do you think we can get the kids to bed tonight?"

"Uh . . . well . . . regular bedtime is nine, but the older kids get to stay up to read or watch television until ten."

"Meet you in the living room at ten-thirty," Matt said, feeling as if he'd just arranged a forbidden tryst. Of course that was ridiculous. Once the kids were in bed, all they had to do was be available in case of an emergency.

"I'll be there right after I get the girls settled for the night. Are we going to discuss activities?"

"Oh yes," Matt said, putting on his best guileless smile and hoping she couldn't guess the activity that was foremost in his mind.

"Oh good! Matt wants apple crisp," Lisa said, glancing down at the list of desserts that Julie had given Hannah. They'd just closed for the night and were sharing a last cup of coffee before Herb came to pick her up.

"Why are you so happy he wants apple crisp?"

"Because I just found Grandmother Herman's recipe. I'll make two double batches of it tonight, and you can take it out there for tomorrow night's dessert. They can warm it up in the oven and serve it with ice cream."

"Perfect. I'll pick up some vanilla to go on top."

Lisa shook her head. "Get cinnamon instead. It's even better that way."

"Does the Red Owl have cinnamon ice cream?"

"Sure. Florence always stocks it over Christmas."

"Why does she stock it for Christmas?" Hannah asked, trying to figure out what cinnamon ice cream had to do with Santa and Christmas.

"They use it in Hot Candy Canes," Lisa explained.

"What are those?"

"They're drinks that Hank serves down at the Lake Eden Municipal Liquor Store."

"You've had one?"

"No, but Herb told me about it. Hank mixes hot coffee with peppermint schnapps in a big mug, and then he tops it with a scoop of cinnamon ice cream. He sticks in a candy cane for a stirrer, and it's really popular over the holidays. Herb said it brings in more revenue for the town than his parking tickets do in a whole year."

"Got it," Hannah said, jotting a note to stop by the Red Owl before Florence closed and pick up some cinnamon ice cream. Then she made a second note to fight like a Tasmanian devil if anyone ever tried to talk her into tasting anything called a Hot Candy Cane.

Lisa glanced back down at the list. "Somebody wants blueberry muffins? They're not exactly a dessert."

"I know, but one of the twins is crazy about them. I think it was Larry, but it could have been Gary. They're identical. How about the strawberry shortcake for Serena? Do you have any strawberries in your greenhouse?"

"Not right now. But you can use frozen, can't you?"

"Sure. We'll need two days to make it. My Pound Plus Cake needs to age that long."

Lisa glanced down at the next item on the list. "Fudge cupcakes should be easy. You can use the recipe you made up for Beatrice Koester."

"Right. And the peach cobbler's no problem. We'll bake our special Minnesota Peach Cobbler."

"Christmas sugar cookies are easy, and we certainly know how to make cherry cheesecake. What recipes do we have to punt on?"

"Punt?"

"You know what I mean. The ones where we're out of options and all we can do is hope everything turns out all right."

Hannah laughed. Lisa had obviously been watching football with her new husband. "I'll tell you if you'll read the rest of the list to me."

"Brownies," Lisa obliged her. "We've got that one covered. I'll make Bon-Bon Brownies the way I'm going to do for the Brownie Scouts."

"Great. What else?"

"Somebody named Spenser wants Christmas Cake. What are we going to do for that?"

"I'll make Grandma Ingrid's Date Cake, the one with the chocolate chips and nuts on top. All I have to do is figure out a way to make it really special. Is there anything else?"

"Julie's surprise. You put a little star in front of that."

"Pretend that star is a football, because that's where we have to punt. Julie wants me to teach her how to make a dessert so she can surprise Matt and the kids. And Julie's culinary skills are on a par with Andrea's."

"That'll be a punt all right! You may have to resort to ice cream sundaes with lots of store-bought toppings."

"Maybe, but I hope it doesn't come to that." Hannah

glanced out the window as a car pulled up in front of the shop. Even through the lightly blowing snow, she could see who it was. "There's Herb."

"Oh *good!*"

Hannah felt a slight stab of envy as Lisa gave a delighted smile and ran to get her coat. It wasn't that she was jealous. Far from it. Herb had been a classmate of hers at Jordan High and they'd never been more than friends. But the expression on Lisa's face spoke volumes about how happy she was with her husband. Hannah wondered if she'd ever be so happily married. Despite her mother's belief that the goal was marriage and any man who was single would do in a pinch, Hannah wasn't about to go marching with Mendelssohn until she'd decided on her perfect groom.

"What?" Lisa said, coming back into the coffee shop and catching Hannah's pensive expression.

"I think I should mix up my Pound Plus Cake," Hannah said, letting Lisa think that was what had been on her mind. "If I bake it tonight, I can take it out to the academy and stick it in Julie's freezer. Then she can serve it if the weather gets bad and we can't get out there to deliver a dessert."

"Good idea. You'd better take the frozen strawberries along too. And the whipping cream and sour cream for the crème fraîche . . . unless you don't think she can whip the cream."

Hannah thought about that for a minute and then she shrugged. "That's a possibility. I'll take along a couple of cans of whipped cream, just in case. And I'll give her the instructions for thawing the berries and making the topping."

"Sounds good to me. Bye, Hannah. Don't work too late."

"I won't. Tell Herb hi for me." Hannah saw her partner out and locked the door behind her. Then she headed for the kitchen with thoughts of marriage still on her mind.

After a quick trip to the pantry and the walk-in cooler, Hannah assembled the necessary ingredients in the order her recipe listed and got out one of her largest stainless steel mixing bowls. As she mixed the softened butter with the sugar, she decided that Julie was absolutely right. Matt did appear to be perfect for her.

Hannah added eggs to her bowl and beat them in thoroughly before she mixed in the sour cream. The baking powder and vanilla were next, and as she measured out the cake flour, she wondered what would happen between Julie and Matt when all of the kids had been put to bed for the night.

DOUBLE APPLE CRISP

Preheat oven to 375 degrees F.,
rack in the middle position.

For the bottom:
8 large apples, cored, peeled, and sliced***
¾ cup white *(granulated)* sugar
1 tablespoon lemon juice
½ cup honey

For the topping:
1 cup flour
½ cup brown sugar, firmly packed
½ teaspoon salt
½ cup *(1 stick, ¼ pound)* softened butter

***I used 4 Granny Smith and 4 Fuji, but any combination will do. Half of the apples should be tart and the other half sweeter.*

Spray a 9-inch by 13-inch cake pan with Pam or other nonstick spray. The pan can be metal, glass, or disposable foil.

Spread the sliced apples over the bottom of the pan. Sprinkle them with the white sugar and then the lemon juice.

Measure out the honey. *(I always spray my measuring cup with Pam first, so the honey won't stick to the sides as much.)* Drizzle the honey over the apples.

Mix the flour, brown sugar, and salt together in a small bowl. Use a fork to work in the softened butter, stirring until you have a crumbly mixture. *(You can also do this in a food processor using the steel blade and a stick of chilled butter cut into 8 pieces.)*

Sprinkle the topping evenly over the apples in the pan.

Bake at 375 degrees F. for 30 to 40 minutes, or until the apples are tender when pierced with a fork and the topping is golden brown.

Serve warm with whipped cream, regular cream, vanilla ice cream, or cinnamon ice cream.

Hannah's Note: If you take this out of the oven twenty minutes or so before the meal begins, it'll be a perfect temperature to serve for dessert. If you're not that organized (and who is?), dish up the apple crisp and heat it in individual bowls in the microwave. It holds up very well when reheated.

It's also good at room temperature or even cold, right out of the refrigerator. There is no wrong way to serve this Double Apple Crisp.

STRAWBERRY SHORTCAKE SWENSEN

Pound Plus Cake
The Strawberries
Hannah's Whipped Crème Fraiche

Pound Plus Cake

  WARNING: This cake must chill for at least 48 hours. Bake it 2 days before you plan to serve it. You can also bake it ahead of time, cool it, wrap it in plastic wrap and then in foil, and freeze it until the day before you need it. At that time, remove it from the freezer and let it thaw in the refrigerator for at least 24 hours.

  Pound Plus Cake will keep in the freezer for up to 4 months. This recipe makes two cakes. Each cake serves six people.

Preheat oven to 325 degrees F.,
rack in the middle position.

1½ cups softened butter *(3 sticks)*
2 cups white sugar
4 eggs
1 cup sour cream *(you can substitute unflavored yogurt for a lighter cake)*
½ teaspoon baking powder
1 teaspoon vanilla

2 cups cake flour *(DO NOT SIFT—use it right out of the box.)*

Generously butter and flour two 9-inch round cake pans. *(Don't use Pam or spray shortening—it won't work.)*

Cream softened butter and sugar in the bowl of an electric mixer. *(You can mix this cake by hand, but it takes some muscle.)* Add the eggs, one at a time, and beat until they're nice and fluffy. Then add the sour cream, baking powder, and vanilla. Mix it all up and then add the flour, one cup at a time, and beat until the batter is smooth and has no lumps.

Pour the batter into the pans and bake at 325 degrees F. for 45 to 50 minutes. *(The cakes should be golden brown on top.)*

Cool in the pans on a rack for 20 minutes. Run a knife around the inside edges of the pans to loosen the cakes and turn them out on the rack.

After the cakes are completely cool, wrap each one in plastic wrap, sealing tightly. Wrap these packages in foil and store them in the refrigerator for 48 hours.

Take them out an hour before you serve, but don't un-wrap them until you're ready to assemble the dessert.

The Strawberries
 (Prepare these several hours before you serve.)

Wash 3 boxes of berries and remove stems. *(The easiest way to do this is to use a paring knife to cut off the top part of the berry.)* Slice all but a dozen or so, reserving the biggest and best berries to top each portion. Taste the berries and add sugar if they're too tart. Stir and refrigerate, covered tightly.

If you use frozen berries, thaw them in the refriger-ator overnight by placing the whole package in a bowl. Test them for sweetness several hours before dessert and add sugar if they're too tart. Stir and refrigerate the berries in a covered container.

Hannah's Whipped Crème Fraîche
 (This will hold for several hours. Make it
 ahead of time and refrigerate it.)

2 cups heavy whipping cream
½ cup white sugar

½ cup sour cream *(you can substitute unflavored yogurt, but it won't hold as well and you'll have to do it at the last minute)*

½ cup brown sugar *(to sprinkle on top after you assemble the dessert)*

Whip the cream with the white sugar. When it holds a firm peak *(test it by dipping in your spatula)*, fold in the sour cream. You can do this by hand or by using the slowest speed on the mixer.

If you use canned whipped cream, just squirt it out until you have 2 cups and then fold in the half-cup of sour cream. Cover and refrigerate until it's time to serve.

Assembling Strawberry Shortcake Swensen

Cut each *Pound Plus Cake* into 6 pie-shaped wedges and place the cake on dessert plates. Top with the sliced strawberries. Put several generous dollops of *Hannah's Whipped Crème Fraiche* on top and sprinkle with the brown sugar. Garnish with the whole berries you reserved *(unless you used frozen and don't have any perfect berries)*. Serve and receive rave reviews.

Chapter Four

"This is just heaven." Julie stretched luxuriously and snuggled a little closer to Matt. They were sitting on the overstuffed couch in the living room of Aames House, a relatively new structure that had been built for parents who were staying overnight at the school. "I wonder if parents feel like this when their kids are in bed."

Matt hugged her a little tighter. Her comment about parents and children was making him feel very fatherly. Not to Julie, of course. As far as Julie was concerned, his feelings were about as far from fatherly as . . .

"Do you think I should check to make sure they're sleeping?" Julie asked, interrupting the fantasy that was just starting to form in his mind.

"I don't think it's necessary. You told them we'd be watching a movie down here. If something's wrong, they'll come down the stairs to get us."

"You're right. Maybe it's a good thing I don't have children. I'd probably be an overprotective mother."

"That's okay. I tend to give kids their independence early. We'd balance each other out." Matt kissed the top of her head. Her hair smelled sweet, like flowers. As he tipped her face up to kiss her, he wondered idly whether she used some kind of special shampoo or if the woodsy sweetness was her own individual scent. It reminded him of morning dew, and freshly mown grasses, and precious little violets hiding deep in the forest. Then Julie gave a little sigh and molded her body to his, and Matt stopped thinking altogether.

It had been an innocent comment on her part. She'd realized she'd been worrying about the kids and she'd told him she'd probably be an overprotective mother. And then he'd said it was all right, that they'd balance each other out. Did that mean Matt wanted to have children with her? And even more important, did he even *know* what he'd said? Was it merely a slip of the tongue? Or could it be a slip of the heart?

Julie's mind spun as their kiss deepened. It was impossible to think when she was this blissful. Matt's arms were warm and protective around her, and she took delight in hearing the beat of his heart. All of her senses were alive. Every nerve and sinew was thrumming in anticipation. There would be time to think later. Right now all she wanted to do was enjoy this wonderful moment and hope it never stopped.

"They're kissing," Spenser reported, sticking his head in the girls' room where they all waited for the latest news.

Serena snorted. "That's what you said the last time."

"Well, they're still doing it. That's all they've done for the last five minutes. The movie's going, but they're not watching. They're just kissing."

Joy looked puzzled. "Don't they have to stop sometime so they can come up for air?"

"You can breathe while you're kissing," Serena told her. "You kiss with your lips and breathe through your nose."

"Is it like snorkeling?" Larry wanted to know.

"No, it's the other way around," Spenser explained. "You have to breathe through your mouth when you snorkel. If you breathe through your nose, you'll drown."

Serena looked dubious. "How do you know so much about snorkeling? People in Minnesota don't do it."

"I know, but they do it down in Florida. My dad used to live there, and we went snorkeling in the Keys before he died. But how do *you* know so much about kissing?"

"Uh . . . well . . ." Serena sputtered slightly. It was clear she didn't know what to say.

"I think it's because she reads those books all the time," Joy explained.

"What books?"

"Love books. You know . . . the ones that are all romantic. Serena's got one under her pillow right now."

For a moment, Serena looked as if she might deny it, but then she just nodded. "I like them. They're a lot more fun than doing homework. But this isn't about me. It's about Mr. Sherwood and Miss Jansen. You watched them for a long time, Spense. Do you think he's going to ask her to marry him?"

Spenser shrugged. "How would I know?"

"There are ways to tell. I'd better go with you to see for myself." Serena led the way to the door. "The rest of you stay here and be quiet. We'll be back in five minutes and I'll tell you what's *really* going on."

"What was *that*?" Matt asked, sitting back, startled.

Julie laughed breathlessly. "My cell phone. I put it on vibrate so it wouldn't disturb us."

"Well . . . it did." Matt started to chuckle too. "For a second there, I thought we were having an earthquake."

Julie clamped her lips shut to keep from making a quip

about how the earth had moved, or anything similar. But Matt seemed to be waiting for her response, so she said, "I don't think we have earthquakes in Minnesota."

"Sure we do. I was just reading about it on the Internet with the kids. They're not as noticeable as the temblors they have in California, but that's because the magnitude is much lower. Are you going to get that, Julie?"

"Get what?"

"Your cell phone. It's still vibrating."

"Oh. I guess I'd better. I gave Dr. Caulder my number before he left in case he wanted to check in with us."

"Don't you mean *check up on us*?"

"That too." Julie retrieved her phone. "Hello?" There was a pause while she listened, and then she laughed. "Nothing's wrong. As a matter of fact, things are going very well. It just took me a minute to answer the phone, that's all."

Matt cocked his head slightly, and Julie knew he was wondering if she was talking to Dr. Caulder. Her eyes began to sparkle as her mischievous side came out. It wouldn't hurt to tease Matt a bit. "They're all in bed, so this is our personal time alone together. We were just sitting here on the couch, watching a movie that we weren't really watching."

Matt's jaw dropped like a character in a Saturday morning cartoon, and Julie gave a little chuckle under her breath as she turned back to the phone. "Sure thing. I'll go look tomorrow. Tonight Matt and I are . . . busy."

There was a strangled sound from her fellow teacher and Julie had all she could do not to laugh out loud. "What's the matter?" she asked, as she ended the call.

"You weren't talking to . . ."

"Of course not," Julie cut him off before he could get too worried. "That was Hannah. She wanted to find out if Mrs. Dryer had any cookie cutters in the kitchen, and I'm supposed to call her back tomorrow. I was just teasing you, Matt. I'd never say anything to Dr. Caulder that would embarrass you."

Matt gave a relieved sigh, and then he looked a little sheepish. "I guess I should have known."

"Don't be so hard on yourself. There's really no way you *could* have known. We're not familiar enough with each other yet."

"That's fixable," Matt said, pulling her back into his arms and picking up right where they'd left off before Julie's phone had interrupted them.

Hannah hung up the phone with a grin. Julie was every bit as much a tease as she'd been in high school, and it was clear she'd been playing some sort of joke on Matt. She just hoped that Matt had a good sense of humor.

She'd just dumped the contents of two nearly empty containers of take-out Chinese food on top of the rice in the third container to make a sort of Oriental hotdish from the leftovers of her dinner when there was an irate yowl from her resident feline. Moishe, the orange and white tomcat she'd found shivering on her doorstep over two years ago, had cornered the duck's foot she'd bought for him between the refrigerator and the stove. He'd tried to hook it, but it was back, out of paw's reach.

"Okay, hold on a second." Hannah retrieved the yardstick that hung on a nail next to the broom closet and attempted to extricate the oriental treat. Moishe didn't eat duck's feet. He simply played with them until he got bored and then he buried them in his litter box.

Moishe gave her his best kitty smile as she fished around with the yardstick, attempting to snag it without dislodging the dust mice that were surely lurking in the small narrow space that never saw the light of day. The smile consisted of a crinkling of his eyes and a slight opening of his mouth, but that was good enough for Hannah. She got the aquatic appendage on the fourth try, grabbed it before Moishe could get it, and gave it a quick rinse under the kitchen faucet.

There was another yowl before Hannah was through drying it with a paper towel. "Here you go," she said, holding it out to him. "You can take it into the living room, but it's curtains for quackers if you lose it in back of the television. There must be a hundred wires back there, and there's no way I'm going to even try to get it out until daylight."

Moishe took the duck's foot with another kitty smile that Hannah interpreted as a thank-you. Then he turned and headed for the living room with his head held high and his tail gently switching back and forth.

There were three high-pitched electronic dings in rhythmic succession and Hannah reached up to turn off her stove timer. She'd mixed up one of her famous cherry cheesecakes to save time tomorrow at The Cookie Jar. The cheesecake was best if it was chilled for at least a day, and two days was even better. She'd store it in her own refrigerator overnight and put it in the walk-in cooler at the shop tomorrow.

The cheesecake looked good, and Hannah set it on a wire rack to cool. Then she went off to join her furry roommate who'd managed to flip the duck's foot into the commode and was standing there staring at it balefully.

CHERRY CHEESECAKE

Preheat oven to 350 degrees F.,
rack in the middle position.

For the Crust:
2 cups vanilla wafer cookie crumbs *(measure
AFTER crushing)*
¾ stick melted butter *(6 tablespoons)*
1 teaspoon almond extract

Pour melted butter and almond extract over cookie
crumbs. Mix with a fork until they're evenly moistened.

Cut a circle of parchment paper *(or wax paper)* to
fit inside the bottom of a 9-inch Springform pan.
Spray the pan with Pam or other nonstick cooking
spray, set the paper circle in place, and spray with Pam
again.

Dump the moistened cookie crumbs in the pan and
press them down over the paper circle and one inch up
the sides. Put the pan in the freezer for 15 to 30 minutes while you prepare the rest of the cheesecake.

For the Topping:
2 cups sour cream
½ cup sugar
1 teaspoon vanilla

One 21-ounce can cherry pie filling*** *(I used Comstock Dark Sweet Cherry)*.

*** If you don't like canned pie filling, make your own with canned or frozen cherries, sugar, and cornstarch.

Mix the sour cream, sugar, and vanilla together in a small bowl. Cover and refrigerate. Set the unopened can of cherry pie filling in the refrigerator for later.

For the Cheesecake Batter:
1 cup white *(granulated)* sugar
3 eight-ounce packages cream cheese at room temperature *(total 24 ounces)*
1 cup mayonnaise
4 eggs
2 cups white chocolate chips *(I used Ghirardelli's 11-ounce bag)*
2 teaspoons vanilla

Place the sugar in the bowl of an electric mixer. Add the blocks of cream cheese and the mayonnaise,

and whip it up at medium speed until it's smooth. Add the eggs, one at a time, beating after each addition.

Melt the white chocolate chips in a microwave-safe bowl for 2 minutes. *(Chips may retain their shape, so stir to see if they're melted—if not, microwave in 15-second increments until you can stir them smooth.)* Cool the melted white chocolate for a minute or two and then mix it in gradually at slow speed. Scrape down the bowl and add the vanilla, mixing it in thoroughly.

Pour the batter on top of the chilled crust, set the pan on a cookie sheet to catch any drips, and bake it at 350 degrees F. for 55 to 60 minutes. Remove the pan from the oven, but DON'T SHUT OFF THE OVEN.

Starting in the center, spoon the sour cream topping over the top of the cheesecake, spreading it out to within a half-inch of the rim. Return the pan to the oven and bake for an additional 5 minutes.

Cool the cheesecake in the pan on a wire rack. When the pan is cool enough to pick up with your bare hands, place it in the refrigerator and chill it, uncovered, for at least 8 hours.

To serve, run a knife around the inside rim of the pan, release the Springform catch, and lift off the rim. Place a piece of waxed paper on a flat plate and tip it upside down over the top of your cheesecake. Invert the cheesecake so that it rests on the paper.

Carefully pry off the bottom of the Springform pan and remove the paper from the bottom crust.

Invert a serving platter over the bottom crust of your cheesecake. Flip the cheesecake right side up, take off the top plate, and remove the waxed paper.

Spread the cherry pie filling over the sour cream topping on your cheesecake. You can drizzle a little down the sides if you wish.

Chapter Five

"They're in love," Serena said, sounding very sure of herself. "You don't kiss like that unless you're in love."

"Kiss like *what?*" Gary wanted to know.

"Like a raging fire that sears the emotions and scorches every inhibition to a cinder. That's the way they described it in the book I'm reading."

There was silence for a moment while everyone digested Serena's response. Then Spenser gave a little laugh. "Can you tell us in plain English?"

"Of course. They kissed like they were trying to swallow each other's tonsils."

"Yuck!" both twins exclaimed in unison.

"I feel sick," Hope added, folding her arms over her stomach.

"I know it sounds gross, but just wait until you're older," Serena advised. "Then it'll seem like fun."

Gary and Larry locked eyes. They stared at each other for a moment, and then both of them shook their heads in tandem.

"There's no way I could . . ." Gary started the thought.

". . . be *that* old." Larry finished the sentence for him.

"You'll see," Serena said, still supremely confident. "It'll happen to you too. But let's get back to Miss Jansen and Mr. Sherwood. They're in love and they're going to get married. You just watch and see if I'm right."

Joy began to frown. "But you can be in love without getting married."

"You're only seven. How do *you* know?" Spenser asked her.

"Our mother told us," Hope spoke up. "She's been in love lots of times, but she's only been married twice."

"Three times," Joy corrected her.

"Not yet!" Hope insisted, her lower lip beginning to quiver. "It won't be three times until tomorrow. And that's why we couldn't go home for Christmas. She's going on her honeymoon."

The twins glanced at each other, and then Larry said, "It's the same for us, except . . ."

". . . opposite," Gary finished his sentence. "Mom and Dad are getting divorced and they fought so much over . . ."

". . . which one got to take us, the judge said we'd be better off staying here." Larry ended the story.

"I'm here because I've got nowhere else to go," Spenser declared. "My dad's dead and Mom's on assignment in Africa."

"What's she doing *there?*" Serena asked the question that was plain on all their faces.

"She's a photographer, a good one too. She didn't want to work over Christmas, but she just switched jobs and they might have fired her, or something like that. I wanted to go over there to be with her, but she said it was too dangerous." Spenser stopped speaking and gave a deep sigh. "I should've talked her into it so I could protect her."

There was another silence, broken only when Serena cleared her throat. "You did the right thing by staying here, Spense. She would've worried about you the whole time you were there, and neither one of you would've had a good time."

"I guess . . ." Spenser shrugged, but it was clear he felt better. "What about you, Serena? Nowhere to go?"

"I've got somewhere to go. I just didn't want to, that's all. I spent enough Christmases in the Home. Believe me, this is a lot better!"

"Maybe, but it's not very exciting," Gary complained. "I wish something really . . ."

". . . exciting would happen," Larry finished the thought for his twin.

"Something exciting *is* going to happen," Serena declared. "Mr. Sherwood is going to ask Miss Jansen to marry him. And we're going to know about it before anyone else in the whole school!"

Hope started to smile. "We'll know first and we can tell everybody else when they come back."

"That's right," Joy said, sounding delighted. "All our friends will wish they'd stayed here."

Spenser looked doubtful as he turned to Serena. "How do you know Mr. Sherwood's really going to ask her?"

"I just know, that's all."

"Then it's like my dad used to say . . . put your money where you mouth is."

"You mean you want to bet?"

"Why not? If you're so sure you're going to win, you should go for it, right?"

"Right. But . . . I don't have any money."

"Then bet something else."

"Like what?"

"Like how about doing my chores for a month if you lose?"

Serena glanced around at the rest of the kids who were intent on their conversation. It was clear she didn't want to back down. "It all depends on what you have to do."

"I have to pick up after Queenie every day."

"Mrs. Caulder's toy poodle?"

"Right," Spenser answered what he knew would be her next question. "I know she's small, but she can . . . well . . . let's just say it takes me at least a half hour to do it."

Serena shrugged. "That doesn't sound so bad. I wouldn't mind walking Queenie around."

"Oh, you don't get to walk her. Mrs. Caulder does that. What you have to do is pick up all the . . . uh . . . *stuff* in Dr. Caulder's backyard. And if you miss any, he's not exactly delighted, if you get what I mean. So is it a bet?"

Serena thought about that for a minute. "Not unless you have to pay if you're wrong."

"What do you mean?"

"This goes both ways. If you lose and I win, you have to do my chores for a month."

"Deal," Spenser declared, holding out his hand.

"But don't you want to know what my chores are?"

"Doesn't matter, since I'm not going to lose. But just for the purposes of discussion, what are they?"

"I have to help Mrs. Dryer clean up the kitchen after supper."

Spenser's hand quivered with the effort not to pull it back. He'd heard that Mrs. Dryer made her helpers scour every surface of the kitchen after every meal.

"So do you want to back out?" Serena asked smugly.

"No way. It's a deal by me. Let's shake on it."

The other four watched as Serena and Spenser shook hands. Then Joy hopped off the bed.

"I want to bet too," she said. "I'll do Gary's chores if we lose, and he can do mine if we win."

"Deal," Gary said quickly, holding out his hand so that Joy could shake it.

"Me too," Hope declared, holding out her hand to Larry.

"That's it then," Spenser said. "It's the boys against the

girls. If Mr. Sherwood asks Miss Jansen to marry him before Christmas is over, we have to do the girls' chores. Is that right, men?"

"Right!" the twins chorused.

"And if they don't get engaged before Christmas is over, the girls have to do *our* chores. Right, girls?"

"Right," Hope said.

"Yes," Joy added, turning to Serena.

"It's a bet," Serena confirmed. "We'll write it down so there won't be any misunderstandings, and we'll all sign it. And then you boys have to go to your own room. It's late and we need to get some sleep."

Hope waited until the boys had left and then she turned to Serena. "You're not sleepy, are you?"

"No. I think I'll read another chapter in my book. But first I want to get a glass of water."

Joy gave a little giggle as she caught on. "From the front bathroom at the top of the stairs?"

"So you can see how our bet is going?" Hope added.

"You girls are pretty smart for your age," Serena said as she got up and headed for the door.

"Don't they ever get tired of kissing?" Gary asked, as Spenser returned to their room.

"I guess not. They're still at it."

"You'd think their lips would start . . ." Gary stopped and waited for his twin to finish the sentence, but Larry was sitting in front of his laptop computer, surfing the net.

"Forget him. He's in another world. You'd think their lips would start to what?" Spenser asked.

"Swell up, or get chapped, or something," Gary completed the thought by himself, but he started to look a bit worried. "They're doing an awful lot of kissing down there. Do you think Serena might be right and we could lose?"

"The only way we'll lose is if we sit back and don't do anything to break things up."

"What things?"

"Them. We have to figure out a way to break up Miss Jansen and Mr. Sherwood."

"But that's not fair!"

"I know, but if we don't do it, we'll lose. Do you and Larry really want to spend a month doing chores for the girls?"

Gary wavered. "I don't know. What do they have to do?"

"Hope and Joy have to go to Mrs. Caulder's house and pass around trays at her Wednesday night musicales."

"That's not horrible."

"You wouldn't say that if you'd ever heard Mrs. Caulder sing. And she sings at every musicale."

"We could always wear earplugs."

"Wait. There's more. On Saturday afternoons, they have to go shopping with her and carry her packages."

"No way Larry and I want to do that!" Gary made a face that perfectly expressed his feelings. "But I still hate to break up Mr. Sherwood and Miss Jansen."

"So do I, but it won't be permanent. They're doomed to get together eventually. But not until we've won our bet."

Julie was snuggled warm in Matt's arms, half-watching the movie. Normally, she would have been engrossed in the silver screen classic, but the beating of Matt's heart was so comforting, she just wanted to close her eyes, relish the moment, and dream of the future. If Matt asked her to marry him, she'd say yes. There was no doubt about that. They were perfectly compatible, and she was perfectly in love. All she had to do was hope that Matt was beginning to feel the same way.

Her sleepy mind drifted off to thoughts of a perfect wedding. Matt stood in the front, unbelievably handsome in a black tux, waiting for his bride. And there she was, a lovely vision in a white lace tablecloth and tiara. One hand rested on her father's arm, and the other was holding a beautiful bridal bouquet of dandelions.

Dr. Caulder was officiating. She hadn't known he had the authority, but it wasn't surprising with the long string of initials after his name. And there was her mother in the front row, smiling and happy in a lovely dress, sitting next to Joy.

Julie turned slightly so that she could see her bridesmaids. There was Serena, looking quite lovely in her school uniform. Her partner was Spenser, one of Matt's groomsmen, and he cut a dashing figure in his hockey gear. Hope was the flower girl, holding a white basket of pine needles to strew in her wake, and one of the twins was the ring bearer. Julie wasn't sure which twin it was, but that didn't really matter because he was much too old for the honor anyway. The other twin, Gary or Larry, whichever this one wasn't, would be really upset. Julie didn't see him and suspected he'd stayed in his room to pout. She should have invited him, because he might just come here to disrupt the whole thing and . . .

"Miss Jansen?"

Julie's eyes flickered, and she did her best to banish him from her dream. This was her wedding. He shouldn't be here if he couldn't behave.

"Miss Jansen?"

There was no help for it. She had to take time to explain that there could be only one ring bearer per wedding and he'd just have to wait until the next faculty member got married.

"Something's wrong, Miss Jansen!"

Julie sat up with a start. Gary or Larry was leaning over the back of the couch and he looked worried. "What's wrong?"

"Gary's not in his bed. He isn't in the bathroom either. Spenser and I checked."

Julie glanced at Matt. He was sleeping peacefully, his chest rising slowly up and down. His hair was tousled like a little boy, and he looked years younger than he did when he was awake. "Matt?" she said, reaching out to shake his arm. "Wake up, Matt. We need you."

"What?"

Julie could barely believe her eyes when Matt straightened up, blinked twice, and was fully alert. "What is it, Larry?"

"I just told Miss Jansen. I woke up and Gary wasn't in his bed. Spense and I looked, but he's not in the bathroom. We wanted to search the house, but Spense thought we should come and get you first."

"Spenser thought right. Has Gary ever done any sleepwalking?"

"I don't think so."

"That's good. It's cold out there." Matt turned to Julie. "Would you check the front door, Miss Jansen? I threw the deadbolt when we were all in for the night. If it's still locked, that means Gary's somewhere inside. I'll go check the back door with Larry."

The door was securely locked, and Julie gave a huge sigh of relief. She was very glad Gary hadn't gone out in the dead of winter. The wind had kicked up, and it was howling so loud, she could hear it inside the snug walls of Aames House. While she was there, she pulled back the curtains and checked the thermometer mounted on the outside frame of the window next to the door. It was eleven below zero, and she hoped Gary hadn't gone out the back way.

"The bolt was still thrown." Matt came back looking relieved.

Julie nodded. "Same with the front door."

"Good. That means he's got to be here somewhere. Will you check the downstairs, Miss Jansen? And when you're through, come up and find us. We'll be checking all the vacant rooms on the second floor."

278   *Joanne Fluke*

"While you're at it, you'd better check the girls' room. Gary could be there."

"Why would he be in the girls' room?" Larry wanted to know.

"He could have gotten up for some reason and taken a wrong turn when he tried to get back to your room. This is the first night we've spent at Aames House, and he's used to being in the dorm."

Matt gave her an approving smile. "I wouldn't have thought of that, but you're right. We'll check the girls' room last. No sense in waking them up if we find him somewhere else."

When Matt and Larry had gone up the stairs, Julie headed for the kitchen. Aames House was designed like a very large private residence with more upstairs bedrooms than the normal-size family would require, but with a single kitchen, a giant living room, a dining room that would easily seat twenty, and several fully equipped offices for the convenience of working parents who had come to visit their children.

Julie switched on the kitchen lights and blinked in the sudden flood that illuminated the marble-topped counters and gleaming appliances. She'd expected to find Gary here. It was a natural place to look. She hadn't forgotten her nights as a child and the times she'd stolen downstairs in the middle of the night for a snack.

But Gary wasn't in the kitchen. That was apparent at a glance. Julie checked the pantry and even opened the broom closet, but no one was hiding there.

The laundry room was next, and then the dining room. Julie went through the offices and even double-checked the living room, but Gary was nowhere to be found. She was halfway up the stairs when she heard Matt start to laugh. They must have found him!

"Gary!" Julie arrived at the boys' room in a rush and hurried to put her arms around him. "Thank goodness you're safe. We were worried about you."

Gary squirmed slightly and Julie let him go, suddenly remembering that ten-year-old boys didn't like to be held for long. She turned to Matt. "Where was he?"

"Under his bed. He must have tumbled out, rolled under it, and fallen asleep again."

Once the boys were back in bed, Julie and Matt went back downstairs. Matt checked the doors again, to make sure they were secure, and Julie folded the afghan and placed it on the back of the couch.

"Now that the crisis is over, I think I'd better call it a night," Julie said. "The girls slept right through everything and they'll probably be up early tomorrow."

"You're probably right. I'll just stay here for a while and see if I can find some late news. I'd really like to hear the weather report."

"Mostly overcast, temperatures below zero, and variable winds," Julie recited.

"And that means it'll be sunny, unusually warm, and perfectly calm?"

"You got it," Julie said, blowing him a kiss before she headed up the stairs to the guest room she'd staked out as her own.

Chapter Six

It was the kind of perfectly beautiful winter day that painters loved and weathermen hated. The temperature had climbed to slightly above thirty degrees and the sunlight gleamed on the icy banks of snow, making them shimmer as if they were studded with diamonds. The icicles that hung from the stark black branches of the trees glistened like silver Christmas ornaments, and brightly colored winter birds flitted from branch to branch turning black and white to Technicolor.

Hannah turned into the driveway that led to Lakes Academy. It was the fourth round-trip she'd made in as many days, but she really didn't mind. She opened her window to enjoy the fresh pine scent that Christmas trees in warmer climates could never begin to replicate when she noticed another more subtle scent on the breeze. It was that indefinable something that some people claimed they could smell when snow was on the way. Hannah could smell it, her grandmother had taught her, and she hoped that the winter storm wouldn't hit too hard. It would be a pity if Julie, Matt, and the kids were snowed in and she couldn't carry out the Christmas plans she'd made for them.

Hannah had just pulled up and was preparing to unload when she heard the sound of childish laughter on the wind. Curious, she got out of her truck and followed the sound through the tall pine trees to Aames House. It seemed to be coming from the rear and Hannah walked around the red brick structure. What she saw when she came around the corner made her blink several times in surprise.

Julie and Matt were helping the kids make snowmen, but they were unlike any other snowmen Hannah had ever seen. They had the traditional stacked snowballs—a large one for the body, a medium one for the chest, and a smaller one for the head. But instead of white snowmen, these icy creations were in rollicking colors. One snowman had a red body with a yellow chest and an orange head. Another had a green body with a peach middle and a blue head. The one that they were working on now had a blue body and a yellow chest. Hope was rolling the head, and it was still white.

"Is this the right size?" Hope called out, sitting back on her heels to look at her work.

"Perfect," Matt replied, and he helped Hope move the head to a small gardener's tarp that had been spread out on the snow at the foot of the uncompleted snowman.

"What color do you want for his head, Hope?" Julie asked.

"I want purple."

"I need the grape, please," Julie called out to Spenser, who was holding a tray containing several thermoses.

Spenser hurried over with a thermos, and Hannah watched as Julie shook it. Then she uncorked it and poured a thin stream of liquid all over the top of the snowman's head until it was streaked with purple. A few moments later the color began to spread, and within a minute or two the snowman's head resembled the top of a huge grape snow cone.

"Okay?" Matt asked Julie.

"Go ahead. It should be cold enough by now."

Matt lifted the slightly irregular ball of snow and carefully placed it on top of the larger yellow ball. "That does it, except for dressing them. I found some old hats and scarves."

"And I found some little pinecones we can use for the eyes," Serena said.

"Let's wait until after lunch to do that. I want to make sure they're frozen hard." Julie turned to Spenser. "Will you bring in the thermoses, Spenser?"

"Sure, right after I take a picture to send to my mom. I sent her an instant message about the snowmen, and she wants me to e-mail some photos."

"Okay. Come in when you're through then."

Julie headed for the back door with Matt and the kids, and that was when she spotted Hannah. "Hi, Hannah. Did you see our snowmen?"

"I did. They're pretty colorful characters. How did you do that?"

"Jell-O. The kids got tired of eating Jell-O with fruit cocktail for lunch, so we thought we'd use it up another way."

"Very clever. I had no idea it would color the snow that evenly."

"Neither did I, but I hoped it would. And believe me, it took some doing! The temperature of the Jell-O liquid has to be just right, and the snow needs to be really icy. I don't think I would have figured it out if I hadn't spent one whole summer at Eden Lake Bait and Tackle making snow cones."

"I'll do the sandwiches, Miss Jansen," Serena offered, catching up with them. "I know you want to talk to Miss Swensen."

"Thanks, Serena. I was going to make peanut butter and jelly on toast."

"Okay. I'll make the toast, Joy can spread the peanut butter, and Hope will put on the jam. Gary and Larry can set the table and pour the milk."

"There's a big box of cookies in the back of my truck if someone wants to go out and get them," Hannah told Matt. "It's the box with the cutout handles. The bakery boxes are filled with Blue Blueberry Muffins for tonight's dessert and they can come in too."

Matt turned around and motioned to Spense, who'd just finished taking his pictures. "We'll rinse out the thermoses, and then Spense and I'll carry them in."

Hannah waited until the back door had closed behind the kids and Matt, and then she turned to Julie. "So?"

"So what?" Julie started to grin.

"So how's the romance going?"

Julie's grin faded abruptly. "It's not," she said.

"You had a fight with Matt?"

"Oh, no. It's nothing like that. It's just that we can't seem to get any time alone. Every time we think we've got them all settled down and tucked in for the night, one of them wants something or other."

"I think that's pretty common with kids. They want to be the center of attention twenty-four hours a day. I remember Andrea saying that it was really hard to get any time alone with Bill after Tracey was born. And you and Matt have that problem times six!"

"That's true. I really didn't think the kids would be that needy, but I guess it's understandable. I'd feel pretty lonely too if I had to stay at boarding school over Christmas."

"You *do* have to stay at boarding school over Christmas."

Julie laughed and Hannah was glad. Andrea's high school friend had looked just a bit depressed.

"I wonder if it bothers Matt as much as it bothers me," Julie mused. "I'd come right out and ask, but I think that's a little blatant, don't you?"

"Maybe," Hannah conceded, although that was probably what she would have done in the same circumstance.

"Why don't *you* ask him for me? You can kind of approach the subject obliquely, so he won't know I asked you to."

"You mean I should be tactful?"

"Exactly."

Hannah sighed. If Julie expected her to be tactful, she was in deep trouble. She'd been told often enough by many people that there wasn't a tactful bone in her body.

"Will you at least try to find out?"

How could she resist a plea like that? Hannah caved in without a whimper. "Okay. I'm not very good at things like that, but I guess I can try."

There was no chance for Hannah to talk to Matt during lunch. The kids were in high spirits and the noon meal was filled with laughter and wisecracks. But after they'd finished eating, Julie organized the cleanup, and Hannah found herself straightening the chairs and putting on a clean tablecloth with Matt.

"Do you have a second?" she asked, moving as far away from the kitchen door as the confines of the room would allow.

"Sure. I figured you'd want to ask about the peach cobbler when Julie wasn't around."

Hannah started to say that wasn't what had been on her mind, but she quickly changed tactics. A discussion of Julie's culinary limitations might give her a clue to their relationship. "Did she manage to heat it in the oven?"

"Yes. She did a good job too. Only one corner got a little brown, and I ate it before she could notice."

Love, Hannah thought to herself. She'd thought it was love before, but now she had the proof. Any man who would eat the corner of a burned dessert rather than embarrass the woman who'd heated it was definitely in love. "Then it doesn't really bother you that Julie can't cook?"

"Not at all. I like to cook, and I don't think Julie would

mind being my helper. She's better than I am with a knife, and she's great at plating. All I can do is follow a recipe."

"But you're not doing the cooking here."

"I would have offered, but I thought it might make Julie feel bad. She's very proud of being able to make lunches and snacks for the kids."

Definitely love, Hannah decided, giving Matt an approving smile. "Do you bake?"

"I never really learned, but I'd like to get into it. Maybe later, when I have more time."

Time. Hannah heard her cue word and picked up on it. "Julie said the kids are needy right now, and they demand almost constant attention."

"She's right. Not the girls so much, but the boys seem to really need us. We've been trying to watch *Roman Holiday* for three nights now, and Gregory Peck's still got his arm in the gargoyle."

Hannah laughed and so did Matt, but she quickly sobered. "About the kids . . . Julie thinks they're probably lonely, missing their parents and all that."

"Well . . ." Matt sounded as if he'd been about to agree when he'd had second thoughts. "That *does* make perfect sense, but I don't think it's the only reason."

"Why not?"

"It's a whole bunch of things. Let me give you some examples. Last night, an hour after he was supposed to be asleep, Spenser came down to tell us the window in their room was stuck and Larry wanted it open a crack."

"It wasn't stuck?" Hannah guessed.

"It slid right up when I tried it. Spense said he must have loosened it up and he should have tried it one more time before he came to get me, but I noticed that he couldn't look me in the eye when he said it."

"You found that a little suspicious?"

"Yes, in light of everything else. The night before that, Gary came down to tell us that the faucet in their connecting bathroom was dripping and he couldn't get to sleep. I went up to fix it, and all I had to do was tighten it with my hand."

"And Gary could have done that?"

"Of course. It's almost as if the boys are jealous of the time I spend alone with Julie."

"That's interesting. And it must be frustrating for you and Julie, never getting any time alone together."

"You have *no* idea!" Matt said, sighing deeply. "The only time we can talk without one of the boys standing there listening is when they're eating dessert."

"Good thing I brought extra Blue Blueberry Muffins," Hannah said, proud of the way she'd managed to gather the information Julie wanted. "The next time I drive out, I'll bring triple dessert and you might actually have time to finish that movie."

BLUE BLUEBERRY MUFFINS

Preheat oven to 375 degrees F.,
rack in the middle position.

The Batter:
¾ cup melted butter *(1½ sticks)*
1 cup sugar
2 beaten eggs *(just whip them up with a fork)*
2 teaspoons baking powder
½ teaspoon salt
1 cup fresh or frozen blueberries *(no need to thaw if
    they're frozen)*
2 cups plus one tablespoon flour *(no need to sift)*
½ cup milk
½ cup blueberry pie filling

Crumb Topping:
½ cup sugar
⅓ cup flour
¼ cup softened butter *(½ stick)*

Grease the <u>bottoms only</u> of a 12-cup muffin pan *(or
line the cups with double cupcake papers—that's
what I do at The Cookie Jar).* Melt the butter. Mix in
the sugar. Then add the beaten eggs, baking powder,
and salt. Mix it all up thoroughly.

Put one tablespoon of flour in a baggie with your cup of fresh or frozen blueberries. Shake it gently to coat the blueberries and leave them in the bag for now.

Add half of the remaining two cups of flour to your bowl and mix it in with half of the milk. Then add the rest of the flour and the milk and mix thoroughly.

Here comes the fun part: Add ½ cup of blueberry pie filling to your bowl and mix it in. *(Your dough will turn a shade of blue, but don't let that stop you—once the muffins are baked, they'll look just fine.)* When your dough is thoroughly mixed, fold in the flour-coated fresh or frozen blueberries.

Fill the muffin tins three-quarters full and set them aside. If you have dough left over, grease the bottom of a small tea-bread loaf pan and fill it with your remaining dough.

The crumb topping: Mix the sugar and the flour in a small bowl. Add the softened butter and cut it in until it's crumbly. *(You can also do this in a food processor with chilled butter and the steel blade.)*

Fill the remaining space in the muffin cups with the crumb topping. Then bake the muffins in a 375 degree F. oven for 25 to 30 minutes. *(The tea-bread should bake about 10 minutes longer than the muffins.)*

While your muffins are baking, divide the rest of your blueberry pie filling into half-cup portions and pop it in the freezer. I use paper cups to hold it and freeze them inside a freezer bag. All you have to do is thaw a cup the next time you want to make a batch of Blue Blueberry Muffins.

When your muffins are baked, set the muffin pan on a wire rack to cool for at least 30 minutes. *(The muffins need to cool in the pan for easy removal.)* Then just tip them out of the cups and enjoy.

These are wonderful when they're slightly warm, but the blueberry flavor will intensify if you store them in a covered container overnight.

Hannah's Note: Grandma Ingrid's muffin pans were large enough to hold all the dough from this recipe. My muffin tins are smaller and I always make a loaf of Blue Blueberry tea-bread with the leftover dough. If I make it for Mother, I leave off the crumb topping. She loves to eat it sliced, toasted, and buttered for breakfast.

MINNESOTA PEACH COBBLER

Preheat oven to 350 degrees F.,
rack in the middle position.

Hannah's Note: Don't thaw your peaches before you make this—leave them frozen.

Spray a 13-inch by 9-inch cake pan with Pam or other nonstick cooking spray.

10 cups frozen sliced peaches *(approximately 2½ pounds)*
⅛ cup lemon juice *(2 tablespoons)*
1½ cups white *(granulated)* sugar
¼ teaspoon salt
¾ cup flour *(no need to sift)*
½ teaspoon cinnamon
½ cup melted butter *(1 stick, ¼ pound)*

Measure the peaches and put them in a large mixing bowl. Let them sit on the counter and thaw for 10 minutes. Then sprinkle them with lemon juice and toss.

In another smaller bowl combine white sugar, salt, flour, and cinnamon. Mix them together with a fork until they're evenly combined.

Pour the dry mixture over the peaches and toss them. *(This works best if you use your impeccably clean hands.)* Once most of the dry mixture is clinging to the peaches, dump them into the cake pan you've prepared. Sprinkle any dry mixture left in the bowl on top of the peaches in the pan.

Melt the butter. Drizzle it over the peaches. Then cover the cake pan tightly with foil.

Bake the peach mixture at 350 degrees F., for 40 minutes. Take it out of the oven and set it on a heat-proof surface, but DON'T TURN OFF THE OVEN!

Top Crust:
1 cup flour *(no need to sift)*
1 cup white *(granulated)* sugar
1½ teaspoons baking powder
¼ teaspoon cinnamon
½ teaspoon salt
½ stick softened butter *(¼ cup, ⅛ pound)*
2 beaten eggs *(just stir them up in a glass with a fork)*

Combine the flour, sugar, baking powder, cinnamon, and salt in the smaller bowl you used earlier. Cut in the softened butter with a couple of forks until the

mixture looks like coarse cornmeal. Add the beaten eggs and mix them in with a fork. For those of you who remember your school library with fondness, the result will resemble library paste but it'll smell a whole lot better! *(If you have a food processor, you can also make the crust using the steel blade and chilled butter cut into 4 chunks.)*

Remove the foil cover from the peaches and drop on spoonfuls of the topping. Because the topping is thick, you'll have to do this in little dibs and dabs scraped from the spoon with another spoon, a rubber spatula, or with your freshly washed finger. Dab on the topping until the whole pan is polka-dotted. *(Don't worry if some spots aren't covered very well—the batter will spread out and fill in as it bakes and result in a crunchy crust.)*

Bake at 350 degrees F., uncovered, for an additional 50 minutes.

Minnesota Peach Cobbler can be eaten hot, warm, room temperature, or chilled. It can be served by itself in a bowl, or topped with cream or ice cream.

Chapter Seven

"Maybe tonight is our lucky night," Matt said, sitting down on the couch next to Julie and reaching for the remote control. "Hannah brought us a quadruple batch of fudge cupcakes, and the boys ate four apiece. With stomachs that full, they should sleep for hours."

"Don't count on anything when it comes to the kids. Even after we put them to bed, there's always something they need."

"There's always something *the boys* need," Matt corrected her. "It's never the girls."

"That's true. The girls are no trouble at all." Julie glanced at the screen where *The Quiet Man* was playing without sound. "Where were we anyway?"

"I think I was kissing you and you were making those little purring noises in your throat, the ones that make me feel like I'm the most important guy in the world."

Julie laughed, but her cheeks turned pink "Well, you *are* the most important guy in the world, but I was talking about the movie. What scene were we watching the last time the boys interrupted us?"

"The one where Maureen O'Hara bolts the door and John

Wayne breaks it open. But I don't really care about that. I'd rather research those little purring noises."

"Research is very important for a teacher," Julie replied, snuggling into his arms and leaving John and Maureen to their own devices.

"Mr. Sherwood?"

Matt groaned. This couldn't be real. No one was that unlucky. He must be imagining the night's worst scenario, because he was afraid it might happen again.

"Mr. Sherwood?"

Yup. It was happening. That was Larry's voice, and the boys were interrupting his night with Julie again.

Resolutely, Matt pulled away from Julie's willing arms and turned to face his ten-year-old tormentor. "What is it, Larry?"

"Gary had a nightmare."

There was a beat of silence while Matt considered the logic of that statement. "I'm sorry to hear that. But if Gary had a nightmare, why didn't *he* come down here to get us?"

"Because he's hiding in the closet and he won't come out. He thinks Spense and I are aliens. We think he's still dreaming."

It was the lamest excuse Matt had ever heard, and he was about to say so when Julie interrupted.

"I'll go," she offered, standing up and moving past him. "You find the scene where John Wayne fights with Victor McLaglen while I'm gone. When I come back, we can start watching everything all over again."

"Of course I'm sure," Larry said, once Julie had gone back downstairs. "We broke them up, but not for long. They're just going to start kissing again."

Spenser nodded. "I think you're right. And if they keep

this up, we're going to lose to the girls for sure. It's time to pull out the big guns."

"What big guns?" Gary and Larry asked together.

"I'm not sure yet, but I'll come up with something. Just give me a little time to think about it."

Larry looked worried. "Better think fast, before . . ."

". . . Mr. Sherwood asks her to marry him and we have to wear aprons and listen to Mrs. Caulder sing," Gary finished.

FUDGE CUPCAKES

Preheat oven to 350 degrees F.,
rack in the middle position.

4 squares unsweetened baking chocolate *(1 ounce each)*
¼ cup white *(granulated)* sugar
½ cup raspberry syrup *(for pancakes—I used Knott's red raspberry)****
1⅔ cups flour *(unsifted)*
1½ teaspoons baking powder
½ teaspoon salt
½ cup butter, room temperature *(one stick, ¼ pound)*
1½ cups white sugar *(not a misprint—you'll use one and three-quarters cups sugar in all)*
3 eggs
⅓ cup milk

   *** *If you can't find raspberry syrup, mix ¼ cup seedless raspberry jam with ¼ cup light Karo syrup and use that.*

Line a 12-cup muffin pan with double cupcake papers. Since this recipe makes 18 cupcakes, you can use an additional 6-cup muffin pan lined with double papers, or you can butter and flour an 8-inch square cake pan or the equivalent.

Microwave the chocolate, raspberry syrup and ¼ cup sugar in a microwave-safe bowl on high for 1 minute. Stir. Microwave again, for another minute. At this point, the chocolate will be almost melted, but it will maintain its shape. Stir the mixture until smooth and let cool to lukewarm. *(You can also do this in a double boiler on the stove.)*

Measure the flour, mix in the baking powder and salt, and set it aside. With an electric mixer *(or with a VERY strong arm)* beat the butter and 1½ cups sugar until light and fluffy. *(About 3 minutes with a mixer—an additional 2 minutes if you're doing it by hand.)* Add the eggs, one at a time, beating after each addition to make sure they're thoroughly incorporated. Add approximately a third of the flour mixture and a third of the milk. *(You don't have to be exact—adding the flour and milk in increments makes the batter smoother.)* When that's all mixed in, add another third of the flour and another third of the milk. And when that's incorporated, add the remainder of the flour and the remainder of the milk. Mix thoroughly.

Test your chocolate mixture to make sure it's cool enough to add. *(You don't want to cook the eggs!)* If it's fairly warm to the touch but not so hot you have to

pull your hand away, you can add it at this point. Stir thoroughly and you're done.

Let the batter rest for five minutes. Then stir it again by hand and fill each cupcake paper three-quarters full. If you decided to use the 8-inch cake pan instead of the 6-cup muffin tin, fill it with the remaining batter.

Bake the cupcakes in a 350 degree F. oven for 20 to 25 minutes. The 8-inch cake should bake an additional 5 minutes.

Fudge Frosting:
2 cups semi-sweet *(regular)* chocolate chips *(a 12-ounce package)*
One 14-ounce can sweetened condensed milk

18 cupcakes, or 12 cupcakes and 1 small cake, cooled to room temperature and ready to frost.

If you use a double boiler for this frosting, it's fool-proof. You can also make it in a heavy saucepan over low to medium heat on the stovetop, but you'll have to stir it constantly with a spatula to keep it from scorching.

Fill the bottom part of the double boiler with water. Make sure it doesn't touch the underside of the top.

Put the chocolate chips in the top of the double boiler, set it over the bottom, and place the double boiler on the stovetop at medium heat. Stir occasionally until the chocolate chips are melted.

Stir in the can of sweetened condensed milk and cook approximately 2 minutes, stirring constantly, until the frosting is shiny and of spreading consistency.

Spread it on the cupcakes, making sure to fill in the "frosting pocket."

Give the frosting pan to your favorite person to scrape.

These cupcakes are even better if you cool them, cover them, and let them sit for several hours (or even overnight) before frosting them.

Hannah's Note: If you want to make them in mini-cupcake tins, fill those ⅔ full and bake them at 350 degrees F. for 15 minutes.

Chapter Eight

"Do you know how to preheat the oven to three hundred and fifty degrees?" Hannah asked, taking nothing for granted as far as Julie's domestic skills were concerned.

Julie nodded. "I can handle that part of it. It's the job they used to give me when we baked in a group in high school. Do I have to do something with the rack?"

"It should be in the middle position," Serena told her after glancing down at the recipe Hannah had brought. "Do you want us to unpack the box with the ingredients, Miss Swensen?"

"Not until Miss Jansen's had time to read through the recipe," Hannah said, handing the recipe to Julie as she came back to the workstation in the middle of the kitchen.

Julie scanned the recipe and started to smile. "What fun! I've never heard of Multiple-Choice Bar Cookies before."

"You mean it's like a test?" Serena asked.

"No, it's like a buffet," Julie said, placing the recipe on the surface of the workstation and motioning for the girls to come closer. "Just look. There are four columns, and you get to choose one ingredient from each column. You could make a lot of different bar cookies from this recipe."

"One thousand five hundred and eighty-two," Hannah said.

"You figured it out that fast?" Serena looked impressed.

"No, I made it up. Whenever I do math problems like that, I forget to subtract for the number of factors to avoid the duplicates."

"Right," Julie said, looking every bit as confused as the kids. "Whenever I see a math problem like that, I'm glad I majored in English."

Serena cracked up, and so did the two younger girls. Hannah could tell that Julie had a good relationship with them. It would be an unusual child indeed who didn't like Julie. She was funny and caring at the same time.

"Since there are four columns, let's split this up," Julie continued. "You can choose one from each column. Take the first column, Serena. Hope? You've got the second column. And you've got the third column, Joy. I'll take the fourth, and we'll have our own creation."

Leaving the girls to discuss their choices and argue the merits of graham cracker crumbs over chocolate wafer crumbs, Hannah pulled Julie aside to teach her how to melt butter in the microwave and pour it in the pan. Once that was done, they had time for a brief, private conversation.

"How are things developing with Matt?" Hannah discarded any fleeting notion she might have had at subtlety and waded in with both feet.

"We'd be fine if the kids would just leave us alone," Julie said, and then she shook her head. "Matt and I talked about it, and he pointed out that it's just the boys. The girls have been perfect angels. They never interrupt us when we're together. I think they're really sensitive to the way we feel about each other. It's almost as if they're encouraging us to get together."

"Miss Jansen?" Hope called out. "Can I use M&Ms *and* raisins? It says two cups, and Serena thought it might be okay if I used one cup of each."

"Hannah?" Julie turned to her.

"Absolutely. And that makes one thousand five hundred and eighty-*three* ways to make them. You're a natural-born baker, Hope."

"Thanks, Miss Swensen."

While Julie was sprinkling the chosen ingredient from column A in the pan, Hannah thought about how the boys didn't want Julie and Matt to get together and the girls did. It was a little strange, considering that both the boys and the girls seemed to like Matt and Julie a lot. Something didn't make sense, but Hannah couldn't quite put her finger on what it was. Then Julie asked about the best way to cover the pan evenly with sweetened condensed milk, and Hannah shoved the romantic puzzle aside to consider later.

Spenser was worried. He'd thought it was suspicious when Mr. Sherwood said he was going out for supplies. The storeroom was fully stocked and there really wasn't anything they needed. It was the reason he'd offered to help Mr. Sherwood unload when he came back, and just as he'd expected, Mr. Sherwood had insisted that he could handle it himself.

His curiosity aroused, Spenser had watched from an upstairs window as his teacher carried things in. Most of the packages Mr. Sherwood had bought were for them. Spenser recognized the toy store logo on the bags. But then Mr. Sherwood had gone back out to his car to retrieve a red bag with a logo on the side. It was a silver heart with an arrow, the trademark symbol of Cupid's Jewelry. Since there was no way Mr. Sherwood had purchased jewelry for one of them, it had to be for Miss Jansen. And Spenser was pretty sure the bag contained a diamond engagement ring.

Spenser ducked around a corner as Mr. Sherwood came up the stairs to stash the bag in his room. Things were coming to a head much too fast. It was time for them to act, or all was lost.

"Something's wrong in the office, Mr. Sherwood." Gary arrived at his teacher's side panting slightly, with Larry following a second or two behind him.

"What office?"

"The one down the hall," Larry answered. "Gary and I were walking down . . ."

". . . the hall when we heard this loud noise," Gary finished.

"It was sort of like a ringing sound," Larry tried to describe, "except it buzzed too. We thought it was . . ."

". . . a phone off the hook, or something like that."

"Thanks for telling me," Matt said. "It sounds like a fax machine, or something electronic. I've got the master keys in my pocket. Show me which office it is, and we'll go take a look."

This time it seemed that the twins had a legitimate reason for needing him. As they neared the office that Julie used to check her e-mail and generate daily reports to Dr. Caulder, he could hear the beeping noise Larry and Gary had told him about.

"It's definitely electronic," Matt said, making short work of unlocking the door and flicking on the lights.

Gary headed straight for the computer desk. "It's coming from here."

"What is it?" Matt asked.

Larry gave a little laugh. "It's an alarm clock. One of the guests must have left it in here . . ."

". . . and it got turned on accidentally," Gary finished. "But it's a good thing we came in. This is the computer Miss Jansen used, and she . . ."

". . . must have forgotten to turn it off," Larry completed the thought. "Do you want me to do it, Mr. Sherwood?"

Matt nodded. Both Gary and Larry were computer gurus. Even though they were only ten, they'd already written several small programs, and they knew more about the computers in the offices than Matt did. "Go ahead. Just make sure you save any files Miss Jansen might have open."

"Don't worry about that. We always check everything to . . ." Gary stopped and stared at the screen. "What do you think . . . ?"

"I don't know. Maybe it's some kind of security . . ."

"No way! It looks more like an illegal operation that led into an internal conflict with . . ."

"No, it doesn't. Just let me . . ."

"Better not. Look at that . . ."

"Uh-oh," Larry groaned.

Matt began to frown. "Uh-oh what?"

"Miss Jansen's computer just went to the blue screen of death."

"*What* blue screen of death?" Matt interjected before they could revert to twin talk again.

"You know, Mr. Sherwood," Larry started to explain. "You only get the bright blue screen when . . ."

". . . your operating system's compromised," Gary ended the explanation.

"That sounds bad," Matt said, remembering his old college roommate talking about getting a blue screen and not being able to access the term paper he'd just finished.

Gary gave a short laugh. "It's always bad, and sometimes it's a disaster. But we know a couple of fixes that might . . ."

". . . get it back online again," Larry took over. "Just give us a minute, and we'll get into the CMOS and run some internal checks."

"Take your time," Matt said, sitting down on the couch by the window.

The twins worked in silence for a moment, and then Gary gave a little cheer. "Okay. It's up."

"That's just the operating system," Larry pointed out. "How about her files and her Internet provider?"

"The files are here. Let me just sign on and see if . . ." Gary stopped speaking as the computer rang like a bell several times in succession. "It's an instant message."

Larry frowned. "Better retrieve it and save it. If you don't, she might lose it."

"Okay. I'll just pull it up and . . . Wow!"

"Wow, what?" Matt asked, leaning forward slightly.

"I didn't know Miss Jansen was engaged!"

"Engaged?" both Matt and Larry asked at once.

"Well, she must be. He's asking her questions about their wedding."

Matt felt sick, and he was glad he was sitting down. "You shouldn't read somebody else's e-mail," he said weakly.

"But he's talking about *you*," Gary insisted. "You want to know what he says, don't you?"

"Yes, but we really ought to respect her privacy." Matt's voice trailed off. Of course he wanted to know what the message said. He'd been about to propose to Julie and that meant he *needed* to know.

"How can it be private if it's about you?" Larry challenged, and then he turned to his twin. "Go ahead and tell Mr. Sherwood what it says. Don't read it out loud 'cause that would be snooping, but tell him the important parts."

"Okay. His name is Dan and he's talking about something called a bachelor party. Do you know what that is?"

"Oh, yes," Matt said, the sick feeling rising in his stomach.

"The wedding's going to be in June, and Dan's telling Miss Jansen that he just sent an e-mail to her colleague to invite him to the bachelor party."

"Me?" Matt managed to ask.

"That's right. He says, *your colleague, Mr. Sherwood.* And then he says something about how he's looking forward to meeting you, and how glad he is that you're keeping her amused over Christmas."

Amused? Julie had told her fiancé that he'd *amused* her? Matt felt like swearing a blue streak, or throwing something through the picture window that overlooked the quad, or tracking down Julie's fiancé and taking him out with his bare hands. Any one of the three might have made him feel better, but he did none of them. Instead, Matt took a deep breath and let it out again slowly, hoping that his equilibrium would return and the twins wouldn't notice how his hands were shaking.

"That's very interesting," he said, pleased that his voice sounded calm, "but it's really none of our business. Save the message and then go find Spenser. Tell him I'm going to drive you boys out to the mall for hamburgers, and after that we'll take in a movie, or go bowling, or something."

"How about the girls?" Larry asked.

"They can stay here with Miss Jansen. It'll be boys night out, no girls allowed."

"Like a bachelor party?" Gary wanted to know.

"'Course not," Larry corrected him. "Spense told me about bachelor parties. All the guys drink a lot, and a lady in a bikini pops out of a cake."

"Do they eat the cake after she pops out?"

"Spense didn't say. Come on, Gary. Let's go find him."

Gary started to join his twin, but then he turned back to the computer. "Do you want me to shut this off, Mr. Sherwood?"

"I'll do it. I've got an e-mail I have to send, and I need to check something in that last report Miss Jansen wrote for Dr. Caulder. Just meet me by the car at five o'clock sharp and we'll leave."

"Thanks, Mr. Sherwood," Gary said.

"It'll be fun," Larry added.

The twins headed for the door, but just as they got there,

Matt thought of something else. "Better not say anything to anybody about that e-mail from Miss Jansen's fiancé."

"Right," Larry agreed.

"We won't," Gary promised. "She might not understand how we had to open it to save it."

Once the boys had left and closed the door behind them, Matt sat down at the computer desk and opened Julie's e-mail. He was going to do something he knew he shouldn't do, but in the interests of his own sanity, he had to know exactly what was going on with the woman he'd intended to make his wife.

MULTIPLE-CHOICE BAR COOKIES

Preheat oven to 350 degrees F.,
rack in the middle position.

½ cup butter *(one stick, ¼ pound)*
1 can *(14 ounces)* sweetened condensed milk

Column A
(1½ cups of)
Graham Cracker Crumbs
Vanilla Wafer Crumbs
Chocolate Wafer Crumbs
Animal Cracker Crumbs
Sugar Cookie Crumbs

Column B
(2 cups of)
Chocolate Chips
Butterscotch Chips
Peanut Butter Chips
Raisins *(regular or golden)*
M & M's *(without nuts)*

Column C
(1 ½ cups of)
Flaked Coconut *(5 oz.)*
Rice Krispies
Miniature Marshmallows
    (2 ½ cups)
Frosted Cornflakes *(crum-
    bled)*

Column D
(1 cup of)
Chopped Walnuts
Chopped Pecans
Chopped Peanuts
Chopped Cashews

Melt the butter and pour it into in a 9-inch by 13-
inch cake pan. Tip the pan to coat the bottom.

1. Evenly sprinkle one from Column A over the melted butter.

2. Drizzle sweetened condensed milk over the crumbs.

3. Evenly sprinkle one from Column B on top.

4. Evenly sprinkle one from Column C on top of that.

5. Evenly sprinkle something from Column D over the very top.

Press everything down with the palms of your impeccably clean hands. Bake at 350 degrees F. for 30 minutes. Cool thoroughly on a wire rack and cut into brownie-sized bars.

Make sure you cut these before you refrigerate them or they'll be very difficult to cut.

Hannah's Note: Kids love to help make these bars when they get to choose the ingredients.

Chapter Nine

The moment that Hannah pulled open the heavy front door of Aames House, she knew that something was wrong. Instead of the childish laughter that had greeted her on every other visit, there was only the sound of quiet voices from the kitchen where Julie and the girls were waiting for her. The group baking yesterday afternoon had been so much fun, the girls had asked if they could do it again today. Of course Hannah had agreed. Tonight was Christmas Eve, and The Cookie Jar was closed. Hannah and Lisa had plenty of time to start the holiday fun by baking Christmas sugar cookies with Julie and the girls.

"What's the matter?" Lisa asked, as Hannah stopped and listened.

"It's quiet . . . too quiet."

"Like in an old western when the Indians are about to ride up over the top of the hill and attack?"

"Not exactly, but the general concept's the same. Something's wrong, and I've got the feeling it's something big. Let's go find out if I'm right or if I've seen too many movies."

Hannah led the way down the hallway to the kitchen and pushed open the door. Julie was standing at the central work-station with the girls, who were talking quietly among themselves.

"Uh-oh," Hannah said under her breath as she caught sight of Julie. Even though she'd tried to cover the traces of tears with makeup and there was a brave little smile on her face, Julie's eyelids were puffy, and Hannah suspected she'd been crying most of the night.

Lisa nudged Hannah and moved closer so she wouldn't be overheard. "You're right. It's something big. I'll take over with the cookies and the girls if you want to have coffee with Julie in the dining room and find out what's wrong."

"Good idea." Hannah took a deep breath and waded into deep waters. Julie might resist her probing, but she looked so miserable, they couldn't just stand by and pretend nothing was wrong.

"Hi, Hannah," Julie said as Hannah approached her. "The girls are all ready to bake Christmas cookies."

"And Lisa's all ready to teach them how to do it. Let's get a cup of coffee and go into the dining room."

It was proof of Julie's misery that she didn't even voice an objection or say something about how she should help to supervise her students. She just poured coffee for both of them and carried the cups into the adjoining room.

"I guess the makeup didn't work," Julie said, setting the cups down on place mats.

"It might fool someone who was visually challenged on a night with no moon." Hannah opened one of the bakery boxes she'd carried in with her. "We brought along all the leftover cookies for the kids. These are Twin Chocolate Delights. Eat one."

"Thanks, Hannah, but I'm not really hungry."

"You don't have to be hungry. Just eat one. The endorphins in the chocolate will help."

"Help what?"

"Whatever it is that's making you cry. You want to feel better, don't you?"

"Of course I do, but . . ."

"Then take a bite. It'll work, I almost guarantee it. Chocolate creates a feeling of well-being, calms frazzled nerves, relieves stress, and puts daily problems into perspective."

Julie gave a brief little smile, and Hannah was very glad to see it. "You sound like a commercial for a new drug. The only thing you're missing is the part about the side effects."

"You may experience a slight weight gain if you overdose," Hannah said in her best announcer's voice. "Ask your local baker if chocolate is right for you."

This time Julie's smile was a bit wider. She reached into the box, chose a cookie, and took a bite. "These are good," she said, after she'd swallowed.

"Of course they are. If I calculated right, they're over seventy percent good stuff."

"What's *good stuff?*"

"Chocolate, butter, and sugar. But let's not talk about nutrition."

"Or the lack of it," Julie countered, finishing her first cookie and reaching for a second.

"Right." Hannah was pleased as Julie's second cookie began to go the way of the first. "Now tell me what's got you so upset. I'm assuming you had a fight with Matt?"

"Yes."

"Over what?"

"Over e-mail."

Hannah thought fast. Asking Julie questions was a little like cracking almonds. If she applied too much pressure, Julie might be crushed by the weight of her problem and start crying again. Still, she had to know the facts. "You mean Matt's been sending you e-mail?"

"No, he's been getting e-mail . . ." Julie stopped to take a deep breath, ". . . from my fiancé. And I don't even *have* a fiancé!"

"Then how did . . . What . . . Did he . . ." Hannah sputtered while she went through the possibilities in her mind. "Let me get this straight. Matt got an e-mail from a guy who said he was your fiancé, and now he thinks you're engaged?"

"Exactly. And Matt also thinks I was just amusing myself with him because I was bored and this Dan who claims to be my fiancé is all the way out in Montana."

"Uh-oh."

"Uh-oh is right. I tried to tell Matt that it must be a case of mistaken identity, that there must be another Julie Jansen and that I don't even *know* a guy named Dan. But he wouldn't listen." Julie's eyes filled with tears.

Hannah thought about that for a moment, and then she stood up. "Okay. I'm going to go talk to Matt."

"It won't do any good," Julie warned.

"Maybe not, but I have to try. You stay here and eat a couple more cookies. I'll be back just as soon as I can."

"I really don't want to talk about it. Not only that, it's really none of your business."

"Yes, it is," Hannah countered. Matt was being rude, but she didn't take offense. It was clear by his expression that believing Julie was engaged had wounded him deeply. "I talked to Julie and she told me about the man who claims to be her fiancé."

"The man who *is* her fiancé."

"Whatever. Let's leave that open for now. I'd like to see the e-mail he sent, if you still have it."

"Why?"

"Because I just can't believe that Julie would lie to both of us about being engaged. I admit I haven't seen her since she was in high school, but it seems so out of character for her."

Matt hesitated, but then he nodded. "Okay. I understand how you feel, Hannah. I was taken in by her too. Come with me. It's in the room I'm using as an office."

It was only a few steps to Matt's office, and Hannah waited while he unlocked the door. Once she was seated on the couch next to the windows, Matt brought her a sheaf of papers. "What's all this?" she asked.

"The top one's the e-mail I got from Dan. The others are copies of the messages he sent to Julie. I know it was wrong to do it, but I read them and printed them out."

"I don't understand how you got her e-mail."

"The twins must have known her password or gotten around it somehow. They're both computer whizzes."

"You asked the boys to break into Julie's computer?" Hannah asked, clearly shocked.

"No. The whole thing was accidental. The boys came to me because they heard something buzzing in Julie's office and the door was locked. It turned out to be an alarm clock, but her computer was on. While we were there, the computer started acting up and the twins tried to fix it. They got it back online, but then an e-mail message came in and they were afraid that if they didn't open it and save it, Julie would lose it."

"I see," Hannah said, and both meanings of the word applied. While they'd been talking, she'd paged through the messages, and one thing had popped out loud and clear. "So the twins are computer experts?"

"That's right. They even dabble in programming. Both of their parents are in the technology field."

"So if anyone could make a computer act up, it would be the twins."

"True." Matt's eyes narrowed slightly. "But they don't have a key to Julie's office. How could they get the alarm clock to go off?"

"I'm not sure, but I bet if you check you'll find out that they went into Julie's office while she was there. If one twin did or said something to distract her, it would be easy for the other one to set that alarm clock."

"You could be right, but how about all these messages from Julie's fiancé? I've got them right here in black and white."

"Let me read you something," Hannah said, paging through the stack to find the one she wanted. "According to the date, this one came in yesterday. *I yearn for you more each day and fervently anticipate the instance when we can be united continually.* Does that sound like something a guy would write to his fiancée?"

"Not really. I guess I was too upset to notice it before, but the wording's very awkward."

"How about this one?" Hannah located a second sheet of paper. "*The moments we're estranged are anguish, but the future will soon arrive. I adore you more with each second that elapses.*"

Matt began to frown. "That's even worse. It reminds me of something, but I can't quite put my finger on it."

"It's writing for Roget," Hannah told him. "Somebody looked up some perfectly good words in the thesaurus and substituted bigger ones."

"You're right! But who'd go to all that trouble for an e-mail?"

Matt and Hannah exchanged glances. And then he answered his own question. "There's only one person who'd do it. It was a kid who was trying to sound like an adult."

Hannah headed for the kitchen at a trot. She'd check in with Lisa and the girls, tell Julie what was going on, and then she'd confront the boys. Matt said they were watching television in the lounge and that was a perfect place to elicit a confession from the three pranksters who'd almost been Julie and Matt's undoing.

A lovely scent wafted down the hallway as Hannah neared

the kitchen. The girls were already baking. She'd mixed up the dough at The Cookie Jar before she'd left last night. Today the only thing to do was roll it out, cut it in Christmas shapes, bake it, and then frost it. From the mouthwatering aroma that hit her nostrils as she pushed the kitchen door open, Hannah could tell that the girls were well on their way to finishing the sugary Christmas treats.

"Will you come look at my cookies, Miss Swensen?" Hope asked, running up to grab Hannah's hand and pull her to the far end of the workstation. "I'm decorating the bells."

"And you're doing a wonderful job, Hope. I especially like that one." Hannah pointed to a red and green bell with markedly irregular stripes.

"Serena likes that one too. She wants it for her Christmas present."

To the girls' delight, Hannah inspected all the cookies and pronounced them good enough to eat. Then Lisa shooed her out of the kitchen and into the dining room to talk to Julie.

"What did Matt say?" Julie sounded calm, but the way her hands twisted in her lap was testament to her anxiety.

"He believes you now."

"It's about time! He should have believed me when I first said that . . ."

"Stop!" Hannah held up her hand and Julie fell silent. "Let's not compound the problem. Matt didn't want to believe it, but he was tricked."

"Who tricked him?"

"We don't know for sure, but we think it was the boys."

"But . . . I thought the boys liked me," Julie said, looking very confused.

"Oh, they do. And they like Matt too."

"Then why did they try to break us up?"

"That's what I'm about to find out. You wait here. Matt's coming to ask you to forgive him, and I want you to do it. It's true that he should have trusted you, but everyone makes mistakes."

Julie thought about that for a minute. "You're right, Hannah. I just hate to think the boys did this deliberately, though. Maybe they were just playing a prank and it got out of control."

"Maybe," Hannah said. Julie was kind, giving the boys the benefit of the doubt, but Hannah didn't believe it for a second. The boys had planned all this very carefully and she was determined to find out why.

CHRISTMAS SUGAR COOKIES

Do not preheat oven—this dough must
chill before baking.

*I came up with the cookie recipe and Lisa did the
frosting.*

1½ cups melted butter *(3 sticks, ¾ pound)*
2 cups white *(granulated)* sugar
4 beaten eggs
2 teaspoons baking powder
1½ teaspoons salt
1 teaspoon flavor extract *(lemon, almond, vanilla,
orange, rum, whatever)*
5 cups flour *(no need to sift)*

Mix the melted butter with the sugar. Let cool. Add
the beaten eggs, baking powder, salt, and flavoring.

Add the flour in one-cup increments, stirring after
each addition.

Refrigerate dough for at least two hours. Overnight is fine, too.

When you're ready to bake, preheat the oven to 375 degrees F., rack in the center position.

Divide the dough into four parts for ease in rolling. Roll out the first part of the dough on a floured board. It should be approximately ⅛ inch thick.

Dip the cookie cutters in flour and cut out cookies, getting as many as you can from the sheet of dough. *(If you don't have cookie cutters, you can cut free-form cookies with a sharp knife.)* Use a metal spatula to remove the cookies from the rest of the sheet of dough and place them on an UNGREASED cookie sheet. Leave at least an inch and a half between cookies.

If you want to use colored sugar or sprinkles to decorate, put it on now, before baking. If you'd rather frost the cookies, wait until they're baked and cooled.

Bake at 375 degrees F. for 8 to 10 minutes, or just until delicately golden in color. Leave them on the sheet for a minute or two and then transfer them to a wire rack to complete cooling.

Icing:
2 cups sifted confectioner's sugar *(powdered sugar)*
Pinch of salt
½ teaspoon vanilla *(or other flavoring)*
¼ cup cream

Mix up icing, adding a little more cream if it's too thick and a little more powdered sugar if it's too thin.

If you'd like to frost the cookies in different colors, divide the icing and put it in several small bowls. Add drops of the desired food coloring to each bowl.

Use a frosting knife or a brush to "paint" the cookies you've baked.

Chapter Ten

"Hello, boys," Hannah said.

"Hi, Miss Swensen," the boys chorused, and three faces with identical innocent expressions turned to greet her.

"So why did you do it?"

"Do what?" one of the twins asked, but a dull red stain crept up his neck and spread to his cheeks.

"Yes, what?" the other twin chimed in, pulling his collar up a bit to hide his telltale color.

"You know what you did. What I want to know is why."

"It was my fault," Spenser said manfully, squaring his shoulders a bit. "I talked them into making the bet, and these guys had no choice but to go along with me."

"Yes we did," one of the twins said. "We could have . . ."

". . . said we didn't want to bet," the other twin finished the explanation.

"Tell me about the bet," Hannah said, sitting down in the chair next to the couch and switching off the television with the remote control.

Spenser drew a folded piece of paper from his pocket.

"You can read all about it. I've got our copy right here. All of us signed it to make it official."

Hannah took the paper and read it. "The girls win if Mr. Sherwood asks Miss Jansen to marry him. And you win if they don't get engaged. Is that right?"

"That's right," Spenser said, and the twins nodded.

"I don't get it. You must not like Mr. Sherwood and Miss Jansen."

Spenser shook his head. "We like them a lot," he said.

"It's just that the girls were being so . . ." one twin started the thought, but he got stuck for a word.

". . . confident," the other twin provided it. "And stuck up. They thought they knew better than we did."

"They *did* know better than we did," Spenser pointed out. "Mr. Sherwood was going to propose to Miss Jansen. I saw him carry in the jeweler's bag with the ring that he bought at the mall. The girls were right and we were wrong, and that meant we had to do their chores for a month. We couldn't let that happen. It was just too awful."

"What do the girls have to do for chores?" Hannah asked, thinking that it must be pretty bad for the boys to go to such lengths to win.

"Hope and Joy have to go shopping with Mrs. Caulder every Saturday and carry her packages," one twin said, shuddering slightly.

"And they have to pass trays of sandwiches with their crusts cut off on Wednesday at her musical sorry," the other twin added.

"Soirée," Spenser corrected. "Serena's chores are pretty bad too. She has to help Mrs. Dryer clean up the kitchen after dinner."

"When does this bet end?" Hannah said, an idea beginning to form in her mind.

"The day after Christmas," Spenser told her. "We didn't know that Mr. Sherwood and Miss Jansen would feel this bad. Now we wish we hadn't done it."

"Okay," Hannah said, handing the remote control to Spenser and standing up. "I've got to go. I need to bake a dessert for tonight's dinner."

"Are we busted?" one of the twins wanted to know.

"I'm not going to punish you, if that's what you mean. Your own consciences will do that."

"Do you think Mr. Sherwood will propose before Christmas is over?" Spenser wanted to know.

"I have no idea. All we can do is wait and see," Hannah said, heading for the hallway and leaving the three guilty boys to think about the havoc they'd caused.

"Hannah's right," Julie confirmed it when Matt told her Hannah's theory. "The twins came into my office yesterday morning while I was getting my e-mail. Larry said he wanted to see if I had the latest virus protection and he offered to teach me how to check. I was busy with him, and I didn't pay much attention to Gary."

"That must be when Larry got your password and Gary set the alarm clock."

Julie thought about it for a moment. "I remember Larry asking me to type in my password so he could download an update to my security program. It all makes sense."

"I think Spenser must have planned it. He's quite the strategist. That boy is going to go far."

"Let's just hope he doesn't turn to a life of crime. He might just get away with it. He almost did this time."

"That was my fault." Matt slipped his arm around Julie's shoulders. "I should have trusted you when you said you didn't have a fiancé."

"And I should have been more insistent that you listen to me. I just gave up without a fight."

"We'll learn," Matt promised, bending down to kiss her. "With every day that passes, we'll trust each other more."

"Yes, we will," Julie agreed. And as he pulled her tightly

into his arms, it was as if the whole misunderstanding had been a bad dream and they'd never been apart for an instant.

Hannah pulled aside the curtains and peered out at the driveway. Her family and friends should arrive any minute. When Jordan High's cook, Edna Ferguson, had heard that Julie and her young charges were going to eat frozen dinners for the holiday, she'd volunteered to come out and cook a "proper" Christmas Eve dinner.

The two men Hannah was dating, Mike Kingston and Norman Rhodes, had volunteered next. Along with Lisa's husband, Herb, and Andrea's husband, Bill, they were bringing out snowmobiles to entertain the boys. Not to be outdone, Andrea had offered to take charge of the girls and decorate Aames House for Christmas. There would be presents, of course. Hannah's mother had organized that. And Hannah would bake her special Christmas Date Cake complete with the surprises her mother had suggested.

The big grandfather clock in the lobby had just struck noon when the first car drove up with Edna Ferguson and her sister, Hattie. Hannah rushed to the door to greet them, and then she called for Matt and the boys to help them carry in their load of goodies for the holiday feast.

The next to arrive was Andrea, and she brought Tracey, baby Bethany, and her live-in nanny, "Grandma" McCann. Once Julie and the girls had exclaimed over the baby and made Tracey feel welcome, Hannah got baby and nanny settled in the lounge while Andrea took the girls off to unpack the decorations she'd brought.

Just about the time good smells were beginning to waft in from the kitchen, Bill and Mike drove in, towing a large three-passenger snowmobile behind Mike's Hummer. Hannah's other boyfriend, Norman, was next, and he was also towing a snowmobile. Lisa's husband, Herb, was right behind him with the third, and when the boys raced out to look at the snowmobiles, Matt turned to Hannah.

"Is all this for us?" he asked.

Hannah shrugged, but she was smiling. "I just mentioned that I was coming out to spend Christmas Eve with you, and the word spread. The guys decided to take the boys out for a ride and give you a little break this afternoon."

"That's really nice of them."

"They're all nice guys. Mike's got a Christmas tree in the back of his Hummer. Why don't you go out and help him carry it in before he takes off on his snowmobile with the kids?"

Once the tree was inside and securely fixed in the stand, Andrea and the girls began to decorate it. Matt watched the boys leave with the four men, and Hannah thought he looked a bit lost.

"Is there anything you need me to do while they're gone?" Matt asked her.

"Yes," Hannah said, her mind racing to think of something he could do with Julie. "Andrea could use some mistletoe for her decorations. I spotted some hanging from the old oak tree near the end of the driveway when I drove in. Would you and Julie go out to cut some?"

With everyone busy and happy, Hannah was about to head for the kitchen to bake her cake when her mother arrived. Delores was dressed for the occasion in a red satin pantsuit that would have looked ridiculous on any other Lake Eden woman even approaching her age. She wore gold high-heeled shoes and carried a gold-beaded purse. Anyone who saw her for the first time immediately knew how Andrea had acquired her perfect petite figure and her sense of fashion.

"Nice outfit, Mother," Hannah said, taking her mother's coat.

"Thank you, dear. I wanted to be festive." Delores reached

in her purse and drew out a tissue-wrapped packet. "I brought the silver charms for the cake, dear."

"Thanks. And speaking of the cake, I'd better go make it." Hannah headed for the kitchen at a trot. Once there, she worked fast, getting out the ingredients she'd brought with her and mixing up her batter. She was just slipping the cake into the oven when Julie came into the kitchen.

"You look happy," Hannah remarked, noticing that her younger friend was practically glowing.

"That's because I *am* happy. I think Matt's going to ask me to marry him, Hannah. And I wouldn't be surprised if it's tonight."

"Uh-oh," Hannah said, thinking of the boys and their bet. Then she noticed the frown on Julie's face and hurried to re-assure her. "I'm delighted, Julie. I think you and Matt are perfect for each other. There's just one small problem. Come over to the sink with me while I wash these things, and I'll tell you all about it."

Hannah finished explaining the terms of the bet about the same time Julie dried the last bowl. "I know they deserve to lose for what they've done. And doing the girls' chores won't be that bad."

"Oh yes it will. You have no idea how the other boys will tease Spenser when he has to work for Mrs. Dryer in the kitchen. And the twins will just die if they have to follow Mrs. Caulder around the mall. I want Matt to ask me to marry him, but I don't want the boys to suffer. Isn't there a way that the boys and the girls could both win?"

Hannah thought about that for a minute, and then she started to smile. "No, but there's a way they could both lose. It'll take some doing and you'll have to clue in Matt, but I think it should work."

When the last succulent bite of roast turkey had been eaten, and the final morsel of sweet potato with marshmallow and brown sugar topping had found a willing mouth, it was time to serve the dessert.

"Will you explain dessert, Mother?" Hannah asked, turning to Delores.

"Yes, dear," Delores stood up and smiled at everyone seated around the oval table. "We're having a Regency Love Cake for dessert."

"What's that, Mrs. Swensen?" Serena asked, clearly enthralled by the concept.

"It's a little something they served at parties in England in the early nineteenth century. Hannah has baked the modern-day version, a Christmas Date Cake. Each piece has a little prize inside, a small keepsake to remind you of this marvelous Christmas Eve. It's wrapped in a foil packet so you won't inadvertently eat it."

"That's good," Norman said, and everyone laughed.

"All the prizes are the same," Delores went on, "except for one. And that special prize is what makes it a Regency Love Cake."

"What's the special prize, Mrs. Swensen?" Joy asked.

"A gold ring. Is everybody here willing to abide by the old Regency rules and reveal the name of the person they love if they get the piece with the gold ring?"

The adults at the table laughed and nodded. In sharp contrast, the kids looked very uncomfortable.

"But Mrs. Swensen," Spenser gulped slightly. "What if we don't have someone we love?"

Delores smiled to reassure him. "Don't worry, Spenser. The gold ring is only for adults. If you or one of your friends gets it, just give it to me and I'll pass it on to Hannah."

Hannah gave her mother a dirty look. Delores was matchmaking again.

"And now it's time for the Regency Love Cake." Delores walked over to dim the lights, and Hannah ducked in the kitchen to light the candles on the platter of cake. Each piece had a dollop of whipped cream on top to camouflage the spot where she'd inserted the prize. She quickly located the piece with the double swirl of whipped cream and carried the platter out to the applause of the kids and the assembled guests.

Once the candles were blown out and the lights were back on, Hannah plated the cake the way they'd planned, making certain that Julie got the piece with the double swirl. She gave Julie a conspiratorial wink, and then she put on her best guileless smile.

Everyone tasted the cake and pronounced it excellent, and one by one, they found their prizes, a little silver whistle for everyone except . . .

Julie unwrapped her prize and let out a little shriek. "Oh my!" she exclaimed, acting very surprised. "I've got the gold ring!"

"How marvelous, dear!" Delores reached over to pat her on the shoulder. "You're our lucky winner. Will you tell us the name of the person you love?"

Julie nodded, blushing slightly as she smiled at Matt. "It's Matt and I'll give him this ring if he'll marry me."

Matt did a good job of feigning surprise, but he quickly recovered. "Yes, I will. Remember the day I went out to the mall to pick up a few gifts for the kids? Well, I stopped at the jewelry store and bought an engagement ring for you. I was planning on asking you to marry me later tonight, but you beat me to the punch."

"Oh no!" Spenser groaned as Matt reached over and placed the ring on Julie's finger. "Mr. Sherwood asked her to marry him!"

"No, he didn't," Larry pointed out. "Miss Jansen asked . . ."

". . . Mr. Sherwood to marry *her*," Gary finished the thought.

"Then we win the bet?" It was clear that Spenser could scarcely believe his good fortune.

"What bet?" Delores asked.

"I'll explain later," Hannah told her, and then she turned

to Spenser. "You lose the bet, Spenser. You bet the girls that Mr. Sherwood and Miss Jansen wouldn't get engaged until after Christmas was over. Take a look at that ring on her finger. They're engaged."

"So you have to do *our* chores!" Serena crowed, giving Joy and Hope a high five. "We win!"

"No, you don't," Hannah said, taking great relish in pointing it out. "You bet that Mr. Sherwood would ask Miss Jansen to marry him, and that didn't happen. Miss Jansen asked Mr. Sherwood instead."

"So we both lost?" Spenser asked, looking very confused.

"That depends on your point of view. I think you both won. The important thing is that no one has to do anyone else's chores."

"Right!" Spenser said, smiling again. "I don't think I want to bet on anything again for a really long time."

"Good idea," Hannah said, glad that he'd learned something from the experience.

"There's one more thing we have to do before this Christmas Eve dinner is over," Andrea said, nudging Bill.

Bill stood up and lifted Tracey onto his shoulders. He walked over to the beam where the ball of mistletoe was hanging, and Tracey reached up to remove it. Then Bill took her over to Matt and Julie, and she leaned forward to hold the mistletoe over Julie's head.

"You know what mistletoe means, don't you?" she asked.

"I certainly do," Matt said, taking his cue and leaning over to kiss his bride-to-be to the accompaniment of cheers from everyone there.

CHRISTMAS DATE CAKE

Preheat oven to 325 degrees F.,
rack in the middle position.

Hannah's Note: This recipe is from my Grandma Ingrid. She used to make this cake every Christmas.

2 cups chopped pitted dates *(You can buy chopped dates, or sprinkle whole pitted dates with flour and then chop them in a food processo.)*
3 cups boiling water
2 teaspoons baking soda

Pour the boiling water over the dates, add the soda *(it foams up a bit),* and set them aside to cool. While they're cooling, cream the following ingredients together in a large mixing bowl:

1 cup soft or melted butter *(2 sticks, ½ pound)*
2 cups white *(granulated)* sugar
4 eggs
½ teaspoon salt
3 cups flour *(don't sift—pack it down in the cup when you measure it)*

Once the above are thoroughly mixed, add the cooled date mixture to your bowl and stir thoroughly.

Butter and flour a 9-inch by 13-inch rectangular cake pan. *(This cake rises about an inch and a half, so make sure the sides are tall enough.)* Pour the batter into the pan. Then sprinkle the following on the top, in this order, BEFORE baking:

12 ounces chocolate chips *(2 cups)*
1 cup white *(granulated)* sugar
1 cup chopped nuts *(use any nuts you like—I prefer walnuts or pecans)*

Bake at 325 degrees F. for 80 minutes. A cake tester or a long toothpick should come out clean one inch from the center when the cake is done. *(If you happen to stick the toothpick in and hit a chocolate chip, it'll come out covered with melted chocolate—just wipe it off and stick it in again to test the actual cake batter.)*

Let the cake cool in the pan on a wire rack. It can be served slightly warm, at room temperature, or chilled.

If you want to be truly decadent, serve it the way Hannah did in the story, with a generous dollop of sweetened whipped cream on each slice.

Index of Recipes

Baking Conversion Chart

These conversions are approximate, but they'll work just fine for Hannah Swensen's recipes.

VOLUME:

U.S.	Metric
½ teaspoon	2 milliliters
1 teaspoon	5 milliliters
1 tablespoon	15 milliliters
¼ cup	50 milliliters
⅓ cup	75 milliliters
½ cup	125 milliliters
¾ cup	175 milliliters
1 cup	¼ liter

WEIGHT:

U.S.	Metric
1 ounce	28 grams
1 pound	454 grams

OVEN TEMPERATURE:

Degrees Fahrenheit	Degrees Centigrade	British (Regulo) Gas Mark
325 degrees F.	165 degrees C.	3
350 degrees F.	175 degrees C.	4
375 degrees F.	190 degrees C.	5

Note: Hannah's rectangular sheet cake pan, 9 inches by 13 inches, is approximately 23 centimeters by 32.5 centimeters.

Twelve Days

SHIRLEY JUMP

Shirley Jump's
White Chocolate Raspberry Thumbprints

½ cup butter
½ cup shortening
½ cup granulated sugar
½ cup powdered sugar
½ teaspoon baking soda
½ teaspoon cream of tartar
⅛ teaspoon salt
1 egg
½ teaspoon vanilla
2 cups all-purpose flour
⅓ cup seedless raspberry jam
1 cup white chocolate chips
Red sugar sprinkles

Trust me, these ones are so good, you won't have any left for guests (and whoever invented that rule about sharing your cookies, anyhow? It's Christmas, indulge yourself a little). In a large mixing bowl, beat the butter and the shortening with an electric mixier (or use a stand mixer and let the machine do the work), then add the sugar, powdered sugar, baking soda, cream of tartar, and the salt. Beat just until combined.

Add the egg and vanilla, then mix in the flour gradually. Cover the dough and refrigerate for 3 hours. I know, it's a long wait, but it'll be worth it later. Heat the oven to 375 degrees F. Roll the dough into ¾-inch balls and put them on an ungreased cookie sheet. With your thumb or the end of a wooden spoon, press a circular indentation into the center of each cookie. Drop a ¼ teaspoon of jam into each thumbprint. Bake cookies for 8 to 10 minutes, then cool on a wire rack for 5 minutes.

Meanwhile, pour yourself a glass of milk and get into serious cookie-eating mode. Skip lunch if you have to—there's no way a tuna on rye can compete.

Put the white chocolate chips in a microwave-safe bowl and microwave on high in 30-second bursts, stirring each time, until the chips are melted. Pour the white chocolate into a resealable plastic bag and snip off a tiny bit of one corner. Drizzle the white chocolate over the cookies. Sprinkle cookies with red sugar to add a festive flair.

Now you're ready to indulge—don't worry about the calories until January 1st. Makes 3 dozen, just enough for you and a very special, handsome friend!

Chapter One

Natalie Harris knew exactly what Santa could bring her this year. Jake Lyons. Wrapped with a red bow—

And nothing else. No need for a stocking or, hell, so much as a piece of tissue paper. Boxers—or briefs—all completely optional.

If she woke up December 25th and found Jake beside the tiny tabletop tree in her breadbox-size apartment in Boston, she'd grab him by that bow, haul him off to her bedroom and make sure he made a few of her bells jingle. Many, many times over.

Blame it on hormones. That peppermint mocha latte she'd bought at Starbucks this morning. The fact that he'd worn the blue shirt that set off his eyes. There was just something . . . different about Jake today, something that had taken her interest in him from bemused curiosity to full-out cubicle-born fantasy.

"What did he do after that?"

The little voice reminded her she wasn't supposed to be staring at the man five feet away. She was supposed to be reading *Bear's Christmas Wish* and focusing on G-rated material instead of the NC–17 thoughts of a woman who had clearly gone way too long without a little something under her tree.

Natalie cleared her throat and refocused her attention on the book, dipping her head to read the words from above the out-turned pages. "And then, the bear cuddled up with the boy and went to sleep, all snug in a bed. The very type of bed he had dreamed about when he'd been sitting in McGuffy's Toy Shop, waiting for someone just like this boy to take him home. The bear's Christmas wish had come true. He had someone to love and someone who loved him in return." Natalie closed the book, laid it across her lap and faced the circle of children at her feet. "The end."

The book might be finished, but her hormones sure weren't. Every single one of them was zeroed in on Jake, like some kind of estrogen sonar. He had one hip against a scarred wooden desk, his intent blue eyes watching her read to the children of Our Hope Shelter. His dark hair was a bit longer than he usually kept it, which made one lock sweep across his brow. Beneath the well-pressed, slightly starched shirt lurked a pair of six-pack abs and a trim, tight waist.

In other words, one manly slice of heaven.

She and Jake had been coming to the shelter in Boston for four months, always on the third Wednesday at eleven. While Natalie hurried to be with the children, Jake usually stayed away from the room's pandemonium, opting for the director's office. There, he lent a hand in balancing the shelter's books, saving them the cost of a CPA, and often made a corporate donation while he waited for Natalie to finish story time. But today—of all days—he'd followed Natalie into the vast, open "family" room of the shelter.

Making her nervous as hell and sending her thoughts down Under the Sheets Lane.

"Didn't the bear have a name?" asked David, who was sitting at her feet, as close as he could get without actually climbing in her lap. David Wilkins had latched onto her from the very first day. His was a story much like that of the others in the room—raised in a single-parent home that had slipped through the cracks of government-support programs and ended up here, after spending an entire season living out of a car. His dark brown eyes were sharp and attentive, yet tinged with a weariness that seemed sadly very grown up. Natalie wanted to reach out, tug him into her arms and stuff him full of cookies.

"The author didn't name the bear in the story," Natalie said, smiling down at David. "So you can make up your own name."

Ariana popped her thumb out of her mouth. "Let's call him Teddy!"

"No, Buster!" piped up Jacob. The towheaded five-year-old had read every book in the popular *Arthur* series at least three times and thought everyone in the world should be named after the aardvark's best bunny friend.

A name debate sprung up among the two dozen children, rising in volume with every idea. Natalie tried to restore order, looking around hopefully for the shelter's assistant director, who usually did crowd control. But there was no sign of Kitty Planter, which meant she'd probably taken advantage of story hour to grab a few minutes of peace or to check in on the job-hunting class most of the parents were attending in another room. "Children," Natalie called to the scattering, chatty bunch. "If you don't sit down, I can't read you another story."

They didn't listen. Filled with cabin fever from the freezing December weather, they'd been antsy the whole story hour. Natalie's voice had about as much impact as a gnat trying to hold back a herd of elephants. Plus, they all knew Natalie was a complete pushover who'd do encore readings until the director kicked her out. "Children, I—"

Jake pushed off from the desk and crossed the room. He

had the walk of a man who had the world at his fingertips—
but the confidence not to flaunt it. Natalie's eyes met his, and
for a second, she forgot to breathe.

"Want some help?" he asked.

"Sh-sh-sh . . . sure." Oh hell, there she went again. Whenever she got near a man, particularly one who gave goose-
bumps a whole 'nother meaning, she stuttered. Not just
stumbling over a couple of words, but full out Porky Pig bab-
ble.

It had been that way since she'd been a kid. Only then,
she'd stuttered with everyone and everything. A couple
dozen years of speech therapy and she'd learned coping
techniques. They'd always worked—

Until she got around Jake.

But if Jake noticed, he didn't show it. Instead, he smiled,
then pivoted toward the children. At six-foot-two, he towered
over them, like Gulliver in the land of Lilliputians. "Everyone
who sits quietly and listens to Miss Harris read another story,"
Jake said, his deep voice automatically commanding attention, "gets a dollar."

En masse, the group scrambled back onto their carpet
squares, hands clasped, faces upturned, waiting and expectant.

"You're *p-p-paying* them to be g-g-good?" Natalie whispered. Or rather, jerked out like a complete social moron.

If Jake noticed her vocal ineptitude, he didn't mention it.
"Money talks a hel—" he cut off the curse before the curious
ears around them heard it, "a whole *lot* louder than words."

"Yeah, b-b-but . . ."

"Your audience awaits, Miss Harris," he said, sweeping a
hand toward the children. Then he smiled at her.

Holy cow. Natalie had thought he looked sexy in a blue
shirt. Found him mesmerizing when he stood across the
room and watched her. But when he smiled . . .

The unnamed bear wasn't the only one dreaming of a bed

tonight. Only her thoughts involved a whole lot more than cuddling.

As Jake dispensed the promised George Washingtons, Natalie moved toward the chair, about to sit down with another book from the stack on the table, when Bobby tugged at her sleeve. "We want him to read to us." He pointed at Jake.

"I really think Miss Harris is a better choice." Jake gestured toward her.

If she hadn't known better, Natalie would have sworn Jake looked nervous. But Jake never got flustered, never lost his cool, no matter what idiot decision his CEO cousin had made that day at the accounting firm where she worked. "Here," she said, pressing a book into his hands. "You'll do fine. They're an easy audience to please."

"I, ah, don't do well with kids," he said, leaning over to whisper in her ear.

"What's to do? You read, you pull a few Sh-sh-shakespearean stunts here and there, and t-t-toss everyone a c-c-candy cane when you're done. Easy as ch-ch-cherry pie."

He grinned. "I don't bake either."

"Well, maybe someday, I'll make you dessert." She'd meant it as a joke, one of those offhand comments thrown into a conversation, but the promise inherent in the words held innuendo. Anticipation.

They were also the first words she'd spoken that hadn't come out sounding like they'd been through a shredder.

Every time she got near Jake, she wanted to take the thoughts in her brain and put them into action, to actually *act* as aggressive as she felt. But the minute she opened her mouth and started stuttering like a car with a bad battery, her self-confidence went running.

"Come *on*," Bobby said, impatient with the adults. He tugged at Jake, dragging him away from Natalie and over to the chair, with all the timing of a drunk rooster. Natalie would have liked to see where the conversation would have gone. Start with dessert . . . move onto the beefcake?

But Jake was already surrounded by children, like a bread crumb in an anthill. As soon as Jake sat down, the kids scooched and squished back into a semicircle.

Jake sent a helpless look toward Natalie. She gave him an encouraging grin, then stepped back, taking his place against the desk.

"Uh, this book is, ah, about . . ." Jake looked down at the slim colorful hardcover on his lap as if he'd forgotten Natalie handing it to him, "Santa Claus. And, ah, his favorite . . . ah . . . reindeer."

Natalie bit back a laugh. Jake sounded more like her than he knew. For a man who could handle office politics with the finesse of a piano tuner, who managed to insert some calming sense into Brad's insane bright ideas and who had done more for Lyons Corporation in the last five months than anyone had in the last five years, he seemed positively out of his element when it came to children.

"I believe in Santa," Ariana said, her big brown eyes looking up at him. "Do you?"

"Uh, sure." Jake flipped through the first couple pages to get to the beginning of the story.

"What's he bringing you this year?"

Jake glanced at Natalie, "help me" clear in his eyes.

"Ariana," Natalie said, "you know Santa only brings things to kids, not grown-ups."

The little girl digested that, then turned to Jake again. "Then what'd he bring you when you were a kid?" Ariana pressed on, a terrier with a Nylabone.

Jake cleared his throat and shifted in his seat. "He, ah, didn't come to my house."

Natalie sat back against the desk, watching Jake and wondering what kind of childhood lacked a visit from the jolly red guy. As far as she knew, he was the kind of man who had everything—

Everything except Santa visits, apparently.

"Haven't you seen the movie?" Ariana said. "If you have a house, he *always* comes. 'Cept not for me, 'cuz we don't have a house now."

"Well, ah—" He glanced up at Natalie, panic in his eyes.

She couldn't let him flounder anymore, even if she was as curious as the children to know about the lack of a Claus presence. "Mr. Lyons traveled a lot as a child," she said, throwing out the first excuse she could come up with that seemed to fit with what little she knew about Jake, "so sometimes it was hard for Santa to find him."

The kids pondered this, connecting the information with all their Santa legends. "Does that mean he won't find us here?" Ariana said.

"He will," Natalie assured the children. "I've talked to him myself and let him know that all of you are living here for now."

"Thank you," Ariana said, her voice sweet and soft, and making Natalie wish she had twice the Christmas gift budget from Lyons Corp that she did. These children needed so much, beyond a few toys. They needed homes and help.

Despite spending most of her weekends and most of her time off there, helping the families with everything from job applications to welfare forms, Natalie realized she was only one woman and she could only do so much without big-time corporate support.

Unfortunately, Brad held onto every tax deductible penny like he had Super Glue stuck to his fingers.

Natalie glanced at the clock. "Mr. Lyons doesn't have a lot of time, so we better start the story. Okay?" The kids nodded, resettled themselves in position and looked up, expectant. "Do we get paid to listen to the story too?" Victor asked from the back.

"No," Natalie said, then laughed and leaned down to whisper in Jake's ear, taking her time with the words so they came out right. "I think you've created a monster."

He chuckled. "At least it's one driven by capitalism. We could be breeding future entrepreneurs here."

"Or bank r-r-robbers." He laughed again, then she waved a flourishing hand in Jake's direction. "Mr. Lyons?"

He cleared his throat, then began the book. The first few pages were filled with the same nervous pauses, but then, just as the reindeer in the story found his footing, Jake did too, adding some flourish to his words, a few dramatic gestures and noises. The children leaned forward, rapt and still, as captured by Jake's voice as Natalie.

Did this man have any faults? If so, she couldn't see them, not right now, not while the six-foot hunk was crunched into a preschooler chair, making reindeer grunts.

Two minutes later, the shelter's director came into the room, effectively ending the session in time for lunch. Jake rose and handed the book back to Natalie. "Thanks for rescuing me back there."

She shrugged. "It was n-n-nothing." Oh, hell, there she went again.

"This was fun. Really fun. I had no idea reading a book could be so . . . rewarding." A smile crossed his face. Not an ordinary smile, but the kind that socked her in her stomach, putting Tom Cruise's famous dimples to shame.

"It is," she agreed. "The k-k-kind of experience that s-s-stays with you."

Much the way Jake was looking at her right now was going to stay in her memory for a long time.

"Those kids love you," he said. "You must be here a lot more than once a month."

"I help out. Th-th-the kids, they're like f-f-family, I guess."

He watched as the children filed out of the room, chattering happily about the upcoming holiday. Pots and pans clattered in the kitchen, someone's name was announced on the loudspeaker system for a phone call on line two, but Natalie barely heard any of it.

All she noticed was Jake Lyons and the way he was staring at her.

"I can see that," he said. "But you . . . you really wowed me today. You're great with them."

"Th-th-thanks." Damn that stutter. She'd be better off taping her mouth shut.

He took a step closer, his deep blue gaze sweeping over her, as if he'd just noticed her—*really* noticed her—for the first time. "We'll have to do this again sometime."

"I'll do it anytime with you," she said, the words a whisper. Too late, she realized what she'd said. Lacking a recall button for verbal idiots, she had to stand there, watching Jake's lips curve up into a grin as the meaning hit him.

"You're not what I expected, Natalie Harris," he said, then chucked her under the chin. "See you around the office."

Chapter Two

Brad Lyons entered the front office of Lyons Corporation, stopping by the first cubicle in his notice-me light blue suit, the one that made him look more like Merv Griffin than Diddy. If Natalie hadn't seen the family photos hanging in Brad's office, she'd never have believed Jake shared a bloodline with his wannabee-pimpin' cousin.

As Brad approached, Natalie ducked down into her cubicle and feigned busyness. Kind of hard to do, considering she, Angie, and Tim were all in there, sharing a Harry & David gift box that had arrived in that day's mail.

The chocolate was a necessary medical intervention after her encounter with Jake earlier. The man she had a total lust crush on had chucked her under the chin, for God's sake, like she was a five-year-old who'd presented him with a Crayola masterpiece.

Brad stopped in the center of cubicle world and cleared his throat. "Has anyone seen the *effulgence* of the lobby Christmas tree?" He pressed a hand to his chest. "I ordered it to be decorated myself. It has a certain *joie de vivre,* don't you agree?"

Not one of the two dozen people working for Lyons Corporation did so much as pop up a gopher head out of their cubicle, long since unimpressed with Brad's mangling of *Merriam-Webster*.

"I thought you blocked the Word of the Day from his computer," Angie muttered to Tim, the resident techno-geek.

"I did. Suck-up Sam probably found a way around it." Tim pushed off with his heels, sending his rolling chair across the puce carpet and back into his own square space.

As if on cue, Sam, an intern from Boston College who had clearly paid attention in Sycophant 101, stood and sent an air high five toward Brad. "Great word, boss."

"Thanks." Brad straightened his tie, proud as a dog who'd just unearthed a muddy tennis ball. "Or should I say, I extend my gratitude to your commendation?"

Natalie bit back a groan. She was all for increasing vocabulary, but not at the expense of perfectly good words.

"*Tim,*" Angie hissed. "If you don't block that site from the servers, I swear, I will shove your gigabytes up your—"

"I know, I know. I'll get right on it." Tim turned to his computer. "I promise, by morning, Brad will be back to two-syllable words."

Natalie asked herself for the hundredth time why she still worked here. She'd spent a year at the supersized accounting firm, stuck in a box no bigger than her apartment's bathroom, shuffling paperwork for billion dollar businesses. When she'd come to work for Brad, he had promised her a position overseeing the nonprofit side of Lyons Corp.

A side that had never materialized. The closest Brad had come to philanthropic work had been his support of her shelter reading program, something she had spent six months lobbying for, pestering him on a daily basis until he'd relented, agreeing only if she made up every hour she invested in the program.

Since she'd started volunteering at the shelter, Natalie had finally started feeling like she was doing something that had meaning. That she was repaying, just a little, all that had been done for her.

Still, it wasn't enough. She wanted to do more, to accomplish more. The taste of charity had created a need in her for a life that was more. More fulfilling, more adventurous, more than just an existence.

To that end, it was time to move on, to find a job that was more meaningful than a Kleenex.

And to take a chance with her love life instead of being so held back by her stuttering issues.

Natalie's gaze strayed across the room to the man sitting behind the glass walls, and she knew why she was still here, stuck in a dead-end job working for Brad the Buffoon.

Because of the view. A bird's-eye one of Jake, all day, every day. He'd started here five months ago, just when Natalie had started dusting off her resume.

And promptly put it back in the drawer the first time Jake talked to her.

Today, after they'd finished at the shelter and she'd returned to the office, she'd hoped Jake would say something—anything— to explain his new interest in her reading abilities and to capitalize on her growing lust for a man who could bond with kids as easily as he could send her heart racing.

But he'd hopped in a separate cab, telling her he had a meeting. By the time he came back to the office, she was busy sorting out a client's depreciation mess and didn't get a chance to talk to him, never mind brush by him at the watercooler. He'd been holed up in the glass office ever since.

Besides, it was clear the man had no interest in her, Natalie told herself as she popped a fourth chocolate truffle into her mouth. He clearly found her about as sexy as a pair of fuzzy dice.

"All right, everyone, attention on me," Brad said, straightening his maroon tie. "I have a couple of announcements that will surely bedazzle the holidays for all you office drones."

The gopher heads popped up. "Everyone gets a raise because it's Christmas?" said Joe, who hadn't mastered a thing in the office except FreeCell. Above him, one of the fluorescent lights flickered like a strobe at a cheesy disco.

The boss laughed. "Good one, Matthews. I'll have to remember that for April Fool's Day."

Angie groaned and popped another handful of Moose Munch into her mouth. "Asshole," she muttered through the crunching.

"First," Brad went on, "we're going to instigate a Secret Santa exchange." He raised his hands as if warding off objections. "I know, I know, all of you want to amass the presents on me this year, but in the spirit of the holidays, I'm going to share the wealth."

"Damn. There goes my Fruitcake of the Month idea," Angie whispered.

"Each of you will retain and will become a Secret Santa. Tomorrow marks twelve days until Christmas, so we'll embark on a Twelve Days of Christmas theme. Isn't that a brilliant initiative?"

"Technically, Mr. Lyons," Natalie said, "the Twelve Days of Christmas fall after Christmas and lead up to—"

"I say *these* are the twelve days before Christmas." He eyed her, daring her to disagree.

Angie handed her a Post-it with "Monster.com" written on it. "You and me, we'll make a break for it," she whispered.

Natalie glanced again at Jake, on a call in his glass-walled office. He was standing, talking into the earbud of his cell phone, commanding attention, even across cellular lines. She was crazy to think she'd seen interest in him earlier. And she was even crazier for hanging onto a sucky job just because she had a crush.

"Do you want to draw names?" Sam said, rushing toward Brad, nearly salivating with enthusiasm. "Here, I can put them all down." He grabbed a yellow legal pad off Natalie's desk.

"Hey! Those are my notes."

Sam ignored her, tearing the yellow paper into tiny pieces, scribbling the names of everyone in the office on them, then dumped Natalie's deep—and full—in-box onto her desk. He thrust the names inside the now-empty mesh container, then rushed over to the boss, like the simpering fool that he was. "Here you are."

"Good assessment, Sam." Brad might as well have patted the intern on his head and handed him a Milk-Bone. "For that, you can select the first nomenclature."

Sam made a big production of rooting around, then pulling out a slip of paper. He opened it, read the name, smiled to himself and walked away.

"What do you bet he drew the boss?" Tim said.

"Better him than us," Natalie said.

"What, and miss an opportunity for a good suck-up? There could be a raise in it for you, Miss Harris," Tim mocked.

One by one, they each went up and drew a name. Everyone except Karl, who called himself a "conscientious objector to the overt capitalism of the holiday season."

"No fruitcake for him," Natalie whispered to Angie.

Her friend laughed, then headed up to pull a name out of the box. She flashed "Sam" and a frown at Natalie. "At least it's better than having Jonathan," Angie said when she reached her desk again.

"I thought they fired him."

"Nope, he's still here. He seals himself in the janitor's closet every day. Something about the radiation levels in the office or something. I think Brad's afraid of a workers' comp suit."

"Dena?" Brad called, then made no secret of watching her flagrant approach.

The new receptionist trotted forward, her breast implants

high and prominent, like a one-woman billboard for *Dr. 90210*. Her leather miniskirt sashayed, and with it, the eyes of every man in the room, except for Waldo, who was on a one-man quest for a lifetime of celibacy. Judging by the XXX movies Waldo rented on his lunch breaks, he had the one-man thing down.

"I hate her," Natalie said, gesturing toward Dena.

"Hey, I'm president of her non–fan club. Especially since she stole Joe before I could even get out the door to go to lunch with him."

Dena's flirting had drawn the UPS driver's attention last month, never to return again to Angie, not after he'd taken a few spins down Dena Drive.

Now he delivered all his packages personally to Dena—who gave the words *confirmation signature* a whole new meaning.

Brad gestured toward Natalie. "Nettie," he said.

One year here and the boss had yet to learn her name. Clearly a sign she should leave.

"Good luck," Angie whispered.

Natalie strode across the room. She hoped she didn't draw Clive's name. Clive was convinced he was a Klingon and therefore not allowed to speak English. With a sigh, she closed her eyes, dipped her hand into the box and pulled out a folded slip of paper.

"Aren't you going to look and see who it is?" Angie asked when Natalie walked back to her cubicle. "You could have drawn my name."

"Fate isn't that kind, believe me. I bet I got the new mail room guy."

"The one who brings fried bugs for his lunch? Isn't he trying out for *Fear Factor* or something?"

Natalie grinned. "I could get him an ant farm. Or an exterminator's license."

"Now you're stalling," Angie said, reaching forward and

yanking the tiny slip of paper out of Natalie's hand before she could stop her. "Holy shit."

"What?"

Angie turned the paper toward Natalie.

She looked at the name, blinked, then looked again. But the four letters hadn't changed. "Oh God, I can't have him. I'll—"

"Take this as the awesome opportunity it is and run with it. How long are you going to have a crush and not act on it? Besides, if we stick to our plan to ditch this place after the first, you can't leave without at least giving Jake a ride around the moon."

"I couldn't." Natalie paused. "I shouldn't."

"Come on, Nat. Live a little. Take a chance. What's the worst that could happen? You could end up with that"—she pointed toward Jake, who had loosened his tie and the top two buttons of his shirt, making him sexier than anything Calvin Klein had ever put on a billboard—"in your bed?"

"Well, now that you put it that way . . ." Natalie said, grinning. She had gone way too long complaining about her stagnant life. She'd finally broken off her on-again, off-again relationship with Steve this past summer. Making that change had left her feeling empowered. Finally, she, Natalie Harris, master stutterer, was taking the reins.

Maybe she could do the same with Jake. After all, hadn't he been a huge help to her in the last couple of months? Helping her work her way up in the company? Whenever she asked him a question or didn't understand a transaction, he took his time to explain things to make sure she had a grasp on the task before she left his office.

If he took that much time explaining the ins and outs of corporate tax laws, what would he do with a very different kind of education? The kind that happened in her bedroom, between the sheets?

"As a Secret Santa, you don't have to talk to him," Angie said, her voice low in Natalie's ear. "But you can communicate in other ways. Like by sending him a garter belt and directions to your apartment."

Natalie wasn't going to go that far, but maybe she could play a different game. She was creative. Surely she could come up with a solution that would give her cake and a bite of it too.

Because if she didn't do it now, she'd never have another chance. After the holidays, she was going to take Angie's advice and find a new job, one that allowed her to repay the community that had helped her so many years ago. The shelter program was a start, but it wasn't enough. Natalie wanted—no, needed—to make a bigger impact.

To do that, she had to do what Angie had said. Live a little. Take some risks. With her life, her career and most of all with the sexy man in the glass office.

If she didn't do it now, when would she?

"Remember, this is a secret only for twelve days," Angie said. "What are you going to do after that?"

Natalie grinned. "If all goes well, I'll be taking Jake Lyons for a sleigh ride. Or two."

Chapter Three

Jake would have preferred to skip Christmas altogether.

In fact, he had done exactly that in years past, jetting off to the Bahamas, the Caribbean or anywhere that didn't have a bunch of fat guys in red chortling ho, ho, ho.

But this year, before he could rack up some frequent flyer miles, he'd gone and promised his cousin he'd stay through the holidays to help with the company. Things had been going south for a long time. Brad needed him to help set them straight.

And then there was this Secret Santa thing. As part of a company effort to increase morale, Brad said Jake was expected to participate. Jake never bought presents. Never bothered with a tree. Never found a lot of use for a holiday that put a cheery red hat on creating credit card debt.

But here he was on Thursday morning, holding a box wrapped by one of the staff in Bath Essentials, marked for Natalie Harris in the salesperson's curly script.

Of all names to draw, that had been the last one he'd expected.

Until today, he hadn't exchanged more than a handful of

words with the shy account manager. He knew her mainly for her attention to detail, her commitment to staying until the job was done and her avoidance of him.

But then his curiosity had gotten the better of him and he'd found himself following her into the family center, to see what it was that made the children watch her, still and quiet, wrapped in the magic of her voice and her story-telling. He'd seen a different side of Natalie, one that had intrigued him. She was fun and inventive, with a creative edge that he'd never realized existed.

There was something about this woman, about the way she acted so shy yet seemed to be masking a side of herself that was a little wild. When she was passionate about something, like the Our Hope Shelter, Natalie displayed a very alluring tiger beneath her kitten exterior.

It had all ignited his imagination, along with the kind of continual need to see her that he hadn't felt since his first crush in seventh grade.

A soft knock sounded on his door, and he looked up. She was there, as if conjured up by his imagination. He gave the box a gentle push under his desk with his foot, then cleared his throat. "Natalie. How can I help you?"

"I-I-I—"

She was stuttering again. She only seemed to do that around him. Perhaps he made her nervous, though he couldn't for the life of him think of a reason why. Either way, for some weird reason, Jake found her stammered words endearing, not annoying.

Definitely a sign he needed to book a flight to Jamaica. Too much holiday Muzak and he was getting all sentimental.

"Do you need something?" he supplied when she kept doing the single-vowel dance.

"I-I-I want t-t-t—" Helpless, she held up a sheaf of papers he'd left for her to complete.

"Want my signature on the Maxten paperwork?"

She nodded, then moved forward and around his desk,

circumventing the piles of work that Brad had dumped on him over the last few days. The only clean space was directly in front of him. Reaching for it would topple the work mountains. Natalie paused a split second, then slipped into the space beside him, avoiding a teetering pile with the grace only a woman had, and laid the papers down.

Her perfume floated lightly on the air between them, a scent so warm and homey, it made him think of chocolate chip cookies and milk. The woman who wore the scent, however, had a body that took his mind to a place that had nothing to do with a kitchen or anything June Cleaver ever baked.

She wore a straight red skirt that ended at her knees, revealing strong, long legs set off by strappy black heels. A sparkling black holiday sweater grazed her curves, dipping a little in the front as she bent over to retrieve a pen and hand it to him, giving him a view of perfectly shaped breasts fringed by black lace.

Sexy. Intriguing. And definitely evidence of a lurking jungle cat.

"Jake?"

Her soft voice made him jerk his gaze away from her chest and back up to her face. "Sorry. Daydreaming."

More like fantasizing, but he kept that to himself.

"C-c-can you—" She gave up on the sentence and directed the pen toward him.

"Sure." He looked down at the document, and for a second, his mind went blank. "Where?"

She laughed, a quiet, very merry sound. "H-h-here." She flipped a couple of pages and pointed. Right beside the "Sign Here" Post-it.

Duh.

He scrawled his name across the line, then handed the papers up to her. When he did, their hands touched, sending an electric jolt through him.

Hell, you'd think he'd never touched a woman before the

way his body was reacting. It had to be the crooning of Dean Martin coming through the office speakers. Or maybe the sushi bordering on sashimi he'd had for lunch.

Or maybe he was getting soft. First he was reading stories to preschoolers, now he was actually *shopping* for Christmas and thinking about one of the employees in a way that had nothing to do with work.

"Someone gave you a poinsettia," she said, gesturing to the plant that had arrived that morning and was sitting in the corner, because he'd yet to clear a space for it. "I love them, don't you?"

"I'd love it a lot more if it could file and organize for me, but yeah, they're nice."

"When I was a little girl," she said softly, "my mother always had a pointsettia at Christmas. She said they brought good luck or something. But then . . . well, it wasn't true." A wistfulness appeared in her eyes.

"Take it," he said, gesturing to the plant. "I'm sure you'll give it a much better home than I will."

"Are you sure?"

With her smiling like that at him, he'd have bought her a whole damned nursery. "Absolutely."

"Thanks." She picked up the plant, then started to head out of his office. That smile, however, was the kind that stayed with a man, that starred in his fantasies. A smile he didn't want to see disappear, not yet. "Natalie?"

She pivoted back, her long brown hair swirling around her shoulders as she did. Jake had always thought of himself as a blonde man.

Until now.

"Y-y-yeah?"

"Uh, someone left your Secret Santa gift in here." He pulled the box out from under his desk and held it out to her.

For a second, she didn't move, just looked at the box, then at him. Oh shit. He'd just given out his secret. He hadn't thought about how "coincidental" this would be. All he'd been thinking about was seeing whether she smiled like that when she unwrapped the lotion or whatever the hell it was that he'd bought at the Bath Essentials store. Women's products weren't his forte.

Natalie reached for the box, took it out of his hands, then smiled again. He saw her swallow, then purse her lips, pause, then push a word out. "Thanks."

She turned to go again. "Aren't you going to open it?"

"I have t-t-to," she paused, drew in a breath. "Get back to work."

Then she was gone, leaving Jake's fantasy of seeing her smile again unfulfilled.

Damn.

He shook his head, then pulled one of the piles in front of him and vowed to tackle it instead of thinking about the pretty brunette. For one, she was too . . . nice. The kind of woman who had white picket fence expectations written all over her. For another, she worked in the same office and he knew all too well the disaster spelled by putting office and romance together.

And for a third—

He couldn't think of a third. But he was sure there was another really good reason for him to stop thinking about her, stop being mesmerized by this woman who had captured the hearts of the Our Hope Shelter under-eight set.

Not to mention every ounce of his attention. He sighed again, then opened the first file his hands touched. Time to focus on getting this company back up and running with the profitability it had had during his grandfather's tenure.

It didn't matter if Jake hated working with numbers, if every day he'd spent in college going after an accounting degree his father had chosen for him had been torture. The company was in trouble, it was part of the Lyons family, and Jake would suck it up and do what his father had asked of him because he was a Lyons and that meant something.

A quick rap sounded on his door. "Hey, Jakey, this one's for you." Brad ticktocked a brightly wrapped package.

Being a Lyons clearly meant something else to Brad, who had to be from a whole other gene pool.

Jake gritted his teeth, both against the nickname and the intrusion of his cousin. Brad thought nothing of popping in, propping his feet up on the desk and rambling on for two or three hours about nothing. No matter how many times Jake tried to tell him he had work to do, Brad still did it.

Because Brad didn't do a damned thing around the office and everyone knew it. Leaving things squarely in "Jakey's" lap.

He took the gift from his cousin. "Thanks."

"I know something you don't know," Brad said, leaning forward and grinning. "Like who your Secret Santa is."

"All right, I'll bite. Who?"

"Dena. Don't know why I didn't think to snag her myself. I wouldn't mind her thanking me under the mistletoe." He grinned. "I might have even gone over the ten dollar limit just to have that happen."

"Dena?" Jake looked down at the gift. It was small, perhaps three inches on each side, and wrapped in a velvety festive paper, secured by a thick crimson ribbon. Attached to that was a small white envelope, his name and FROM YOUR SECRET SANTA written precisely across the front.

The word *Santa* brought up the memory of the shelter and the kids asking him about the jolly guy visits. Then Natalie, coming to his rescue, saving him from explaining that his father was too often out of town, off with the woman of the week, and his stepmother of that year was too busy socializing to think of perpetuating the myth for a little boy who was only one more thing underfoot.

No one in his life had ever gone to this much trouble, not for a present, and certainly not for Christmas.

For a man who didn't do Christmas, he was feeling downright nostalgic right now, looking at the jolly paper and the carefully tied bow.

None of which seemed to go along with the receptionist, who had all the organizational skills of a barrel of monkeys.

"Why do you think Dena is my Secret Santa?" Jake asked.

"I saw her, with this gift in her hands. She was going to try to deliver it personally, but I stopped her, so I could give you the heads up."

"Dena," Jake repeated, wondering why he felt so disappointed. On any other day, the thought of the busty Dena being interested in him would have had him planning a cozy weekend at a B&B and picking out a bottle of good champagne. Dena was his usual type—uncommitted, undemanding and yet, if he were honest with himself, also uninteresting.

Dena should have been the one he'd fantasized about last night. But for some reason, the woman starring in his late-night mind movies had been a leggy brunette who got all tangled up in her words.

"Mr. Lyons," Velma, Brad's assistant, poked her gray-haired head into the room and gave her boss a stern look. "You have kept a client on hold for ten minutes. I have already pulled his file, laid the paperwork on your desk and flagged the relevant information. Do you think you could possibly answer the phone?"

No one in the office messed with Velma. She'd been here since the dawn of time and made Nurse Ratchet look about as menacing as Gidget.

"Be sure to thank Dena in person," Brad said, giving him a wink-wink before leaving. Velma followed, shooing Brad back into his office like a mother goose.

Instead of getting back to work, Jake detached the card from the ribbon. Good paper stock. Careful writing. Clearly this was someone who had gone to more work than tipping the counter staff at Bath Essentials to slap some wrapping paper on a box.

Putting the card aside for now, Jake opened the package.

Inside, he found a small inscribed clock, set in a triangular-shaped stone. "True leaders climb the ladder of success," it read, "always keeping one hand free to help those behind them."

True leaders. He wouldn't say he was one of those, not even on his best day. Nevertheless, the thought that someone thought he was one—or had that potential—sent a smile to his face.

He went to put the clock back in the box, then stopped. He grabbed a stack of papers and files, looked around for a new location and finally put them on the floor, leaving a clear space. He took the clock and planted it squarely in the center of his desk.

He toyed with the card, weighing the wisdom of reading instead of tackling the long To Do list he had yet to conquer today.

The To Do list would be there tomorrow. He slit the envelope with a pearl-handled letter opener and then slid out the single sheet of paper inside.

Dear Jake,

A million times, I've wanted to tell you face-to-face how I feel. To put into words how much I admire you, and not just for your looks.

Okay, so I do admire your looks. Often. Especially that blue shirt that sets off your eyes and those gray pinstriped trousers—

Whoops. Got a little sidetracked there. Anyway, on this the "first" day of Christmas, I wanted to tell you something about firsts. You're the first thing I think of in the morning. The first man I've met who has sent me so off-kilter, I end up forgetting the simplest thing. The first man I've put this much thought into for a Christmas gift in . . . forever.

Maybe, when my identity is revealed, we can have coffee. Tea. More?

*In the meantime, this clock is here as a thank-you
for taking the time to look for those behind you and
offer them a hand up the ladder. I see a true leader in
you, in the way you handle everything around you.*

*As I write this, I don't know what you'll wear today
(the blue shirt . . . can I get that lucky twice?) but
knowing you as I do, I bet it will be a blend of both determination and compromise.*

*Just don't dry that shirt I love on cotton. I'd hate to
see anything about you shrink. ;-)*

SpiceGirl, your Secret Santa

A secret admirer. Hell, he hadn't had one of those in . . .
never. He turned the card over, looking for a hint, a clue.
Nothing. Jake glanced up, looking out at the cubicles. Same
as every day. Jerry was eating a pen cap, Ken had his cell
phone held up to one ear, his desk phone held up to the other,
feigning a business call. Brad was wandering the floor, chest
thrust forward like a peacock, and Dena, the receptionist,
was—

Staring at him.

She gave him a smile, then a two-finger wave.

Jake glanced down at the box, the card. Nah, it couldn't
be. Could it?

"Uh, Mr. Lyons?"

Natalie was back in his office, another pile of papers in
her hands.

"Yes?"

"I forgot. I needed you t-t-to," she drew in a breath, concentrated, then started again, "s-s-sign this one too."

"Oh, sure." He took the papers from her, gave them a
glance, then scrawled his signature across the bottom.

"Nice c-c-c—" Natalie let out a gust and with it, the word
that had gotten lodged on her tongue. "Cock."

Had he just heard what he thought? "Nice *what?*"

She flushed crimson. "Clock." She pointed toward the newest addition to his desk.

"Oh, yeah." Jake cleared his throat, trying to rid his mind of the mental images of Natalie Harris in his bedroom, helped along by her missing consonant. It was definitely time for some bourbon. "It was my Secret Santa gift." Then he remembered his unthoughtful, unimaginative, un-carded gift to her. "Did you open yours?"

She nodded. "It was a b-b-body spray. I l-l-love it."

He got up, came around his desk, laying the papers in her hand. Before he could think about what he was doing, Jake leaned down and inhaled the soft fragrance drifting off her warm skin, a complement to the scent she normally wore. "Very nice." Why was his voice so damned gruff?

She smiled, then stepped away. "Th-th-thank you."

And then she was gone, back to her cubicle.

Ten minutes ago, all Jake had wanted was to dispense with the Secret Santa thing and get back to work. But as the memory of that quiet, mesmerizing scent ran through him— Peach Simmer or Summer or something—he found himself doing nothing but staring.

And wondering what Natalie Harris would do if he gave her that warming body cream the saleswoman had been trying to push. Or even better, what she might do to *and* with him.

He had a business to rescue, a secret admirer to uncover and a holiday to avoid. He didn't have time for a fantasy.

Even one that gave peaches a whole new meaning.

Chapter Four

"How'd it go?" Angie said when Natalie hurried back to her desk, took a seat and let out a burst of air.

Natalie sighed. "You know how Tom Cruise crashed and burned in *Top Gun?*"

Angie nodded.

"I went nuclear."

"You didn't tell him you wrote the letter?"

"I didn't even get past saying 'M-M-Mr. Lyons.' Damned stuttering." It had been her own personal curse to carry around all her life, as bad as Cyrano de Bergerac's nose. Only more vocal. In the sixth-grade play, it had given her performance as Tinkerbell a whole new dimension. Poor Peter Pan hung so long from the ceiling, waiting for her to finish her line, that he ended up losing circulation in his toes.

That had effectively ended her career in acting.

During the seventh-grade spelling bee, she'd gotten so stuck on the first letter of *bicentennial* that the program director had ended up escorting her off the stage, still trying to blubber out anything beyond *b-b-b.*

The Titanic had gone down with more grace.

And at graduation, her salutatorian speech had taken so long to get through, the principal had dozed off, setting off a chain reaction of snorers on the stage. Finally, the band director stepped up, cuing the brass section to play a rousing version of "Pomp and Circumstance." Mrs. Beetleman, the guidance counselor, had tugged Natalie off the stage as if she were Michael Moore at the Oscars.

She'd spent her life being teased and haunted by the possibility that her stuttering could pop up at the worst possible time. It had restricted her, made her hold back on fully living.

No more, dammit (or d-d-dammit, as she might say). She was determined to conquer this stuttering thing once and for all, starting with the main cause of her twisted tongue.

Jake Lyons.

"And now, I have another problem," Natalie said. "Dena. I saw her snag my present out from under the Christmas tree in the lobby and try to hand it off to Jake, like it was from her."

"Well, that's it then. We're just going to have to kill her."

"Don't plot her murder yet. Brad intercepted her."

"He apparently does have a brain cell or two." Angie grinned.

"Let's not overestimate now."

Angie laughed, then nodded in Dena's direction as the receptionist toodled another wave at Jake. "You're going to have to watch out for her. And beat her to the playboy."

"Yeah, if I can get a word out," Natalie said. "I don't know what it is about him. It's like hives or something."

Angie patted Natalie's hand. "I think it's kind of cute."

"Cute is when a Bichon Frise sits up and begs for a cocktail wiener, Angie. I want Jake to look at me and think: sexy, gotta have her." She shook her head. "Kind of hard to do when I sound like a scratched Celine Dion CD."

Angie laughed. "Just keep talking to him. It'll get easier."

"It can't get worse." Natalie dropped her head into her

hands. "When I went in there, I noticed the gift I got him on his desk and thought maybe I could be clever about it. You know, notice it, all cool, like I had nothing to do with it. So I told him he had a nice—" She held up her hands.

"What, clock?"

"Drop a consonant."

Angie's mouth rounded into a little O. "Well, look on the bright side. At least you made an unforgettable impression. It'll be a hell of an addition to your year-end review."

"Oh God." Natalie groaned. "Shoot me now."

"Did someone say guns?" Tony Harris poked his head over the gray cubicle wall. "I've got a Ruger, a Colt and a Magnum. Pick your method."

"Tony, are you stocking up for Armageddon? *War of the Worlds* was fiction, you know."

Tony looked around the office, then back at them, cupping his hand over his mouth. "I'm not worried about the end of the world. I'm packing heat because of the rats."

"Rats? Since when did you need a *Magnum* to take out a rat?"

"These are smart rats," Tony said. "Escaped lab experiments."

Natalie and Angie exchanged a glance. Tony had always been a little on the psycho side of weird. Angie was convinced Brad employed the eenie-meenie-moe method on resumes based on the selection of employees at Lyons. "Uh, okay, Tony. Escaped rats. I'll keep an eye out."

"You mark my words," Tony said. "One of these days, rodents will take over the world." He wagged a finger of warning, then dipped back into his space.

"I think we need to talk to Brad about his hiring policies," Angie whispered. "And you, girlfriend, need to snag that." She pointed in Jake's direction.

"No, I need to buy a muzzle. It's my only hope."

Tony poked his head over again. "Did someone say muzzle loader?"

"*No!*" Angie and Natalie said together.

"Sheesh. Try to help someone ward off a rodent invasion and get blasted." Tony went back to work.

"What are you going to get him tomorrow?" Angie asked.

"I'm not going to get him anything. This is an insane idea. I don't know why I ever thought it would work. And besides, he's going to think it's all from Dena, not me."

Angie took hold of Natalie's hands and forced her friend to look at her. "Do you want him?"

"Does Anna Nicole Smith want public exposure?"

"All right, then. You gotta work it. You have eleven days. Plenty of time." Angie grinned. "God only needed six to pull off his miracles."

Angie was right. Natalie couldn't let a little setback—well, two if she counted both of Dena's 38D's—stop her. "I need to find another way to reach him, something he won't expect," Natalie said, thinking.

After that afternoon at the shelter, she hadn't been able to put Jake from her mind. If she left Lyons Corporation without ever dating him, at least once, she'd always have that what-if in her life. If there was one thing Natalie was done doing, it was wondering what might have happened if she'd just taken a chance. "I know what I'll do. Text."

"Text? As in a big heavy book thrown at his head?"

"I don't think that would go over so well." Natalie grinned. "Text his cell. I'll do it from mine, yours, Tim's . . . that way he doesn't guess who it is."

Angie draped an arm around Natalie's shoulders. "Your brilliance is what makes you such a great friend."

Natalie thought of Jake, picturing him at the shelter, reading to the children. She'd started out wanting him for his looks, for the way he sent a thrill down her spine, but ended up wanting him for the way he'd been so tender, so sweet with the children. Seeing that other side of him hadn't dampened her desire; if anything, the event had quadrupled her want.

Caring about him, however, added a complication she hadn't considered. Natalie had no intentions of taking this beyond Christmas. Being involved with Jake would only give her an excuse to stay here longer, instead of conquering her fears and moving on to a more meaningful job.

But until then, she wouldn't mind having a little fun under the mistletoe.

She took Angie's cell phone, flipped through the office directory until she came across the cell listings for management—the only one listed was Jake, since Brad never wanted to be bothered outside of these walls—and began to type.

> **Hope U liked Ur gift & if U have the time for a little fun, I have the ideas that will put a real jingle in your stocking. In 11 days, let's meet and greet. ;-)**

She signed it, as she had the note, with "SpiceGirl."

"Well done," Angie said. "A little sexy, a little mysterious. Now watch what happens."

The two of them rose and crossed to the communal coffeepot, keeping an eye on Jake the entire time they poured drinks they didn't need. Natalie saw him flip open his phone, read the message, smile a little—causing her heart to do backflips—then look around, as if wondering where that had come from.

"You're right," Natalie said. "I'd be crazy to give up just because Dena inserted her breasts into the deal. Now, if I can get my mouth to cooperate, I'll be fine."

"If you're smart, you won't use your mouth for *talking* to Jake Lyons," Angie said, a devilish gleam in her eyes. "Believe me, you can get your point across in many other ways."

Natalie laughed. "You are a bad influence. A smart one, but still, very, very bad."

Angie blew on her fingers. "We all have our talents."

Chapter Five

Jake had spent three hours with Dena on Saturday night, eating a dinner he didn't like at an overpriced restaurant, waiting for some hint that she was his Secret Santa, as Brad had claimed. Because whoever his mysterious gifter was, she had him intrigued.

More intrigued than he'd been in a long time. Friday's gift, the second in the Twelve Days, had been a set of Mozart bookends, a sign his secret someone knew he listened to classical music in his office. He'd read the attached letter so many times, he'd practically memorized it.

Dear Jake,

According to the song, today I should be giving you two French hens, something I don't think you'd appreciate, unless they had good typing skills.

Did you know the song "The Twelve Days of Christmas" was first published in 1780? Although the twelve days are an English tradition, the French created the music, using the dozen items to symbolize biblical events.

Enough trivia. We can save those kinds of conver-

*sations for afterward, when we're cuddled up together,
killing time until we can make your jingle bells rise
again. I'd love to show you exactly how merry a
Christmas night can be.*

The letter went on, detailing several methods of ringing
in the holidays. Some in a closet, a kitchen and one in a
place even he hadn't thought of. His sender had an imagination all right.

One he wanted to try out.

Then, later that day, another text message, just as cryptic
and fun as the one on Thursday. He'd texted back, asking for
more hints, and all he'd gotten in reply was "you already
know me; just open your eyes and come find me."

So he'd done that, going up to Dena's desk at the end of
the day. She'd readily accepted the invitation, saying something about what had taken him so long to notice her. He'd
had a flash of doubt, but Brad sent him a huge thumbs-up,
and Jake made dinner reservations.

During dinner, he'd asked Dena what books she liked to
read, and she'd answered "*Vogue.*"

He'd brought up the concept of good leaders and she'd
cited Mary Kay as someone who had changed America.

He'd tried to talk about music, but she'd gotten sidetracked in a lengthy soliloquy about her favorite Menudo song.

By the time the crème brûlée arrived, Jake knew his
Secret Santa couldn't possibly be Dena. But then, she'd gone
and thrown a monkey wrench into everything.

"You know, Jake," Dena said, laying a hand on his, "I really
appreciate you asking me out. Things have been tough for
me this year. After my boyfriend left me, I thought my love
life was over, heck, my whole life. I felt so . . . lonely, worth-
less." A tear glistened in her eye. "But now, you've given me
hope." She smiled, squeezed his palm. "You've restored my
faith in men. I just have to hope"—at this, she'd sighed—
"that you aren't another one of those eat-and-leave kind of

guys. Well, most of them stay through dessert, if you know what I mean, but then they're gone. I just couldn't handle another broken heart."

He'd cringed inwardly, knowing he had intended to sign his name to the bill and get the hell out of there. He and Dena had nothing in common, even though she was the kind of woman he usually chose. Lately, he found he wanted more. Less crème brûlée and more honey-baked ham.

The problem—he wasn't so sure he had the commitment gene. He'd started with becoming more responsible within the family business. Taking on the whole wife and family thing, however, was another story.

The word story brought up a mental image of Natalie, reading to the children. *That* was what he wanted, a little of that . . . certainty.

Dena sat across from him, giving him the wide doelike eyes. She was everything he'd always wanted—before he'd come to work at Lyons. "Dena, I—"

"Oh please don't break up with me. Not now. Let's just pretend we have another date for . . . next Tuesday. Okay?"

"Uh—"

"Good!" she'd said, overriding any objections before Jake could voice them. He'd ended up leaving it at that. A woman like Dena, who dated men in the office like some people went through drive-throughs, would undoubtedly be on to someone else before the week was out.

Now, as the office began to pick up tempo on Monday morning, Jake did no work, instead holding that day's letter, his thumb tracing over the neat script of his name on the envelope. Day five and he wasn't a whole lot closer to knowing who his Secret Santa could be. He'd eliminated Dena, but that still left Angela; Natalie; the new girl . . . Janie, he thought her name was; and Shelly, who pretty much kept to herself and her cubicle, seeming to be a lot happier with numbers than humans.

The gift attached to today's letter had been on his desk

when he'd come in this morning, as neatly wrapped as the one before, with another letter dangling from the bow. In the box had been a file organization system, one of those kinds that sat on his desk and corralled his paperwork into neatness.

The gift had been thoughtful, practical. But it was the letter that had him the most intrigued.

Dear Jake,

I came across a quote today and thought of not only you, but also myself.

"Life is so full of meaning and of purpose, so full of beauty—beneath its covering—that you will find that earth but cloaks your heaven. Courage, then to claim it: that is all!"—Fra Giovanni Giocondo

Ironically, although the quote is attributed to Giocondo, experts think it was actually written by the son of a novelist. A secret hidden behind a pearl. Sounds very much like what we are doing here. Secrets and pearls . . . but will you find me to be a pearl at the end? Or just the shucked shell of an oyster?

Have you ever been afraid to claim what you want? I have been, and still am, every day of my life. I know what I want . . . but going after it is another story. It's like I'm afraid that if I do it, I'll jump into a pool and forget how to swim.

So I've tacked that quote over my mirror at home, so I see it every day and remember that courage is all I need. Well, that and a kiss from you ;-). But that will have to wait until we get to Day Twelve.

The wait seems impossibly long. But as they say, anticipation is half the fun.
SpiceGirl

He looked up. Through the glass walls that surrounded him, he didn't see a single guilty-looking person whom he could pinpoint as the letter's John Hancock. From the conversation he'd had with Dena, where none of the words consisted of more than two syllables, he doubted even more that she had written this.

Jake fiddled with the organizer for a few minutes, sorting the files, setting them to rights and creating a clear working space on his desk. He moved the clock in front of it, then sat back and enjoyed the newly cleared space. For a few minutes, Jake fiddled with some work but accomplished very little, too busy wondering about the identity of SpiceGirl.

There were fourteen women on this floor of Lyons Corp., half of whom he could rule out. Velma, who had been married for fifty years and served as guardian of Brad. Coco, the temp, who had made her preferences known when she started dating Kitty, who worked in the mail room.

He didn't know much about the other women, but he knew enough that a good chunk of them were married or nearing retirement. Or both.

That left Angela, Dena, Natalie and a couple of other women with whom he hadn't exchanged more than three words in the last five months.

Once again, he looked out at the office but saw no one but Dena looking his way. She smiled and waved, then winked. Could it be Dena?

He considered Natalie, then rejected the idea. Surely she would have given off some clue that her alter ego was SpiceGirl. The thought of Natalie created an odd craving in his gut.

He picked up the receiver and punched in an extension he'd already memorized. A melodious hello greeted him a second later, sending a smile across his face. "Miss Harris," he said, trying to keep things businesslike, to keep those dreams he'd had last night to himself, where they couldn't do any damage in the workplace, "could you bring me the file on Wharton? They're an old client, maybe five, six years back. It might be hard to track down."

"Certainly," she said, then disconnected. He popped back in his chair, watched her rise, skirt the gray cubicle wall, then stride across the office toward the file room at the back. Too fast for him to see if she'd found his gift today as interesting as the one before.

He waited, drumming his fingers on his desk. Five minutes passed. Ten.

As he got up and headed in the same direction, he told himself it was only because he was in a hurry for the Wharton information. That it wasn't because he'd been thinking about the identity of his Secret Santa, and also about Natalie Harris and her stammered shyness, all weekend long. That he hadn't spent far too much time in a department store, selecting gifts for Natalie, wanting only to see her smile again.

He entered the file room. The door shut behind him, closing him and Natalie into the cramped space that housed hundreds of files in stacked lateral cabinets. At one end, he saw Natalie, knees bent, searching through a drawer.

"Miss Harris?"

She popped up so fast, her knee banged against the drawer, sending the metal winging back into the cabinet with a slam. She spun around, a slight flush filling her face. "Y-y-you startled m-m-me."

"Sorry." He moved forward, his gaze sweeping over her slim frame, accentuated by a straight black skirt and a V-neck red sweater decorated with beaded ornaments—which had him thinking about a whole other kind of ornamentation on her chest. "Are you okay?"

"Sh-sh-sure."

"Let me check your knee, just in case." Before she could protest, he bent down, placed his palm against the reddened skin on her kneecap and feigned doctor. "Looks good to me."

Actually, it looked more than good. Her entire leg, from

ankle on up, looked good enough to eat. He hadn't been thinking broken bones or displaced kneecaps when he'd been down there. He'd been thinking about running his hand up her leg, under that pencil-thin skirt and—

"Th-th-thank you."

"Sure," Jake said, rising before he did something stupid, like act on his thoughts. "Did you, ah, find the file?"

She nodded. Her green eyes met his, clear, direct and unabashed.

Jake inhaled. What the hell had he wanted that file for anyway? He had no idea. He couldn't have told the time, the date or the address of the building, not while Natalie Harris's bright emerald eyes were watching his with such intensity.

Before he could think better of it, Jake stepped forward, the small room closing in, seeming to tighten the circle around them even more. He lifted his hand, brushed back her hair. Dangling from her ears were twin silver snowflakes.

She'd worn them. The thought that Natalie had liked his second gift too sent an odd thrill through Jake's chest. "Nice earrings," he said.

"Th-th-thanks." Her voice may have faltered, but her gaze never did.

They stood there, still as statues, his hand still caught in the tendrils of her hair, aware, so very aware of her every breath, of the scent of peaches and cream. His gaze locked with hers, building the heat between them, arcing the temperature upward two degrees, three, maybe even five. His hand strayed down from her earlobe to her jaw, thumb tracing the outline of her lower lip. Natalie parted her lips, took in a sharp, fast breath.

Want surged within him, crashing past the sensible roadblocks he'd put into place earlier. In an instant, his mouth was on hers, a flame of desire ignited by a knee and a file drawer and a pair of eyes that were more vibrant and deep than the Atlantic. She tasted sweet beneath his lips, like honey melting into tea.

The scent of peaches whispered under his nose, telling Jake that for a Secret Santa, he was currently two and oh.

And what an oh it was, he thought, as he brought her closer to him, the kiss deepening, his tongue sliding into her mouth in invitation and then hers, no longer tied up by words, slipping along his in a dance that had Jake considering the merits of the nearest flat surface.

The muffled sound of conversation outside the door injected a few senses back into his brain, with reluctance. He pulled back, allowing his lips to linger against hers for just one sweet second longer. "Sorry. That, ah, shouldn't have—"

"D-d-don't," she said. "Don't apologize." She gave him a grin of confidence, one that told him the ball had somehow left his court, along with his racket. "It's C-C-Christmas. Let's call th-th-that a gift."

Then she swung around, grabbed a file out of the cabinet and thrust it into his hands before he could respond.

If there were prizes for man screwups, Jake would have gotten the gold medal.

Chapter Six

Jake stood outside the file room, wondering what the hell he'd just done.

Okay, he knew what he'd just done—kissed an employee. The question was why. In every how-to-be-a-boss book in the universe, that was a no-no. And not just kissed any employee, but *Natalie Harris,* who might as well be wearing a T-shirt saying DANGER: BREAKABLE HEART.

Jake wasn't a man who stayed with women. He was, by and large, a one-woman-at-a-time man, with his time frame lasting roughly six weeks. Anything longer than that meant talk about mortgages, Labrador puppies, and worse, children.

If there was one man who shouldn't breed, it was definitely him.

And yet, after that kiss with Natalie, every one of his bodily instincts was telling him to do just that—or at least practice—a lot—with her. Natalie Harris might get tongue-tied talking to him, but she didn't have that problem when it came to kissing. In fact, he thought her tongue had been decidedly flexible and sweet, fueling a few thousand fantasies in Jake's mind.

Fantasies that were still simmering in certain parts of his body, making him stall instead of cross the room to his office.

Still, it had been a stupid thing to do. He'd never gotten involved with an employee before, and he wasn't about to start now.

Really.

"Jakey, there you are." Cousin Brad strode over, his black-and-white striped suit making him look more like a zebra than a Lyons. Where the hell did the man shop? "Come on into the conference room for a bit. I have to break some bad news and want you there to soften the blow. You play Mutt to my Jeff." He thought a second. "Maybe it's the other way around. Anyway, come be the good cop."

Jake waited until they had entered the dark, foreboding conference room before speaking. "Bad news? Just before Christmas?"

Brad waved a hand of dismissal. "I can't base my profit and loss on a damned holiday. Besides, when did you care about Christmas? Or Easter, or hell, Valentine's Day for that matter?"

"Still, firing someone before Christmas—"

"Oh, I'm not firing anyone. I'll save that one for Christmas Eve." He chuckled. "Right now, I'm just ending the company's support of that stupid shelter. God, talk about a drain on resources. What those people need is bus fare to the unemployment line, not turkeys and 'story time.'" He put sarcastic air quotes around the last two words.

Jake happened to think the story time wasn't a bad idea, and as far as he knew, it didn't cost the company more than a couple of hours of Natalie's time, time she always made up by staying late. The book reading worked out to be a wash in the financial river, and the donations from Lyons Corporation were small enough that they couldn't possibly be making a dent in the bottom line, but Jake didn't quibble. Once Brad latched onto a cost-cutting measure, there was no talking him out of it.

It was probably the same stubborn streak that had him convinced he was a dapper dresser.

Still, he hated to see Natalie's project get axed, especially now. He knew that shelter meant a lot to her, just by the amount of time she invested in it.

He shouldn't care. He should be smart and remember that he was here to run a business, not save a woman he barely knew from a little disappointment. "Brad, you can't do that. Not to—" He'd been about to say Natalie but pulled himself back. What was *with* him lately? Was Starbucks throwing in some estrogen-laced soy milk into his daily morning latte?

He should agree with axing the program because they definitely needed to cut back on expenses. Brad was still handling the books, despite Jake bugging him to see them. Either way, it didn't take a genius to see that the company was doing poorly.

If Jake didn't keep his focus on that, he wouldn't be able to pull Lyons out of the financial pits. Doing so would prove, once and for all, that Jake Lyons was more than just a pretty face who'd inherited a lot of money and not a lot of brains. It would prove it to his family, to the tabloids that loved to latch onto his life and, most of all, to himself.

"Some other sucker will come along and toss those homeless some coins, believe me. Anyway, I only did it for the publicity." Brad snorted. "Fat lot of good that did me. Not one paper ran an article on Lyons Corp's philanthropic efforts."

"What a shocker," Jake deadpanned. Over the last few months, the company had donated the equivalent of one half-filled Salvation Army kettle. The checks were small, but Jake noted that the shelter's director was always grateful, regardless of the number of zeroes.

"You stay here," Brad said. "I'll go get Natasha—"

"Natalie."

"Whatever. I'll get her and tell her that her little pet project is kaput. She'll probably thank me. One less thing to worry about. Besides, this little Christmas shindig she was planning over there would have cost us a fortune. Hiring a Santa, for God's sake, and buying a present for every one of those ungrateful brats. It's a ridiculous expenditure when we need to be watching our own dimes instead of tossing them to the poor."

"Brad," Jake said, grabbing his cousin's sleeve before he could depress the intercom button on the speakerphone in the center of the table, "why not continue supporting the shelter? Both of us have enough personal wealth to—"

Brad laughed. "Why the hell would I give my own money to the poor? I worked hard to earn it."

"You mean inherit it."

"Hey, it's not easy to be born into the right family. All that Lyons sperm floating around, you and I are lucky we're legit."

His cousin was right. Brad's father as well as his father before him, Jake and Brad's grandfather, had been a notorious womanizer. A tabloid had once done a story on him, estimating the number of potential illegitimate heirs. After a hundred, the reporter had stopped counting. Only because Grandfather's will had been ironclad had the money passed on to his siblings and grandchildren. Jake's father had inherited more than a few mill from his *paterfamilias*. He'd also downloaded the infidelity gene.

John Lyons had been a distant father, never putting any time into his relationship with his son until last year, when a heart attack scared him into catching up. Before the second attack took his life, he'd asked only one thing of his son—to work with Brad and restore Lyons Corporation to its former glory.

There were other companies, dozens of them, in the Lyons family portfolio, but this one had formed the core of it all. It was the source of the Lyons fortune, the kind of rags to riches story that magazines loved to report on. Before his death, John Lyons had finally seen what his brother's incompetence had done to the company and asked his son to step in.

To save the family name. The cornerstone of the family wealth. And in doing so, Jake saw himself redeemed for all those years of playing instead of caring. And most of all, it would give him the purpose he'd been searching for ever since his father had passed away.

If it hadn't been for all that, Jake would have walked out on his cousin a hundred times over. But Lyons Corporation was part of his family's legacy and he'd be damned if he'd watch it drain away.

Despite that, he hated to see Natalie hurt in the process. "Brad, I still think—"

"Jake, we're rich and we're bastards. Thinking isn't required. Just back me up while I protect the company assets." Brad chuckled as he left the room. "And while I take a peek at Dena's assets."

Jake reached a hand into his shirt pocket, where he'd put that day's Secret Santa missive. Someone here thought he was an honorable, smart man.

He hoped like hell he wasn't about to prove that wrong.

"Dish," Angie said. "You left this desk wearing lipstick and now most of it's on your chin, so you better tell me what just happened in the file room. I saw Jake go in there about three seconds after you did. What happened behind closed doors? Enquiring minds want to know."

Natalie shrugged. "We kissed."

Angie plopped down on the corner of Natalie's desk. "No, no, no. That's not the way you tell a story like that. I need details, Nat. You know my life is about as exciting as balsa wood. If I don't live vicariously, I might as well go buy an oversized cable-knit sweater and eighty cats."

Natalie laughed. "Okay, I'll tell you. But only for the betterment of feline kind."

Angie put her hands on her hips. "Hey, I could take care of a cat."

"Ang," Natalie said, laying a hand across her best friend's, "I love you dearly, but you can't even keep your philodendron alive."

"It would help if the plant could talk and tell me it needs water. I mean, it just sits there. I've had boyfriends like that, just sat on the sofa and clicked my remote. I didn't give them any tender loving care either. I want a man who acts, not one who potatoes."

Natalie cast a dubious brow toward the shriveled brown leaves of the plant sitting on the shelf above Angie's desk, but let it go. It was the third plant to be tortured in that spot, despite Natalie's furtive attempts to sneak the greenery a drink and some sunshine time. The poinsettia Jake had given Natalie was thriving well, bringing a vibrant crimson burst to the drab gray walls of her office box.

"Really, the whole thing was nothing," she said. "Jake came in, told me he was looking for a file, and he noticed my earrings, and then, before I knew it, we were kissing."

"Was he good?"

Natalie grinned, unable to keep the memory from showing on her face. "Does Elton John know how to sing?"

Angie laughed. "I knew it. He looks like a good kisser. Nice lips, nice hands. It all spells awesome in bed."

Natalie had been thinking the exact same thing, before Jake kissed her, during . . . and after. "Well, we didn't go that far. He was the one to break it off, to *apologize*, for Pete's sake." She sighed. "I must have been really terrible."

"Or he just felt bad about a little office hanky-panky." Angie drew closer. "If that's the case, then it's time to add a little bam! to your Secret Santa plan. Send him a vibrator, something that gets his imagination rolling."

"Trust me," Natalie said, thinking again of the feel of Jake Lyons against her, "he needs no help in that department."

Angie grabbed Natalie's arm. "Then take a bigger risk, Nat. Or you'll end up sitting under the mistletoe, sipping eggnog and cuddling with a Shih Tzu."

"Angie, I—"

Brad popped his head over her desk. "Miss Harris, may I have a word?"

Angie slid her copy of *Webster's* onto the corner of her desk, sending Natalie a conspiratorial grin.

"Sure," Natalie said, rising and following Brad into the small conference room. Brad probably had a bone to pick with the way she filled out some paperwork or something. Brad Lyons had a way of taking the tiniest infraction and turning it into a drama worthy of Broadway.

But when she entered the room, she stopped cold, realizing instantly that this was no chastising about using blue ink over black. Jake sat at one end of the long, dark table, looking as uncomfortable as a man could.

She was being fired. For fraternizing—both mind and body—with the boss. Well, if Brad tried that, she'd make it clear that it hadn't been a one-sided event.

"Please, have a seat," Jake said, gesturing toward the chair across from him.

She sat, but not all the way, ready to spring up at any second and argue her point.

Brad slid into the chair at the head of the table, cleared his throat, looked at Jake, then back at Natalie. He readjusted his suit's lapels three times before he was satisfied with their placement. "Miss Harris, I want you to work on the Simpson account this afternoon. We have a meeting with the client at two."

"But I'm supposed to be going to the Our Hope Shelter, remember? I have a meeting with the director to talk about the Christmas party for the children. If I miss it, we'll be cutting it awfully close. We need time to hire a Santa and buy all the gifts."

"We're not doing that." Brad placed his palms flat on the cherry surface. "This company is done with that silly shelter. It's been nothing but a drain on company resources."

The heat left Natalie's body. "Did you just say you were ending the program? Before *Christmas?*"

"Yeah. I don't want to waste a bunch of money on presents for ungrateful leeches." Brad picked a piece of lint off his jacket sleeve, then flicked it toward the floor, watching the fluff's slow journey down. Jake sat immobile, his face unreadable.

Natalie rose, forgetting her job, her place, seeing nothing but red fury in front of her. "Those children are *needy*. They aren't leeches, nor are they ungrateful. If we don't provide a Christmas for them, they won't have one. They're homeless, for God's sake. Do you know how that affects a child?"

Brad shrugged. "Might as well learn about the cruel, cold world at an early age. Don't want them holding onto illusions forever. No more solatium from this company. Let 'em get their own damned money."

She cringed at the bastardization of another Word of the Day. Someone needed to give Brad a *Webster's* all right— and shove it into a place a dictionary never ventured. She turned to Jake. "Do you support this decision?"

His gaze wouldn't meet hers. "I'm sorry, Natalie. I really am."

"Bullshit." She shook her head. "I thought you were different. But you're just like all the rest, aren't you? Out for Numero Uno. The rest of the world be damned." She gave her chair a hard push back into place, then stormed out of the room.

She refused to cry, refused to dwell on the thought that moments ago she had been kissing the very same man who had just betrayed the one thing that meant something to her.

As soon as she reached her cubicle, she pulled up Internet Explorer and zoomed over to Monster.com, posting her resume with several angry keystrokes.

"Hey, what'd that keyboard ever do to you?" Angie said, sliding back to poke her head around the paneled wall separating them.

"It's not the keyboard. It's *him*."

"Jake?"

"*Jerk* is more like it."

Angie held up a hand. "Whoa, Nelly. Five minutes ago you were starry eyed and well kissed. How'd he go from Romeo to Benedict Arnold so fast?"

"He let Brad cut off the Our Hope Shelter. Before Christmas. Before we bought gifts for the kids."

"He did?" Her jaw dropped. "For real?"

"Technically, Brad did. Jake just stood by and watched the train wreck."

"Hey, go easy on him," Angie said. "Jake is the brains behind the operation, but Brad is where the buck stops. He has the majority share, remember?"

"Jake could have argued with Brad more. Anything but sit there like the village idiot and let this happen." She shook her head, then pushed back from the desk, watching as her job search posting went into cyberspace. "I thought I knew him."

"Maybe you do. There could be more to the story than you're hearing. Some reason he supported Brad." Angie paused. "Though I can't think of one right now, I'm sure there is a reason."

Natalie snorted. "I doubt that." Then she sagged in her chair, wondering if she could find a way to leave work early. Just hole up in her apartment with a pint of Ben & Jerry's and some Turning Leaf and forget she ever thought Jake Lyons was a good idea.

"Why is this shelter so important to you?" Angie asked,

her voice soft, concerned. "It's about more than just poor kids, isn't it?"

"No." Natalie shook her head. "Yes." But she didn't elaborate. She didn't want to tell Angie about her childhood, about the events that had driven her to passionately support anything that helped needy children. A few days ago, when Jake had sat in that chair and read a silly book about a reindeer to the children, she'd thought he might have felt the same way, but now . . .

It was clear he didn't.

"Well, why didn't you tell Brad and Jake that?" Angie asked. "Maybe Brad the Bozo would have reconsidered cutting the program support."

"Brad let me do this only because he thought it would be a great PR stunt. Apparently, Jake agrees." She cursed under her breath. "It's all about the freakin' bottom line."

"Listen, you should talk to Jake." Angie gave her friend a light jab in the arm. "Ask him to dinner. Lunch. A scone at Starbucks. And *talk* to him."

Natalie laughed. "Yeah, right. With me and him, it's more like playing verbal ping-pong. And I don't have a paddle." She rose, and grabbed a pad of paper and a pencil. "Either way, I'm not letting them stop me. I'm going to give those kids a Christmas no matter what."

"And Jake?"

She grinned. She had a plan now. There was nothing like taking action to make her feel better. "For him, I do believe a lump of coal is in order."

Chapter Seven

He'd gone too far. The small blue box in Jake's hands was much too expensive for a Secret Santa gift and would definitely give him away as the gifter. Until now, he'd done little things—the Peach Shimmer body spray, the silver earrings, a book of poetry, a snowglobe with a scene that reminded him of the cityscape just outside the shelter's windows.

But after he'd watched Natalie walk away from the conference room two days ago, disappointment and frustration sitting squarely on her shoulders, he'd wanted to do something, anything, to undo the damage Brad had just done.

Brad hadn't acted alone. Jake had screwed up too, particularly by not putting his foot down about his cousin's penny-pinching. Why'd he let this one slip by when he'd argued a hundred other financial decisions in the past?

He knew why. Because he'd been more worried about the fate of the company than the feelings of Natalie Harris. It had been a business decision, plain and simple.

Either way, guilt had driven him over to a jewelry store, made him linger so long the salesman got annoyed and had him racking up his credit card to buy something that was supposed to be office entertainment.

He'd never put so much damned thought into a gift in his life. For his father, who had everything—and everything everyone else wished for but couldn't afford—Jake had always done something tax deductible, like buying a sheep in Indonesia. For his past girlfriends, he'd always called Tiffany's or Cartier and let the experts there pick out a gift, wrap it, sign his name and ship it to him in time for a planned evening on the town. Shiny things always went over well with the women in his life, which meant he also had a Merry Christmas, sometimes under the blankets, but more often than not, under the tree, or wherever the diamonds had been dispensed.

This time, though, he'd spent four hours at the mall, battling crowds and bargain hunters, until he found the perfect gift, choosing it himself, right down to the wrapping paper. Not caring about what he might get in return but only wanting to see a smile cross Natalie's lips again.

"Whatcha got there, Jake?" Sam the Suck-Up asked, poking his head into Jake's office.

"Here," he said, tossing the gift to Sam as if he didn't care about it one whit, "put this on that girl's desk. Someone gave it to me by accident."

Sam caught the box, then read the name inscribed on the card. "Oh, Natalie. The troublemaker."

"What do you mean, troublemaker?"

"Did you hear how she argued with Brad over the Twelve Days of Christmas? It's like she never read Working in an Office 101."

"I bet you memorized it."

Sam beamed. "Even better. I wrote it *and* self-published it. If you're interested, I can—"

"I'm not."

Sam shrugged. "Suit yourself." He turned away, his head held in high superiority, the kind that came with knowing he was secure in his job because he had his head so far up Brad's ass, he could probably measure the boss's intestinal tract.

From behind his glass wall, Jake watched as Sam slipped the gift onto Natalie's desk. Instead of getting to work or tackling the long list of calls he needed to return, Jake left the room and crossed by the central coffeepot, waiting until she entered the office a few minutes later.

Her hair was tousled from the winter wind, her cheeks red and bright. He'd never thought anyone could look so sexy and so innocent at the same time.

He wanted to kiss her again until the cold left her lips and she melted into his arms, drawing from his warmth. And maybe drawing a little more than that out of him. Desire for Natalie Harris wasn't a problem—the ramifications of getting involved with her, particularly when the company needed a lot of TLC, were.

As she had for dozens of days, Natalie hung her long black coat in the closet, folded her knitted blue scarf and put it in the pocket. Neat, precise movements, all very good at ignoring him as she made her way to her cubicle.

He remained rooted to the spot, pretending to sip a cup of coffee, watching for the soft smile of discovery that took over her face when she found, then picked up the box. A smile curved across his features in concert with hers. Hell, now he was turning into the After Grinch, the one with the tripled heart.

He'd stopped thinking about his own Secret Santa and how intrigued SpiceGirl made him feel. Instead, he was more interested in Natalie and her responses to his gifts. In the last few days, he'd found out it was definitely way better to give than to receive.

With agonizing slowness, she removed the silver ribbon, the navy paper, then ran a thumb over the hinge of the long, thin velvet box before finally opening it. Everything within him stood still, waiting for her gasp of surprise.

The woman at the next desk—Angela, Jake thought her name was—let out a shriek. "Holy crap, Nat! That's some quality zirc."

Cubic zirconium? She thought the tennis bracelet, made up of tiny diamonds and rubies in the shape of poinsettias, was a *fake?*

"It's beautiful," Natalie said, fingering the gems. "It doesn't matter what it's made out of."

"Well, you got the long end of the Secret Santa stick. This is what was on my desk this morning." Angie held up a Yard-O-Beef.

Jake chuckled, then covered with a cough when the women looked in his direction. "Uh, allergies." He took the Styrofoam cup and headed back to his glass walls.

He lasted all of five minutes in his office before he depressed the intercom button and asked Natalie to come in. She did as he asked, her back ramrod stiff, her anger at him still clear on her face. For a second, he was tempted to tell her he was her Secret Santa.

But he'd rather not see his privates strung up on a diamond bracelet.

"You wanted to see me, M-M-Mr. Lyons?"

"Jake, please." When she paused, he added a smile. "Please."

She drew in a breath, then released it with his name. "Jake."

The soft, throaty sound sent his thoughts spiraling back down Bedroom Boulevard. Somehow, he needed to make peace with her. Not so he could repeat the moment in the file room—

Who was he kidding? He wanted that particular event to go into multiple reruns. His mind might know better than to get involved with an employee right now, but the rest of him didn't care. "I want to talk to you, but I don't want to do it here, in the fishbowl. Would you like to get some coffee?"

The delicate arch of her eyebrows raised. "C-c-coffee?"

"You know, that warm caffeinated beverage that people use to start their day?"

"No, thank you. I have w-w-work to do. And you already h-h-have some."

Oh yeah. He'd forgotten the cup from earlier. "You know the coffee here. Brad buys the cheapest crap he can. It's more colored water than caffeine."

That at least coaxed a smile out of her, albeit fleeting.

"We can talk about work if you like. Most of the time." He tried smiling again, but she shook her head.

"I c-c-can't. Sorry."

"Listen, I know I was a jerk the other day. But if you'll let me explain, over a cappuccino or whatever you want, I'd appreciate it." He looked at her wrist, saw the sparkles dangling from her thin, delicate frame and considered again telling her it had been him who'd given her that "quality zirc." But if he did that, he knew she'd only think he was buying her and she'd be out of his office before he could get another word out. "Please."

She smiled at him, socking him in the chest once again. "Okay. Some c-c-coffee would be n-n-nice."

"Then grab your coat and let's go."

"N-n-now?"

"Sure. I'm the boss, or one of them anyway, and I say you can take a break right now."

She opened her mouth to protest, then shut it again, sending another smile his way. "Okay."

A few minutes later, they had snagged a table at the Starbucks on the corner. A peppermint mocha latte sat in front of Natalie, a regular Kenyan roast in front of Jake. Shoppers and workers bustled in and out of the shop, ushering in a cold winter wind. Some used-to-be-popular pop star was on the store radio, singing a Christmas song, something about love and loneliness.

Jake wrapped his hands around his mug and realized he had no real reason to have asked her here. Presumably, if the boss asked an employee to coffee, he had intentions.

Jake had intentions all right. None of them work related.

"So," he began, scrambling for something to discuss, anything that didn't revolve around his "clock." "Tell me why this shelter is so important to you."

She bristled, and immediately he knew he'd asked the wrong question. Where was his brain? Couldn't he have started with some small talk? Something like, "Hey, think the Pats will make it to the Super Bowl again this year?"

"Why do you care?" she asked, her ire immediately peaking again. Clearly, he'd hit a sore spot. "We're not involved with that 'silly' place anymore. A few homeless kids will go without for Christmas, but the company will sure look good on its profit and loss, and that's what's *really* important, isn't it?"

"I didn't mean that. I—" What had he meant?

She rose, shoving her arms back into her coat. "This wasn't a good idea. I have work to do anyway."

"Natalie, wait." He reached for her wrist, but she was too quick. Leaving the coffees behind, he hurried after her, pulling on his coat as he did. He caught up with her just outside the coffee shop. "Natalie, wait," he repeated, taking her arm and inadvertently hauling her against him, sending a spark of fire roaring down his arm. She drew in a sharp breath.

"What?"

"Stay." When she hesitated, he pressed on. "Please."

Her sharp gaze narrowed. "Only if you tell me why you let Brad ax the shelter p-p-program."

Through the outdoor speakers, Amy Grant's version of "Rockin' Around the Christmas Tree" started playing. Natalie had worked hard on the shelter program, investing, he knew, many of her off-work hours to create crafts for the kids or to find a new book to entertain them.

He may not have been in the room to hear her read every week, but he had heard the shelter's director sing Natalie's praises every week. To the workers at the Our Hope Shelter, Natalie Harris was an angel.

A light snowfall started up, dusting her dark hair with fluffy white flakes. Maybe the people at the shelter weren't too far off in their assessment.

He drew in a breath. "Do you want to know why I work for my cousin?"

She seemed startled by the question, so far off the topic, but she took it in stride. "Why?"

It took him a moment, even though he'd been the one to open this conversational can of worms. He'd never told anyone, much less a woman he wasn't even technically dating, about his family history. Or his own part in it.

"I'm known as the family screwup," Jake said finally. "I finished college, but just barely. I hated accounting, fell asleep during half my classes. Add that to the fact that I haven't settled down, haven't gone off and invented a cure for cancer or a car that drives itself, like the other Lyons men, or at least the ones who aren't my cousin. I've just been . . ." he looked away, watching the bustle of shoppers hurrying down the street, "ordinary."

"There's nothing wrong with th-th-that," she said, the stutter back in her voice. When she was angry with him, it disappeared, but when her frustration dissipated, he noticed she was back to the nervous tick.

"My father disagreed. He was a fighter pilot in Vietnam, even got a Purple Heart and a commendation from the president himself. When he came back, he created StarAir." When her eyes widened, he nodded. "Yeah, *that* StarAir. So, as the next generation, he wanted me—no, expected me—to be more, to carry on the legacy. To make my mark." Jake paused for a second as a woman with a baby stroller circumvented them. "Just before he died this summer—"

"I'm sorry to hear that," she said, softly cutting in and

laying a hand on his shoulder, a hand that carried as much weight as her words. "This must be a hard holiday for you."

He blinked several times, refusing to acknowledge how her words had opened a crack in his heart, a break he promptly sealed back up. "Thank you." He cleared his throat. "Anyway, at that time, he asked me to come here, to work with Brad, the other family screwup."

Natalie chuckled. "He's the industrial size, though."

Jake echoed her laughter, then sobered. "I thought, though, when I came to work here, that I could make my father proud by turning the company around. In my grandfather's day, Lyons Corp was the equivalent of E.F. Hutton. It's always been the family gem, at least until Brad took over. That's why I stepped in. But working with Brad . . ."

"Is a lot like trying to truss a badger with dental floss."

He grinned. "Another Word of the Day fan?"

She smiled back, sharing the joke, the connection. "No, c-c-crosswords."

"In ink?"

She nodded.

"Of course." He marveled at this woman with whom he had worked for the past few months and never really noticed, not until now, until this week. Now he saw so much, saw that she was a pearl in a room full of bricks. She was smart and witty, and so far out of the league of the normal woman he dated.

And that meant trouble.

"Y-y-you still h-h-haven't told me why you d-d-didn-n-n—" She shook her head, giving up on the word with a muttered curse.

A gang of shoppers, wielding stuffed red bags from Macy's, came heading down the sidewalk, four abreast. Jake tugged Natalie out of the way before she could get sideswiped by a Liz purse. She collided gently against him, sending another fire racing up his spine, igniting other parts.

He wanted nothing more than to kiss her again, to finish

what they had started in the file room. But if he did that, he
was sure she'd run. And probably slug him before she did.
He could still see the simmering anger in her eyes, the disappointment that he'd let her down.

"Natalie, you're completely justified in hating me," he
said, hoping like hell that she didn't, because he was enjoying the feeling of her in his arms. Very much.

Too much.

"I should have said something," he went on, "and I was
wrong for not doing it. At the time, it seemed like just another bottom-line decision. I won't lie to you—the company
is struggling. Brad has made a lot of bad decisions in the
past, and they're starting to come back to bite us." He drew
in a breath. "And, in his infinite wisdom, my grandfather left
his two sons nearly equal parts of the company, which was
then passed down to the next two males in the family. Brad
has half and I, as my father's heir, have the other half. Brad,
however, with his 51 percent, is used to having the whole enchilada. Even when his brother was alive and after Brad took
over, my father liked tinkering with planes, not money, so he
never interfered."

"And n-n-n-now you're trying to be the kn-n-night on the
shiny steed?"

He chuckled. "Maybe the battered knight on the old gray
mare, but yeah, something like that. So, forgive me if I got
all corporate instead of—"

"Human."

"Yeah." Jake Lyons hadn't been human in a long time, if
he thought about it. Before he'd come to work here, he'd
been the quintessential rich playboy, discarding relationships as easily as tissues. His apartment, his address book,
his social calendar had all been filled with things, people and
events that had about as much substance as Jell-O.

And then he'd met Natalie Harris, who took her life seri-
ously, who had invested herself into a purpose. A purpose
he'd helped yank away from her. "Natalie," he said, taking

one of her hands, feeling the beat of her pulse, watching the delicate cloud of warm air around her lips. "Will you forgive me?"

"I—"

He put a finger to her lips, shushing her before she could say no. "Give me a second chance, Natalie."

Then, before he could remember his promise not to get involved with an employee, he leaned forward, hauling her closer to his chest, and did what he'd wanted to do ever since he'd had his first taste.

He kissed her. Thoroughly. Completely ignoring the people around them, the Christmas music playing in the background, the busy, bustling city.

She tasted of candy and chocolate, a sweet, tempting combination. He slid his tongue into her mouth, a thrill rushing through him when she responded in kind. His hands reached up, fingers dancing in her hair, pulling her head closer, deepening their kiss, taking it from a tease to something that bordered on seduction.

She curved against him, her wool coat parting as she did, pressing her breasts to his chest. He went hard with want and cursed his timing, the location. If he'd been in his apartment, he'd have had her in his bed and naked faster than a couch potato could change the channel.

After a long, sweet second, Natalie pulled back and leaned her head against his shoulder. "Th-th-that was nice," she whispered.

With her, the surge of want was supplanted by something deeper, something that seemed to cut into his heart and create a space that had never been there before. He found himself wrapping his arms around her, drawing her warmth to his, creating a small island of just the two of them against the increasing winter snowfall. It was magical, the kind of comfortable coziness Jake had thought only came as a scripted part of a movie.

Oh, this was a mistake. A really big mistake.

"I'm su-su-supposed to h-ha-hate you," she said into his coat.

He chuckled. "Hate me? Why?"

She drew back, met his eyes. "B-b-because you cut the p-p-program."

"We'll have to find a way to fix that."

"Really?" The smile that spread across her face was wide and contagious. She raised herself on her toes, placed a kiss against his lips, then drew back. Their gazes met, held, and she leaned forward again, this time kissing him with more . . . more everything.

He was jostled from behind by a stack of shopping bags, the crinkle of paper and poke of something sharp and hard drawing him away from Natalie. And back to his senses.

"Thank you," she whispered.

He caught himself before he said he'd done it because it was important to her. Doing that implied he cared, that he would take this kiss beyond a street corner and a morning latte.

He couldn't do that. He wasn't the kind of man who had staying power. Hell, philandering was part of his genes. Natalie Harris deserved more.

And even if he did take this further, if he took her home and spent the night with her, even one night to erase this constant want from his mind, there would be consequences. Beyond the office gossip, there would be the look in Natalie's eyes, the same look he'd seen this morning and had no desire to duplicate.

"The shelter's a good tax write-off," he said, knowing as he watched the impact of the words on her face that he had effectively ended any hope of something more with Natalie Harris.

Chapter Eight

When Natalie got back to the office, the peppermint mocha was sitting heavy in her gut, along with a hefty topping of disappointment. She should have been pleased when Jake made it clear there was nothing between them but saving a few cents on his IRS bill. That he wasn't starting to fall for her, something she'd insanely thought when he'd kissed her, so well and so tenderly.

She didn't want a man to fall in love with her. She didn't want to settle down, to start looking for permanence. The minute she did that, she became complacent, as she had in the past year she'd worked at Lyons Corp. It had gotten easier to stay than to move on, and if there was one thing Natalie wanted, it was to move onward and upward.

She had plans. Ambitions that involved doing more than tallying accounts receivables numbers.

When she got back to her desk, she logged onto her e-mail account and there, in her in-box, was the change she'd been seeking. "Oh my God. I got a job offer," she told Angie.

"Already? Without an interview?"

"I interviewed with them before I came to Lyons. Apparently, they remembered me, saw the posting and 'didn't want to let me get away again.'"

"Wow. I wish I could have that kind of luck with men. Maybe that's what I need. A Monster.com for my dating resume." Angie laughed. "Though mine might crash the server."

"I can start the week after Christmas if I want, he said," Natalie said, reading the rest of the enthusiastic note from Charles McGraw, the man who had interviewed her. "I could be out of here in a week."

"And on to a real job." Angie winked.

It was exactly the kind of real job Natalie had wanted, with a nonprofit, which would allow her to continue her charitable work, and maybe make a difference in the city. Clearly, she wasn't going to be able to do that while working at Lyons. The promises Brad had made to her when she'd been hired, about working with nonprofits and about the shelter, had each been rescinded when it became clear company income mattered more than people.

"What are you waiting for? Hit Reply and tell him yes." Angie nudged Natalie's mouse.

"I'm going to miss it here." She glanced around the office, saw Ted hunkered over his jar of colored paper clips, very carefully picking out all the black ones and putting them into a separate container. "Okay, I won't miss this office, or the people who think they're Klingons, but I will miss you."

Angie gave her a quick hug. "Don't worry. You won't get rid of me that easily. I know where you live." She winked. "Now, that hunk over there in the corner office . . ." She gestured toward Jake, who had once again worn a blue shirt. Definitely Natalie's undoing. "It's too bad you can't take him with you. Make him your office boy. Keep him in the mail room and only take him out when he's been very, very good."

"There's an idea." Natalie laughed.

"Are you still going to give Jake a spin around the block before you leave?"

"Maybe." Natalie spun the wheel on the mouse. "Maybe not."

"Oh no." Angie studied her friend. "Don't tell me you're falling for him. You read the tabloids, you know the reputation of Lyons men. They have about as much sticking power as oil."

"I know. And I'm not falling for him. Really."

"Good. Take a piece of advice from Angie Central. When you have your fling, be smart and get the hell out of there afterward. No spending the night. That spooning will mess with your emotions, I tell ya."

"Oh, I'm not planning to fall in love or anything like that," she told Angie and herself. "Besides, I wouldn't be able to tell him even if I did. He'd fall asleep before I got past I-I-I."

Angie laughed. "Once you get cozy with him, I bet that little stutter thing will go away."

"That's the problem," Natalie said. "It hasn't gone away, which makes getting cozy a problem. I mean, he's kissed me, but I can't seem to make any sense when I'm around him. It's kinda hard to be sexy when you're a blubbering idiot."

"Then Secret Santa needs to kick it up a notch."

Natalie looked at the job offer before her, then took a second glance around the office. Brad was strutting through the room, a peacock at the zoo, and serving about as much purpose. Jake was in his office, on the phone. Dena came in from lunch and made a beeline for Jake's office.

Jealousy whipped through Natalie, the emotion coming so hard and so fast it surprised her. She had no claims to Jake Lyons. She wanted no claims to Jake.

And what better way to prove it to herself than to accept this job offer and, before she left, have that fling? A Merry Christmas all around, with no broken hearts to repair after the new year. Natalie hit Reply and started typing.

"Look at Dena," Angie said. "Isn't that illegal in certain states?"

The receptionist was now hanging on the edge of Jake's doorframe like a stripper going down a brass pole.

"I heard he took her out to dinner on Saturday," Angie added.

Natalie drew in a breath. She hadn't known about that. She shouldn't care, shouldn't be affected. "Why would he take her out? They don't seem to have a lot in common."

"*Hello*. He's a guy with a heartbeat. That's reason enough. Besides, have you seen how she's been dressing lately? It's like she's shopping at Hookers 'R Us." Angie shook her head. "Between how short her skirts have gotten and how high her shirts are riding, you can see her belly ring from any angle."

Natalie laughed. "You are so mean."

"It's true. And you know it." She spun Natalie around to face her. "If you want that man, you better get him now. You let Dena get her claws into him and he'll never be fit for womankind again." Angie gave Natalie a little push. "So go on over there and interrupt them."

"Oh yeah, he's going to pick N-N-Natalie over Holy-cow-those-are-huge Dena."

"You have a point." Angie chewed on the end of her acrylic nail, thinking. "Take my cell, text him again."

Natalie glanced at the reply message she'd composed to the nonprofit. It was about damned time she started acting on her thoughts instead of being a bystander while other people, like Dena, did what they wanted and did it with more oomph. She needed, as Angie had said, to be more risky. "No, no texting. I want to keep him on his toes." She grinned. "IM."

"I am what?"

"Instant message. He's at his computer right now; it'll pop right up and be more in his face than Dena will ever be."

Angie grinned. "You should be president."

Natalie glanced again at Dena, who had her leg wrapped around the jam in ways Natalie didn't think a leg could go. "Tim," she said to the techno-guru behind her, "I need help."

One minute later, Tim's wizard fingers had given her a new instant messaging ID, one that cloaked her real identity. She logged onto the system and hit Jake's name. The little window popped up. Natalie poised her fingers over the keyboard—and froze. Doing this was so out of her normal range of activity that, for a second, she panicked. She reached for her mouse, about to shut the program down, when she stopped herself.

When had living on the sidelines ever gotten her anywhere? She was stuck in a job she hated, in a too-small apartment, and she was about to spend her third Christmas in a row alone, considering Steve had found it convenient to break up just before any and all gift-giving holidays. She hadn't dated a man in six months because no male in his right mind found a woman who sounded like a stuck record sexy.

And to be honest, she hadn't gone after another job because the entire interview process was a major stress. Worrying that she might stutter in the middle of a meeting with the CEO or get stuck on something simple like her name. Only through lots of deep breathing and calm focus had she been able to get through the last set of interviews a year ago.

About the only person in the world with a life worse than hers had been Quasimodo.

Conjuring up every romance novel she'd ever read—and a few episodes of *Real Sex* from HBO—Natalie composed an IM and hit Send before she could stop herself.

The game was on. The problem?

Natalie wasn't so sure she had the guts to see it through.

* * *

Jake had been trying to get Dena to leave for the last ten minutes. The woman seemed determined to stay, and the quiet phones hadn't helped the situation. He prayed for a phone call, a visitor, a meteor to drop from the sky—anything that would get the chatty receptionist out of his office.

He didn't mind talking with women; he just preferred the kind that had something to say.

"And so then, I told that woman at Macy's I was not going to pay full retail for something I knew was so last season. I read my *Vogue*, you know."

"Uh-huh." He pulled his keyboard in front of him, then clicked his mouse, sending his screensaver scurrying away. "I have work—"

"Like she even knew the difference. She was clearly wearing a knockoff Donna Karan. Who does that when they work at Macy's, for God's sake? It's the Mecca of fashion." Dena drew in a breath, which only served to rev her mouth engine. "And then . . ."

But Jake had stopped listening. The interoffice instant messaging program had popped up, along with a greeting from someone named "SpiceGirl," the same one who'd been texting him from three different phone numbers, a trick he admired for the way it threw him off her identity. He looked up, glanced around the office, but no one looked guilty.

Thinking about me? SpiceGirl wrote. Because I'm thinking about you.

Hell, yeah, he was thinking about her. Had been since last night. And the night before that. What are you thinking? he typed.

That there's more to you than meets the eye.

And when I meet you, what will I see?

There was a long pause. He waited, fingers at the ready on his keyboard, Dena still going on about Macy's in the background. A minute passed, the hand on the desk clock she'd given him sweeping around, as if mocking him.

Another minute. A third.

Not what you expect, came the cryptic answer. Before he could respond, another IM popped up. I had a dream about you last night, SpiceGirl said. Want to know what you were wearing? Or rather, not wearing?

His fingers hesitated over his keyboard as the receptionist continued her litany against the fashion world. Unless Dena had telekinesis, she wasn't the one sending him the messages.

"Picking out a purse is like choosing a career," Dena was saying. "I mean, being a receptionist is a really hard job. You can't have just anyone answer the phones. Just like I can't use my credit cards to buy something made," she waved her hands vaguely, "somewhere across the Specific."

Okay, *definitely* not Dena.

I'll bite, he wrote back. What was I wearing?

Mmmm, SpiceGirl wrote back. Nibble on me anytime.

The temperature in his office climbed a couple of degrees.

You had on a bow, she continued. A big, red, gorgeous bow. And nothing else.

And what about you?

It was a hot dream, so I was hot too. Very hot. I had to take *everything* off, except this teeny tiny lace—

"Hey, Jakey, I necessitate you in the conference room," Brad called. "Monumental client crisis."

Damn Brad's timing. Reluctantly, Jake left his office, leaving the IM program up and running in case SpiceGirl had more to say. Dena sure did; she didn't stop talking even as he said he had to go and headed into the conference room.

SpiceGirl, he'd noticed, was a woman of few words. But every single one had one hell of an impact. At first, he'd been intrigued, but now, the curiosity to meet her—and see what she meant by teeny tiny lace—had consumed his every thought.

Before the twelve days were up, he was going to figure out who his Secret Santa was. And take her up on her offer.

If he was smart, he'd go for SpiceGirl, and her no-strings attached offer, rather than knit himself up anymore with Natalie. He was already pretty damned tangled up, considering how often Natalie crossed his thoughts—and had him considering the very thing he shouldn't be.

Commitment.

Chapter Nine

It was the tenth day of Christmas, or at least it was in Brad's strange little world, and Natalie's nerves were shot.

She'd texted. She'd IM'd. She'd written letters that were a combination of seduction and conversation. And in the last couple days, she'd even gotten a few messages back from Jake. He'd enjoyed the letters, he told her, found her to be a juxtaposition of brains and sass, and he looked forward to finding out who she was . . . and taking her up on her offer.

She never had sent the threatened coal, because deep down, she was having fun with her SpiceGirl persona, keeping Jake on his toes, doing and saying all the things she'd never had the guts to do in her daily life, afraid the words would come out wrong and that he would laugh.

When this had started, all she'd imagined doing was priming the pump with the Secret Santa gifts, then, at the end, revealing her identity, enjoying one very hot and sexy night with Jake Lyons and then moving on.

"Let's meet, today," Jake had written this morning in a reply to her text, this time sent from her new cell phone, a number Jake didn't have. "I can't wait any longer."

Neither could she. She started to type a message back, then stopped. There was still one little problem.

Actually a b-b-big problem. There was no way she was going to tell Jake who she was and try to launch a one-night seduction scene while she was still master of the Porky Pig impersonation.

No wonder her sex life had been about as exciting as a congressional memo.

Natalie turned and noticed a large, wrapped box addressed to her, sitting on the floor by her chair. Her Secret Santa.

A thrill of anticipation rocketed through her. She still had no idea who her mystery giver was and found she was looking forward to the beginning of each day, to finding out how he—or she—would surprise her.

Each gift from her Secret Santa had been right on target, as if it were from someone who knew her well. The only one here Natalie had gotten close to had been Angie, who was suffering in her own private hell after drawing Sam the Suck-Up's name and hearing him broadcast each of her gifts to the whole office. Angie had finally stopped his bullhorning by presenting him with a lifetime supply of edible underwear.

Today's box was the biggest yet for Natalie, the wrapping clearly not done by a professional, because the edges weren't exactly square and there were seven pieces of tape on one end. Natalie chuckled. Clearly, her Secret Santa had Scotch tape issues.

As always, her name was inscribed across the front in neat handwriting that looked awfully familiar. She fingered the tag for a moment, thinking. She *knew* this tight cursive hand, had seen it a hundred times. But where?

Then she drew back the paper and opened the box.

And knew.

The box was filled with children's books, all the classics that she'd read as a little girl, the kind she loved sharing with the kids at the shelter. *Where the Wild Things Are, The Cat in the Hat, The Wizard of Oz* . . . the pile was huge, a veritable collector's library, and then, at the bottom, an autographed and highly valuable copy of the first *Arthur* book, with a note that read, "You know who would love this the most. Give him a smile this Christmas."

A tear slipped down her cheek. And as it did, the pieces fell into place.

So did another problem. The one complication she hadn't thought of when she'd started this whole game.

That she might fall in love.

Natalie picked up the Marc Brown book, clutched it to her chest, then headed into Jake's office and shut the door. "It's you, isn't it?"

Jake looked up from his work, his blue eyes a mixture of tease and, she hoped, a little joy at seeing her. "It's me . . . what?"

"You're my Secret San-san-santa."

He grinned and wagged a finger at her. "Now, you know it wouldn't be a secret if I told you."

She could just pretend to go along with the joke and drop the subject before it went too much further. But the book was hard against her palms, a solid reminder of this man and his simple gift. A gift that hadn't been about books but about who Natalie Harris really was, and what mattered to her.

Without even knowing, Jake had upped the stakes. And taken this into a realm Natalie hadn't considered. Inaction simply wasn't an option, not while every inch of her was craving the next step.

She skirted his desk and slipped into the space before him, not caring if the entire office was watching. Her gaze met his, locked onto those deep blue eyes.

There wasn't any doubt. Natalie Harris had fallen in love and fallen good.

Before she could think twice, Natalie leaned forward and placed a soft, tender kiss on his lips. "Thank you."

"You're very welcome." A smile crossed his face and he

pulled her closer, brushing his lips against hers, then giving her a kiss that whispered a promise. Of more. Of a night she'd never forget. Of a man who knew very well how to take care of a woman.

After a long, sweet second, he drew back. "If I'd known books would get this reaction, I would have bought you a Barnes & Noble."

She laughed, then sobered, connecting again with his steady gaze. "I'm glad it was y-y-you."

Damn that stuttering. If she could have cut off her own tongue, she would have. How the heck was she supposed to seduce a man with a mouth like this?

"I'm glad it was me, too." He reached up, caught a tendril of her hair in his hand, exposing the silver stars dangling from her lobes. A long, heated second passed, filled with anticipation that maybe, just maybe, she wasn't alone in these feelings and the one-night stand she'd planned would turn into two, three, a hundred.

He swallowed, then that familiar grin appeared on his face. "It was fun being your Secret Santa," he said, with about as much emotion as a car wash. "I'll have to thank Velma for picking out such great gifts."

Velma had done all the shopping? He'd sponged her gifts off onto Brad's *assistant*?

What had she expected? Jake Lyons had done nothing more than live up to his reputation. Stayed exactly the same as he had been when she'd launched this plan to get the man she wanted.

Only now, she wanted more.

He released her, stepping back as he glanced down at the present on his desk, the very one Natalie had wrapped early that morning and slipped into his office before he arrived. "Now, if I can just figure out who my Secret Santa is, I'll be all set. I know it's not Velma." That grin again, but for the first time, his smile seemed to put distance between them.

Here was her opportunity. To tell him, to grab that sleigh

by the reins and finally take Jake Lyons on the ride to her bedroom. She opened her mouth, intending to do just that, and all that came out was, "I-I-I . . ." like a record stuck on the alphabet song.

Because the only words that wanted to come out were "I'm falling in love with you."

For once, her mouth was smarter than her brain.

"Brad told me it was Dena," Jake said, "so I took her out—"

Thunder crashed in Natalie's head, rocks slammed against her heart, obliterating the rest of Jake's words. Of course he'd think it was Dena. Any man with a pulse would. Dena of the big breasts and the smooth, albeit limited in vocabulary, speech.

Before he could finish the sentence, she was backing up, leaving the office. "S-s-sorry, work to do," she said, then ducked out of there before she could make a total fool of herself.

She'd already hit 98 percent in that department. No need to go any further.

Natalie feigned a fatal attack of intestinal issues and went home for the day. She turned off her phone, didn't answer her doorbell and didn't budge from the sofa except to refill her ice cream dish.

It wasn't until Angie practically beat down the door that Natalie finally opened up. "What the hell happened? I saw you kissing Jake Lyons just before you ditched and claimed instant flu." Angie plopped onto the couch.

"He's my Secret Santa."

"Really? How cool! Did you tell him you were his?"

She shook her head. "He thinks it's Dena. He's dating her."

"No, he's not. They only went out the one time; she told me all about it when I waved a Godiva bar under her nose.

Apparently, there wasn't much chemistry there, on either end, and by the next day, she was already getting cozy with Eric on the fourth floor."

"Doesn't matter," Natalie said, stabbing her spoon into a pint of Ben & Jerry's. Her voice sounded as thick as the ice cream. "I'm not going after him."

"Why not?" Angie leaned forward, then tipped Natalie's chin up and caught a tear on her finger. "Aw, hell, Nat. You fell for him, didn't you?"

"He was a really good Secret Santa," Natalie sobbed.

"What'd he give you? The Hope Diamond?"

Natalie shook her head. "He pays *attention*, Ang. Or at least I think he does. But after today, I don't know what to think." She rose, crossed to the sofa table and came back with the box filled with the nine gifts. "Remember this bracelet?" She held it up. "It's made of poinsettias because I told him I used to love them when I was a little girl."

"Oh my God. Really?" Angie cut in. "Then that's definitely not zirc. It's the real freakin' thing."

"See these star earrings?" Natalie continued, pulling back her hair. "I mentioned once last month, I think, that I liked to stay up late and watch the stars come out at night. Here's a copy of the poems of Emily Dickinson." She held up a book. "I have a quote from her taped over my computer monitor. And then, today, books."

"*Books?* That's what has you overdosing on ice cream?"

"Books for the kids at the shelter. All the ones I love to read to them. The shelter copies had been donations, and they were all worn and falling apart. He replaced each and every one. And then, he bought Jacob an *autographed* copy of an *Arthur* book." She shook her head. "He's paid attention, even when I thought he wasn't looking. But then he went and told me Velma picked out all the gifts."

"Velma? Honey, I've seen Velma at the vending machines. She can't pick out a package of Doritos without help. She's all left brain, Natalie."

"Then why would Jake say she did the shopping?"

"He's a guy," Angie said, nabbing an Oreo and munching on the cookie. "It's in his genes to avoid so much as the appearance of commitment."

Natalie sighed. "Which is exactly the problem."

Angie put her thumbs and forefingers together, forming a square that she squinted through. "I see you, as a vision in white, walking down an aisle."

"Angie, just because he's not dating Dena doesn't mean he's in love with me."

"So? Rich men who take notes on what you like don't come along more than once a millennium."

"It doesn't matter if he's George Clooney and Viggo Mortensen wrapped into one, with the Oscars *and* the paychecks. I'm done with having a half-baked life and half-baked relationships. And I don't want to fall in love with a man who doesn't love me."

Angie patted Natalie's hand. "I think it's a little late for that, sweetie. At least have the fling, get him out of your system, and move on. Starting next week, you don't have to see him anymore, right?"

Natalie nodded, although the thought of starting her job at the nonprofit didn't fill her with eagerness, not anymore. Instead, the feeling in her gut was an awful lot like loss. "What if I can't get him out of my system?"

"Simple. Call George Clooney. He's still single."

Natalie laughed. "That easy, huh?"

"Yep." Angie grabbed an Oreo off the plate on the coffee table. "So, are you going to the office Christmas party tomorrow? Or rather the annual Suck-Up-To-Brad-with-gifts-he's-just-going-to-return, Cheetos-and-store-brand-soda office gala?"

Natalie put the half-eaten pint of ice cream on the table. What was the good of making a resolution if she didn't put it into action? "Yes, I am. And this time, I'm taking your advice. Maybe all I have is a bad case of infatuation and one night with Jake will cure me." Yet, even as she said the words, Natalie knew what she felt for Jake Lyons was so much more. "Either way, I'm done being stuck in my life and definitely done letting a few stuck words hold me back."

"You go, girl! Always trust your heart. Everything you need to know is right there." Angie rose and grabbed her purse off the floor. "Speaking of hearts, I have to go. I have a date."

"You do? With who?"

"Tim." A flush filled Angie's cheeks. "Sometimes Mr. Right is right under your nose, or in my case, right under my keyboard."

Chapter Ten

The office Christmas party was in full swing by the time Jake arrived. It should have been a costume party so that he could have come dressed as an idiot, the one part he seemed to be playing pretty well lately.

After yesterday, when he'd gone and lied to Natalie, telling her it was Velma—Velma, of all people—who had picked out the gifts, he'd wanted to smack himself, and then take the words back. Tell Natalie it was simply a measure of his insanity, brought about by spending ridiculous amounts of time in Man Hell—that is, the mall.

He'd meant to tell her that as sexy as SpiceGirl sounded, and as fun as a little rendezvous with her might be, the only one he wanted under his mistletoe was Natalie.

However, she was the kind of woman who meant taking things further than one night. He saw it in her eyes, tasted it in her kiss. She wasn't the kind of woman a man loved and left.

She was also the kind any sane man held onto for the rest of his life.

What if he wasn't that kind of man, though? What if, in the end, he turned out exactly like his father and grandfather?

He had yet to prove himself with the company. The late night he'd spent with the books last night, after finally prying them out of Brad's controlling hands, had proved to him that Lyons Corp was in even worse shape than he'd thought. All the effort he'd put in over the last five months hadn't made more than a dent in profitability. If anything, the company was hemorrhaging faster than before.

It was going to take some serious work to get it back on track. First, an in-house promotional campaign to let their old customers know that, yes, Lyons was still alive, and second, a significant reduction in management salaries and benefits.

Maybe then, at next year's Christmas party, Jake could relax. Think about having a personal life again. Until then, he'd be putting in some long days. Any relationship he might try to have with Natalie would undoubtedly end up relegated to second place. If there was one thing Jake knew about Natalie Harris, it was that she deserved a man who would put her first.

"Hey, Jakey, loosen up," Brad said, coming up to him and clapping him on the back, then shoving a plastic cup of undoubtedly cheap champagne into his hands. "You worry too much."

"Brad, if I don't worry, this company will tank. Do you know how much market share we've lost this year alone?"

Brad waved a dismissive hand, making his red silk shirt flip-flop against his wrist. "Tomorrow's another day."

"No, Brad, it's not. This company is going down the tubes and you're just sitting there, sucking it dry." Jake leaned in closer so the other employees wouldn't hear. "I saw your 'expense' reports for the last three months. Women are not an expense item, neither are limos."

Brad shrugged. "What do I care? It's the family feed bucket. Pull up a bowl."

Anger boiled inside of Jake. "It's a legacy, Brad. Why don't you want to protect it instead of destroy it?"

"I'm just taking my share, before there's nothing left."

"You're not doing it while I'm here," Jake said, his voice low. "We're going to buckle down, cut back on our salaries and—"

Brad snorted. "Cut back? Are you nuts? I'm not trimming anything. You want to cut your salary, be my guest. But I own 51 percent, so that means I own all the decisions too. And I decide I need a raise, starting immediately."

Jake's first thought was to quit, walk away and let Brad do what he wanted with Lyons Corp. But just as he opened his mouth, he thought of what his father had asked of him. To restore the family business, at all costs.

So he turned and walked away, leaving his champagne on Dena's desk and the argument unfinished.

He worked his way in and out of the crowd; it seemed every person who worked for Lyons, and a few who probably didn't, had crowded into the fifth-floor corporate offices. Tension crackled in his veins. He didn't need champagne to loosen him up, to take his mind off the general ledger. He needed only one thing—

Natalie.

And then, he saw her, in the corner, talking with her friend Angela. "Natalie," he said, after he reached her. Angela drifted away, a knowing smile on her face. "I was looking for you."

He saw her draw in a breath, center herself, then speak without hesitation. "Why?"

"Because I want to offer you a job. A promotion, really." The words came out, as if the thought had been there all the time. It had, he realized, he just hadn't vocalized it until now.

"A-a-a job?"

"I want you to head up the marketing department at Lyons. You're inventive, you're fun and you're good with numbers. If you ask me, you're wasting your time stuck in that cubicle, doing whatever Brad throws your way. Plus, you'll need to work side by side with me in the next year as I put more time into expanding Lyons Corp's reach."

He waited, sure she'd say yes on the spot. Wanting her to say yes, so that he could see that smile on her face.

She swallowed hard, then shook her head. "I c-c-can't. I'm sorry."

"Don't tell me you love your cubicle so much that you don't want to leave it?" He added a grin, hoping the surprise at her refusal didn't show.

"I already took another job. I s-s-start next week."

She was leaving? Hell, he couldn't blame her. If Brad hadn't been family, he would have left a long time ago too. "Next week? That soon?"

"Where I'm going, I can make a difference," she said softly. "I can't d-d-do that here."

But you *can* make a difference, he wanted to say, you already do. In his days, in the way he looked at Monday mornings, and the disappointment he felt on Fridays and—

"Natalie, tell me I can talk you into staying," he said. "If it's pay, don't worry. We can negotiate a raise."

She opened her mouth to speak, then changed her mind and led him back into the maze of cubicles. Behind one of the gray walls, a woman giggled and a man murmured. Apparently, they'd found the mistletoe.

"Why are you leaving?" he asked.

She considered him for a long second. "You r-r-really want to know?"

"Yes."

Again, she paused, inhaled, then went on. "Meaning. That's what I want. I don't find meaning in filing paperwork or making sure all the credits and debits balance. I want to wake up in the morning knowing I am going to do something good that day and when I go to sleep at night that I made a tiny difference to one person." She drew in a breath. "I don't want a job, Jake, I want a vocation."

420   Shirley Jump

As she always did when she was fired up about something, Jake noticed, she stopped stuttering. It had to be hard, he was sure, to conquer something like that. He realized anew what a strong, compelling woman Natalie Harris was. He wanted just a little of that—of her determination, her desire, for more.

"What drives you, Natalie Harris?" he asked, moving closer to her, seeking answers in her gaze, wondering if someday he, too, could find that magic elixir for a life.

Natalie sank onto the edge of the desk, toying for a moment with a stray paper clip. "When I was a little girl, my mother married and married. And *married.* She pretty much made it a career. But she never married a man who was worth a dime. They'd all leave, and she'd be stuck with the bills and the credit card debt and the car payments. Finally, we ended up running out of money; it all happened so fast. We ended up living in a car for a while, camping out wherever we could, bathing in gas station restrooms. The whole nine yards. If it hadn't been my life, I would have thought it was a movie."

Shock rippled through him, at how different her life had been from his, despite their both growing up in homes of serial marriers. "I had no idea. Natalie, I'm so sorry."

"That's when I started . . ." she paused, and he saw the pain in her eyes, "stuttering. The doctor said it was the trauma of the whole thing. I was a little kid, and it was scary. I ended up going to speech therapy and learned how to get it under control." Her smile spread across her lips and socked him in the gut. "Most of the time. Now I only do it when I get nervous."

He took a step closer. "And *I* make you nervous?"

"Sometimes." She laughed. "Okay, most of the time. But not anymore."

Around them, the holiday Muzak continued to play, the party continued its happy chatter. The couple in the next cubicle kept on doing whatever they were doing.

"Why not?" Jake asked.

"Because last night I made some decisions, and once I did that, I felt . . . empowered. Stronger. Able to take on tall conversations in a single bound."

He chuckled. "Still, when you were a kid, all of that must have been really hard."

She shrugged. "It's okay, I survived. It taught me a lot, actually, about life and being strong."

"And that's why this shelter is so important to you." He let out a gust. "I'm sorry we axed it. If I had known—"

"Don't tell me about the bottom line again," she said, putting up a hand, cutting him off. "If you truly wanted to, you could do anything, Jake. You could even walk away from this place."

He shook his head. "You don't understand, Natalie. I have to take care of this company."

"Why?" She took a step forward. "Tell me honestly, do you feel like this," she swept her hand in a semicircle, indicating the building, "is your purpose? Or just a job?"

"It's . . ." his voice trailed off as he realized his only reason for being here was to live up to someone else's legacy, to make someone else happy. Someone who had died and thus couldn't even see what was happening. He realized then that he hadn't just been trying to rebuild a company but also to create the family bonds he'd never had. "I'm trying to continue what my grandfather started. What my father inherited and passed on to me."

"But is it what makes you jump out of bed in the morning, raring to start the day? Is that what your passion is, Jake?" She searched his gaze, and in that look, he knew he was connecting with a stronger Natalie than he had before. "Because I know what mine is."

With both hands, she clasped his face, then leaned forward and kissed him. This time, her kiss was even deeper, more intimate than before, as if her new resolutions had extended to this too. Desire ignited within him, hot and fast, making him draw her closer, his hands slipping down her back, along her waist, craving the feel of her against him. She was soft in all the right places, her body carved into the spaces of need.

He opened his mouth, letting his tongue do a hell of a polka with hers. In response, she grasped his shoulders, pulling him down on top of her, across the desk. The aggressive move surprised him, stoking a fire that didn't need any additional flame. Natalie's hands roamed his back, sliding down his pants, over his hips, his buttocks, every reachable inch. He followed her lead, sneaking a hand between them and up under her sweater, cupping one of her perfect breasts against the delicate lace of her bra. It wasn't enough. He wanted more, and wanted it now, to hell with waiting.

He slid one silken strap to the side, then, finally, his hand was there, the palm encompassing her fullness, his thumb teasing across the nipple. She moaned and arched against him, sliding upward on the desk, allowing him more access to slip into the space between her legs.

Clearly, there were more dimensions to Natalie Harris than he had realized. Really sexy, absolutely incredible dimensions.

Before they rounded any other bases, Natalie broke away. He backed up, releasing her. She got to her feet, pausing for a moment, before connecting again with his gaze. "I want you," she said, clear and sure and sending another spark of desire rocketing through him. "Or, rather, I *wanted* you."

He arched a brow. "As in past tense?"

"The Jake Lyons I've been fantasizing about wouldn't compromise people for profit. And he wouldn't try to hold onto a sinking ship when it wasn't even a ship he wanted to be on."

He refused to acknowledge that he hated working here, that he had been questioning whether this was the right path since the day he walked into the building. If he did, then where did that leave the Lyons legacy? "Do you know what makes me get out of bed in the morning and come rushing in here? It's not the job." He took her hands in his, rubbing his thumbs over her warm, peach-scented skin. "It's you. But you expect a lot out of me, Natalie. More than I think I'm capable of giving you."

Her smile was fleeting, gone too fast. "I understand. Maybe someday down the road, we can try this again."

"But that kiss—" he said, gesturing toward the desk.

"Was a kiss good-bye. Before today, I wanted a fling with you. A one-night stand. I was too afraid to say anything, because I was too worried that those damned words would get caught on my tongue. I'm done being afraid, Jake. I'm done waiting for what I want." She smiled, shook her head, then looked back at him. "This is going to sound crazy after everything that's happened, but I've realized that it's okay to want more. To want the whole enchilada instead of just the beef." She placed a palm against his cheek, her gaze bittersweet. "That's why I'm leaving the company. And you. If I don't stand up for and go after what I want, I'll never get it."

He envied her that confidence, that surety in what she was pursuing. Hell, most of his life he'd been seeking a purpose and thought he'd found it when he came to work with his cousin. But the empty feeling in his gut told him Natalie had hit his nail on its head.

The only problem was he didn't have a backup plan.

Natalie gave him a quick kiss on the cheek. "Bye, Jake. I wish you well."

"Wait," he said, reaching for her, wishing he could rewind their conversation. "Don't go. Not yet."

"I have to. I have some serious shopping to do. I can't produce Santa, but I can sure blow my last paycheck on giving those kids at Our Hope Shelter the best damned Christmas they've ever had."

And then she was gone, leaving the millionaire feeling, for the first time in his life, as if he was lacking something very important.

Jake turned to go back to the party, then stopped when a glint of metal caught his eye.

Natalie's cell phone. He picked it up, stepped out of the cubicles to look for her, but she was gone.

It wasn't until he flipped the lid and saw the text message displayed across the screen that he realized he'd just lost a lot more than a good employee.

Chapter Eleven

Natalie had left the party early, spent the rest of the day and all of Christmas Eve shopping and wrapping. She'd thought, when she walked out of the Lyons building, that she would feel free, ready to embark on something new.

Instead, a nagging sense of loss had dogged her every step. She'd woken up early that morning and hurried over to the shelter with her bundles of gifts, determined to make this Christmas Day wonderful for twelve boys and girls.

And just as determined to forget about Jake Lyons.

She readied her pile of gifts and faced the closed doors that led to the family room, waiting for the shelter's director to finish with a phone call and start the festivities.

"Merry Christmas, SpiceGirl."

Natalie pivoted at the sound of a familiar male voice in her ear, nearly dropping the gifts in her arms. "Santa?" she asked, raising a brow.

The man in the red suit and white beard just winked—a wink she recognized. "Ho, ho, ho. Yes, indeed, I'm Santa. And if you've been good, little girl, I've got a present for you." When she opened her mouth to speak, he tick-tocked a gloved finger at her. "No, no, not now. You have to wait until we hand out all *these* presents first."

Jake took a step to the right, revealing a huge red sack on the floor behind him, filled to the brim with toys. Dolls, remote control cars, Game Boys, books, puzzles. She stood there, stunned. First, because he was here, and second, because he had gone to so much trouble for the children. Hope thudded in her chest. Maybe she didn't have to settle for just the appetizer. Maybe there was still a possibility she could have the whole Jake entrée. "I bet you just raised Toys 'R' Us's stock a hundred points," she teased.

"Great! You *did* get a Santa." Kitty Planter entered the room and beamed at Natalie. "The kids are going to love it. Are you ready?"

"I need a second," Natalie said. She turned back to Jake. "Why are you here, really? And don't tell me it's for a tax deduction."

"Nope. I'm not even going to ask for a receipt. It's because someone inspired me to find *my* passion." Beneath the fake beard she could just make out his grin. "Now, let's get to work, and then you'll see what Santa has in store for you."

Curiosity bloomed inside her. All she could do, though, was look at the man beside her and wonder if he was real or just a Christmas miracle.

Natalie nodded toward Kitty, who turned the handle of the family room door. The second it opened, the children rushed forward, squealing with surprise at the appearance of Santa and his toys.

They were swarmed in an instant, but Jake held his cool and maintained his Santa persona, dispensing the gifts with clear enjoyment of the task. Each toy widened a smile, brightened the red in their cheeks, and turned the eyes that had seemed so weary before to ones filled with joy. Parents joined in on the fun, and laughter rung its happy peals in the room for the first time in forever.

When the gift frenzy had died down, David approached Santa, a huge stuffed bear clutched tight to his chest, along with a copy of the book that Natalie had read to them the last time she was here. Every child had received a copy of *Bear's Christmas Wish* from Santa Jake, a sweet touch that had melted Natalie's heart.

David squinted up at Jake, assessing his suit and his beard while his mother waited a few feet away, a beam of pride on her face. "Are you really him?"

Jake nodded. "Yes, sir, I am."

"Then how'd you find us? We don't have a house, not anymore," David said. "That's why we gotta live here."

Jake put a finger beneath David's chin, lifting the boy's sad face up, and Natalie's heart constricted again at Jake's tender touch and care for one of the most traumatized children in the room. "Well, David, Miss Natalie helped me find you. You don't have to worry, though, about next year. As of today, you *do* have a home. Santa got all of you an extra special gift." Over the boy's head, he caught his mother's eye. "A deed."

Natalie froze. Had Jake just said what she'd thought he did?

David's mother gasped as the words sunk in. "A deed? For a *house?* But how? Why?"

Jake's gaze connected with Natalie's, the blue eyes twinkling above the snowy beard. Her heart expanded a hundred times, filled with love for this man, who had gone to greater lengths than she would have ever dreamed. "Santa heard from this lady here that you all were very, very good. And she also told me that what you needed, more than books, more than dolls, was a place to call home." The room was silent, as if no one could believe what was happening. The parents looked from one to the other, eyes wide with disbelief. In the back of the room, Kitty Planter had slumped into a chair, her mouth agape.

Jake reached into the bag, rooted around at the bottom, and with a flourish pulled out several large, thick envelopes filled with the promised papers and a set of house keys. Each of them, Natalie saw, had been addressed to the families who resided at the shelter.

Santa Jake made his way through the room, handing one to each struggling parent. To the single mothers who had done their best to make ends meet. To the grandmothers who were living their retirement years raising a whole other generation. To the dads who had been beaten down by failure but whose faces brightened when they realized they held a new start in their hands. "Merry Christmas," Jake said.

Ariana's mother, tears streaming down her cheeks, reached out, took his arm and gave him a squeeze. "Thank you. Oh, thank you."

"You're welcome," he said, with a short, quick nod. But when he turned away, Natalie was sure the twinkle she saw in his eyes now had nothing to do with being jolly.

"Well, children, my bag is empty now," Jake said, swinging the red velvet sack over his shoulder, "and I've got some mighty tired reindeer waiting for me, so I'm heading back to the North Pole. You all have a good Christmas."

He turned and headed back out the door he'd entered, followed by waving hands and chattering children shouting Christmas greetings.

A moment later, Natalie followed, waiting until the door had shut behind her before she spoke. "What was all that?"

Jake pulled off the beard, then the hat, revealing the face that had become as familiar as her own in the last few weeks. "*That* is my new job."

She quirked a brow at him. "You're a professional Santa?"

"No. I'm the new head of the Natalie Lyons Foundation, dedicated to helping families stay off the streets and find homes."

"The . . ." her voice trailed off as the words sunk in. "Natalie Lyons Foundation? What are you talking about?"

"Oh, would you look at that?" Jake said, ignoring her question and once again reaching into the sack. "Santa has one more gift in his bag." He withdrew a tiny velvet box; then, as Natalie watched in stunned, silent surprise, he lowered himself to one knee, pulled off his gloves and tipped back the lid of the box.

A perfect round diamond, nestled in a plain, perfect setting, gleamed back at her. She gasped. "An engagement ring? Holy cow."

"Natalie Lyons, will you be my Mrs. Claus?"

She opened her mouth to speak, then shut it again when no words would come forward. She stared at the ring, at the man bearing it, and waited for it all to hit her. "M-m-marry you?" This time, the stuttering was perfectly understandable, given the circumstances.

"I know it's a little sudden, but a very wise woman told me that if I don't stand up for and go after what I want, I'll never get it." He grinned, flinging out an arm in surrender. "This time, I'm on my knees."

She laughed, still not believing the sight before her. "But, Jake, I'm leaving the company and—"

"Yes, you are. And you're coming to work with me." He grinned. "I can't very well run the Natalie Lyons Foundation without Natalie Lyons, now can I?"

"But this is so sudden, so . . . crazy."

"Yeah, it is. And that's what makes it so perfect. I want you, Natalie, and the SpiceGirl underneath. But most of all, the woman who showed me that finding my right path is just about looking in the right direction." He rose, withdrew the ring from the box, then took her left hand in his. "So, are you ready to try the whole enchilada?"

She nodded, for the first time in her life, unable to speak at all for a good twenty seconds while she processed it all, taking in the ring that he slipped onto her finger, the meaning of his words. "But what about Lyons Corporation and Brad and your father's legacy?"

"I thought about my father's legacy a lot after you left. I realized there was no better way to honor him, and my grandfather, than to start something that gave back to the very community that built Lyons rather than trying to chase someone else's dream." He drew in a breath, then went on. "I had no family as a kid, not really, and when I was here, with you that day, I got a true sense of what family is really about. It's not money or bloodlines, it's about connections and creating a home. So, I sold my shares to Velma. She worked under my grandfather and knows more about the firm than anyone. And she's the only one who can make Brad quake in his boots."

Natalie laughed. "That was brilliant."

"Besides, Brad can't even add to twelve. He shouldn't be in charge of an accounting firm." Jake took her hand, the one with the ring on it, and clasped it between both of his. "You know, today is the twelfth of Brad's little days."

"And since it's Christmas," Natalie said, teasing him, "the office is closed. Oh well, I guess you won't find out who SpiceGirl was after all."

"Oh, I have my suspicions," Jake said, his voice low and dark and so incredibly sexy, Natalie was sure she was going to melt on the spot. "I found your cell phone after you left."

"Were you . . ." she paused, "disappointed it was me?"

"I was hoping it was you." The smile that took over her face erased any lingering doubts in Natalie's mind. "I love you, Natalie Harris."

Joy soared in her chest. "I love you, too," she said, the words coming out clear and strong, without a trace of hesitation.

As she stepped into Jake's arms, Natalie realized that the unnamed bear in the story wasn't the only one getting his true Christmas wish fulfilled this year. "Jake," she said, drawing back, her voice husky. "Do you have a big red bow?"

"Of course. I'll give you one guess where I'm wearing it."

The grin on his face just before he kissed her promised they would be ringing in a very merry holiday tonight.

Santa had brought Natalie exactly what she wanted for Christmas. She was sure she'd be tipping him extra for the personal delivery for many, many holidays to come.